HEARTLAND RETRIBUTION

By:

Michael Lee Williams

Dedication and Thank You

I want to dedicate this book and whatever success may come from it to those in my life who have helped support me throughout this journey.

To my mother and father for all of their love and support, and to my biggest supporter, Olivia, who's always encouraged me to keep moving forward and have confidence in myself.

I want to thank all the people who have helped on this journey, including my beta readers, Lisa, in particular.

Last but most importantly, thank you to all of you who've purchased the book. I hope you will enjoy the story that follows as much as I have enjoyed creating it.

PROLOGUE

PORT OF SALALAH, OMAN

The night was crisp; despite the bright illumination of the Ports lights, stars were visible in the night sky. A constant clacking of buoy bells chimed in the distance, followed by the gentle crashing of waves in the harbor. The acrid smell of diesel wafted over the dock, fluttering in on the back of the breeze sweeping in from the Arabian Sea.

The sound of diesel engines running was almost deafening. Massive cranes shuttled large shipping containers. Loading and unloading untold cargo from the dock to ships and vice versa. The plethora of colorful containers was too dazzling to the eye. It was like a rainbow—red, blue, orange, yellow, white, and in the hundreds.

The whole shipping yard was a buzz of activity; trucks and rail cars moved workers and materials about. Men shouted orders, with others following. Several men dressed in bright yellow vests silently directed container haulers to specific locations through a complex series of hand signals.

Despite the chaotic appearance on the ground, everything seemed to operate like a finely tuned symphony of movements. One false move here, though, wouldn't stir a quiet chorus of boos. It could cost someone their life.

The flurry of night activity meant the intel that was received was correct. The US Navy was using the Port of Salalah as a refueling and transport dock and supplying the Omani government with weapons in the process. This was apparent by the crates that were being offloaded onto pickup trucks emblazoned with the word 'munitions,' accompanied by the US insignia.

Walid Althani watched the frantic movements below, perched atop one of the thousands of shipping containers, with a half snarl, the hairs of his thick black beard prickled against his grizzled bare cheekbones. He bristled with hatred and animosity at the sight of a few dozen American Sailors standing around watching the chaos before them, chatting without a care in the world.

Their nonchalance would be their undoing this night, that, he vowed.

A large gray vessel began to take shape as he shifted his gaze upward, staring intently into the harbor and bringing up a set of binoculars, peering down the left side with his right eye. His left eye had been rendered blind from an explosion several years ago. The gray, blocky mass took on a solid, defined shape under the device's magnification.

The US Naval frigate gently bobbed and weaved in the harbor. Through the lens, he could see the ship's hull illuminated under the bright lights of the cranes unloading containers, watching the enlarged sailors aboard conduct their silent movie. He cursed under his breath. Walid adjusted position, swinging the binoculars toward the ship's rear, stopping at what he was looking for. Along the side, in substantial bold black stenciling, LSD-51.

Walid pulled the binoculars away from his face, lifted himself to one side, and retrieved a slip of paper from his thawb. Opening the folded square, he examined the contents of the slip, running his finger down the left column of the printed table of ship names and designations.

"There," he whispered, finding what he was looking for, shuffling backward with a happy smirk, reaching the end of the container. He dropped down a level, aided by two other men in dark military fatigues, landing with a softened thud against the container below. He turned to face a collected group of twenty military-clad figures with AK47s. Some also sported RPGs. Another was wearing a backpack that was clearly too heavy for him. The man finagled with the straps, trying to reposition it to make the hefty object easier to lug around.

"The USS Oak Hill," Walid addressed the group. "Is just over there." He violently jabbed a finger behind him. The assembled group had taken up hiding in a cleared-out square surrounded by other shipping containers. "Tonight, my brothers, we strike and show the West that we are still a threat without Amell. Hasan has made us stronger. And thanks to our new allies, we will now have the means to enact our jihad. Doing so with the very weapons

America uses on us. We will turn them on our enemies. Tonight, we kill as many infidels as Allah wishes."

The men quietly celebrated and readied themselves. The goal of the evening was to take out a US Navy ship, letting it be known that they could strike anywhere at any given time—even at America's mighty Navy. They'd do so in an explosive fashion in the process.

"Walid?" the man with the backpack whispered. Again, he tried to shift the weight of his pack.

"What is it, Kadar," Walid answered, pulling back the charging hammer of his AK, chambering the first of what he hoped would be many more rounds.

"This pack, it's too heavy for me, cousin." Kadar Sayed was Walid's and Hasan's cousin. He was a young man of small stature, skinny and lanky, with curly black hair and a bare face. Barely twenty years old. "Why can't Ferran carry it?" he asked, thumbing to a large, bulky man with long, dark, wavy hair and a beard to match.

Walid forcefully clamped his hands down on Kadar's shoulders, pressing him where he stood. "It is because, cousin, we need his gun, but you still have the most important job. Get this bag on the ship," he said, removing a hand and tapping the backpack. "Then get back out, and we blow that American ship up. Every man must play their part." Walid patted his cousin on the shoulder, smiling at him. He then turned to face the rest of the men. With a hand gesture, the group of terrorists moved out to commence their assault.

****

Thirty minutes later, a Toyota Highlander barreled through a chain-link fence. The padlock and chain that secured the two halves of the gate exploded, flinging the doors wide open.

The truck bounced over a speed bump at nearly sixty miles an hour, jarring the occupants. The bottom chassis smashed against the ground in a firework show of sparks. Walid held onto the handle above the passenger's door, steadying himself as the vehicle veered sharply to its left, then right, swerving around a set of concrete barricades.

He looked over his shoulder at his cousin, then at the cargo in the truck bed—several containers of weapons they'd stolen. A second truck burst through the gate, smashing it even further. The gate wobbled ferociously as it hit the apex of its arc, swinging back violently. Seconds later, a third truck blew through, ending the barriers tortured life.

It crashed upon the front end of the third Highlander. The impact of steel on steel burst the gates from their hinges. Sending both pieces hurtling through the air. The two trail vehicles easily swerved around the barricades, speeding away from Salalah—their raid successful, having gunned down several dozen Navy sailors, absconding with their prizes.

Walid couldn't wait to see them in action, thoughts about the carnage he could do with his new toys. But they had to finish the job first and get back to Hasan. "Kadar," he said, shifting his gaze from the cargo to his cousin. "The honor should be all yours." He handed the younger man a detonator switch.

Kadar took the small box from his cousin. Carefully handling the object, he felt a slight hesitation rise inside. He knew what would happen the second he pressed the button. The good and bad that would come from it. The good, finishing off what remained of the Navy sailors.

That wasn't causing the pause. It was knowing that fellow Arabs would be killed in the blast as well. Although they were helping the Americans, they were still Arabs and Muslims, and he wasn't too keen on killing his own ilk.

The young man took a deep breath, flipping over the clear plastic cover and exposing the red button underneath. "Allahu Akbar, Allahu Akbar," screamed the others inside the vehicle. Kadar joined in with cries of "Allahu Akbar." Then, depressed the button.

For a moment, nothing. Then, a thunderous explosion rumbled from behind. Walid's gaze shifted to the rearview mirror to see a cloud of fire rising from where the USS Oak Hill had been docked. A blast wave chased after the trio of speeding Highlanders, stopping just behind the last vehicle.

A roiling dust cloud succeeded the shock wave, partially obscuring Walid's view of the carnage. However, a sinister smile arched across his face. He didn't need to see it to know he'd delivered a striking blow against the infidels.

"Good job, my cousin," he said, setting his one working eye on Kadar through the mirror. "Hasan will be most pleased. We shall give him the good news together when we see him tomorrow."

Kadar nodded before shifting in his seat to watch the raging inferno until it vanished as they drove off into the desert towards Sarfayt, a city bordering Yemen.

****

The Omani sun reached its Apex in the desert country, beaming its harsh rays onto the typically scorched-out lands. However, the city of Sarfayt lay on the coastline of Oman, which granted it an unusual amount of green vegetation for the region. You could see out over the Arabian Sea from the cliff face where the city was situated. The breeze from the ocean lent its hand to cooling off the oppressive heat. However, today, it wasn't doing its job very well.

A wave of heat blasted into the back seat of a parked tinted-out black Range Rover, swooping in on a gust of wind, spraying its main occupant in the face with a sharp smack of dust and grit, disrupting his immaculately groomed slicked back hair.

"Hurry up and close the fucking door, Grant," barked Jonathan West, taking out a comb from his button-up shirt's front pocket, running it through his hair, putting every strand back in its place. "We need to go now, or we'll be late."

West was the CEO of Sotor Corps, the former top Paramilitary Company of the US Department of Defense. That was until he was ousted from the country for his involvement in his father-in-law's, the former Oklahoma Senator Roy Stone's plan. They plotted to use a terrorist faction they funded to drum up and stoke fear in the American people—all to funnel billions of dollars to themselves.

He hated being late. It was a pet peeve of his.

"Yes, sir," Grant responded, closing the door and handing his boss a water bottle.

"Briggs, let's go," West ordered, tapping the headrest of the driver's seat in front of him. "I don't want to miss this meeting. There's no telling where Hasan will be off to next. This Haji moves every four fucking weeks," he sniped, annoyed.

Hasan was now the leader of the Abyan Islamic Army, the AIA, since Amell al-Garshi's death. They needed to stay hopping between locations so as not to be captured by the CIA, which was heavily pursuing both parties.

"Yes, sir, on the move," Briggs, a large, bulky African American with a shiny bald head, said. He reached for a walkie-talkie sitting on the dashboard and keyed the mic. "We're moving again," he announced into the device.

"Copy, Oscar Mike," a voice called back.

The Range Rover pulled away from the small gas station onto the main road that went straight through the coastal city. Briggs checked his rearview, watching a second black Range Rover pull out of the parking lot behind him. The two vehicles turned onto As Sultan Qaboss Street.

"We're about ten minutes out, sir," the fourth occupant of the vehicle, a Hispanic man of medium height and build sporting a crewcut, said, checking the GPS coordinates on his phone and relaying the information to West while showing the screen to Briggs, who nodded in agreement.

"Good, thanks, Sanchez," West said, drawing a sip from his bottle before reaching into his pocket upon feeling a vibration. He retrieved a phone. "Shit," he cursed, seeing the name on the caller ID. "Yes, Dad," West answered, annoyed. It was his Father-in-law, Roy Stone.

"Jonathan, I need you to deal with this situation accordingly," Stone emphasized with a dark undertone. "We didn't give Hasan the docking locations for him to blow everything to hell. It's drawing too much attention to him and, by proxy, us. I thought you told him to lay low after the bombing in Bahrain. Which doesn't mean blowing up a shipping yard in Oman."

West rolled his eyes, even more annoyed at Stone's tone. He'd already had several meets with Hasan since they'd entered into their alliance with the AIA leader after the shootout in DC that Stone barely escaped eight months prior.

"I did, but the fucking Haji doesn't listen."

"Well…" Stone said and paused.

West could hear Stone thinking.

"Maybe it's time we dissolve this partnership then—if he can't be trusted to halt his anger and hatred long enough to see the bigger picture. Then, we don't need someone of that nature jeopardizing our plans. I trust you know what to do," Stone stated.

Jonathan smiled a sinister grin, tapping the Glock stashed into his shoulder holster. He hated putting up with Amell, Hasan, and the AIA. He'd never liked any of them and, in fact, hated all Arabs. He'd seen too many of his former brothers-in-arms killed by their Jihad holy war, having only gone along with Stone's plan because of the money, power, and influence it gave him.

"I do. It'll be done." West hung up. "Boys," he said, and his smirk grew wider. "Be ready; this is going to turn ugly," he warned as Briggs turned off the road, bringing the vehicle to a stop outside of a building nestled into a small strip of shops.

West, Briggs, Diaz, and Grant exited the vehicle as the second Range Rover pulled up. West surveyed the area behind a pair of large, rounded aviator sunglasses as the four members of the second Range Rover filed out. Two men with AKs approached the four men. It was obvious that they despised working with their enemies, much like West. Evident by their sneers.

Besides the two approaching men, West spotted two more on top of the building, which looked like a local restaurant. However, there were no other vehicles parked in the lot. Hasan must've taken it over when he arrived. One of the pair above had an RPG slung around his back. The mercenary leader quickly glanced at Grant, who spotted and acknowledged it immediately with a slight nod.

"You are West?" one of the two men asked, eying the businessman, unimpressed. They both wore military-style fatigues and were practically indistinguishable from each other.

"I am. Where's Hasan? We need to talk," he said, taking a sharp tone with his greeting party.

"He's inside, waiting for you. We take you to him. Your men wait out here."

"No, my men come with me." The retort drew ire from the two men. Sensing the tension, the pair on the roof took aim at West's men. The two groups stared each other down for a brief moment.

"Fine, but not all," finally came a response from one of the Arabs.

West faced his men. "Grant, Hart, Diaz, you keep an eye on the vehicles," he ordered, facing his greeters. "Let's go."

The two Arabs led West and his quintet into the building. It was indeed a restaurant. He could smell the remnants of whatever meal had last been prepared. They followed the escort to the rear of the building, entering a back room through a set of swinging doors. It was the kitchen. The two men circled back around West's group, taking up positions on either side of the doors as they came to a rest.

West and his men quickly fanned out into a wedge formation with the CEO at the point, flanked by Perry to his left and Briggs to his right. Stevens and Jones stood nearest to the two escorts in the back of the formation.

In the center of the room, Hasan Althani stood behind a metal food-prepping table with a meat cleaver hacking down on what remained of a goat's leg. Two other men flanked him, Walid to his left and Kadar to his right. West recognized each from having dealt with them on two other occasions. Two other men also accompanied them, standing beside Walid and Kadar.

Hasan delivered another hack at the leg, sheering off a huge chunk of meat, scooping it up, and dropping it into a pot before looking up to address the new arrivals.

"Mr. West, the AIA want to thank you and Mr. Stone for supplying the information on the USS Oak Hill and its cargo. The weapons taken from the ship will greatly aid us in our war," the terrorist leader said, dropping the cleaver down again.

"Hasan," West addressed, removing his sunglasses. The

weight of his shoulder-holstered Glock shifted with the movement. Walid picked up on it, feeling an uneasy air of tension in West's voice. "We supplied that information months ago and told you after the attack on the base in Bahrain to lay low. Your attacks are drawing too much *fucking* attention. That CIA bitch is snipping at our heels."

Hasan looked up from the table, tossing the newly hacked meat into the pot. "That is not my problem. The CIA, Army, Navy, Marines, British SAS, and all of your Western military and law enforcement have been hounding us for decades. It's nothing new to our people." Dropping the clever again, he sliced off the last vestiges of flesh from the bone before chucking it aside. Turning the cleaver towards his guests. "You, too, must learn to live with it."

West stood up straighter, arching his back, glowering at the Arab, taking the gesture as a threat more than anything. His fingers tensed, wiggling, readying at any moment to draw down on the Arab. "Your actions are jeopardizing our plans, Hasan," West scathed through gritted teeth. "You need to *cease* your operations for a bit. The Senator is working on something."

"Former Senator," Hasan corrected. "And I don't know what that means," adding with a shrug, looking toward his men for confirmation of the meaning. They, too, shrugged.

A sigh escaped West's lips, shaking his head. "It means knock it the fuck off," West shouted, pounding the steel table with his left fist, hunching over to conceal the movement of his right hand. His fingers curled around the grip of his Glock. Walid had seen it, though, having been intently watching West the whole time.

"No!" came Hasan's reply. "You come to me-"

"Oh, fuck it," West shouted, whipping out the gun, pointing the Glock directly at Hasan's head. "I am done with you Haji pricks." He pulled the trigger.

"No!" Shouted Walid, jumping in front of his brother and taking the slug directly to the forehead. Blood and brain matter splattered over Hasan's face.

In a split second, the kitchen erupted into a maelstrom of action. Two of West's men, Stevens and Jones, spun weapons drawn, firing simultaneously at the two men who'd escorted them in—hitting both square in the forehead, spraying the walls with a coat of red.

One of them managed to squeeze off a shot from his AK before he was felled.

A stream of fire from the assault rifle immediately cut down Stevens. Jones managed to leap clear of the blast.

"Shit," West cursed, watching Walid's body drop, aiming at the momentarily dazed Hasan, who was in a state of shock, watching his brother's head explode. "Fuck you." He fired again.

Perry, the man standing to West's left, sprang into action, seeing Kadar draw a weapon. "Boss," he said, shoving his leader aside, causing his round to miss its target wide, and taking a gouge out of the concrete wall behind them.

Kadar's shot hit a target, though. Not it's intended, but it still struck true. The 7.62mm round tore a ragged hole from Perry's neck, ripping the flesh apart. A spray of bright red atrial blood sprouted from the gaping maw.

On his way down, the merc managed to squeeze off two rounds, both striking the man to Kadar's right: one center mass, the other burrowing through his left eye socket. The two men fell to the floor.

Kadar stood mouth agape at Perry's body, blood oozing across the slopped floor to a drain. He'd never directly killed a person before. Pressing a button was completely different than squeezing a trigger and instantly seeing the person on the other side die before your eyes.

West staggered from the shove, hit the ground with a thud, and slid across the tiled floor as Briggs and Jones exchanged fire with the man who had been standing to Walid's left. He'd since taken cover behind a refrigerator in the room's far corner.

West, still sliding, realized he had an open shot at Hasan and quickly snapped up his Glock; coming to a stop, he fired.

Hasan recovered from the initial shock of watching his beloved brother's head explode in front of him in the nick of time. He quickly flipped over the prep table just before the round hit him and, in the process, managed to pull the stunned Kadar down. The two took cover behind the table.

West's round crashed into the steel, denting it, but the slug fell harmlessly to the ground—another curse. He'd missed again.

"Sir, we've got to go," Briggs called out, backing to the door, keeping the other Arab pinned down. "Jonesy, move!"

"Come on, sir!" Jones stopped shooting, helping West to his feet, before firing several rounds over his shoulder into the corner as well as keeping the other man behind cover.

"No!" West tried to pull away. "Hasan's got to die," he shouted before being pushed through the swinging door by Jones, with Briggs following suit.

The three stumbled into the dining room of the restaurant as chunks of the door blew out, sending wood chips flying under the barrage of AK fire.

"Go, go!" Jones pushed his boss forward as Briggs sent a blind volley of gunfire into the kitchen. The rounds struck nothing but concrete walls and steel appliances.

Inside, rounds pinged off the table that Hasan and Kadar were taking cover behind. "You need to leave, my cousin," Kadar said, watching the Americans flee the embattled kitchen. "Go out the back, Fadil, and I will cover you." Hasan reluctantly agreed, with his cousin nodding. "Go with Allah."

Staying low, Hasan moved to the back wall, opened the door slowly, and peeked out to make sure West didn't have anyone covering the rear exit. Seeing no one, he slipped out the doorway, running to one of the Highlanders parked in the backlot.

Kadar watched Hasan leave before turning to face Fadil. The two men gave each other knowing looks, silently commending each other for their impending sacrifice. "For Allah," they intoned.

In the dining room, Jones and Briggs quickly reloaded. The front door swung open. Against the sun's backdrop, two silhouetted men entered, guns drawn at the ready. Briggs and Jones turned about to fire on the newcomers.

"Friendlies," one of the figures shouted. The dark plots came into focus as they approached. It was Grant and Hart. "Threats outside neutralized," Grant said. Diaz is securing the vehicles.

"We've got to go back in and eliminate Hasan. Stone's

orders." West barked, sliding a fresh magazine in, chambering a round. It was now five against three. He liked his odds.

The group readied to go back into the kitchen. Before they could move, though, Kadar and Fadil exploded out from the kitchen, charging through what was left of the swinging doors, AKs blazing. All five Americans whipped around, emptying their magazines into the pair. Their bullet-riddle corpses dropped side by side.

"What the fuck was that?" Briggs asked, sliding in a magazine.

"Martyrdom," shrugged Jones.

"No, diversion," West stated, brushing past Briggs and Grant entering the kitchen. "Fuck." The others followed. "Fuck, he's gone. Shit." He kicked a pot across the room upon seeing that the back door was open and a set of tire tracks led away from the building. He pulled his phone from his pocket, activated the screen, and tapped on Stone's name.

****

"Is it done?" Stone asked curtly.

"He got away," West answered with a tone of defeat in his voice, staring off in the distance at the road, running a hand through his hair, fixing it.

"Get back here then. We need to find where he's going."

"And when we do. Me and my men will be ready." West looked around at the four gathered around him, all nodding in agreement they wanted revenge.

"No, I've got a better idea." Stone's smirk was evident even through the phone. "Enemy of my enemy. We'll send that CIA bitch Sophia Evans after him. Get her off our trail for a bit."

It was West's turn to smirk. "Good idea."

****

Hasan looked back in the mirror, watching the coastal town disappear. A sense of rage and fury swelled inside him as he wiped his brother's blood from his face. He pulled out a cell phone and dialed a number.

"Umar, I need you to find out where the American Stone is hiding out. They've betrayed us. So we will betray them. Find me his location and figure out how to get in touch with Amell's killer, that CIA infidel." Hasan hung up without waiting for a response.

He figured, why not follow one of the oldest rules in warfare? The enemy of my enemy. He'll just set the snake on itself. Watch the two sides consume each other while he plots his revenge on both.

CHAPTER ONE CAMP DARBY, ITALY

SOPHIA Evans could feel her heart thumping in the deep recesses of her chest as she bent over the sink, bracing the countertop with her hands and feeling them slide from the damp, clamminess of her sweat-laced palms. She took a deep breath, following the instructions of her therapist. She steadied, lifting her shirt and running her right hand across her abdomen.

Her fingers gently caressed her smooth skin, finding a ripple of her muscle first. A small sign of the hard work she'd put in during physical therapy. Then, a less pleasing feeling. The outer edges of a scar.

The physical after-effect of being shot. A small one. The wound's diameter was less than 2 centimeters, taking a split second to graze over. The mental effects, however, were and had been far larger.

A spark of anger flushed over Sophia as her finger brushed over the surface of the matted skin. She closed her eyes, reaching back into the recollection of her memory, finding the right file like it had been stored as a video to be played repeatedly, fueling a deep-seated rage and drive. The video played, and she found herself lying on the asphalt, searing pain in her stomach—a faint voice telling her to hold on. Yet her eyes were not fixated on the person talking or the hole in her stomach. They were trained on one man being ushered away from the carnage—Senator Roy Stone, or now, former Senator.

He hadn't been the one that shot her. No, that person was already dead. However, he was responsible for setting in motion the events that led to the shootout in Washington, D.C. The firefight resulted in the scar being placed on her stomach. The very man that had eluded her for the past five months, as well as her team, dubbed Joint Task Force (JTF) 200. They had been tasked with bringing to justice Stone, his son-in-law Jonathan West, CEO of Sotor Corps and PMC, and the new leader of the Abyan Islamic Army, a terrorist group propped up and funded by Sotor Corps' Hasan Althani. Somehow, the trio had managed to stay one step ahead of her.

"Sof, they're approaching," called a voice from beyond the restroom door, followed by a gentle tap.

"Coming," Sophia fired back. "We'll get you asshole," she murmured. Opening her eyes, effectively ending the video playback. A glance in the mirror caused an almost repulsive reflex. Her body may have been made right by physical therapy and her mind by mental therapy, but her face told a different story. Finding a paler-than-normal reflection staring back at her. The dark circles of many sleepless nights burned through the slight amount of makeup she wore. She was tired, near burnt out after the months-long international manhunt. The highs of having Stone within her grasp, only for the inevitable letdown of him slipping away. This time would be different. For once, they had a solid lead on his and West's whereabouts. Turning away from her ghostly doppelganger and swiping a key card, the latch to the restroom door sprung open.

The door led out into her team's temporary base and home. Knowing that Stone and his cohorts' area of operations would most likely be limited to countries with non-extradition treaties with the US, they'd most likely be operating out of the Middle Eastern regions. In an agreement with the US Army, JTF 200 would be allowed to operate out of their base in Italy, Camp Darby, making it easier and quicker to launch operations.

The room wasn't much bigger than a standard apartment living room, but it had been fully transformed into a state-of-the-art tactical operations center for Sophia's team. Nine forty-two-inch TVs covered the back wall, creating one massive monitoring station. Several workstations were on either side of a main aisle leading to the room's front—each complete with a full accouterment of computer equipment.

She took a moment to let her eyes adjust to the darkened room before setting off, strolling down the aisle, arms folded across her chest, right hand to her mouth, biting pensively on her index finger. As she headed up the aisle, Sophia passed two people with their heads down, eyes glued to their computer screens: Jerry Dickerson and Gaby Wise, two analysts she'd hand-picked for

JTF 200. James Owens, the Director of the Central Intelligence Agency, had given her carte blanche in choosing her team of analysts.

Jerry had been part of Sophia's class at 'The Farm,' the CIA's training facility. They'd gotten along pretty well, and he'd been a part of a few higher-profile cases in the past. Plus, he was an excellent translator who spoke several languages and was a top-notch drone pilot. Physically, he was a man of smaller stature with thick-framed glasses, completely unassuming, but he was a technical whiz.

The other member, Gaby Wise, was suggested by Owens—a slightly more seasoned analyst with an impeccable track record and an almost unnatural ability to parse through high volumes of data due to her eidetic memory. She was in her early forties but looked much younger. As Sophia passed, glancing at Gaby's screen, it looked like she was reviewing area statistics.

Sophia continued up the aisle, stopping beside a third analyst. Richard Sparks was the youngest member of the team at twenty-two. However, he was easily the smartest of the group, graduating from MIT at twenty with several degrees. A kid of average height, slightly overweight, and shaggy blond hair, which he refused to cut. He was clacking away at his keyboard, linking communications, and simultaneously maneuvering a satellite into position. With a few strokes of his keyboard, the right half of the monitor wall lit up with an overview of an island in the middle of a lake.

The team's intel suggested that Stone had been hiding on a small island in the middle of Lake Slansko in Montenegro. The image Richard had brought up was of the area. With a few more key clicks and a scroll of his mouse, the island grew bigger, showing a structure on the island's east side and a dock not far away. As Richard continued to scroll, the structure took on form. It was a mansion. Sophia grew more disgusted. The mastermind behind so many deaths—deaths of friends, gets to hide out in style and wealth-despicable. Subconsciously, she bit harder on her finger at the thought.

"Sof, here," a tall blonde with a German accent and

supermodel looks said as she suddenly appeared beside Sophia, handing her a cup of coffee. She was taller than Sophia by several inches, with shoulder-length hair and piercing gray eyes. She walked back to her console, brushing Richard's shoulder. The man instantly reddened in the face.

Sophia barely managed to suppress a smile. She knew the German loved to play flirt with Richard. Guessing it was her way to help the man. "Thanks, Mila," taking a sip, looking over the image of the mansion.

Sophia had met Mila Koch while on assignment trailing a Russian billionaire. He'd recruited Mila and her hacker commune to hack into several US banks to unfreeze his accounts. Sophia had traced one of the hacks back to Mila. Instead of arresting the hacker, she turned her into an asset, and later, the two became close friends. Since then, Mila had always been loyal to Sophia, which was specifically why she wanted the German brought to the task force despite her inexperience. It was for her loyalty and their friendship—two things in short supply in her line of work.

"I just know you've been up all night," Mila added, sitting and setting her cup down. "I'll take over comms," she said to Richard. The kid flashed a thumbs up, not breaking eye contact with his screen. In fact, he rarely looked at Mila, finding her almost too attractive to look at. It didn't help that she never dressed like a professional, always wearing skin-tight or revealing clothing. Something that both Richard and Sophia found distracting—the latter more for the frustration of the image it portrayed. But Mila loved to play the dumb blonde shtick as much as she could, knowing her looks would help.

"Are we set?" Sophia asked.

"About to bring the team online in…" Mila situated herself in her seat before typing in a command code. "Three…two…one, we're online with the team."

****

Master Chief Petty Officer Marshall Wallace peered through his night-vision scope lying hidden amongst tall, untamed grass,

20

perched atop a hilled outcrop of the lake's shore. The scope emblazoned the otherwise pitch-black night with a dazzling display of green, illuminating the area. The scope also served to enlarge what he was looking at, which wasn't particularly needed as the house he'd set his sights on loomed large enough on the island ahead without the lens. Describing the structure as a house was as disingenuous a descriptor as calling a Lamborghini a car. It was more equivalent to what one would see if watching an episode of MTV's Cribs.

The mansion stretched almost the length of a football field. The backside sat a dozen yards up from the island's shoreline and a small dock on top of an embankment, just in case the lake flooded. It'd be harder for the water to reach the extravagant house. Floor-to-ceiling windows dotted the façade of the first and second floors. The only separator between the lower and upper was a wrap-around balcony that stretched the length of the house.

No self-respecting mansion would come without a pool, right? No worries, this one had one nestled between the house and the dock. A smaller, less lavish house was off to the distant right of the main building. Wallace figured this would be for the house staff and the mercenaries that guarded the house's living quarters.

Several of those mercenaries appeared to be roaming the grounds. Two were circling the balcony, one more roaming around the pool area, and one was pacing back and forth between the main and staff houses, with most likely one or two more around the front—not to mention however many may be inside, which was a good sign to Wallace. At least someone was home worth guarding.

"Alpha-one, we're live." Came a crackle in Wallace's ear. "Tactical is on, TOC's ready," Senior Chief Petty Officer Ryan Sands, otherwise known as Alpha-two, radioed.

SEAL team six had been assigned to JTF 200 upon their request after working with Sophia to help capture the AIA's figurehead, Amell al-Gharsi, on Perim Island. During the last six months, they'd help track down and follow up on every lead they could to capture Stone, West, and Hasan.

"Hello, MTV, and welcome to my crib," chirped Bobby Jenkins, aka Tex, Petty Officer First Class (Alpha-three,) who was lying in the grass beside Wallace, surveying their target.

"Stow it, Tex, let's move."

"Rich, crooked assholes," Tex muttered, following Wallace as they departed the outcrop.

The two low crawled back several yards into a small clearing where the other six team members the team had set up. Each team member had a camera rigged on the side of their head attached to a headband. Facing the group, Wallace saw red lights flick on. The lights indicated they'd been switched on. "Alpha-one to TOC, good copy?"

In the Tactical Operations Center, the second half of the monitor wall flickered, and eight smaller screens backlit in green appeared. The names of the SEALs, along with their current vital signs, popped up in the boxes. The box labeled 'Sands' displayed Wallace's image as the operator centered his team leader in his field of vision—a man with sharp facial features hidden under a thick black beard.

"Hey, girlie, what up?" Tex cut in, fixing another monitor onto his face—this one belonging to another member of the team, Walsh (Alpha-seven.). "Stop, focus on me, Walshy. Jeez. What up, baby."

Sophia shook her head. Was the man ever going to stop trying for her? It'd become almost a running joke between the two. "Ceiling tiles and dingy lighting," Sophia answered, eyes shifting to the ceiling, scanning for anything else she could throw in, finding nothing worth noting. The whole room was very bland. "You?"

"Trees and clouds, and…possibly some skinny dipping-"

"Alpha-three, knock it off," Wallace scolded. "We could use some intelligence," Wallace interrupted, glowing at Tex, then looking up, knowing he could never see what he hoped was above him with his naked eye.

Sophia rounded, looking back at Jerry's workstation. His head was buried in his screen, and his hand was wrapped around a joystick. No response. She impatiently snapped her fingers in his direction. "Jerry," she hissed. The analyst broke concentration. "Drone?" He flashed a thumbs up. Sophia twisted away, screwing her eyes. "Richard sat?"

"Good to go," the young man replied.

Sophia turned back to the monitors. "You're all set, Alpha-one. We've got eyes on you. Eagle above and sat imagery. We are looking at the target building now." She took a sip of her coffee, inspecting the image.

"From our location, we can see four tangos. Would like to know if there are more in the area. And possibly inside."

"Copy Alpha one, give us a moment. Richard, thermal." The young man tapped a few keys. The green images on the monitors swapped over to a rainbow of colors.

The colors were read in a spectrum, with the darker and blue shades read as objects emitting lower heat thresholds. Yellows, oranges, and reds are associated with those that emit heat. Generally, heat sources such as stoves, heaters, and, most importantly, people were more easily discernible. Thermal imaging has been used in military and law enforcement since its creation, helping assess potential enemy troop numbers and locations even through structures and heavy fog or smoke.

Sophia scanned the area. Seeing the four men that Wallace had most likely already identified. "I see an additional eleven heat sources. It looks like there are two more guards up front and three in the house. Plus, several more in their bedrooms. It must be the Stone's and West's. I think we've got'em," she declared, swapping smiles with Mila. "You know what to do commander. Take them, preferably alive. But *if* you have to shoot'em. You know what they say."

"*Shit* happens out there… *SHOT*." Sophia and Wallace simultaneously said. Drawing on a shared memory.

"Happy hunting. We'll monitor. Over and out."

Wallace turned to his team. "Alright, men, you heard the lady. Clean, fast, and easy. Just the way we like. Tex, Johns, I want you on the hill. Take out the balcony guards. Everyone else… we're going for a swim."

"Copy that," Petty Officer First Class (Alpha-six) Damon Johns said, tapping Tex on the shoulder and telling him to follow.

The two stealthily headed for the hill Wallace had pointed out.

****

Ten minutes later, a figure quietly and slowly rose from the lake, water dripping down his camouflaged face. Emerging from the serenely still waters, Wallace brought up his silenced SIG Sauer MCX before pulling his night vision goggles back down over his eyes. The area once again lit in a field of green. Several more heads broke the water line—the rest of the SEAL team.

Ryan first, followed by Petty Officer Marcus Tyus (Alpha-four), Petty Officer Second Class Victor Gutierrez (Alpha-five), Petty Officer Second Class Ahmed Alwani (Alpha-eight), and Petty Officer First Class Michael Walsh (Alpha-seven) emerged, bringing their weapons to bear and donning goggles.

Back in the TOC, Sophia clenched, seeing the view from their video feeds come up. They were now a few dozen yards from the mansion and ending their months-long mission. The six SEALs crept out of the water and onto the sand-crusted bank using the tall grasses as cover.

"Ry, Ty, Gut, circle to the front. Take out the guards. Walsh, Al, and I will eliminate the grotto guard and breach from the rear. Tex and Johns take out the two on the balcony. Sophia, count us down when Bravo is in position at the front door. Everyone copy their assignments?"

The team flashed a thumbs-up.

"Move out."

Ryan took his team and moved up the bank toward the staff house. Wallace, Walsh, and Alwani moved up the embankment leading from the shoreline to the house, angling to the right and making their way to the pool, which was angled slightly away from the house.

Wallace peeked his head up to see the guard keeping a regular pace going from the pool area, moving down the backside of the house before disappearing amongst trees that obscured most of the house. Checking his watch to see the timing of the guard's route, he noted that it took the guard approximately five minutes to complete it.

The guard entered the pool area. The pool was an interesting design—a rectangular zero entrance that led out into a semicircle head. Within the circular area was a section out of the water with a fire pit. Several glass bridges ran from the side of the pool out into the center section. The back of the circular area was walled with a fake rock wall. Once the guard entered the pool section, he would be out of sight from anyone inside, giving a window to take him out without being seen.

As the guard made his way back toward the men, Wallace peered down his sights, taking the man into his crosshairs, waiting for him to pass the last of the mansion windows and enter the pool area. Wallace took a breath, holding it.

The guard strode past the window down the bricked path toward the pool, oblivious that he'd be taking his last steps. Wallace paused, giving a few extra seconds for the guard to get further away from the house so that when his body hit the ground, the two men on the balcony wouldn't hear it. He squeezed the trigger.

Pfft.

The guard dropped a red splatter on the rock wall behind him. "Pool guard down," Wallace reported. "Tex, now."

****

On the opposite bank, Tex and Johns were lying in the grasses. Each of the two snipers had the sights of their M91A2 rifles pointed at the roaming guards on the second-floor balcony. Waiting for the command to fire. They needed to fire roughly the same time so neither could sound an alarm upon seeing their buddy go down.

Upon hearing Wallace's order, they fired in concert. Both guards hit the floor at the same time.

"One," Tex called out.

"Dude?" Johns shook his head. "Seriously, not a competition, bro."

Tex shrugged. "Alpha-one, you're clear," he reported, turning to Johns. "You only say that because you never win." No one knew exactly why Tex loved to keep track of his kill counts during missions; he just did. It was something else to add to the minor details that something wasn't quite right in the head of the Texan.

"Keep the channel clear," Wallace demanded, moving his team to the rear of the house, looking for the back door.

****

Ryan, Ty, and Gut made their way up the shoreline, away from the main house, toward the staff quarters. They came around the backside of the building, using it for cover, shielding their advancement from the roving guard. It was dark outside, and the moon had been shrouded with thick clouds, making it darker than normal. There wasn't much man-made light either—a few garden lights lining the path from the staff house to the main. With Ryan and the others clad in all black, it would've been difficult for anyone without night vision to have seen their approach on a normal night, let alone in the current conditions. Still, they didn't want to take the chance to be seen and kick-start a full-fledged firefight. *Too soon.*

Stacking up against the side of the house, Ryan peered around the corner, spotting the guard. He was walking away with his back turned to the SEALs, headed up the walkway toward the main house. He could hear the guard whistling a tone. Listening carefully, he picked out it was from a hard rock song but didn't remember the band name. *So much for night discipline,* Ryan thought.

Giving the signal for Tyus and Gut to stay put, Ryan unsheathed his knife from the front of his tactical vest. Handing his Sig to Ty. He didn't want anything on him to possibly make a sound. He could sneak up on the man while his back was turned.

Breaking from cover in a crouch, Ryan stalked his prey, moving stealthily over the open terrain, staying off the bricked path, fearing his footsteps would give him away. He knew from watching the guard's patrol that he wouldn't reach the end of the path for another ten yards, which gave him plenty of time.

Drawing nearer, ten feet… five… three. Ryan brought the blade up, ready to pounce—one foot.

Now!

The SEAL reached out, wrapping his left hand over the stunned guard's mouth, muffling a shocked yelp, running the blade across the man's throat, unleashing a sprout of blood severing the carotid artery. The man gurgled as he struggled for a few seconds before going lifeless in Ryan's arms.

The commando gently laid the corpse on the ground, wiping his blade on the man's sleeve, sheathing his knife, retreating to his compatriots, and taking his Sig back from Ty.

"Let's move," he ordered.

The group headed for the front of the house. Approaching the side, they stopped. Peeking around the edge, Ryan spotted the two guards that Sophia had seen on satellite. One stood by the front door; the other paced the drive. There were two cars parked in front, backed up near the doors, making it easier to evacuate at a moment's notice. The way they were parked also conveniently gave the team cover while they made their approach. Plus, they blocked the pacing guard's view of the man by the door. *Amateurs*.

"Ty, take the doorman, Gut driveway." Both men nodded in agreement.

They tore around the corner in a low crouch, using the SUV as cover, approaching rapidly, getting as close as possible before opening fire. Gutierrez broke away, heading to the front of the SUV to get a clearer shot at the rover. Tyus and Ryan continued forward with Tyus running point.

The doorman noticed movement in his peripheral, turning to see Gutierrez streak across through the SUV's window. The man spun, whipping up his rifle, about to shoot.

He wouldn't get the chance.

Two high-velocity 5.56mm rounds struck the side of his head, burrowing through his motor cortex and severing his brain's ability to contract his finger muscles. The guard hit the ground with a thud. The two SEALs continued their advance to the front door without breaking stride.

Gutierrez, meanwhile, had lined up his own shot with a light squeeze of his trigger. Two rounds punched through the pacing man's chest, a third through his neck, tearing a rent from his throat. With a gurgle, he, too, fell. Gutierrez rounded the front of the SUV, joining Ryan and Tyus by the front door.

"Front tangos down. Ready to breach," Reported Ryan.

"Copy." Sophia watched their feeds, seeing Wallace's team was already on standby near the back door. "Remember, there's three gunmen inside—one in the kitchen near the fridge. Wallace, when you breach, he's immediately to your right. Ryan goes straight ahead through the hallway, and there's one sitting on a couch. The third is by the stairs. You're not going to have a clear shot right away. It may get loud. Over."

****

The mansion, for all its size and extravagance, had a simple layout. It was long but not wide. The kitchen was offset to the main living room area down a long hall. The front door opened into a short vestibule before dumping into a large gallery area of the main living room, surrounded by an atrium with pillars supporting the upper section. A set of stairs leading to the second-floor balcony overlooked the living room that was set off the left of the vestibule exit.

"Copy, count us down."

Sophia glanced around the TOC. Everyone's eyes were glued to the monitors. They were about to achieve their objective. "Three…two…All Alphas breach."

On that order, both Wallace and Ryan kicked in the back and front doors, respectively.

Breaching the back door, Wallace entered the kitchen, cutting right as Walsh, second to enter, turned left; Alwani continued straight. Wallace scanned his field of fire, searching for the threat he knew was there. He Spotted the guard standing in front of the refrigerator door with a carton of orange juice in hand, wearing a stunned, disbelieving look on his face.

It was a mere seconds of shock before training retook his body, zapping him out of paralysis. But, against a highly trained Navy SEAL, a tenth of a second of hesitation meant death. The man dropped the carton, swinging up his M4. Only to take two rounds to his chest. He jerked back, hitting the steel fridge with a thud, before sliding down the front, leaving a red streak, dropping out of sight.

Alwani and Walsh advanced further into the house as Wallace moved to ensure the man he'd just shot was dead. He rounded the center island, finding the guard sitting propped up by the fridge, head slumped, chin to chest. No rise from the latter. Dead. He spun, following his men into the hall and advancing to the living room.

****

Ryan busted through the front door, darting through the vestibule, catching the man on the couch by surprise. However, he was a little quicker than his dead friend in the kitchen. He sprang into action faster, managing to get off several rounds as Ryan, Tyus, and Gutierrez poured in, looking for anything to take cover behind.

Ryan threw himself to the floor in a slide, stopping behind a couch—Tyus dove for cover behind one of the pillars supporting the atrium. Gut, the last through the door, hadn't made it out of the vestibule, throwing himself against the wall, tucking into the 'L' corner before exiting the vestibule threshold.

The first fusillade sprayed over their heads, shattering the chandelier above the entrance and sending crystal fragments showering down on the intruders. The man saw one figure slide behind a couch, another taking refuge behind a pillar. The third was trapped in the vestibule, having to choose between which of the three to exact his rage on. The shooter shifted position, opening fire on Tyus behind the squared pillar.

Unleashing a barrage of fully automatic fire at the marble pillar, the rounds smacked against the hard stone, gnawing away at the intruder's cover until his magazine ran dry.

Ryan sprang from behind the couch, hearing the *click, click* of the shooter's empty magazine. Propping his MCX on the back of the couch, he set the shooter in his sights as he fumbled the new magazine. Ryan fired. The man took three slugs to the chest, falling backward and crashing through a glass coffee table, shattering it to pieces.

The cushions beside Ryan exploded in a mist of foam padding as slugs pounded into the couch, sending the SEAL diving back down for cover.

The upstairs man appeared, firing wildly in Ryan's direction before darting behind the wall at the top of the staircase. Ryan signaled to Tyus to take a shot the next time the shooter popped back out. Which he was about to force.

Getting to his feet, crouching behind the shredded sofa, he identified another pillar in the grand living room a few feet away. Leaping to his feet, he ran for the marble pillar. The shooter above, seeing this, exposed himself to fire, only to take several rounds of his own and slump out from behind the wall.

Wallace and his team burst from a hallway, guns raised, and saw the two dead men. "Good job."

"Thanks. You're a little late there."

"It's a long fucking hallway," Wallace retorted. "This place is huge."

"Probably going to be haunted now," said Tex over the radio.

"Not done yet, boys," Sophia cut in. "Looks like the West's and Stone's are moving," she said, seeing activity from the upstairs heat signatures. "Wallace, when you hit the top, go left. The master bedroom is down that hall; it dead ends into the room. There are two signatures. It must be Stone and his wife. Ryan, you're going to take four and break right." Wallace pointed to Ty, Gut, and Walsh to go with Ryan.

"The first door on the left. It's a bedroom, and there is one signature inside. Bypass the second door; it looks like a bathroom. The third must be a second bedroom. There is one signature inside, and another room appears to be a little further up the hall—the first door on the right. There are two more heat sigs inside. Probably

Johnathan and Megan West. Remember, there are kids. Trigger discipline, gents," Sophia directed.

"Copy. Go, go." The team bounded up the staircase, stepping over the corpse of the Sotor Corps guard. Wallace and Alwani took the left hallway as Sophia instructed. Ryan, Tyus, Gutierrez, and Walsh went right.

Walsh kicked in the door to the first room, finding its occupant. Gutierrez broke down his door, securing the person inside. Ryan and Tyus kicked in the third door seconds later. The pair, bewildered at their findings, expected the CEO of Sotor Corps to have put up a fight.

Wallace and Alwani smashed through the French doors into the master bedroom, guns drawn, ready to take their prize into custody.

CHAPTER TWO

WALLACE burst through the door. "Get down, get on the ground," he shouted, angling towards one side of the bed, where a man-shaped figure startled by the sudden intrusion had leaped. Alwani moved toward the opposite side, where a slender female-looking person was still groggily coming out of their sleep, sitting up. Wallace pounced on his target with snake-like speed. "On your knees," he screamed, forcing the man down at gunpoint, jabbing the barrel in the man's face, tossing a sideways glance to Alwani, checking he'd secured his prisoner.

The other SEAL was helping the woman out of the bed, bringing her over. "On your knees too, Ma'am," he ordered. "Lights."

"Stop moving," Sophia hissed angrily. With all the movement the two were doing, she couldn't get a good look at the man they'd just taken into custody. She eagerly waited for Alwani to throw the light switch. When they finally flicked on, her body convulsed with a wrath she'd never experienced.

"What the fuck!" Sophia spat. She was expecting the cold, callous face of Roy Stone to be looking at her through Wallace's video feed. Instead, it was the frightened expressions of an older couple. Not the Stones. "Son of bitch," she roared, snatching her empty coffee cup and chucking it. The cup slapped against a wall with a thud, shattering into a million pieces.

"Who the fuck are you?" Wallace demanded, taken aback by the couple, who were both terrified and trembling with fear.

"Chief, I think we've been had," Ryan said, entering with the occupants of the other rooms—none of them being the Stones or Wests. The SEALs corralled the seven terrified people together, putting them all down on their knees.

"Mr.… Mr. Soldier Man," the oldest of the group. The man that had leaped from the bed upon Wallace's intrusion spoke up, raising his hands. "We… we have a message."

"Shut up," the Wallace retorted with a glower. "Sof, what do you want us to do?"

The blonde slumped into a chair, burying her head into her

hands. The all-too-familiar feeling of defeat washed over her soul. Yet again, Stone had managed to evade capture somehow. "Let him speak," she sighed.

"Go ahead, what's the message?" Wallace still held his gun trained on the man, as did the rest of his men on their captors.

The man pointed to his breast pocket. Wallace nodded to go ahead. He reached inside, sliding out a piece of paper, clearing his throat nervously, trembling, sweat beading on his forehead, clearly not wanting to read what it contained.

"To my shadow, the CIA bitch."

Sophia tensed, pursing her lips and clinching her fist, and the man read.

"Always a step behind. You'll never catch me. Give up before you get more people killed." The man dropped the paper, fearing what retribution he'd suffer for having read the words.

"That's it?" Wallace asked. The man stared blankly at him. "This asshole," Wallace muttered. "Watch them." He gestured for his team to keep a close eye on the group. The SEALs surrounded them at gunpoint. Wallace strode out into the hallway, shaking his head. "What a dick," Wallace mumbled, keying his mic. "Sof, what's the call here?" he asked, running a hand through his damp, close-cropped brown hair, knowing they'd been had again.

The analyst sat contemplating for a moment. She wanted to question all of them. However, going over every possible scenario in her head, there wasn't a way to legally do so. Technically, they hadn't committed any crimes and weren't US citizens. Plus, Montenegro had no extraditions with the US, and her team had no authority to operate in the country. Bringing them in for interrogation would be tantamount to kidnapping. She fell into thought, biting her index finger.

"Bring them in," she finally answered. *What the hell*, she figured. Knowing the CIA had a long history of similar acts. What's one more if it meant capturing America's most wanted man? "Bring them all in."

"You sure on this?" Wallace asked, himself knowing that doing so would be illegal. "You know, we'd be breaking several international laws."

"Sometimes you have to break an egg to make an omelet," came her tart reply.

"Alright, we'll bring them in." Wallace returned to the room. "Everyone to their feet. We're all going on a field trip." The team helped the prisoners to their feet and, one by one led them from the room. "We'll see you in a few hours. Wallace over and out."

The video feeds cut out as Richard terminated the connection.

Mila swiveled in her chair, signaling for the others to leave. They abruptly did so, filing out. Waiting for the door to close, she approached her friend, who was trembling in rage. "Don't bite my head off." Sophia's face turned up to her friend. "It's just a minor setback."

"*Another* setback, Mila. When do setbacks just become plain fuck ups?" the blonde spat. "When do *I* admit I am a fuck up and in over my head."

"We'll get him. Don't worry." The German put a hand on Sophia's shoulder, trying to comfort her friend. She'd seen this level of questioning of her abilities after the Belgrade mission went sideways, and she took responsibility for the deaths of several of her team members.

"I know," Sophia said, shaking her head. "I just… just *really* thought it'd be today." Sophia stood, shoulders slumped, head down, and she padded toward the door. Twisting before opening it. "Call me when the boys are back."

"Where are you going?"

"Type out the report. Owens is going to want an update, too. This was supposed to be the day we brought an end to all of this. And… I failed. Again."

"You didn't-" Before Mila could finish, the door slammed. "Fail." She continued, knowing that Sophia couldn't hear her. She returned to her terminal, bringing up the case file and clacking away at her keyboard.

Sophia stepped into the hallway, where the rest of her team had been waiting, seeing their half-shocked, half-pity-filled expressions. She felt a need to address them. "I am sorry, guys. That wasn't… professional of me. I know." Lowering her head, she continued down the hall, ashamed of her outburst.

Reaching the door to her room, swiping her key card, she entered. The agent set her eyes on the nicely made bed—one she hadn't slept in for over twenty-four hours. Shambling to it, she threw herself upon it like an angry teenager.

Letting herself sink into the surprisingly comfortable bed, she stared up at the ceiling. She wondered what went wrong. *How was Stone always a step ahead? Could there be a traitor in the group? How?* They were all hand-picked by either herself or Owens. And there was no way any of Wallace's team would be the culprit if there was a leak in the group.

Thoughts raced around her brain.

It wasn't long before those racing thoughts subsided into slow-moving contemplations as the adrenaline of the mission had worn off. Sophia's tired eyes succumbed to the inevitableness. She dozed off into a long-awaited sleep.

****

Sophia's phone trilled across the nightstand, arousing the agent from her deep sleep. A dream-filled slumber. One in which her greatest desire was being fulfilled.

Standing at a podium in the deep recesses of the George Bush Center for Intelligence, at the CIA's home office in Virginia, receiving the Distinguished Intelligence Cross from her boss, James Owens, given to her and her team for the capture of Roy Stone. Preparing to give a rehearsed speech, only for it to be broken up by the rattling of the phone skipping across the tabletop. She snatched it before it fell over the precipice. Staring bleary at the caller ID, she let her eyes adjust.

The collection of colors and shapes slowly began to take form as her mind merged them into a coherent image. "Oh shit," she snapped, sitting up. What had formed was one word on the screen, 'Boss.' Checking the time, it was already one in the afternoon, two hours past her mission report due time. She rubbed the sleep from her eyes, composing herself.

She answered. "Good morning, sir."

"Agent Evans," James Owens, the CIA's Clandestine Services Director, and Sophia's direct report, spoke. The tone in his voice was somewhere between concern and irritation.

"Yes… yes sir," came her groggy reply.

Try as she may, it wasn't easy to sound wide awake on the phone when you've only just been awoken. Plus, she was upset for allowing herself to fall asleep. Sophia despised lateness of any sort. So, being two hours late to file her operations report was particularly flustering as well.

"Can you please tell me why I am not currently reading over your mission report? As the mission should've been over seven hours ago. I hoped to be reading about how your team captured Stone."

No excuses, Sophia, she told herself before answering. "Sir-" she gulped. "He wasn't at the location… again."

She pulled the phone from her ear in expectation of a deserved tongue-lashing. No immediate response came—a few seconds of awkward silence.

"Well," came Owens' reply finally. "That's a shame."

Sophia could almost hear him thinking as another unpalatable silence fell. "I know this the fourth time we've struck out, sir. But I assure-"

"What do you think this means?" the DCS interrupted, cutting her off. "Is he possibly getting feed information somehow?"

"I… I uh." Sophia was confused. She'd expected to be scolded, possibly told she would be taken off the mission. She wasn't prepared for that question. "I am sorry, sir, but you're not going to pull me. It's been six months-"

"Sophia," his tone sharp, "Let me stop you there before you dig yourself a hole that you shouldn't. I am not going to pull you from this mission. I *gave* it to you because I know you're the best person for the task. It's taken a few months—something like this will. The man you're chasing, men you're chasing," quickly correcting himself. "Have a lot of resources at their disposal. You still have my complete confidence. So, again, I ask, what do you think this means?"

Sophia stiffened a bit, hearing the vote of confidence. "Normally, I'd say there's a leak," she answered. "But the team was hand-picked by just the two of us. So, I...I don't want to believe that. But...I'd be remiss if I completely dismissed it, sir." She had to admit that it could be possible as no one, not even a former US Senator, could be this lucky to stay a step ahead continuously.

"Ok, let me look into that possibility," he said. "In the meantime, you focus on finding these assholes and bringing them to justice."

"Will do, sir."

"Great, oh, and I still want my report," he added.

Sophia could picture a sly smile on his gaunt, bespectacled face. "Yes, sir." She hung up, then retrieved her laptop from the desk table to start typing the 'After Action Report.'

A knock at the door. "Agent Evans, your presence is requested in the TOC."

The voice didn't sound familiar at all. It was most likely a building staffer sent to fetch her. "I am a little busy right now. I'll get back to them when I can."

"Ma'am, Ms. Koch sounded pretty adamant that I get you to return to the TOC ASAP," the staffer added.

"Why didn't you say that first." Sophia rolled her eyes, getting up. "I'll be there in five." She could hear the sound of his feet retreating. She got up and quickly changed, gliding to the mirror trying to fix her bedhead. "Oh, screw it." She tied her hair back into a ponytail.

****

Sophia approached the TOC's door, digging into her pocket for her keycard. Finding it, she swiped the card in front of the reader, wondering what could've been so urgent. The door latch released, and Sophia walked in. Mila whirled upon her arrival, a huge grin across her face. The tall blond rushed over.

"You're not going to believe this," the young woman eagerly

spattered out. "Talk about a twist." She grabbed Sophia by the arm and led her down the aisle to one of the front desks, practically skipping. "Our luck is turning."

"What are you going on about?" Sophia cried, pulling her arm away as Mila pointed at a phone on the desk. The red call waiting button was lit. "So," she added, a little disturbed by Mila's giddiness. "It's a phone. We've used them before," adding with condescension.

Mila threw her hands up in mock offense. "Can never make you happy. Jeez," she said, rolling her eyes. "It's Stone." Sophia's eyes widened, giving Mila a *shut the fuck up look.* The German picked up on the look. "I am not kidding."

Stunned, Sophia shifted glances between the phone and her friend. "What does he want?"

"He uh…" she said, thinking about the nicest way to put it. "Wants to speak to the woman in charge," she settled on.

"We're tracing the call. Right?" Sophia sat down, waiting for a response, looking over at Richard.

"We're trying," Mila added. "It's being bounced all over the world. But we'll get it."

"Hopefully," Sophia hissed and then pushed the hold button, taking the call off hold. "Senator Roy Stone. Or should I address you as former Senator Roy Stone?" Adding an emphasis to the word 'former.'

"Ah, how I've missed your usual curtness, Agent Evans, or should I say my CIA shadow or CIA *bitch*?" he asked, spitting the words acidly. "How does it feel always being a step behind? I mean, how many chances will your boss give you to find me?" he sniped, feigning concern for her job security. "I wouldn't want anyone losing their job on my behalf."

"As many as it takes. In fact, I just spoke to him. Got a full vote of confidence. So, don't get too comfy."

"Oh, my, how far has our mighty intelligence apparatus fallen that a major screw-up like you can keep getting chance after chance? I must admit I like your spirit, kid. The way you keep standing up, or…" he paused. *"Kneeling up."* The sexual insinuation drew a clenching of teeth from Sophia as she fought to keep her composure. "Bet you wish you would've shot me all those months ago in DC. How is our dear old, retired Fred doing?"

Fred Jones, the FBI agent who helped Sophia bring down Stone's plot to drum up fear in America to keep funneling billions of dollars to Sotor Corps, getting the kickbacks from his son-in-law. She hadn't spoken to him much since leaving for the mission.

"He's doing just fine," Sophia said. "In fact, he's making preparations for a 'caught the sleazy scumbag senator celebration' BBQ. I would invite you, but sadly, they don't let prisoners out to attend cookouts. Even if it *is* in their honor."

She glowered over to Richard. The analyst was typing away at his keyboard. He looked up, shaking his head. He still hadn't locked down where the call was coming from, signaling he needed more time.

"So, what do I owe this displeasure to anyhow? Running out of rocks to crawl underneath?"

"I was feeling a little bad for you after your Montenegro strike out. Epic fail, by the way," he said, adding insult to her latest failure. "That I figured I could do something nice for you."

"Oh, what is that? Turning yourself in? I am sure Rebecca can't be fond of all the running. I've seen her closet. All those party and cocktail dresses she has, wait, had. She can't like not being able to go to fundraisers anymore."

"Listen here, you *bitch*," Stone scathed. "Keep my wife's name out of your *bitch* mouth." His usually calm and smug demeanor evaporated at the very mention of his wife's name. Sophia had struck a nerve. Indeed, Rebecca Stone had been growing weary of life on the run.

Sophia smiled, enjoying the revenge taunt, glancing again at Richard. He shook his head. "Now, temper, temper."

"Anyway, back to the point." His tone took a quick turn back to a calmer inflection. A complete polar shift. "Would you like my assistance or not?"

"Sure, depends. What are you giving me?"

"How about Hasan Althani?" Stone replied, letting the reveal set in. Sophia's ears perked. Aside from Stone and West, Hasan was also on her capture list. "Figured that'll get your attention."

Sophia took a moment to ponder. Why now? Why suddenly, out of the blue, call to give up the terrorist leader of the AIA? The group he'd been in bed with for years, helping to fuel his fearmongering.

"Yeah, you've got my attention," she said. "Something happen?" Probing further to keep him on the line. "Honeymoon over? Realized he leaves the seat up?"

"Let's…say…he's outlived his usefulness."

"You mean, his attacks that used to cause the fear you profited off of now don't make you any money. So, time to turn?"

"Not exactly. Call this a good-faith gesture. I am still an American patriot, after all. I still love my country, even if it currently doesn't love me back."

The mere fact that the man still considered himself a patriot drew a scoff from Sophia. "Pfft. What do you mean by currently? The country never forgets. Didn't 9/11 teach you that?"

It was Stone's turn to chortle. "Ha, America, especially today with its thirty-second TikTok, brains have shorter memories. The 24-hour news cycle never falters to bring some new wave of distraction."

Sophia shrugged; he wasn't entirely wrong. He may be delusional in thinking that the country would forget about him and his misdeeds. Still, something struck out at her. He was talking like he really believed that, at some point, he'd be able to go back to the States and live out the rest of his days normally. There was no way she'd let that happen.

"Alright, then." She played along. "Your good faith payment. Where's Hasan?"

"You'll find him in the city of Sana'a, Yemen. He frequently recruits out of there. Now send your attack dogs to get him. After that, we'll talk again about what I want in return. Goodbye, Agent Evans."

Before she could follow up, the line went dead. "Did you get it?" She twisted, glaring at Richard.

"I am sorry," he said apologetically. "He was using some new tech that scrambled the signal all over. The second I thought I had it locked, it'd jump again."

"Fuck," Sophia spat, rubbing her temples with her index finger, running through her head to see if she could really take Stone's word on Hasan's location.

"Sof?" Mila called out from her desk. Sophia looked over, anger in her eyes. Mila had the receiver of her phone to her ear, covering the mouthpiece with her hand. "It's Hasan," she said, pointing at it.

"What the shit?" Sophia stared at her friend, perplexed. "Something must have happened between those three. What are the chances we get calls from both parties on the same day?" Her team shrugged. "Richard, try to get this call, please." The young man cracked his knuckles, preparing to work his computer magic. "Milly transfer." The German did on Sophia's order. "Hasan Althani," she said, picking up.

"Is this the CIA bitch tracking Stone and myself?" he asked, rudely jumping to the point, unlike her usual song and dance of snide marks back and forth with Stone.

Sophia pursed her lips, clutching the phone harder. She hated being called bitch. "Yes," she reluctantly responded. Based on her previous call, she determined that he was calling to give away Stone's location. She didn't want to anger or upset him by getting into an argument.

"Good, you'll find Roy Stone in Tangier, Morocco. I am sure your drone and satellites will be able to pinpoint where exactly."

"Thank-" Sophia pulled her head from the phone as the line went dead. He'd hung up. "Well, that was rude."

"I am sorry I couldn't get that call," Richard exclaimed.

Sophia turned, facing the team. "Don't worry, no one could've. It was too short," she replied, comforting the shaggy-headed man. She then smiled widely, batting her eyebrows. "But we've got them. Now, let's get some confirmations."

****

Several hours later, the TOC was still abuzz with activity. Sophia, Mila, Richard, Gabby, and Jerry were all hard at work confirming the locations of Stone and Hasan when the door to the room opened. Wallace and Tex entered, pausing. They were bewildered by the flurry of movement. It appeared as if something major had happened while they were traveling back. But what could cause this much commotion, they wondered as they sauntered into the bowls of the information center.

Sophia had clocked their arrival, jabbing a finger at them, indicating she'd be with them in a minute before returning to her call.

"Somethings clearly happened," Tex muttered, nodding at Mila and blowing her a kiss. She, in turn, flashed him the middle finger with a grin. "Oh, I am so going to make her my wife," he added, pretending to catch the gesture and pocketing it.

"You wish, bud, in your wildest dreams," Wallace countered. He'd seen Tex snag some beautiful women in the past, especially given his modest looks. However, Mila was on a whole different scale with her supermodel looks.

"Why do you think I go to sleep every night?" he said with a wry grin and chuckle.

"You ever not gonna laugh at your jokes?" Wallace asked.

"Nope."

"Shut up, straighten up." Sophia was headed their way, coming down the middle aisle, cutting off the inappropriate conversation. "Whatever it was that happened, it must've been good. She's smiling for once," Wallace added, speaking out of the side of his mouth.

"I heard that," Sophia said, stopping in front of the pair, jabbing the SEAL in the shoulder. "I would have you know that I generally have a good sense of humor. I smile and laugh." Setting a deadpan expression on Tex. "*When* someone *actually* says something funny."

Tex shrugged, then departed the two, seeing Mila hang up the phone. "But I am glad you're back. And all in one piece."

"All gravy. Sorry, the mission was a bust again, though. We'll get them next time." Wallace looked around the room, flexing an eyebrow. "That time coming sooner than maybe anticipated."

"That's another reason why I am glad you're back. We've…

had some rather interesting developments," she said, indicating for him to follow her.

The pair headed toward a side office off the main TOC floor—Sophia's makeshift office. She sat behind a desk. Wallace took the seat in front of her. The office lacked anything personal despite the team operating out of the base for months. He reckoned that Sophia didn't want to get comfortable. That would've meant admitting the mission would take time. Something he knew she didn't want. At the outset of the formation of the JTF, she'd promised to get the men back home in a couple of months. It'd already taken six.

"What's the development?" Wallace asked, picking up a stapler and fidgeting with it.

"You could never sit still, could you?" Sophia commented, watching the man play around with the object. "Anyway. So… they turned on each other." A hesitation before continuing, giving the reveal a moment to sink in. The stoic SEAL smiled and shook his head. "Wow, not the response I was expecting."

"Not that much of a shock," he countered. "I mean, they were pretty strange bedfellows to begin with."

"True." Sophia had to admit he was right on that front. "Still, they turned on each other. So, hopefully, your team got some rest because we're headed out tomorrow. We just finished confirming both sets of information. And got solid confirmation they are where each said they'd be."

"Where?"

"Stone is holed up in Tangier, and Hasan is in Sana'a," Sophia reported.

"Great. We'll bag Stone, then go get Hasan." He put the stapler down, standing.

"Nope, we're getting both at the same time."

Wallace paused, stiffening his back, affixing a bewildered look at the CIA agent. "That's not possible. I can't be in two places simultaneously. You know how physics works, right?"

"Har, fucking har, smart ass," Sophia retorted. "I know that. You're going to take Alpha Squad to Tangier. I'll take Bravo to

Sana'a."

Wallace's eyes shot wide, betraying his stoic demeanor. "The fuck you will," he spat, sitting back down. "A four-man team in Tangier is fine. They're friendly and adjacent to the US. But, I'll be damned if I send you and four men into Yemen. You know, the terrorist capital of the fucking world. Shit, you were with us on Perim Island. We barely made it out of there. No way." Wallace stood resolute in his stance. Making a show of it by folding his arms across his chest.

"I want them both, Master Chief. I don't want to remind you. I run the operations," Sophia rebuked, meeting his glare.

"Well, considering that you just did remind me. That's moot now." He unfolded his arms, setting a thought in motion. "However, I have a solution since I can't be in two places, and splitting the team would be a terrible idea. We call up Mike's team." Mike Wilks was the head of another SEAL squad that had been put on standby for JTF 200 for situations like the ones they were currently facing.

"No. I don't know them, so I don't trust them."

"Do you trust me?"

Sophia nodded.

"Good, I vouch for Mike's team. But how about this? What if we compromise?"

"I am listening," Sophia said, waiting for him to spit out his idea.

"I'll take Alpha squad with half of Mike's team. You take Bravo with the other half of Mike's team. Sound reasonable?"

Sophia leaned back in her seat, pondering. After a few moments of letting her feelings subside, she was able to see Wallace's plan was the best option. It was one reason she loved working with him. He always saw reason, never letting emotion cloud his judgment. "Ok. Deal." She acquiesced. "I am sorry," she apologized while blushing, mad at herself for blowing up on the man. "I know you're right. As usual. This is a partnership, not a dictatorship." The pair stood. "Thank you. Let's bring Mike's team on."

"Don't worry about it." Wallace waved a dismissive hand at

their disagreement. "Tensions are high. I get that. I'll get him on the line. Get him up to speed, and we'll be off." Wallace dismissed himself.

45

WALLACE crouched low behind the cover of a rocky outcrop, his night-vision goggles casting an eerie green glow over the landscape below. With a silent gesture, he signaled to his team to hold positions as he observed the fortified compound below them.

The layout of the grounds matched everything he'd seen on the image provided to him and his team on the flight from Camp Darby, which didn't ease his hesitation about assaulting such a large compound an ounce. Sometimes, it didn't matter how much planning and preparation you'd done. Once the bullets started flying, anything went.

He eased back into the recesses of the trees, keying his mic. "Alpha one to the TOC, we're on-site, confirming with a Lasso." He signaled to Walsh, who tilted his rifle skyward, depressing a button on the side of a small black box affixed to the bottom of his FN SCAR. He began rotating the rifle like he was preparing to throw a rope, lassoing a hog.

Overhead, high in the night sky above the clouds, lurked a silent force, an eagle-eyed piece of technology that provided America's elite special forces a crucial advantage. A drone. Its infrared cameras picked up the invisible beam being cast from the device on Walsh's rifle.

Gaby, in the Tactical Operations Center back at Camp Darby, stared at the video feed on the wall screen, seeing the light swinging around in the night sky, completely invisible to the naked eye. "Alpha-one, we have your location." She nodded to Jerry, who was seated behind her at his desk, a cue to switch spectrums.

The feed lit up in a dazzling array of colors. Not a single organism was able to hide from the drone's thermal cameras. The sight before her only served to confirm their intelligence reports.

After Hasan had provided Sophia with Stone's location, they set out to learn as much as they could about his activities.

Fortunately for them, the Moroccan government was all too willing to provide any information Sophia had requested.

They confirmed that Stone had arrived in the country three months prior and that he'd purchased a sprawling twenty-acre plot of land, which was formerly owned by a local oil billionaire suspected of running a crime family. He'd then set about refurbishing the compound situated on the plot.

According to customs records, Jonathan West entered the country around the same time. Shortly after that, an influx of foreigners began arriving through the country's airports. They suspected that the two fugitives were setting up shop in Morocco.

That suspicion was now confirmed.

Gaby and Jerry stared at the video monitors, concern growing on their faces as they counted the number of moving reddish-orange blobs.

"One to the TOC, what are you seeing?" Wallace asked.

From his vantage point, Wallace could survey only a fraction of the vast compound sprawled out below. A ten-foot-high brick wall encircled the entire plot of land, its crown adorned with coils of razor wire. Guard towers punctuated the perimeter at precise intervals.

Near the front and back gates, a pair of modest single-story buildings were nestled discreetly against the walls, which likely served as guard quarters. In the heart of this modern-day stronghold, a three-story tower rose into the night sky. Its purpose was a mystery. Was it some new headquarters for Sotor Corps? It was also under some form of construction, indicating that it was new. Something Stone and his men could've started. Scaffolding still surrounded the building, which suggested that it wasn't complete.

But it was the magnificent mansion that truly stole the scene. Its pristine white marble exterior shimmered in the glow of garden lights, casting an aura of regal grandeur upon its surroundings and towering proudly amidst the stark landscape. Elegant archways framed floor-to-ceiling windows that surrounded the house.

Before the mansion's opulent facade, a lush expanse of vibrant greenery unfolded like a verdant oasis, starkly contrasting the arid terrain around it. Each blade of grass was meticulously tended to. A secondary wall, a barrier between luxury and the outside world, further accentuated the mansion, giving it privacy and protection for its privileged inhabitants.

Outside of being able to view the luxury of how the one percent get to live despite being fugitives from the world's most powerful country, he couldn't make out much else, aside from a guard or two in the front and back towers. Fortunately, it didn't appear that any of the other towers were occupied. Making an unseen approach possible.

"Alpha-one, we are counting at least a dozen potential tangos within the compound grounds patrolling. Could definitely be more in the buildings," replied Gaby. She swiveled her chair around to face Jerry, releasing the mic button. "I don't think they should assault this place," she quipped out the side of her mouth.

Jerry nodded in agreement, too concerned to reply verbally, instead settling for the gesture of approval to his co-worker.

Wallace pulled out a satellite picture of the fortress, opened it, and spread it across the ground. The rest of the team drew closer as he clicked on a flashlight, illuminating the photo in a tint of red. Rolling his wrist over, checking the time. It was just past three in the morning. He let his thoughts linger for a moment on Sophia's mission. At this time, she should be preparing to jump from a C-117 over the Yemeni desert. He snapped back to his current mission as the last of his team closed in the circle.

"Alright, boys," he said, looking at each man. "We've got our work cut out for us tonight. We have at least a dozen mercs down there. All probably ex-military. So, not the usual riff-raft, rag-tag band of undisciplined idiots. So, we've got to be on our game."

Everyone nodded.

"Great, here's the plan then. I'll take my team, Walsh, Al, and Johns, and hit the front gate. Thomas, you take your team, Jensen, Johnson, and Smith, around to the back of the compound."

Thomas and his team were part of Wilks' unit. They'd split both of the SEAL teams on Sophia's orders, not trusting anyone other than Wallace to go after Stone.

"You guys will circle around the back. We'll sneak in and

neutralize any and all threats quietly," Wallace ordered.

"Thank god Tex isn't here then," Walsh quipped. "That man can't do shit quiet." Alwani and Johns laughed, nodding their heads in agreement.

"Cut it," Wallace sniped. "Take out whoever we come across quietly. Get into the mansion, grab our targets, and get the hell out of dodge. Bring these assholes home to face justice. Everyone got the plan."

"Hooyah," the team chimed in muted agreement.

"Perfect. Radio when in position Thomas."

"Copy that. Let's go, men." Thomas and Wallace fist-bumped. Then, the former took his team and vanished into the trees. It was a good mile hike on foot to descend from the hilltop that overlooked the bowl in which Stone's compound sat.

"Let's get a move on it." Wallace and his team set off down the hillside toward the front gate. "Alpha-one to TOC, we're en route to the target's location. Let you know when we're in position."

"That's a good copy, Alpha-one," Gaby replied. "I wish them luck. I've seen our boys take on a lot in the past, but assaulting a modern-day castle fortress with one team is insane," she added, sitting at her computer station and tapping away at the keyboard.

****

The SEALs made quick work of the journey down the hillside, making sure to give the main road leading to the compound a wide berth and using the inky night sky for cover. The moon was too busy playing peek-a-boo with the clouds to illuminate the desolate terrain that stretched in front of the compound oasis to bother ruining their day—a good thing for them.

Using a boulder for refuge, Wallace leered out from behind the earthen cover. Peering through his night vision, he spotted one man in the closest guard tower. The tip of his cigarette flared with each drag he took from it, giving away his location. Maybe these weren't the professionals, he thought. Or complacency—the silent killer of many military personnel had just gotten the better of him.

Either way, he knew that the tower only had one occupant. An easy takedown.

Pressing his mic, the radio squelched. "One to all units, in position. I see one tango in the tower."

****

On the other side of the compound, Thomas' team had made their way down into the bowl, quickly encroaching on the fortress at the same time. Using the night to conceal their movements, they reached the south wall of the compound. Pressed against the side, they quietly made their way to a spot on the wall where their movements couldn't be detected by anyone not too curious. He continuously peered down the side of the wall to the gate tower. Much like Wallace's report, he'd only seen one person moving about.

"Bravo units nearly in position," Thomas reported. "Smith, get the ladder."

Jensen spun around, covering their rear as Smith rummaged through Jensen's pack, retrieving a collapsible foldable ladder and tapping his teammate. Jensen dropped to a kneeling position as Smith unfolded the ladder and quietly placed it on the fence. Its hooked top squeezed down the razor wire, smashing flat against the top and eliminating it as a barrier. He gave Thomas a thumbs-up after making sure it was secured. "Bravo units ready for infiltration."

****

"One to TOC status?" Wallace demanded.

Gaby peered up from her screen to the video wall. She'd been noting the intervals of the roving blobs. "Alpha-One, you have one man in the tower to your immediate left—one just outside the guard hutch. You should be able to execute the tower guard without incident. Bravo-two, you also have only one guard in the tower and two more who just entered the guard building. There are three rovers currently. Two were standing guard outside the mansion's gate, one roving in the garden area. So far, that's all we can see."

"One copy. All units on my go execute." He turned to his men. "Johns, on one, take out the tower guard. "Al, Walsh, get the ropes ready." Johns nodded, and the two men swapped positions.

The sniper extended the feet of his bipod stand, finding a level section of the boulder to use, peering down the scope. The world took on an enlarged view. The guard was standing at the front of the parapet, a flare igniting at the front of his face. "Got'em in my sights."

Wallace paused for a moment, taking a deep breath, exhaling one last mental check. His team was ready. Depressing his mic button, "Execute. Execute."

Johns squeezed off the first shot. A flat '*pfft,*' a fraction of a second later, the guard had unknowingly taken his last drag. The bullet penetrated the side of his head; he was dead before he knew what had hit him. His body rocked for a moment, then keeled over.

Wallace, Walsh, and Alwani darted out from behind the rock, running to the wall. Johns quickly packed up his rifle, slinging it over his back and whipping out his M4 Carbine to join the others.

Wallace uncoiled a rope reaching the barrier, winding it twice before launching it up over the side of the parapet. The carbon fiber composite hook landed, barely making a sound. He pulled the line until the hooks dug into some solid. He quickly began scaling the wall as Walsh mimicked his every move.

Seconds later, Wallace cleared the parapet, moving to the back window of the small six-by-six room, pressing up against the side wall. He peeked through the window, spotting the roving guard lazily sauntering back to what appeared to be a gatehouse. Somewhere, guards could take breaks and or get rest before their next shift.

It appeared that the guard had lackadaisically completed a sweep of the area, confirming his earlier suspicion of complacency. They thought they were safe. Wallace peered over his shoulder; Johns was being helped into the room by Walsh and Alwani, bringing up his M4 and switching the fire selector to a single shot. Two *pfft pffts* later, the man crumbled to the ground.

With a silent hand gesture, Walsh took point, and the team rapidly descended the small stone staircase leading to the tower. Hitting the ground, the group moved to the guard room. The door was open, and a strong smell of hookah wafted out from within.

Walsh closed in on the door, lining up just outside near the door frame. Alwani, Johns, and Wallace fell in line behind him. Wallace squeezed Johns's shoulder, signifying he was ready. Johns followed suit, squeezing Alwani's, who repeated the signal on Walsh's.

Go time.

Walsh tore around the corner, barging into the room, rifle raised. As he entered, the dim light forced him to snap up his night vision goggles. Revealing the room. A low-lying round coffee table was at its center. Resting atop the table was an ornate hookah, its smoke tendrils curled lazily into the air, casting a hazy atmosphere over the space, nearly choking the rest of the team as they entered, following behind Walsh.

As he advanced, peeling towards the right side of the room, Alwani cut left. Walsh noticed the corners of the room had been partitioned off into four separate sections, each marked by makeshift barriers offering a semblance of privacy. In each section, sleeping cots were strewn about, some neatly arranged while others lay in disarray. Gear and personal belongings were scattered across the floor.

Walsh continued, Wallace following closely behind. He checked the nearer corner. No one was inside. Maybe it belonged to one of the guards they'd shot outside. Section clear.

He continued progressing deeper into the room. The sheet partitioning the back right corner prevented him from seeing if anyone was inside. He drew closer, peeking around the corner.

Lying on the cot was a man with earbuds on, reading a magazine. He must've sensed a presence; before Walsh could bring his rifle up, he looked up. Eyes wide, startled, the man shot straight up, leaning toward the side of the bed, where his rifle was standing leaning against the wall. Then he paused as Walsh drew his weapon. It was a calculated pause. Knowing that Walsh couldn't shoot him if he were unarmed. The two men gawped at each other, frozen to see who would make the first move.

Walsh broke the stalemate, lunging forward, driving the butt of his rifle into the man's face. With a wet crunch, his nose broke, and his lip split in two. His head lopped back down to the pillow—out cold.

The Walsh quickly retrieved a set of zip ties bounding the man's hands together. Wallace zipped a pair around his ankles as Walsh stuffed his mouth, then secured his hands above his head, zipping them to a wall hook.

"All set," Wallace said, "He'll be out for a bit." Patting the unconscious man's legs. Alwani and Johns approached. "All clear?" Wallace asked.

The pair nodded, with Johns gesturing over his shoulder. Wallace leaned to the side to see another merc lying on his cot, hand dangling over the side, a pool of blood gathering beneath. "He won't be giving us a problem," Johns said.

Wallace shrugged and moved towards the door. "One to TOC, guard house secure moving to main objective building."

"TOC has a good copy," Gaby responded, looking over to Jerry. "Hopefully, this'll be a quick in and out, then. These guys are good."

Wallace gave a signal, and the team stacked back up, donning their NVGs, swiftly moving back into the crisp night.

****

On Wallace's command, Thomas' team sprang into action. Johnson was the first to climb the ladder, dropping on the other side with a light thud, his boots sinking into the soft sand. Smith was second, followed by Thomas, with Jensen bringing up their six.

They shuffled down the length of the wall in a single file line, hugging it as close as possible, using the darkness and shadows to mask their movements, closing in on the guard tower. The man inside was more preoccupied with surveying the desolate landscape outside the wall than monitoring the movements from inside.

The four-man team was double-timing, checking their fields of fire, looking for any motion when movement came from the bushes.

Johnson threw up a closed fist. The group stopped dead in their tracks, dropping to their knees.

Several chest-high shrubs were dotted around the compound's farthest reaches, in various stages of growth or death, the farther away from the main house. This gave a haves vs. have-nots aesthetic in comparison to the lush gardens near the main building.

A merc haphazardly stumbled out of one of the hedgerows drunkenly, staggering around. He reached for his zipper with a bright smile on his face. He slurred out something inaudible before zipping up his pants. He turned and headed toward the bunkhouse, breaking into a whistle as he confidently padded away with a swagger of pride. He had no care in the world.

He continued past the front door to the bunkhouse, though. He turned the far corner and disappeared off to the side of the house.

Johnson watched intently as the man vanished. With another signal, the group continued forward, except at a more cautious pace.

As they got closer to the spot where the mercenary had stumbled out of the hedgerow, Johnson heard a noise from the bushes. He paused the team once more, listening intently. The night was quiet; an eerie blank silence fell upon them. Then the sound came again. It was a faint whimper.

A dark suspicion overcame the point man. Johnson aggressively waved the team forward. As they approached the cutout, a dark figure took shape in the veiled green tint of their NVGs. It was a woman lying in the dirt, her Shirt half torn, exposing her right breast. She was crying.

Seeing four dark-clad figures approach, she instinctively recoiled against the wall, about to scream in fear.

Johnson pounced, wrapping his hand around her mouth. "Shhhh," he whispered, cutting off her scream and putting a finger to his lips. "Good guys, good guys," he added, taking off the goggles. The other three circled around, doing the same, humanizing their form to the frightened woman.

The young woman appeared no more than twenty years old, her eyes wide with terror, curled into a tight ball, desperately trying to cover herself. "Can I remove my hand?" Johnson asked. She nodded. "Good." He slowly removed his hand from her mouth.

"What are we going to do with her?" Jensen whispered, checking the area for any other movement.

Thomas looked at the terrified young woman, trembling, trying to remain covered, holding back sobs.

"What the fuck you mean 'what are we going to do with her'?" Johnson snapped, in a mocking tone, rounding on his teammate.

"Oh god. No, not like that," Jensen drew back in offense. "I mean, she can compromise our mission," he clarified.

"Nothing, we're going to do nothing," Thomas broke in, analyzing her eyes. "English, you speak English?" She shook her head. "Understand?"

The woman shook her trembling hand.

"Ok, good guys." He pointed to himself. "Bad guys." He pointed in the direction of the bunkhouse. "Good guys, kill bad guys. Understand?" He drew a finger across his neck.

She nodded fervently.

"Stay here," he said, pointing to the ground.

Again, she nodded.

Turning to his team. "Alright, we keep moving. The objective is the same."

Johnson took point once more, donning his NVGs again; the other three followed in line. They continued to move down the wall, reaching the bunkhouse. Thomas motioned for Jensen and Smith to ascend the steps to the guard tower. The pair broke off, silently bounding the steps to the top. He motioned for Johnson to keep moving.

They rounded the front side of the concrete bunkhouse. The front door was closed. Johnson tried the door handle. Didn't budge. Locked. Someone was inside. From around the corner, he could hear the merc who'd assaulted the woman still whistling.

The soft sound of liquid hitting the sand tapered off.

Johnson continued to make his way down the edge of the building, staying close to the wall. The sound of the man's whistling grew louder.

The SEAL lowered his rifle, slinging it to his side, unsheathing his K-bar knife from his upper vest, and securing it in his hand.

The whistling sound still growing, Johnson crept to the edge of the building, tightening his grip on the hilt—the man's whistle now practically in his ear.

The merc turned the corner. Johnson snapped forward, grabbing the unsuspecting man by the shoulder. For a brief second, the two locked eyes, stunned revelation meeting Johnson's intense hatred, anger, and wrath. The guard was about to shout for help.

His mouth snapped shut as Johnson's blade impaled through his lower jaw, splicing up through his mouth and up into his brain. The man spasmed, and blood oozed out his mouth. The SEAL ripped the blade back out. The man hit the dirt. Turning around, wiping the blade on his pants before sheathing it. "What?" Johnson shrugged, seeing Thomas staring at him.

"Are you done?"

"Yeah, that was just satisfying," Johnson responded, kicking the corpse and then spitting on it. Adding insult to death. "Fucking pig."

"May we please continue." Thomas subtly nodded towards the door, indicating the other occupant or occupants inside.

"Certainly." Taking his rifle back in his hands, he readied himself in front of the locked door. He silently started counting down from three.

On one, Johnson lunged forward, kicking the door to the bunkhouse. The wooden door shattered off its hinges, falling inside.

Thomas rushed in, stepping over the door, catching a startled merc off guard. The man reached for a weapon. Thomas unleashed a three-round burst. The bullets tore a ragged line across his chest. The man fell inches short of his rifle.

A quick sweep through the bunkhouse revealed no other

occupants. Nothing but three empty cots, plus the one that the man they'd just shot leaped from. That left one guard unaccounted for. Where was he? They'd find out later. With the room secured, Thomas and Johnson exited. Jensen and Smith met them at the base of the steps.

"Guard tower secure," Smith said.

Thomas nodded. "Bravo team to Toc. The rear gate and tower are secure. We are now moving to rendezvous with Alpha-one."

****

After exiting the front bunkhouse with Walsh back on point duty, Wallace's team progressed deeper into the compound. A hundred yards and the inner wall separated the team from the main objective building, with several smaller structures in between. Reconnaissance with the ISR drone suggested they were storage buildings. Probably lawn materials or even weapons and ammunition stashes.

The team reached the first of the structures. Wallace signaled for them to hold position. They took cover behind the building.

"Al, how many explosives do you have?" Wallace asked.

The Explosive Ordinance Disposal specialist thought for a second, doing a quick mental inventory. "I have three extra blocks of C4, other than what we need for the cars. Why?" Alwani gave his team leader a knowing look, not even needing a verbal answer based on Wallace's. "Oh, Gotcha, yeah, Chief," he said with a smirk before unslinging his pack. "Hold one." He rummaged through a side pocket, retrieving a small clay-looking block from his bag. On top of the block sat a small black box with an antenna and a switch on the side. Alwani raised the antennae and flicked the switch, and a small red light appeared on the box. He removed a strip from the back of the device and stuck it to the side of the building. "Charge is set," he whispered, donning his pack and collecting his rifle.

"Good," Wallace added, motioning for Walsh to keep going. The team peeled out from behind the building and continued to the next structure.

At the second building, Alwani placed another charge before continuing.

Reaching the third and final storage building, Alwani removed the last block of C-4 from his pouch, peeling off the adhesive covering on the back. "All set, boss," he said, sticking the last of the explosives onto the wall after prepping it.

Wallace cautiously peeked around the corner. The gate to the estate loomed twenty yards ahead, each side guarded by more of West's mercenaries. Beyond the gate stretched the sprawling manicured lawn, which was bisected by the main driveway, leading to a grand circular forecourt. At its center, a majestic pond was crowned with a bass sculpture, water cascading from its open mouth. Several SUVs and a lone gold golf cart dotted the driveway. Another guard patrolled the interior lawn.

Darkness enveloped the house, its presence marked only by the glow of exterior lights and the harsh beams of floodlights targeting its facade.

Upon the top of the tiered house roved another mercenary, shielded partially by the parapet that crowned the massive house.

Wallace turned to his men. "Ok. We're going to make this quick and easy. Johns?" The sniper perked up. "Take out the man on the roof. Then, bring up the rear. The rest of us will move out on the shot. Take out the two gate guards, cut the lock, and sneak in. Down the rover and pause outside the front door. By then, Bravo should be on our six, just as we planned."

The team nodded.

"On my go." Johns quickly pulled his M91A2, dropping to the ground and extending the bi-pod legs. Wallace meanwhile checked his watch. Bravo should be making their way to them. "Alpha-one to Toc, we are in position outside the front gate, ready to assault. Bravo-one, status?"

"Coming to you, be on your six in about five mikes," Thomas reported.

"TOC copies Alpha-one," Gabby responded. She gazed at the screen, watching intently with Jerry. She couldn't help but feel a surge of adrenaline as she watched the men prepare for their assault.

The plan that had been drawn up was a quick snatch-and-grab. While Wallace's team assaulted the house to grab Stone and, hopefully, West, Bravo would secure their escape. ISR had earlier picked up the SUVs parked in front of the house. They were going to take two of them and drive out with their targets, blowing up the remaining vehicles to prevent any of the mercenaries from being able to follow.

Wallace counted down from three on his hand.

Upon dropping his last finger, Johns fired.

The silenced round barreled ahead at its target at supersonic speed, then bored through the man's skull, punching out the back of his head. He slumped, half hanging over the parapet.

Wallace and the others leaped into go mode. Bounding from behind the structure, they crossed the distance between them and the gate in a flash of a minute. Converging on the two unsuspecting gate guardsmen before they knew it. Wallace fired first, striking the far mercenary in the head with a three-round burst.

The other startled guard twisted, bringing his rifle to bear in the direction of the shots, only to take a three-round burst of his own to the chest from Walsh. The team reached the gate, with Johns bringing up the rear. He, along with Wallace and Walsh, spun around to provide cover for Alwani.

The Arab dropped his pack; it clunked to the ground. He quickly produced a set of bolt cutters and snapped the lock to the gate with a sharp *clink*. The lock dropped to the sand. He pried open the gate slightly, just enough to let him and his comrades slip through.

Re-donning his pack, he slipped through the bared barrier about ten paces, then dropped to a knee, searching the direction they'd last seen the lawn rover. He whispered over his shoulder. "Clear."

Walsh slipped through next, followed by Wallace, then Johns, with Johns whispering, "The last man." With that, the team moved up the driveway, heading toward the forecourt, coming upon the first of the SUVs.

The team stopped; Wallace dug out a C4 brick from Alwani's pack, handing the brick to the EOD. He quickly placed in the rear driver's side wheel well, tapping Walsh on the shoulder to keep moving. The quartet made their way to the second vehicle, following the same procedure.

While moving to the third, movement in Walsh's peripheral caught his attention. The SEAL pivoted, unleashing a burst. His M4 quietly barked. In the night, he heard a thud. "Rover down," he called as they reached the third SUV.

Alwani quickly placed another explosive. "Last one," he yelled, slapping the block to the wheel well.

The team moved to the front door of the house, ascending the steps to the deck. Alwani began picking the lock.

"Alphas in position. Bravo two status?"

****

"We'll be on your six in your two mikes," Thomas reported.

Thomas' team was approaching the three-story building, which currently had an unknown purpose. Four all-terrain golf carts were parked outside the building, though, suggesting there may be people inside. However, it was still deep in the early morning hours. No one inside should be coming out. By the time they knew anything was wrong, the team would be long gone with both of their prizes.

As the team passed the building, a bright, blinding shaft of light shot out from inside it, streaking across the desert, catching Smith in it, who was bringing up the rear.

The SEAL froze, half caught by surprise and half blinded as the light burned his eyes through his NVGs. Jensen quickly doubled back, seeing the burst of light, grabbing Smith and pulling him from the clutches of the light, as Thomas and Johnson dove for cover, sliding down the small embankment of the makeshift dirt road, landing in the shrubbery.

Jensen and Smith tried to follow, but it was too late, and they'd been spotted.

From the light, three men appeared: one man flanked by two others. The one in the center was a man dressed in short track shorts and a tank top, exposing his chiseled arms. The two men on his sides were dressed in guard uniforms, wielding AKs.

The man on the right spotted the two fleeing SEALs, quickly snapping up his AK to fire before he could get the shot off. A line of ragged bullet holes cut across his chest, dropping him.

Thomas shifted his aim to the man in the middle. Then, he quickly realized he was one of their targets.

The man was Jonathan West, judging by the photo they'd seen.

He shifted again to the further man, firing. His burst twanged off the body of one of the golf carts as the two men dove behind it for cover. "Shit," Thomas spat, reaching for his mic.

Before he could say anything, the still quiet of the night erupted as the mercenaries' AK barked in the night. Muzzle flashes filled the darkness as bullets angrily spat from the man's barrel. The rounds flew over the heads of Jensen and Smith as they threw themselves off the road and down the embankment.

Thomas returned fire, seeing one of the men dart back out into the open, retrieving the dead man's AK. His rounds smacked dirt as he retreated to cover.

****

West reached into the cart, snatching a radio off the dashboard, and keyed the mic. "We have intruders sound the alarm, I repeat, sound the alarm.

CHAPTER FOUR

THE sound of automatic gunfire cut through the stillness of the early morning hour. Wallace wheeled at the chatter, scanning the area and searching for the source: no muzzle flashes or the distinct snapping of incoming rounds. Wherever it was, it wasn't directed at them.

"What the fuck!" he exclaimed, reaching for his chest mic.

Bright spotlights flicked on all around the compound in a series. Illuminating the grounds in lights and shadows. A flood light flicked on with a *clack,* exposing him and his men in its gaze at the front door of the mansion. "Shit, cover," he ordered.

The team skittered for anything resembling cover; Wallace himself pressed against one of the many pillars surrounding the house, holding up the wrap-around awning. The other three took cover. Alwani concealed himself behind a pillar as well. Walsh and Tyus threw themselves into the planter bed in front of the porch, hitting with a *plop.*

The rat-a-tat of gunfire that echoed around the compound signaled that Thomas' team had been spotted and were now openly engaging the mercenaries. The bouncing of sound around the desolate desert compound initially made it difficult to determine the location of the skirmish, but after a few more pops, Wallace theorized the source was somewhere near the unknown structure.

Was it a barracks or a control and command center? Had they walked into a trap? How many men were engaging his team?

He couldn't answer the first three questions. The last, however, was indeed answerable. Listening in, he could make out the distinct chattering of an AK: one, no two AKs. Maybe two roving guards had spotted the team. If so, that engagement would be over shortly.

"What do we do, Chief?" Tyus asked, lying in a prone position, looking out over the manicured lawn from behind a rose bush—no one insight in the now shadow-lit lawn.

"Nothing yet. Stay on mission," Wallace replied. "Alpha-one

to TOC, status report. Where is Bravo Two?"

Gabby jumped from her chair in a combination of fright and nervousness; several flashes of gunfire sprinkled the display as she watched the figures of Thomas' team take cover and exchange fire with two unknown entities, who were now hidden behind what appeared to be a golf cart.

"Gabby," Jerry shouted. She turned. "Chief is asking where's Two," he bellowed, pointing at the mic stand on the table.

No immediate response had come to his question, but the gunfire was still ongoing. This wasn't a mere being spotted and taking the shooter out. They were engaged in a firefight. "TOC, where's Two? Need sitrep ASAP," he repeated.

Gabby shook loose from her paralysis, taking in the scene and analyzing the situation. "Uh… uh, Bravo Two is currently engaged with two unknown combatants," she finally spat out. "They are a hundred yards east of the mansion, just outside the three-story building. Enemy combatants are in cover, exchanging fire with Bravo units," she reported.

Wallace took in the situation report for a moment, running over scenarios in his head—their biggest advantage now gone. He knew that operating without the element of surprise on their side would be an obstacle. Putting his team on a truncated time clock. Plus, all of the activity in the compound would make finding and grabbing both of their targets and getting out safely all that more difficult.

"Great, the element of surprise is now gone," Wallace grumbled, noticing his men's eyes were on him. "We continue on mission, for now. Johns, you, and Walsh cover the front. Al, we're going in." Tapping the Arab on the shoulder, the two returned to the front door. "I guess there's no need to be quiet anymore since we've woken the neighbors," Wallace said, giving Alwani a shrug as he reared his leg back about to unleash a devastating blow to kick down the door.

The door swung open.

A man appeared in the door frame armed. He froze, coming almost face-to-face with Alwani and seeing two men in full combat gear standing on the porch. One with his leg raised and cocked back. He gave the two men a puzzled and quizzical look, tilting his head to the side. They gazed at each other for what felt like minutes. Hesitation on both parties—the two sides in a standoff. Then-

The mercenary whipped up his rifle, but before he could get the shot off. Alwani was quicker to react. Putting a round in the man's forehead, with a silenced *pfft*. He crumbled to the floor with a thud. "Guess that's an invitation," he said with a shrug, stepping over the corpse and giving the door a gentle tap. "Solid metal."

Wallace dropped his leg, inspecting the door frame. It was a solid titanium-reinforced frame. "Damn, that would've broken my leg," he remarked, following Alwani inside.

****

"The SEALs are here, I repeat, the SEALs are here," West repeated into the radio between volleys. "Everyone on my location outside central command." He clipped the radio to his shorts and looked at the other man behind the cart. "Now's your time to show the boss what you got, Martin."

"Sir, yes sir," the man shouted back, raising to unleash a volley of AK fire at the enemy. He sent a screaming volley wildly into the bushes.

****

"Jensen, Smith, are you guys okay?" Thomas questioned as the two men slid down the embankment, coming to a rest. Smith flashed a thumbs-up. "Good." He keyed his mic. "Bravo-two to Alpha-one; we're blown. West is at my location. We are outside of the three-story building—permission to corral target.

No response. He and Johnson returned fire. Rounds *clanked* off the ATV. Seconds ticked by, waiting for an answer. Another salvo from West and his guard pounded the top of the dirt embankment; some rounds zinged overhead. Then, a whispered response. "Bravo-two, proceed."

"Alright boys, let's bag this tar-."

Several dozen rounds sliced through the dried vegetation, cutting through the branches of the bushes. The SEALs dropped their heads, letting the rounds sweep over. Branches cascaded down onto them.

Johnson popped up first, seeing the top of a man's head. He'd come out of cover and was wildly spraying rounds into the night. It was like a scene out of a low-budget action movie.

He peered down the scope of his rifle, enlarging his target. He could see the man's face. He was young, his youthful exuberance superseding any training he may have had as he happily let his AK bark at the night—a fatal flaw of inexperienced youth. The sniper zeroed, then depressed his trigger finger.

The shooter's head snapped back. The force of the round sent his body reeling. His rifle swung straight up, sending half a dozen rounds lacing skyward to the heavens. He hit the sand, motionless. The night fell quiet again.

It was a brief moment of respite. Before Thomas' team could advance on West, the building door flashed open again.

****

From the ISR drone, Gabby and Jerry watched and counted at least eighteen to twenty men disgorge from the building and spread out, taking cover behind the vehicles parked outside. The pair looked on in horror. Thomas' team was now squaring off against nearly two dozen armed combatants.

"Gabby," Jerry said, mouth agape. "Should we call for support?" he asked.

The older woman slowly turned to him, "Call who?" she questioned. "The Moroccans don't know we're in the country, remember? We didn't want anyone to tip off Stone. By the time they get over being butt hurt that we didn't deem to inform them that we'd have a special forces team operating in their country. Then, mobilize a force, which is an hour away. This fight will be over one way or another," she said, sitting, shaking her head.

"They are all they got," she added. "Sophia trusts Wallace to get the job done. He'll bring it home." The last said more questioningly than with assured conviction.

****

A couple of West's men joined him behind the cart. The Mercenary leader regarded them both. "Nice of you to join the fight, Grant," he sniped at one in particular.

Jeffery Grant, one of West's most trusted men, gave his boss a sheepish glance. "Sorry, boss. I was in the shower." He shook out his curly hair, throwing water in the face of the other mercenary. "What do we got?"

"That spook bitch found us and sent her lap dogs," came West's acerbic response. "They've clearly infiltrated our base and damn near got to the Senator," he growled, sliding out a fresh magazine from the other merc's vest, slapping it into his AK. "We'll need to talk about your security measures after this." He yanked the charging hammer back. Grant's eyes glazed over, indicating it'd be more than a talking-to. "For now, let's do some spring cleaning."

****

Thomas hesitantly peered over the berm. He felt a brief look of concern wash over his face, watching the new arrivals scatter for cover before a salvo sent him ducking back down. "Two to TOC, I have a dozen or so more tangos on my position," he reported, turning to his men. "How about we show these wannabes how real men fight." The band of four levered themselves to the top of the embankment. "Give him all you got, men." They opened fire, forcing the new arrivals down into cover.

"Hooyah," the SEALs cried out in unison. They all knew they were in for a fight and didn't care—it was what they were trained for.

Thomas ripped open a small pouch on his vest, retrieving a palm-sized round object. He yanked out its pin, holding down the spoon, readying himself, making a brief check of his target location. His brain instinctively called upon learned muscle memory from hundreds of similar throws, judging the distance and deciphering launch angles and force, all in a fraction of a second. Then, he arched his arm back and flung the grenade.

"Frag out," he shouted, ducking back down as a series of rounds hissed over him. He buried his head in the dirt, covering his ears. The other three followed suit.

The grenade silently arched through the air on its trajectory toward the front of the building. It fell back down and landed with a *kerplunk* before rolling.

West heard a thud and spotted a round object rolling over the compacted earth, bounding over the granular path. A spike of fear and adrenaline shot through his body as he recognized what it was.

"Grenade!" he shouted, taking cover, clapping his hands around his ears, and seeing the round object come to rest just in front of the building.

A perfect lob.

It exploded with a thunderous bang. Thousands of pieces of shrapnel were flung in every direction. Several men yelped as white, hot, burning metal slivers penetrated their bodies. One man closest to the blast was thrown against one of the ATVs face first—a sickening crack, as his neck snapped.

Two other mercenaries, dazed by the blast and reeling from shrapnel injuries, were cut down by the SEALs as they stumbled into the open.

The grenade wasn't intended to kill any of the mercenaries—that was a happy coincidence. It did achieve its objective, though.

Where there was once a door to a building, there was now a smoldering pile of debris as the door frame had collapsed in on itself. At least for now, there would be no more reinforcements coming through that way.

West recovered from the blast, gawping at the destruction. Seeing three of his men lying in the dirt. "Return fire he screamed." Giving a look over the ATV. He could see four sets of muzzle flashes. "Grant!" he yelled.

"Yes, sir," came his louder-than-expected response. He hadn't reacted quickly enough to his boss' warning. A small trail of blood oozed from his left ear.

"How many muzzle flashes?" Grant tapped his left ear before cocking his head to the right. "How many fucking muzzle flashes do you see?"

The Merc glanced over. "Four, sir."

"Fuck," West spat, having been a part of the teams before leaving to run Sotor Corps. He knew that on a mission like this, there would most assuredly be more than four men. "There's rats lurking." He deciphered as that realization struck him—the house. "Shit, Hart!" he yelled across to the next ATV. A man in his early thirties peered over. "Take half of the men and beat feet to the mansion. They're going after Stone, too." The man nodded and picked out several men. They started to break away from the group. West grabbed the Walkie. "Briggs, Sanchez, come in."

"Yes, boss," came Briggs' reply. "Where do you need us?"

"Stay in the house. Secure Stone. You probably have intruders. Alert the rest of the men quietly."

"Good copy, boss."

****

Stone had been sitting in front of his computer, sipping on a fresh cup of coffee in his office. Which was initially intended to be a downstairs bedroom in the giant mansion, but he had it turned into an office during the renovations after purchasing the land from the oil billionaire—a man whom he hated having to do any business, to begin with.

He couldn't believe, after all his years of serving his country, that he'd been exiled and banished. When he heard the faint pops of what sounded like a car backfiring, which was impossible, he didn't live in anything resembling a city anymore—something else he despised. Maybe it was one of West's mercenaries working on one of the vehicles again.

Shaking his head at the distraction, movement caught his eye, drawing his attention back to the computer screen. The cursor on the page had begun moving again. The person on the other end of the chat he'd been engaged in was typing a reply to his message.

"Finally," he said, waiting for the rest of the message to type out, reading along as each word appeared. "No word, they might be on to the fact someone is feeding you information. CIA has been poking around. Shit!" he exclaimed. "Will reach out to the powers for further details. Stand by. Fuck." He continued to stare, reading the message again, chin in hand, trying to determine his next course of action. Knowing he couldn't keep staying a step ahead of Sophia without the help the person on the other end had been providing. *Sophia Evans* was a name he'd grown to hate ever more with each passing day. He cursed the woman who ended his perfectly curated life.

Another round of pops drew his attention back away from the computer. An alarm sounded around the compound, and it also went off in his office. A red indicator light pulsed on his desk.

The sounds weren't coming from a backfiring car.

Stone rushed over to another table in the corner of his office. Upon it sat a laptop and a bank of monitors. He tapped in a set of keystrokes. The screens lit up as more pops pierced through the sound-muffled windows. Several images of different locations around the compound flashed over the screens. His eyes examined every frame astutely to discern the cause of the noise.

He paused on one of the camera locations. Stone's heart leaped in his chest at the sight that was be-folding on the screen. A gun battle outside of the compound's control/barracks building. A team of what he could only assume was the SEALs that had been hunting him down like a dog for the past six months and West's mercenaries.

Oh, no, they've found me, was the first thought that came to his mind. He reached for a radio that had been sitting on the desk, flicking over the on switch, when a bright flash on the screen caused him to jump back.

It was an explosion. He watched as the front entrance to the command center caved in.

Flabbergasted, Stone turned away from the monitors and rushed back to his desk. He tore open the bottom drawer, retrieving a PX4 9mm Beretta and slotting in a clip. He wasn't going to be taken back to America to face a kangaroo court—not without a fight.

The door burst open. Stone whipped up his pistol.

"Whoa," shouted a familiar face. Two men had rushed in, only to freeze at gunpoint.

"Senator, we have to go," said one of the two men, quickly recovering from the fact that he'd almost been shot at.

"Briggs, Sanchez." Stone exhaled, lowering the pistol. "What is going on out there?" he shouted demandingly, slipping an extra magazine from the drawer into his pocket.

"The SEALs are here," Briggs exclaimed. The boss says we need to get you out. We'll rendezvous at the rally point. Let's go." Briggs reached to pull Stone along with him. The old man jerked away.

"I am not leaving without my wife or grandkids. They're upstairs." He brushed past the two men, splitting between them and heading for the door. "What are you waiting for?" Seeing that they weren't following.

Briggs and Sanchez regarded each other momentarily. Their orders were to get Stone to safety, but having known the Oklahoman's stubbornness, he wouldn't make it easy if he didn't get his way. They shrugged and followed, with Sanchez quickly taking the lead, exiting the office.

****

Another series of shots impacted the ground in front of Thomas' face, kicking dirt into his eyes. He rolled to his side as West's men had a bead on his location, spitting the crystallized earth out, coming to a stop, and taking aim again. From his new position, he could see a pair of feet beneath the ATV.

Adjusting his angle of fire, he squeezed off a three-round burst. The bullets ripped through the mercenaries' boots in a splatter of blood. The man fell to his side, clutching at his mangled feet. The pain wouldn't last long, as another trigger squeeze quickly released the man of any feeling. A slug slammed through the man's skull: no more writhing, no more pain, and one less gun trained on his men.

"Chief, what are we doing here?" Johnson shouted in between bursts of his own. As they were outgunned and not in an advantageous position, the smart decision would be for them to fall back and regroup.

"We hold them here," Thomas replied to Johnson's shock. Seeing the man's questioning face. "We hold them here, giving Alpha-one time to nab Stone: he's priority one. If we can get this asshole," he said, thumbing over the berm towards the ATV West had been using for cover. "We do so. But capturing Stone is of the utmost importance. You got me?"

A question directed towards the group resulted in another raucous "HOOYAH!" response from his team as they exchanged volleys again with the mercenaries.

"Boss?" Thomas turned to Johnson. "We got rabbiters." He'd seen a small contingent of West's men moving away from the main group.

"Fuck." Thomas slid back down the embankment, clutching for his mic. "Bravo-two, to TOC, I think we have a few early party departers."

"TOC to Bravo-two, we can see them on ISR." Gabby and Jerry had clocked the group a few seconds prior, seeing a dozen men gathering near the far section of the building. Now, they'd set off. The pair watched as they broke away from the skirmish.

"Where are they going?" Jerry asked. "Get vehicles to run, or more men. Jeez, Gabs, what if they have more men." He brushed his hand through his hair, trying not to think about those consequences.

Gabby, meanwhile, continued to stare, contemplatively thinking, before the solution hit her. "Fudgaducker," she exclaimed, depressing the mic button. Bravo-two, we see your last transmission. "Alpha units, you have company en route to your location. A dozen men, how copy?"

Walsh and Johns, still lying in the planter bed, glanced at each other, nodding their heads at the radio transmission. Walsh cracked a smirk. "Guess Bravo's not gonna have all the fun after all. You ready?"

"Fuck yeah, I am ready," Johns replied, pointing ahead to the fountain at the head of the driveway. Walsh acknowledged.

The two SEALs hopped to their feet, sprinting for the fountain and taking cover behind the stone wall.

"Alpha units good copy," Walsh said, readying himself, propping his rifle on the wall, looking out over the lawn, waiting for the new arrivals. Johns followed suit.

"I've never been one for all the sneaking around anyway," Johnson added. I've always preferred a straight-up gunfight."

"Hell yeah, Hooyah," Walsh responded, giving his comrade a fist bump.

****

Wallace threw a hand up, signaling for Alwani to stop. The two had entered the mansion and were making their way through the elaborately decorated and elongated foyer, which was a mix of new-age design and old-age decorations.

"What's up with rich assholes and flaunting their money through things?" Alwani whispered, staring at a mounted bison head. "Especially dead things."

"I don't know," Wallace responded, listening to the last radio transmission. "Walsh, Johns, will you be able to handle that?" he radioed.

"Affirmative Chief, we'll handle any would-be house party crashers."

"Copy, Alwani, let's move." The Arab continued to examine the bison's head like the two were in a staring contest. "Al," Wallace's inflection rose, snapped Alwani back to the moment. "Let's keep moving," Wallace urged. "Or should I set up a date?"

"Nope, all good here, chief."

"Good, let's go then." Wallace continued, subtly shaking his head.

The two SEALs progressed forward, exiting the foyer section, which emptied into a massive living room that seemed sparsely decorated due to its size. In actuality, everything a living room space needed, and then some was present.

The centerpiece of the room was a large floor-to-ceiling standing see-through fireplace that bisected the room. Large 85" TVs were set into the molding on either side. In front of the fireplace on both sides were sectional sofa sets that formed an L shape with round coffee tables situated in the middle. The edges of the room were dotted with bookcases. Several end tables were situated at the ends of the sofas. The exit to the foyer was flanked by two towers topped with vases. Other live plants were dotted around the room. There was an open, airy feeling to the area.

Off to the far-left side of the room was a raised dais with a large black grand piano, and beyond that was a set of French side doors. They were closed, and the curtains had been drawn. Though remembering the layout of the house, they knew the doors didn't lead outside but to another section of the house.

On the far side of the room was a hallway. Despite the activity outside and the compound lights being activated. The house itself sat in relative darkness. The hallway produced a dark, void atmosphere. Beyond the grand fireplace at the center, off to the right side of the room, was a staircase leading to the second floor.

Wallace signaled to Alwani with a quick hand gesture toward the French doors. Knowing that they didn't lead outside, he thought they might lead to an office and Stone's location.

"Let's hope he doesn't have a panic room, or we're boned," Alwani quipped, heading toward the dais.

A light in the hallway flicked on instantly, diverting the SEAL's attention. Three shadowy figures appeared and were headed their way. The two men froze, still standing in the foyer door frame.

Seconds later, the first of the three's figure and face took on form. It was a mercenary. He clearly hadn't seen Wallace or Alwani yet; they were still somewhat shrouded in darkness themselves.

Then Stone appeared, followed by another mercenary. They waited for them to enter the living room fully.

"Freeze Roy Stone!" Wallace shouted. He and Alwani whipped up their rifles. Alwani had his laser sight pinpointed on the lead mercenary, Sanchez. Wallace's trained on Briggs. "Drop your weapons."

The shouted command halted the trio. Stone gawped at the two intruders like a deer in headlights. The two mercs escorting him had frozen, too, knowing if they reacted, they'd be gunned down.

However, the stunned look on Stone's face was quickly replaced with defiant anger. "Come and get me then," he responded.

"Are you fucking serious?" Alwani laughed. "This guy's got balls."

Wallace motioned for them to advance. Alwani took a step forward, and the living room lights flicked on. A flash from the top of the staircase drew their attention. The vase to Alwani's left exploded off the pillar in a hiss, sending ceramic, water, and plant particles spitting in his face.

Wallace quickly shifted targets to the threat. Two mercenaries were at the top of the stairs, and several other people were behind them. Two kids and two women. Wallace opened fire, gunning down the mercenary that had taken the shot while the others retreated.

The vase next to Wallace exploded as he pulled back into the foyer, shifting targets. He could see Sanchez preparing to fire again.

The two unleashed volleys simultaneously. Sanchez's went wide, smacking into the wall. Wallace's hit was a grazing shot, hitting Sanchez in the left arm and sending him reeling.

Alwani recovered from his initial shock of hearing the hiss of the bullet whiz by his face, shattering the vase. He cleared the water and ceramic from his vision. He whipped up about to fire when the French doors burst open.

Two men ran into the room. Alwani redirected and unleashed a three-round burst, cutting the first man down. He fell forward, face-planting, sliding into one of the legs of the piano. The second merc, now aware of where his prey was, turned and fired. Alwani threw himself forward, gliding to a stop behind the sofa as the rounds impacted the wall.

Wallace watched Alwani slide behind the sofa. Aiming for the new arrival. An explosion of drywall splattered into his field of vision, causing him to flinch. Two more rounds impacted near his face. He peered over to see it was Stone shooting, with one of his escorts pulling on him, which is what most likely caused the shots to go wide.

A look of pure rage and anger lit his face as the merc dragged him away. Wallace aimed but hesitated, knowing Sophia wanted him alive.

"Fuck," he spat. Instead, he set Sanchez back in his sights.

****

"Let's go!" Briggs shouted, tugging on Stone and pulling him back into the hallway as the first vase exploded.

"Get off me," the old man shouted, ripping away from Briggs' grip, sending two more shots at Wallace. "Fuck you, I am an American patriot," he spat, taking aim again.

"Get him out of here," Sanchez screamed, holding his bleeding arm. "I'll hold these guys here."

"Not without my family!" Stone raged.

"Ray will bring them out the other way. For now, we have to go." Picking up the smaller older man, Briggs dragged him back into the hallway leading to the kitchen, where there was a back door.

CHAPTER FIVE

THE once quiet living room quickly evolved into a battlefield. Wallace sent a fusillade, screaming at Sanchez. The mercenary threw himself aside, hitting the marble floor hard, sliding sideways, leaving a streaking trail of blood.

He came to a stop on the other side of the standing fireplace. Wallace's rounds impacted the marble crowning with a hard smack, splintering the surface.

A series of rounds punched into the foyer's wall inches in front of Wallace's face. The other mercenary was lining up a clear shot on the SEAL leader. Before he could return fire, a ragged line of bullet holes strafed across his body. The mercenary's body reeled, spinning as he collapsed, falling backward. His head bounced off the piano's keyboard. Sending a piano note eerily vibrating through the room.

"Got you, chief," Alwani yelled, flashing a thumbs up from behind the sectional sofa.

Sanchez had taken cover behind the marble fireplace centerpiece and had opened fire on Alwani's position.

Cotton and foam splattered into the air as a series of shots punched into the sofa and sent Alwani ducking.

Wallace whipped around the foyer corner to fire. Before he could acquire his target, though, Sanchez had seen the move coming, sending two shots hurtling at Wallace. The SEAL leader retreated as the rounds smacked into the wall. From his position, the mercenary had the most advantageous position behind the thick marble wall.

Wallace had been counting the rounds in his head. In the brief seconds before the firefight erupted, he'd clocked the weapons the mercenaries had. They weren't armed with rifles. Each only had a sidearm. He recognized Sanchez' as a Glock 22 .40 Smith & Wesson. A typical magazine held fifteen rounds. He'd already fired three. Then another five were at Alwani, and now two more were at him, leaving five rounds in his mag. Adding that, he'd most likely have a spare magazine or two. He could keep the two pinned down long enough to let Stone escape successfully. He wasn't about to let that happen.

Wallace motioned to get Alwani's attention. The Arab peeked around the end of the couch. The SEAL leader launched into a series of charade-like pantomimes, acting like he was crawling and pointing to the far side of the room. The other man looked at him, confused. Wallace stopped, shooting his team member an annoyed look before going over the series again.

"You know you guys can just walk away from this," Sanchez shouted from behind the wall. "We have more men. My brothers will be on their way."

Wallace continued miming. "Not a chance," he yelled back, mid-crawl motion. You may have more men, but mine are better."

"Some of mine are former SEALs. I myself was a Marine Force Recon. Just give up. I don't want to spill your blood here."

"Your boss is supporting terrorism for money. You all should be ashamed of yourselves, calling yourselves Americans. That's disrespectful and disgraceful to anyone who's worn this uniform," Wallace boomed back.

Alwani finally realized what his leader wanted. He quickly mimed the sequence back to Wallace while he was talking to Sanchez, confirming.

Wallace signaled for Alwani to make his way around the couches and move to the other side of the room to distract their opponent. If he could get Sanchez's attention divided and on Alwani long enough, he could end the standoff.

Alwani began to low-crawl to the other side of the room.

"Hey, brother, we've spilled the same blood in the same places. So, I know you've seen the shit that I have. These politicians are sending us out to die, all the while making big money and pocketing it for themselves while we get killed in some far-off desert. Billions of dollars go missing every week. You know where that shit goes, brother. So, we said fuck that. It was time to get ours," Sanchez continued speaking, peeking around the corner and seeing a part of Wallace's arm.

Wallace watched as Alwani moved into position. "So, you what, sell out your fellow Americans, supply our enemies with the weapons to kill them. All for money. That's wrong, man. You know that's wrong." Alwani signaled to Wallace that he was in position.

"Hey, brother, you gotta get yours while you can. Am I right?"

Wallace gave Alwani the go. The Arab sprang up from his new position, opening fire and catching Sanchez off guard. The mercenary switched positions, sliding to the other side of the wall, unleashing a barrage at the SEAL. Rounds pounded into the sofa.

Wallace rapidly counted off in his head, one… two… three. He waited for the last round to be ejected. A brief moment of silence fell over the room.

The moment he'd been looking for.

Tink, tink, tink.

The sound of the Glock's emptied magazine hitting the hard marble floor.

It was go time. Wallace sprinted around the corner, exiting the foyer, leaping over the fallen pillar, and making a beeline straight for the fireplace wall. Sanchez registered the flurry of movement, shifting positions again, bringing his Glock up toward Wallace, and slamming in a fresh magazine. The mercenary was quicker than he thought.

Sanchez fired two rounds.

The SEAL dropped into a foot-first baseball slide as the slugs narrowly flung over his head. Sliding on his back, Wallace came to an abrupt stop, inches from Sanchez's feet. "I am not your fucking brother, asshole," he said, pulling the trigger and unleashing a three-round burst into the mercenary's gut.

Sanchez's face was full of shock—his mind not yet fully comprehending he'd been shot. He staggered back, one hand pressed to his stomach. His gun hand shook as he tried to point it at Wallace's face, spitting up blood. He dropped the sidearm, then wobbled, spasmed, and fell forward.

Wallace threw up a leg, catching the man with his boot before he could fall forward on him. He kicked the man to the side, and he thudded to the floor.

"You good, chief?" Alwani asked, rushing over and offering a hand.

Wallace took Alwani's hand, and the Arab helped pull him to his feet. "I am all good," Wallace answered, dusting himself off.

"Nice plan, what next?"

"Go upstairs and secure the family," Wallace said, ejecting his magazine and inserting a new one before heading toward the dark hallway.

"What are you going to do?"

Wallace turned. "Go get our target," he announced, then pressed his mic. "One to TOC, Stone is rabbiting. Alpha-one is in pursuit. Eight is going to stay behind and secure the family."

****

Briggs continued to haul Stone down the hallway back toward the office where they'd come from. The old man squirmed and flailed the whole time.

"I am not leaving my family," Stone shouted.

Briggs threw the older man into the office, whirling to slam the door shut. He turned on Stone. "Sir, my orders are to get you out of the house and to rendezvous with Mr. West. So that's what I am doing. I told you that Ray will get your family out. They don't want them. They want you. So, grab your shit, and let's go."

The mercenary walked over to one of the bookcases, pulling on a book. There was a metallic click from behind the wall. In a whoosh, the panel slid open, and the man collected a rifle and two bulletproof vests. He quickly put one on before stomping over to Stone. The old man, taken aback by Briggs' aggressiveness, backed up a few steps.

Briggs grabbed Stone by the shirt, yanking him closer, and forcefully put the second vest on Stone.

"Are you sure?" Stone asked, having calmed down.

"Yes, now get your ass outside." Briggs threw open the back door and shoved the old man out.

The backyard was just as lush and manicured as the front. The pair made their way down a flag-stoned path headed toward the back gate of the interior compound.

****

The shadows continued to dance around the half-illuminated yard as a gust of wind picked up outside. Johns and Walsh peered over the lip of the fountain, staring into the void. A smattering of gunfire still echoed through the compound, which was muffled by the sound of water from the bass fountain decoration spitting water into the pool below.

"This thing really makes me wanna take a piss right now," Walsh quipped. Loud pops of gunfire from the house drew his attention. "Guess they're getting to have a little fun in there," he added, gazing through the mansion's open front door. Muzzle flashes sparked in the windows.

"Don't worry; we're going to get some action in here in a second," said Johns, peering down his scope and snapping for Walsh to pay attention. "I think I see movement."

"About fucking time." Walsh dropped the barrel of his rifle over the lip of the fountain, staring over the lawn.

"Alpha-six to TOC, where's our party crashers?"

Gabby had been watching the monitor, and the group of a dozen white blobs on the ISR had slowly and steadily made their way toward the mansion. Their progress was somewhat slowed, she guessed, by the fact that they had yet to learn where the SEAL team was. Now, they were nearing the inner gate. "Toc to Alpha-six, they are passing the structures now. Will be at your location in minutes."

"TOC, good copy," Johns replied, turning his head to Walsh— a devilish grin stretched across his face.

"What the fuck is that shit-eating grin for?"

"How about we give these assholes an explosive entrance?"

"What a fine idea, my good friend." Walsh pulled out the small black box that controlled the detonation switches to the charges he'd placed earlier, opening the clear plastic button guards. "Alpha-seven to TOC, could you kindly tell us where our visitors are located now?"

Gabby, still monitoring the group's movements, relayed her findings. "Seven, you have two men approaching the first of the structures right about…now."

Walsh depressed the button.

A thunderous explosion rippled through the air, followed by screams, as a ball of fire roiled skyward, casting more light on the garden.

"Two down," Walsh smiled.

"Seven, now, second building," Gabby called out, watching several of the encroaching terrorists run for cover, thinking it could've been an RPG or something that struck the building.

Walsh pressed the second button.

Another flash of a burning fireball engulfed the night sky, followed by more screams.

"Movement," Johns yelled, opening fire at a shadow that crossed the gate threshold. The running figure collapsed.

"They're rushing the gate," Gabby radioed.

"Third time's the charm." Walsh pressed the third button, sparking another explosion accompanied by more screams.

"Contact, contact," Johns called out again, seeing several mercenaries breach the gate and rush past their two fallen comrades.

Walsh and Johns opened fire on the mercs, sending several fusillades lancing across the garden. Several rounds, finding their targets, befalling them.

More men poured over the threshold into the garden, firing back at the SEAL's position. Brick and ceramic shattered upon impact, strafing across the back wall of the fountain and cracking the facade. The Ceramic tiled bass sprout blew apart, raining chunks down, causing a geyser of water to shoot straight up. The barrage sent both SEALs ducking for cover.

"Great, now I am fucking wet," Walsh complained, slapping a fresh magazine in.

"Quit bitching, you're a SEAL," Johns countered. "Go."

Both men popped back up, firing. Walsh spotted a streaking shadow darting for cover behind one of the SUVs. "Gotcha asshole." Stabbing a finger down on the detonator box.

The car exploded, launching the mercenary across the yard in a ball of fire. The body smacked into one of the mercenaries who'd been running for cover, igniting both men. The second mercenary screamed, running, flailing frantically, trying to put himself out, falling to the ground, succumbing to the inferno.

"Seven to TOC, status," Johns radioed, looking over at Walsh. "You're sick, dude."

"What? It's not like I planned that."

"You have five more tangos spreading across the yard," Gabby reported.

****

A deafening explosion, seemingly out of nowhere, in the direction that he'd sent Hart's team drew West's attention. He looked over toward the mansion. A bright fireball had instantaneously lit up the sky, followed by a second boom. Hart's group was in full contact with the other part of the SEAL team that had invaded the compound under the cover of darkness, which meant they'd either gotten to the SEAL team before they entered the mansion or they were already exfilling with Stone.

West's hand darted to the radio on his waistband, tearing it off and pressing the button. "Briggs, Briggs, respond." Silence greeted him; he was about to repeat his call when-

"This is Briggs. I've got the Senator. We've just left the mansion. Sanchez is staying back to hold off the SEALs. Rendezvousing with you to exfil."

"Negative Briggs," West countered. He was currently locked in a standoff with Thomas' team, both sides holding advantageous positions. "I'll rendezvous with you. Meet at the concealed garage bay in the rear." He turned to his two mercs, who had sought refuge behind his ATV. "You two, follow me." The men nodded in unison. "Stubbs," he called out to the merc behind one of the other ATVs. "Provide cover." Without hesitation, the merc agreed, relaying the command down the line.

Every mercenary opened fire simultaneously. West and his

two men fell back into the night, dropping behind the line of fire. Sprinting away from the battle, they headed toward the rear gate with the intention of circling around Thomas' team to gain access to the backyard to rendezvous with Briggs and Stone.

****

"Umm… um, Gabby, Gabby?" Jerry pointed to the screen. Gabby had been fixated on relaying mercenary locations to Johns and Walsh.

"What?" she snapped.

"Something's happening. Three people just pulled back. It looks like they're trying to circle around Thomas' team."

"One to TOC, Stone is rabbiting. Alpha-one is in pursuit. Eight is going to stay behind and secure the family," Wallace's voice cut in.

"Shit!" Gabby knew what West was up to. "They must have an escape plan. He's not circling the team to take them out. He's running. TOC to Bravo-two, your target is rabbiting."

****

Thomas slid in a magazine, slamming the charging hammer forward, chambering a round when he heard Gabby call him. "Go for Two, say again."

"I repeat, your target is running. He's pulled back to circle around your position. He's going after Stone. Who Alpha-one is in pursuit of."

Thomas peered over the berm and looked toward the ATV that West had been taking cover behind to find no one there. He looked back down the road they'd come up from the back gate, catching a glimpse of three dark shadows sleeking away from the battle. "Shit." There was no way he could break off. But Jensen and Smith were a bit further back and could easily disengage. "Jensen, Smith." The two SEALs looked over. "You heard targets running.

84

Go get him.”

“Copy. Cover us.”

“Johnson, frag, and smoke. On my count.” Both men retrieved the objects from their vests. Pulling the pins. “Now.”

The two SEALs chucked smoke canisters into the road several yards back to help obscure Jensen and Smith. They then tossed the high explosive grenades. They landed near the ATVs, with one rolling underneath one, blowing it skyward when it detonated. The smoke quickly filled the area, limiting visibility.

“Let’s go.” Jensen grabbed Smith, pulling him away. The two SEALs retreated down the side of the road. They headed back toward the rear gate when they spotted the three running figures.

****

Jensen and Smith stalked low in the ditch, tracking the three runaways. They’d pulled back from the intense firefight and had now moved behind what appeared to be a motor pool of sorts. The front doors were open, exposing several more ATVs and SUVs inside, a potential escape route for the runaways.

Initially, they thought the trio was going to hop in and try to drive off. Instead, they slipped behind the building. The two SEALs had yet to learn where they were going, but for now, they were content with following.

Cresting the ditch, they crossed the road, giving silent chase. Smith looked back to see a dozen muzzle flashes up the road. “Hold them off, boys,” he whispered as they slid around the building.

The pair kept a distance so as not to be seen, their curiosity growing every second about what they were up to. It didn’t seem as if they were trying to escape, as driving off in one of the vehicles in the garage would’ve been the best way to go.

“Where are these assholes going?” Jensen whispered, still staying low, creeping to the edge of the motor pool building. He peered around the corner to see the three men making their way down another road heading toward the side wall of the interior compound.

The three men stopped in front of the wall. West, in the lead, fumbled with something from his pocket. Seconds later, a gate opened up. There was a side gate to the interior compound.

"Oh, shit, he's meeting up with Stone." Smith realized, darting around the corner, sprinting after the trio. If they got through the gate and closed it behind them, they may not be able to follow. Seeing the last man about to go through. "Hey!" he shouted.

The mercenary turned, seeing two SEALs running straight for him. He drew.

Smith fired first. Two rounds center mass, one to the head. The man fell into the threshold of the gate.

A gun popped around the corner. "Move," Jensen cried out, pushing Smith to the side. The two split up. The round whipping between them. They both let loose a volley at the shooter. Rounds impacted the brick wall, kicking up plumes of dust. But the shooter had evaporated into the interior compound.

The two SEALs converged at the gate entrance, throwing themselves bodily into the wall on either side of the opening. They gave each other a brief nod of acknowledgment. They'd rehearsed entering a new zone a dozen times, their instinctive knowledge taking over.

Smith went first rounding the corner, breaking the threshold to the center courtyard, breaking to his left. The stark contrast of the dried-up desert landscape where he'd just come from to the lush, verdant green landscape inside caught him by surprise. The yard was a lush green carpet dotted with shrubs and plant life. Further ahead to his right was what appeared to be some kind of hedge maze, and a little beyond that, to the left, was another garage-looking structure.

A shot rang out from behind one of the shrubs. An intense burning sensation enveloped his chest. The blow forced all of the oxygen from his lungs. His legs devolved into a jelly-like substance. Smith reeled back, clutching at his chest, and fell to the ground.

Jensen burst through the gate, seeing two figures dart from behind a shrub. He fired. One of the running figures fell. Then he saw his buddy lying on the ground.

"Shit, you hit?" Jensen asked, dropping to a knee beside his buddy, checking on him.

"Yeah… just… fucking took one to the chest plate," Smith said, struggling to respond between gasps for air, writhing on the ground. "I'll be fine, go. Get West." The SEAL waved for Jensen to continue the chase.

"Copy that." Jensen continued giving chase, this time in a full sprint, heading after the mercenary leader.

The two rounded a corner. West tripped over a protruding branch. Before face-planting, he threw himself into a dive, rolling heels over his head. Recovering, he got back to his feet in one fluid motion, still running.

Jensen rapidly closed the gap between the two, knowing they wanted West alive. The SEAL slung his rifle and dove. The two collided like an NFL linebacker taking out a running back. Jensen tackled West to the ground.

The two men rolled over each other. West managed to kick himself free. The pair scrambled to their feet. "You want me? Come get me," West crowed, waving tauntingly for his opponent to attack.

"My pleasure, asshole." Jensen drew into a fighting stance.

They sized each other for a second, circling the lawn. West feigned a punch, checking the SEALs reaction time. Jensen had already moved to block the would-be strike. West drew back quickly. It was Jensen's turn. He threw the first punch. West jinked back, parrying the blow, throwing Jensen slightly off balance.

Recovering, Jensen repealed his hand, attempting a backhanded blow. West caught the SEAL's arm by the wrist. Rotating it, hyper-extending it at the elbow to the breaking point. A snap of ligament and bone. Jensen wailed. West rotated, driving his shoulder under the SEAL's armpit, slinging him over his back, and driving the man into the ground bodily. Jensen involuntarily exhaled upon impact, expelling his oxygen.

Still holding Jensen's wrist. West spotted the SEAL's K-bar knife sheathed on his vest. Ripping the weapon out with his free hand. West drove the knife into Jensen's throat.

Jensen spasmed, spitting up gurgling blood, as West twisted the blade. Jensen's eyes swelled, taking his last breath before falling still.

"Jensen!" Smith yelled, rounding the shrubs to find West sitting atop his friend, holding the hilt of a knife. He drew. Order be damned. Their target had just killed his friend.

West snatched Jensen's sidearm, firing two shots. Smith's head snapped back. His body hit the ground with a thud.

From behind, West heard more rustling in the bushes. He spun, whipping the gun up at the movement. Two figures appeared at the head of the hedge maze. He lowered the pistol.

"Put that fucking thing away," barked Stone, taking in the scene. Maybe if we kill more of them, they'll stop following me," he added, continuing ahead, stepping over Jensen's body.

"Briggs," West addressed his mercenary subordinate. "Where's everyone else?"

"We've got to go," the man said following Stone. "They're probably dead at this point. We need to leave before the Senator realizes that your families aren't coming."

West turned, looking back at the hedge maze and the mansion beyond, where his wife and kids were still trapped. He knew the SEALs weren't after them and wouldn't hurt them, but he'd have to find a way to get them back someday. Sighing, he turned and headed toward the garage, following Stone and Briggs.

****

Wallace barreled down the hallway where Stone and the mercenary had disappeared into, pounding down the marble hall. He had to slow every thirty feet to clear a room quickly, making sure no one would pop out from behind and shoot him in the back.

He reached the end of the hallway. Two large French doors flanked by statues stood like sentient guards. Not slowing, he barged forward, kicking the doors open, bringing his gun to bear, and whipping it around the room.

It was empty.

"Shit," he spat, surveying the room. To his right, a section of the bookcase had opened. A varying cornucopia of weapons was affixed to the wall—several machine guns and pistols. Two were missing. Stone and the mercenary had clearly rearmed.

A breeze hit his face, and he whirled to see the curtains at the back of the room flutter, revealing an open door.

Wallace raced through the door into the rapidly cooling night. Sunup was right around the corner. The temperature normally drops around sunrise.

The SEAL took in the backyard. It was just as well maintained as the front. The walkway was flanked by stretches of grass and flower beds pressed to the sides of the mansion. Ahead was the opening to a hedge maze, one that blocked off the rest of the backyard. Figuring that was the only way for Stone to go. Wallace entered the maze.

He'd noted it on the reconnaissance photos of the compound, thinking how much it stuck out. *Who the fuck builds a hedge maze in the desert*, he'd thought. It was so off the wall and obscured that it stuck out sharply in his memory, allowing the SEAL leader to navigate it expertly.

Wallace picked his way around every corner, checking for signs of his target. There was no glory, but they did have a head start.

Several shots rang out. Wallace paused. They'd come from a Glock 22. Searching his memory bank, he found that it wasn't one of the weapons missing from the office, nor was it one that he'd seen in the two's hands during their earlier engagement. This meant it must be from one of his men. Wallace pressed on faster. The noise had come from way up ahead.

Emerging moments later from the maze to a ghastly scene, Wallace paused, his heart sinking to the pit of his stomach at the sight of two bodies lying on the ground—Jensen, with a knife protruding from his throat, and Smith, a bullet hole in his head.

Overcoming his initial shock, Wallace rushed to the side of Jensen's body, kneeling beside it. The man's eyes were open, staring, glassy-eyed to the night sky. The SEAL closed the man's eyes, noticing his sidearm was missing. That must've been the shots he'd heard.

Another noise quickly drew his attention—the sound of a motor revving. Looking over, he saw another structure twenty yards to his right. He sprinted toward the building.

Just before reaching it, a car zoomed out from behind the building, tires spinning, kicking up a dust cloud, speeding away. Wallace raced after the vehicle, sending a volley after it. Several shots clanked off the back end and rear window. The car fishtailed slightly but held course, speeding toward the rear gate and away from him.

Racing back to the garage, Wallace kicked in the door, found several other vehicles inside, and spotted a Can-Am Maverick R side-by-side UTV. *Perfect,* he thought. Against the wall was a board with several sets of keys dangling. Snatching the set to the UTV, he rushed to hit, throwing his rifle into the passenger seat, leaping into the driver's seat, stabbing the key in the ignition, and flicking it over. The inert vehicle revved to life.

"Bravo-two, to all units. We are under heavy fire and need assistance ASAP," Thomas' voice cracked over the radio. "Repeat; I need backup on my position immediately."

A thought of pure rage enveloped Wallace's mind. He wanted revenge on West for killing two members of his team. But, if he sought that out now, two more would be added to that list of names. Slamming his fist against the steering wheel. "All units converge onto Bravo-two's location. TOC, check the ISR; Stone and West are fleeing. They are in a black sedan last seen speeding toward the rear gate. Johns, Walsh rendezvous on Bravo-two," the leader ordered. Revenge would have to wait.

****

"There, I see them," Jerry shouted, pointing at a blob speeding away from the compound.

The two had been too entranced in keeping watch over the two separate firefights raging on to notice what else had been transpiring.

"Alpha-one, TOC copies," Gabby responded. "Jerry, try to follow with the drone."

"On it." He wheeled back to his workstation, tapping a key command in, grabbing the joystick to his right. "Just remember, if we follow, we'll lose visual on the team."

Gabby stared at him unblinkingly. "I know. But we can't let them get away."

"We may not have a choice. Once they hit the city, it'll be hard to keep track of them, especially with the morning activity."

****

Johns peered down his scope. "I see him," he said to Walsh. "I can't get a good shot, though he's behind the tree."

"I got you," Walsh responded, zeroing in his sights. He fired two quick successive shots. The rounds smacked harmlessly into the trunk of the tree. It was enough to cause the man behind it to flinch, exposing his head on the other side.

Johns fired. The mercenary's head turned into pink mist. "Last man down."

"Johns, Walsh, rendezvous on Bravo-two," Wallace's order cut through the radio.

"Let's bounce."

Johns and Walsh gathered themselves, bounding down the driveway, racing to Bravo-two's aide.

****

"Last mag," Johnson shouted, slapping in his last magazine, firing over the berm. Several rounds *twanged* off one of the battered UTVs—a round managing to skirt through, striking a mercenary on the other side.

"I am out. Switching to sidearm," Thomas called out. "Fuck I hope they get here soon."

"I think they know there are only two of us," Johnson said. Between volleys, he spotted that the mercenaries were seemingly gathering on opposite sides. They're going to try to flank us, divide our fire."

In a moment of near precognition, two separate bands of mercenaries advanced on their location, emerging from the cover of the UTVs and striding across the small road.

"HOOYAH, we fight to the end," Thomas hollered.

The two SEALs opened fire on the two groups of advancing mercenaries, emptying what they had.

Johnson kept firing until his magazine ran dry, quickly switching to his sidearm. He fired several shots, striking down a mercenary who had made a run on his location. A convergence of concentrated fire forced him down. His guns slide locked back, stuck. "I am jammed."

Johnson drew his knife, flinging it at one of the two mercenaries still charging at him. The man jinked out of the way, not breaking stride. The SEAL closed his eyes, about to pull the pin on his last grenade. He wasn't going to give them the satisfaction of killing him, and he'd take them out, too.

He was readying to pull the pin when the two men crumbled to the ground. Johnson looked over to see Walsh and Johns running up the road, sending several more shots toward where the men had come from.

"I am out," Thomas shouted back. Looking over his shoulder, Johnson saw his friend readying a grenade in a last-moment sacrifice, deciding that he wasn't going to go out like that. Thomas unsheathed his knife, seeing another merc break from the pack racing toward him. "Come on fucker!"

The man collapsed feet from the edge of the road—the other three spun, gawking wide-eyed at the sight. A dust cloud was speeding down the road. They opened fire at the new threat.

Wallace chucked his rifle back into the passenger seat and stamped on the gas pedal, ducking. Rounds *pinged* off the front end of the speeding UTV. Wallace held course.

The vehicle struck its first target. The mercenaries were too slow to react, realizing their shots were having no effect. The UTV jumped as the front end thumped over the corpse. Wallace lost control of the steering wheel as he tried to haul it back on course—

another thump as the back axle road over the downed mercenary. The last hit caused it to lurch sideways, the tail whipping out from behind.

The back fender struck the third mercenary full force as it slid to a stop, sending him flying and pitching him off the road and into the ditch.

Thomas pounced on the injured mercenary, running the blade of his K-bar across the man's throat.

The UTV slid sideways to halt perpendicular to the road, tipping. Wallace scrambled across the seat, grabbing his rifle, leaping out before the whole vehicle rolled onto its side.

He landed hard face down, sprawled out like a starfish, spitting out flacks of dirt. Footsteps crunched beneath the boots of someone approaching.

Wallace rolled, snapping his sidearm up, to see the bloodied face of the third mercenary, one of his arms dangling by his side. The man fell to his knees, spitting up blood, struggling to bring his gun up. Wallace looked at him sympathetically, realizing that, at some point, they were on the same side.

The SEAL paused. The man fell face-first. One final gasp, then he stopped breathing.

"Holy shit, are you ok?" Thomas had climbed out of the ditch, racing over to Wallace.

The Commander staggered to his feet, peeking over his shoulder at the tipped-over UTV, unbelievingly knowing that he'd ejected himself out of it just in time. "I am good," the SEAL leader answered with a deep sigh.

"Chief, are we done here? Where's Stone and West?" Walsh asked, arriving with Johns and Johnson by his side. The SEALs took each other in after their grueling fight. Ensuring none of them had sustained any serious injuries masked by the adrenaline flowing through them.

"Alpha-one to TOC, where are our targets?"

Jerry shrugged at Gabby's gaze. He'd been tracking the escape vehicle. However, once it left the desert plane and entered Tangier proper, he lost track of it as it blended into the rest of the stirring early morning traffic.

"We… we lost them in Tangier," the analyst admitted deafeningly.

"Great, so the mission is a complete bust," Johns gripped.

"I have the families," Alwani cut in, announcing over the radio.

Alwani stood watch over Rebecca Stone, Megan West, and two kids, Josie and Jacob West. All four huddled in a room. Their mercenary escort lay dead outside.

"Great job, Alpha-eight. Bring them to the front of the house. Alpha-one to TOC. We are headed back to base with four additional passengers and two KIAs." Johns, Walsh, Jonson, and Thomas all stole stunned looks at each other as Wallace placed a solemn hand on Thomas' shoulder. The five lowered their heads in a moment of silence for their fallen friends.

CHAPTER SIX

Sophia looked down at her wrist, reading the time on her watch. Calculating the time difference. She figured Wallace's team would be getting ready to start their mission to capture Stone and West.

As for her, she was getting ready to H.A.L.O. jump into a terrorist haven of a country. She looked around the cavernous airport hangar, half impressed and half confused as to what was going on. The SEALs all looked so locked into what they were doing. She, on the other hand, had just about no clue. She just found herself mimicking what the others were doing.

Tex was inspecting his weapons and looked to be in a full conversation with his sniper rifle. There's something not right with him, she thought to herself. And not for the first time, either.

Though she'd suspected that was part of the reason she had started to see him in a different light than before. Where she initially viewed him as crass and childlike in attitude and demeanor. Even disgusting, sexiest, and way too forward for any normal human being, she'd started to find herself succumbing to his charm, for lack of a better word, or so she thought.

Shrugging off the feeling she would never dream of telling him any of that, she glanced over to find Ryan. He was inspecting his parachute pack for the third time as he'd done with everything else in his kit bag and combat vest. If she had to profile the team, she'd definitely peg Ryan for having some form of OCD.

She panned her head around to find Tyus and Gutierrez meticulously checking their equipment, swapping items, and communicating in what she could only describe as telepathy. Since neither of them had spoken a word, they just bobbed their heads to whatever music they were listening to on their headphones. Yet their movements seemed to be in perfect concert with each other.

Even the new team members seemed to be going through a series of movements that they'd all done dozens of times before. She wondered if they were as close as Wallace's team was. They seemed like a tight-knit family.

Every one of the men that surrounded her in the spacious hangar wore the same expression on their faces. Unable to place it earlier, it now struck her where she'd seen a similar look before. A memory formed.

It was the only time that her father had taken her to a football game. She was sixteen and couldn't be less interested in sports at the time. Yet, it was a Veteran's Day game, and her father was part of a group of military personnel who were going to be honored before the game.

They were allowed to bring one person onto the field with them, and he'd asked her to be his person. She felt honored that he'd asked her, as they had been arguing in the weeks leading up to the game. About something she couldn't even remember now.

It was several minutes before kickoff, and they were in the tunnel waiting for their names to be called to head onto the field. She glanced down the tunnel to see the team. Their expressions, demeanor, and attitude were all focused and locked into the battle they were about to commence for the next several hours.

That's where she'd seen the look before. It then dawned on Sophia that that's what they were preparing for.

Battle.

A wave of unsureness washed over her now. What was her role in what was to come?

Suddenly, her chest tightened, the world around her began to swirl, and her head felt as light as a feather. She teetered, rocking back on her heels. She gulped only to find her mouth as dry as a desert. Her eyes glazed over as she looked up to the ceiling. The bright illuminance of the bulbs overhead felt like a thousand suns beating down on her. Her chest bobbed up and down as she struggled for breath.

Ring, ring,

The buzz of a phone exploded in the quiet expanse of a room. The ringing echoed. All eyes swiveled and bore down on Sophia like the nocturnal eyes of a dozen forest creatures staring at their prey.

Why was everyone looking at her? Then she remembered. She

had the satellite phone. Snapping out of the brief panic attack that had begun its assault on her, she dove her hand into her backpack, fishing out a blocky black box and looking down at the caller ID. It was Mila.

Sophia thrust a finger into the air, silencing Tex's incoming question. Then she spun and raced out of the hanger. She burst into the warm night. The oppressive heat smacked her square in the face, and a bead of sweat already bubbled up on her forehead.

She paced away from the corrugated building a few yards for privacy before extending the device's thick, stubby antenna. Then, she jabbed her shaky index finger into the answer button, nearly knocking the phone from her hand.

"Mila," exclaimed Sophia. Her voice pitched up several octaves more than she even knew her voice could hit. She could picture her friend yanking the phone away from her ear, cursing under her breath in German. "Sorry, that was louder than I wanted." Her voice now taking on a more sheepish tone of apology.

"No worries," her friend answered. "Just wanted to call to check in on you. Since…" Mila's voice trailed off. The young German wasn't entirely sure how to broach the subject with her friend. She didn't want to make it too obvious that she was worried for her. Or how she'd respond to being back in the field, especially since she'd not done so since the last time. The time she was shot.

Sophia let Mila's last words linger, waiting for the end of the sentence. An eerie silence fell between the two women. When it was clear that Mila wasn't going to say the quiet part out loud, though she was clearly thinking it judging by the call, it would have to be her that brought up the elephant on the call. "You mean since the last time I was out in the field, I got shot." Her hand subconsciously slid toward her midsection, rubbing around the bullet's entry point.

"Yea…yeah," came Mila's hesitant response. "I am just worried about you, that's all. Can't a girl be worried when her best friend is about to parachute into one of the world's most hostile countries?

"I mean…yeah, I guess so," Sophia answered, dragging out

her response. Letting each word drift in the air before hitting the next. "I am actually glad you did."

"Why," Mila asked, picking up on Sophia's timidness. Something she hadn't noticed over the last several months.

"I feel like a sore thumb," Sophia said, "I am watching these men get ready, knowing that at any minute, they could die. And they are all so… calm, like it's another Tuesday. Meanwhile I am here like a duck on the water. Trying to appear serene and calm up top. But, underneath the water, my legs are flailing about, moving a thousand miles an hour on the verge of a panic attack." Mila clasped a hand over her mouth as she'd accidentally let a small chuckle escape. "Oh, har, har, I… am… so glad that my predicament is amusing to you." Sophia snapped, mock offended but also sort of really offended.

"No, no, it's not that, really," Mila stuttered, her face flaring red with embarrassment. She didn't mean to offend Sophia. She could tell that her friend was struggling with the situation. "It's just that it is sort of a normal Tuesday for them," Mila explained. "Honey, they do this all the time. It's what those me do. You can't compare yourself to them. You are not military. Plus, you are not, and I reiterate, not going to be doing the fighting."

Sophia's muscles relaxed; she hadn't even noticed how stiff she was until just now. Her shoulders dropped a few inches as she took a deep breath. "I know, you're right. I am not one of them, and I definitely don't want to get used to this feeling." Sophia rotated her shoulders, trying to work out a knot in them she'd been harboring for months from the stress of the mission. "You always know what to say."

"You know that I've always got your back. It's the least I can do for you since you pulled-"

"We've got each other's backs. Always have since I met you." Sophia said, cutting her friend off, not wanting to rehash exactly how they'd become friends right now. She had a mission to get focused back on. "I'll call you when we touch down in Yemen."

"Ok, safe flight."

"Yeah, ok, I am going to be jumping out of a perfectly good airplane, over thirty thousand feet up. Yeah, that's going to be real safe." Sophia scoffed.

"Tex isn't going to let anything happen to you." Mila retorted with a grin so wide Sophia could detect it over the phone.

"Ha, especially since my ass is going to be up against his crotch. I am sure he's going to be a perfect gentleman." The two continued to share a laugh. "Ok, I've got to go," Sophia said, cutting off their laughter as a large military cargo plane came thundering around the hanger, nearly drowning out her words. "Thanks for the check-in," Sophia shouted. "Talk later."

The team burst through the door, Tex holding Sophia's backpack, waving her over. She flipped the antenna down, jammed the sat phone into one of her vest pouches, and jogged over to meet the team.

****

Wallace stepped out of the airport terminal a few paces and leaned against what he assumed was a power control junction box, judging by the little warmth it was emitting and the faint thrum of coursing electricity. As he let the box take the majority of his body's weight, he let the calmness of the early day encase him.

It was such a stark contrast to the chaotic feeling and events of the wee hours of the day—or the witching hours—where everything bad happens in the dark, as they say. And it was definitely a dark time. Now, he was letting that darkness take hold of him as it swelled internally.

He tilted his head toward the vast sky, taking in the rainbow of colors that coalesced above him—a swirl of oranges, purples, and blues combining to make a beautiful horizon as the sun began to peak. He strained his eyes to make out the retreating constellations as they faded from existence, temporarily phased out by the encroaching sun.

Wallace jerked his head back in confusion, stumbling a bit as he teetered off the power box. He was caught between disbelief and what to do next, as it appeared that one of the stars was not fading but growing in intensity against all logic as it continued its trajectory right at him.

Was it a shooting star? He wondered as he continued to reel back as the object hurtled toward him.

He let out a little gasp of relief and embarrassment as he realized he was at an airport. The 'falling star' that was coming for him was actually a plane with its lights still on.

The cacophonous roar of a Boeing 747's engines pierced what had been a quiet and serene morning as the plane began its effortless glide back down to the earth. The lights danced across Wallace's face, illuminating his downturned, stiff, jutted jaw. He closed his eyes as the beam dazzled his iris.'

Only to immediately force them back open as the images of Jensen and Smith's faces flashed across his mind's eye.

Their expressions were frozen forever, twisted and contorted in death. He let his mind drift to what that feeling must be like. Do you feel the last moment of your life? Or is it there one moment, you are full of life and consciousness, and then. BAM! It's all gone. The brightness of life is there and then, like the plane's lights, just gone, as darkness envelopes you. Do you feel that pain? Or do you feel nothing at all?

Wallace let his mind linger on the topic for far too long this time. The screeching howl of thick rubber tires landing heavily on the asphalt at over one hundred fifty miles per hour snapped him out of contemplation. A cloud of burning rubber exploded in the jet's wake as it lumbered down the runway. The brake pads clamped around the discs in an all-out effort to slow the three-hundred and thirty-plus ton aircraft.

The cloud of smoke drifted across the open expanse of the airfield, wafting on a gust of wind. Its entrails assaulted Wallace's nostrils from dozens of yards away.

The smell of the smoke reminded him of gunpower, flashing him back to the firefight. Why do certain smells trigger memories, and some don't? It'd always baffled Wallace, though he knew it had something to do with the olfactory sense, but he wasn't a medical doctor or a scientist. He didn't really care for the why or how. All he knew was that his senses threatened him with a dangerous chain reaction for any SEAL. Let alone one that just lost two men under his command.

The overnight happenings immediately took over, as he suddenly found himself back at Stone's compound. He replayed every single moment of the mission in his mind's eye, like a football coach going over game tape, trying to find every single flaw or bad call that was made during the game. Questioning everything he did.

Did he do something wrong? Did he make a bad call? Was there something he could've seen or done differently? Anything that would've changed the outcome of the mission.

Were Jensen and Smith dead because of him? He wondered as the 747 continued its lumbered cruise, eventually turning off the runway headed toward the terminal.

The return to the still quietness of the morning lulled the SEAL back to the one place he knew he couldn't and shouldn't go.

Everything inside Wallace told him not to go there. Everything he'd ever learned urged him to run away from the feelings he was going through. "Time machines haven't been invented, so trying to figure out what went wrong is a useless waste of time because you can't change a damned thing. Those men who died are dead and will be dead forever. Stop trying to question or justify it. Because if you don't get out of your head, you'll be next. Just live and learn from it." The words of his former Chief and mentor, Miles Cortez, rang in his head as he fought to abandon the thoughts swirling around.

"Chief," Alwani said, sidling up beside Wallace. "Hey, where'd you go?" He questioned, seeing the thousand-yard stare on Wallace's face as he turned to face him. Wallace, though, looked right past Alwani like he wasn't even standing in front of him. His focus was on the two pine boxes being wheeled out from the terminal toward the hanger where their plane was waiting. "Yo, Chief," Alwani repeated, snapping his fingers several times in front of Wallace's face. "Earth to Chief." Alwani turned his head in the direction that Wallace was staring off in.

"Has everything been arranged?" Wallace questioned finally, his eagle-eyed stare still affixed to the boxes as the crewmen rolled them into the hangar and out of his line of sight. Only now did he realize who was standing in front of him. "Al, they know what to do?"

It was Alwani's turn to stare blankly into the distance at his friends. "You know, I never gave back Jensen's headphones," The SEAL remembered, a corner of his mouth twisting up in thought.

"What," Wallace asked.

"Jensen, during our last deployment, I lost my headphones. I think I left them in a Humvee or something. Anyway, he had an extra pair. So, he gave them to me but made me promise to give them back. I never did." Alwani explained. "Shit, I think I lost them too." He let out a small laugh, racking his memory. "Haha, Yup, I did, now that I am thinking about it." A half smile stretched across his face, still lost in the memory.

"They know how to load the boxes," Wallace questioned again, now eying Alwani.

Alwani turned to face his Chief. "Yeah, they know. They're part of the Moroccan military and, apparently, on loan to us, I guess."

The team contacted the Moroccan government before departing Camp Darby to arrange the mission's arrival and departure details. The Moroccans were more than happy to help and gave their full cooperation. Even agreeing to anything and everything Sophia had requested, including giving the team full access to the private airstrip away from prying eyes.

"Stone and West's families, where are they," Wallace continued, leaning back against the junction box, the heat from it helping to relax the SEAL's battle-weary muscles.

"They're on their way to Rabat, to our Embassy. They are being escorted by a couple of agents from something called the General Directorate for Territorial Surveillance," Alwani answered.

"What the fuck is that?" Wallace asked.

Alwani shrugged, "Not sure, but as far as I can gather, it's Morocco's version of the CIA, I guess," he said. "You know, Chief, there was nothing you could've done differently back at the compound."

Wallace looked back up toward the sky and pointed at one of

the last remaining visible stars above. "You know," he said, "The ancient Egyptians believed that the stars were the souls of deceased people that ascended to the heavens."

"Pharaohs particularly, actually," Alwani interjected. Wallace set his eyes upon him. "I am part Egyptian on my mother's side." The Arab explained; Wallace nodded, knowing that information was somewhere in his mind. "They believed that the Pharaoh's souls returned to the heavens, back to the celestial realm from where they came."

Wallace continued to nod, "Impressive sailor," he said. Pointing back up to the sky, this time, he pointed at two stars next to each other. "Those will be Jensen and Smith, then."

"And so shall they be named," Alwani said. "Doesn't change the fact, there was nothing you could've done."

"What's going on out here?" Johns asked, stepping out from the terminal, Walsh following behind.

"We're naming stars," Alwani answered.

"Listen up, men, gather around," Wallace said, a cold expression on his face as he waved his SEALs closer.

"Oh, shit," Walsh said as the four men gathered closing ranks. Wallace shot him a look. The man cupped a hand over his mouth.

"Listen, today was a rough one, we…" Wallace paused, the words stuck in his throat. "Lost," he forcibly spat the word out. "Two good SEALs and great men today under my command. I'll bear that and add them to the others. Like Gibson, Huff, Wagner and the others before them."

"Nothing you could've done, Chief," Walsh said as the men bowed their heads in respect to their fallen comrades.

"Yeah, Chief, it's as you say, S.H.O.T.," Johns said.

"Shit Happens Out There," the three men intoned, Wallace's saying, which basically meant that you can't change anything, and what happens is what happens.

A small grin stretched across Wallace's face. "I know that. Deep down, I know that, but it is something I'll always carry with me. Anyways," he continued. "As I said, we lost great men today. But let's not make their loss in vain. We still have a mission to complete, and there are still two bad men out there on the loose."

"Hopefully, Ryan's team has a better go at their guy than we did," Johns added.

"Here's to hoping," Walsh said. "I just don't want to be the one that tells Sophia we missed."

"Thanks, I guess that'll be my burden, too," Wallace said, turning towards the east and to Yemen, staring up at the sky. "Here's to hoping."

CHAPTER SEVEN
SANAA, YEMEN

SOPHIA sat strapped into the mesh seat of the C-17 Globemaster III Tactical Transport Aircraft, leg twitching, head and back pushed up against the interior fuselage wall. Her eyes were fixated on the overhead lights, which were currently on but in a dimmed state, dreading the moment the yellow glow switched to a blood red. Judging by the time they'd been airborne, it was coming sooner than later.

Catching movement from her peripheral, a crewman appeared at the head of the bay, sauntering down the staircase that led to the upper section of the plane and the cockpit area. Without saying a word, he crossed the cavernous open expanse of the jump bay. Normally, the plane would be used to transport large numbers of troops and/or equipment. But tonight, the only cargo the craft was ferrying were Sophia and the eight SEALs she was with. The CIA Agent watched the crewman intently as he began checking equipment in preparation for their jump.

After Sophia's team verified the last pieces of information, Hasan was confirmed to be in Sanaa, as Stone had said, which was corroborated by an asset in the city. She informed Owens, who green-lit the operation based on the plans that Wallace and his team drew up on how to either extract or, worst case scenario, eliminate the terrorist leader.

Their first problem, however, was getting the team into Yemen. Driving two truckloads of elite special forces operators across the Saudi border into Yemen wasn't going to work. Their only other viable option was to conduct a high-altitude low-opening drop, otherwise known as a HALO jump. Then, once on the ground in the country, they would be met and picked up by a CIA asset currently in Yemen, who had information on where and when Hasan was going to show up.

Sophia glanced back up, wondering why she had insisted on being present for the mission, then quickly rationalized it was to make better snap judgments, and having boots on the ground in the thick of it was easier. Still, her stomach had been in knots since departing Camp Darby, especially since the last time she was in the field, it resulted in a bullet hole in her abdomen.

"Stop." A hand slapped down on Sophia's leg. Tex blinked his eyes open. "I am trying to sleep."

In her state of hyper adrenaline, Sophia hadn't registered that her leg had been twitching for the past twenty minutes. "Sorry, Tex." Thinking for a second, it hadn't even dawned on her; she'd been the only one awake in the jump bay other than the one crewman. Checking down the row of men, all of their eyes were closed. "How can you guys sleep right now?" she questioned, unable to fathom calming her mind enough to doze off.

"SEALs sleep when and where we can," he responded. Sitting up, arching his back. "Until now," he grumpily said, glancing over at the airmen by the jump door. "Just keep your eye on the Jump Master. When he opens the door, then shit gets real."

"Hey, who's the strap?" asked one of the SEALs further down the row, arousing from his nap. He peered down the line, making eye contact with Sophia, their blue eyes meeting. Sophia guessed he was all of maybe twenty-two. Clean-shaven, close-cropped hair. His tactical vest looked two sizes too big.

"The leader of the team," fired back another SEAL. Master Chief Mike Wilks was the team leader for SEAL Team Six's Bravo squad. He was around Wallace's age, and judging by his expression, he had seen just as much combat. "Sorry, ma'am, new kid. Hasn't learned his manners. That's Petty Officer Second Class Trent Cole," Wilks answered. "And she's our boss right now," he said, directing the comment toward Cole.

The mission had been put together so quickly and at the last minute that they hadn't had much of an opportunity to meet. "Your team comes with a lot of praise. Wallace talks highly of your squad, Master Chief."

With Sophia not trusting anyone else to go after Stone, they'd brought in their relief team, splitting the two squads. Ryan, Tex, Ty, and Gutierrez had been combined with Wilks, Cole, and two other members of Bravo squad, James Simms and Oscar Santiago.

"You too," the Master Chief said with a smirk. "This Hasan

guy, is he the real deal?"

"Fraid so, Master Chief. He's killed a lot of people, a lot of Americans. Your team will be doing a great justice for the country, taking him off the board." The lights switched to red, and the jump master turned and signaled three minutes.

"Oh shit." Sophia could feel her heart skip two beats at the change in the light hue. This was about to really happen.

"Thought all you spooks did jump training at the FARM?" Tex asked, clamping down on Sophia's thigh. She'd subconsciously continued tapping her foot. "And didn't you ace like every assignment?" He remembered an earlier boast from the CIA agent several months back.

She slyly smiled. "All but two—skydiving being one of them."

Tex quizzically raised an eyebrow.

"I didn't jump," Sophia elaborated. "I was first at the door but didn't jump when the instructor said to. I moved to the back of the line and waited till everyone else went. Jumped at the last second before he failed me."

Tex's face stayed locked in.

"Oh, the other course."

He nodded.

"Explosives-"

"Stand up," the Jump Master announced, pulling on a lever. A whirring motor kicked into gear. The airtight seal around the wide rear bay door broke with a hissing sound. The large metal slab began to descend.

A burst of cold air blew into the bay, letting in a howling wind drowning out almost all other sounds. The Jump Master gave the sign to check their equipment.

Tex leaned over. "Don't worry, I've got you," he shouted in Sophia's ear, hooking her harness to his. Both finished checking their equipment. The SEAL tapped her shoulder—the universal sign for all good.

The team filed in a single file line, duck-walking to the open bay door. Ryan, at the head, reached the door first. The Jump Master peeked his head out, Ryan anchoring him, making sure he didn't get sucked out with the wind. Seconds later, Ryan pulled the crewman back inside. As he reentered, he flashed the thumbs up, giving the 'all go' to jump. Everyone quickly donned their breathing apparatus.

Sophia quickly pulled the oxygen mask over her face, gulping in the fresh, pure oxygen, breathing heavily. She could feel the sweat beading down her face. Her mask fogged up more with each breath.

Then Ryan disappeared into the night.

Tyus was next to leap into the dark void, then Cole, followed by Simms. One by one, each member vanished into the abyss. With every disappearance, she and Tex inched closer.

It was their turn.

When they approached, a rough burst of gale-force wind blew in as the plane hit a pocket of turbulence. The jolt staggered Sophia. It might have bowled her over if she had not been attached to Tex, feeling his sturdy, trunky body supporting her svelte frame. The pair forced their way back to the bay opening with Tex as the anchor.

She looked out, expecting to see a sea of bright lights. Sanaa, the capital of Yemen, was a big city with lots of buildings. Instead, she only saw a speckle in the distance, at over thirty-thousand feet up and miles away from the city. It looked more like a small blip in the Yemen desert's empty expanse.

Without warning, Tex pushed off.

The full force of the wind smacked against Sophia; it felt like being snatched off the ground as they were jerked away from the aircraft. The air forces battered against her face as they tumbled away. Tex regained control of their fall, twisting the duo. Sophia was now face down. Taking the brunt of the wind. She could feel her skin contort as it was being pulled back.

The wind whooshed past her ears, berating her eardrums. It sounded like a hurricane and tornado were whipping past her simultaneously.

They continued to free fall for several minutes. The dot of light that Sanaa was before steadily grew in size. She still couldn't see the ground, which didn't matter, as she didn't want to. She didn't want the anticipation of hitting the earth if their chute didn't open.

She'd rather not know the end was coming.

Tex checked his altimeter. "Opening the chute!" he shouted through his mask. He then pulled the rip cord.

In an instant, the weightlessness of their free fall ended abruptly. The re-emergence of gravity took its course. During their entire descent, Sophia couldn't feel Tex's weight. Now, with the parachute unfurled, his two-hundred twenty pounds combined with her one-thirty had them descending faster than the others.

The tandem shot past Simms, then Cole. Next in line was Tyus. They continued to fall, seemingly gaining more speed with each passing second. Below, Sophia could see the canopy of Tyus's chute, then his face as they zipped by him. Another hundred yards, and they'd catch Ryan. Although judging by their speed of descent, Sophia figured they'd probably be on the ground before passing the team leader.

Continuing their fall, the once shapeless ground began to take on subsistence. The flat black landscape's topography shape-shifted with each passing second. Spires of rock jutted from the ground, tree canopies popped like opening umbrellas, and a large rock formation—a small, jagged ridge formed. Yemen was considered a desert country in general. However, the region had huge swaths of mountainous terrain surrounding the capital city, which had reluctantly been designated their landing zone.

Still falling, Sophia checked her altimeter—a thousand feet from the ground. The outcrops of ridges took on more sinister forms. Several of their peaks threatened to end their trip on a gory note. If there is one wrong move or an unseen spike in the dark, the duo could easily find themselves impaled.

She cringed, shuddering at the thought of ramming smack dab into one. The thought caused her heart to skip two beats just thinking about it. Realizing that fear could become a reality, the pair rapidly approached the ground. They were coming in faster than Sophia would've liked.

A tap on her shoulder reminded her she wasn't just a passenger. She had a role to play. Then instinct and trust took over. Tex had instructed her earlier during the flight that when they landed, they'd be doing a butt slide, which meant that she needed to pick her legs up and angle them out ninety degrees so she wouldn't hit the ground first.

That's exactly what she did as the ground drew nearer.

****

They hit the ground, not as hard as Sophia thought. Tex executed the slide perfectly. They came to a stop, seated on the rocky ground. Tex hit the release, unshackling Sophia. She stood watching the other members descend, then land one by one.

The second each man hit the ground, they unfastened their chutes, collected them, wrapped them, and stuffed them back into their packs.

"Here, get us started," Tex whispered, handing Sophia an entrenching tool—a small shovel.

"Copy." She turned in several circles, surveying the ground.

"What are you doing?" Tex asked, stuffing their chute into his pack.

"Looking for a good spot."

"Anywhere is a good spot. Just dig," he whispered.

"Fine." Sophia extended the shovel, jabbing it into the ground, which was softer than she'd expected. Shoveling gobs of dirt, she asked, "Why do you do this again?" She tossed more earth aside.

"To hide the fact that we're here. That's also why we dig a few different holes," Tex answered, pointing out that others were doing the same. "We don't want to put them all in one hole in case the enemy finds it. Then they'd know the exact size of the team." Sophia nodded, admitting that was a smart maneuver. "Here, let me take over." Tex took the shovel from Sophia with no protest.

Sophia slinked away happily, letting the SEAL finish digging the hole, spotting Ryan hunched behind a large rock formation. He'd been the first to hit the ground and had already secured all his equipment and buried his chute. He was looking over a map, checking their location.

"So, are we where we need to be?" Sophia asked, crouching beside the team leader.

"Yup, pretty much right on time, too." He checked his watch, folding the map and pocketing it before donning a mini pair of night vision binoculars, peering over the landscape, and searching for the road. "Our contact should be coming around those rocks over there." He pointed into the distance. A rocky ridge dotted the landscape about five miles in the distance. "This guy reliable?"

Sophia shrugged. "Not my asset, couldn't tell ya." Ryan gave her a side-eyed glance. "He's been vetted, and Gabby's worked with him before. His intel has always been solid," she said. "He's worked with the company for years," she assured him. "I hope," she whispered in a tailing off voice. She did have to admit with a little hesitation herself, she wasn't sure, but trusted Gabby.

Though, what were the odds that an asset would appear out of the blue with knowledge of Hasan's movements the second they learned where he'd be? But it wasn't like they'd been looking for him to have stayed in Yemen after the assault on Perim Island, either. So, they'd not put out a notice for information on his whereabouts.

"Yo, we've got movement," Tyus' voice crackled over the radio.

After hiding their chutes, the team had fanned out and taken up a defensive perimeter. Tex posted up on the highest rock formation. The others took cover behind anything else they could find.

Sophia and Ryan looked out over the pitch-black desert landscape. A bright beam of light bobbed up and down near the ridge Ryan had pointed to earlier. It appeared to be a headlight beam from a vehicle.

"Must be Mohammed," Sophia answered. Mohammed Saeed was the contact they were to meet. She stood, "Ryan signal-." Before she could finish, the SEAL snatched her back down as a van turned the corner, coming around the edge of the ridge. "What the fuck," she hissed.

"Wait," he whispered, putting a finger to his lips. "Tex, tell me what you see."

The sniper peered down his scope. The van took on a greenish tint in his cross hairs. Seconds later, a second van came into view.

"Shit, we've got two technicals."

"The fucker sold us out. Boys, get ready," Wilks said over the radio, yanking back the charging hammer of his FN Scar rifle.

"No, wait," Sophia barked. "That's the signal." She peered out from behind her cover. The lead van was flashing its high beams. Four quick times, followed by two longer bursts. The preset signal code the two sides had agreed upon earlier.

"If he sold us out, he'd give them that code too," Wilks reasoned. "Tex, take out the drivers."

"Tex, belay that order. Do not shoot." Sophia's jaw clenched with tension. "I repeat, do not fire. Wilks, you don't give orders on this mission."

"Petty Officer, take the shot. I am not going to have my team captured, tortured, and killed on a CIA analyst's hunch."

Sophia glared at Ryan. Wallace had given him command of the team despite Wilks outranking him. "Ryan, this is your command," Sophia reminded him.

"Vans are drawing closer. Bravo-one, your call." Tex nestled his nose closer to his scope, aiming it directly at the windshield of the lead van. In the driver seat, an Arab man with a thick beard bobbed his head back and forth, listening to music most likely. *A calm entrance for potential terrorists sent to kill a group of covert special forces operators,* Tex thought. "I've got Mr. Headbanger in my sights," he reported, trigger finger tapping the trigger guard, waiting for the go-ahead.

"Do not shoot," Ryan ordered after several seconds of careful consideration. "That's an order. Do not shoot. Gutierrez, give our signal."

The SEAL flashed the designated return message. A series of two long, followed by four short bursts of flashes, giving the vans their location. The team waited in silence, hoping Sophia was right.

Moments later, the first van pulled up, Arabic music blaring, and the second van pulled in behind him. The driver of the first vehicle turned the music off. Sophia slowly approached, coming out from behind her cover, hands raised. As she drew near the van, the window began rolling down. The driver straining with considerable effort. It was an older model vehicle with no power windows. The man poked his head out.

"Americans, yes?" he asked; his English was broken, and he carried a thick accent.

"Yes, and you are Mohammed, I take it." Sophia tensed, hoping her decision not to shoot was the correct one. A cold chill ran up her spine when there was no immediate reply. She tried looking into the rear of the van, hoping there wasn't a gang of AIA terrorists in the back. But the windows were tinted. Even at night, it was difficult to see inside; some type of curtain appeared to cover the windows.

The driver surveyed the area, looking around, turning his headlights off, not answering. Sophia could feel a bead of sweat trickle down her forehead, suddenly realizing she was out in the open, completely exposed.

"Told there'd be more. Where's the others? I brought cousin to help," he said, thumbing to the driver of the second van, who'd also turned his lights off. "Van only fits six without combat gear. You have lots of gear," he noted.

Sophia, the least kitted out of the group, still had not only a full set of tactical gear on, along with a 9mm Berretta sidearm strapped to her thigh but also an oversized backpack stuffed with clothing and mission-essential gear. All the others had similar belongings, with most of the other guys having far more gear.

"They're here," Sophia answered, putting up a finger on one hand. A red dot slowly crept up the side of the door. The driver watched it closely as it moved up to his face. He could feel it settle on his forehead. "Are you Mohammed Saeed?" The second iteration of the question came out more forcefully.

"Yes, yes, Mohammed," he answered, putting a hand to his chest. "I am Mohammed. That back there is Cousin Anwar."

Sophia gave the second man an irritated look of anger. She hated being caught off guard. "I was told it was only you." She tried to peer into the other van, but its windows also appeared to be blotted out by curtains.

"Too many Americans, not enough room. Bring cousin to

help. It's all good, all good."

Sophia paused, thinking. He did have the signal. And judging by the size of the vans, he was right. They wouldn't all fit in one vehicle. Calculating all the possibilities, she tapped the button on her mic. "He's good, let's move."

The members of the team unveiled themselves from their covers. Without having to say a word, they quickly divided into two teams. Ryan, Tex, Ty, and Guttierrez loaded their gear into the back of Mohammed's van. Wilks, Simms, Cole, and Santiago loading into Anwar's van.

Sophia stepped away, retrieving a sat phone from her cargo pants' pockets, and dialed a number. "Mila, sit, rep." Not wanting to miss their predetermined check-in. "We've touched down and have made contact with our asset. Heading to the safe house. We'll touch base again tomorrow."

"Sophia, good luck and stay safe," was Mila's only reply.

"Need to go. Go now." Mohammed pounded the side of the van. Sophia climbed into the passenger seat. "Area crawls with snitches." He grinned. "Snitches get stitches," he added, singsong like bobbing his head. He handed her a black hijab.

"Oh yeah." Sophia took the silk garment, wrapping it around her head.

"Isn't he technically a snitch? That's a little hypocritical," Gutierrez whispered from the back, drawing a nod from the rest of the team.

Mohammed turned the van on, clearly not hearing the chide remark. The imaginary song in his head was going full blast. "Take to safe house," he said. "Hasan not arriving till later today. I'll take you to place then."

"Thanks," Sophia said, releasing a sigh of breath. She was right.

Mohammed drove off, cutting back across the desert. Part one of their mission was a success. They'd made it safely into Yemen.

CHAPTER EIGHT

THE pop from a backfiring car woke Sophia. The agent stirred in the bed, checking her watch. It had just passed eleven. Thankfully, her few hours of sleep felt like a rejuvenation because she'd most likely need them for the day's events—events that would culminate in the capture of Hasan Althani. She hoped.

Mohammed and Anwar had managed to sneak the team into the oldest part of the city, the heart of Sanaa, during the night. They managed to evade several checkpoints through their exhilarating trip from the outskirts to the safe house.

The jump-in and adrenaline-filled drive through the city had completely tapped Sophia's energy reserves. The brief hours of respite were welcomed. But it was time to accomplish what she'd come for now.

She got up and dressed, wiping the sleep from the corner of her eyes. She could hear commotion from the living room, which wasn't too hard. The walls of the old fire-bricked building weren't very thick or insulated. It sounded like the team was up and moving about already.

Walking into the living room, she was immediately greeted with a cup of coffee. "Thanks, Tex." She took the cup from the burly Texan. "Should we get started?" she asked, taking a sip. Her nose wrinkled, and the corners of her mouth turned up, nearly spitting the coffee out. The unusual blend of tastes attacked her taste buds. "Oh, god, what is that?" she asked, pulling the cup away and sniffing the contents.

"Ghetto mocha," Tex chuckled. "Coffee with hot chocolate," he added with amusement, watching her try another sip. "Just wait for it. It'll hit you. How oh so good it is."

She smacked her lips together after the third sip, allowing her palate to adjust to the chocolate taste while she looked around the room. "Where's Mo-. Oh wow," she said and paused, pulling the cup back, looking at it like she'd just found the greatest-tasting drink in the world. "Oh, my goodness," she exclaimed, greedily taking another gulp.

"Told ya," Tex beamed, walking away, taking up a confident

stroll.

"Where's Mohammed?" she finished asking, another sip later.

The only other members present were Ryan, who was setting up a Frankenstein-looking version of a MacBook on a coffee table in the center of the room. Tex, who'd just handed her the coffee, Wilks, who was standing near a window in the far corner, off to the side, cautiously peering out the window, keeping watch and also, possibly sulking from the night's differing opinions and being overridden by her and a lower-ranked subordinate. Tyus was helping Ryan set up the communications equipment.

"Said he'd be back in a few," Tex answered, sitting on a chair near the small dining table.

The safe house was nothing but an apartment in the center of the city's old district. Peering out the window in the kitchen, Sophia could see they were at least on the top floor of the eight-story building. Not a presidential suite or anything of the sort, but more so for a quick escape if the need arose.

The old part of the city had been continuously inhabited for over twenty-five hundred years. Making it a heavily dense location decorated with hundreds of earth-burned brick towers, all sandwiched together. Some of which had been standing tall against the test of time since the eleventh century. The buildings felt so close to one another that Sophia felt if she reached out the window, her hand would be in the neighbor's apartment the next building over.

It was not great for privacy, but if anything happened and the team was discovered, they could easily jump from building to building to escape. There was no way they could get pinned in.

A series of short knocks at the door drew Sophia's attention along with the others. The SEALs all reached for their weapons. However, the knocks came in the form of a code, similar to the flashing headlights scheme, which indicated it was Mohammed.

Sophia eyed Wilks, expecting him to get the door since he was the closest. He didn't initially move until a second round of knocks finally spurred him into action. With an annoyed look, he padded over, opening it.

"Sorry. Sorry." Mohammed bustled inside; he had two full

grocery bags. He was breathing pretty heavily. Walking up eight stories with hands full of groceries couldn't have been fun. "Got some water and snacks." He sat the bags down, exposing the water bottles and power bars.

"This isn't a picnic," Wilks murmured, retaking his position by the window."

Mohammed gawped at the SEAL, seemingly hurt by the response. "Thank you," Sophia interjected. "Where are the others?"

"Gut and the rest of Wilks's team are in the other room," Tex responded, digging through the bags, pulling several bars out, and slipping them into his pockets.

"Can you get them? I think everyone should be in on this." The SEAL nodded, getting up and crossing the room. "Anwar, where is he?"

For a second, the question seemed to puzzle Mohammed. Wondering why she'd asked. "Preparing."

"For what?"

"Departure," Mohammed responded. "We leave the city after. Once people see Americans, they may suspect. Can't be too cautious."

Before Sophia could follow up, the rest of the team entered, forming a circle around the laptop on the table. She turned her attention to Ryan and Tyus, giving them a nod. With a few button taps, the screen flashed on. Mila's face center screen. "Sophia, how's the team?" the German asked.

"Rested and ready. Are you guys ready?" she asked. "First-time quarterbacking can be nerve-racking." Recognizing this was Mila's first operation where she was in charge of the TOC. The worry was written all over her face.

Mila brushed her blond locks back. "I am just keeping an eye over everyone. You're still calling the shots." The two exchanged smiles. "And speaking of keeping an eye, it's going to be pretty difficult. The area is very dense. We won't be able to see much of what's going on at street level from the sat. The buildings are really tight."

"What if we launch a drone and have Richard take it over?"

asked Tyus.

Mila looked over her shoulder. Richard's voice was barely audible over the link. Whatever he was saying, the German nodded in confirmation. "Should help a bit, Richard says." She turned back to face the camera.

"Good, we'll launch it once we're set up. Speaking of." Sophia turned to Mohammed, and the rest of the room's eyes followed. "Where?" she questioned, "Where are we setting up?"

"Yes, yes, Hasan is in the city. Confirmed by Anwar, too. He is recruiting from the Houthis." The Houthis were followers of the Shia form of Islam and had been in a civil war with the officially recognized governments of Yemen and Saudi Arabia for years. "He comes here every few months to recruit from the rebel ranks," Mohammed continued. "When he is done, he meets his uncle Fayez for lunch at his restaurant."

Sophia motioned for Ryan to get his map. He retrieved it from his backpack and spread it across the dining table. Mohammed pointed to a location on the map. "Here."

"Shit, that's almost smack dab in the heart of Houthi territory," Ryan exclaimed with a heavy sigh. "That's going to be tough to get in and out with this guy." He stepped back from the map, biting his lip. Knowing Sophia wasn't going to wanna hear his next comment. But his team's safety was paramount. "I suggest we switch mission parameters to a kill mission. We set up shop outside the restaurant and wait for him to arrive. Confirm it's him. Tex takes his ass out. In the chaos, we skip town. No one knows we're here. It's the best bet." Wilks nodded in silent confirmation.

Sophia pondered, knowing the risks. If anything went sideways, they were on their own. No backup squad, no one to launch a Quick Reaction Force to bail them out. She weighed the weight of her desire to bring him to justice versus the lives of her men. It was simple arithmetic. One terrorist facing a public trial for his crimes was nothing over the lives of eight of America's Special Operators and their bodies being drug through the streets of Yemen on CNN.

"Ok," she said, finally nodding her head. "Switching from snatch and grab to termination," she announced. "We don't need another Mogadishu. We'll scope it out, Tex; you find an area you can shoot from. Tyus, you spot him. The rest of us will provide support. Gutierrez and Santiago?"

The men perked up hearing their names.

"You'll blend in better than most of everyone else." Most of the team were of lighter complexions. "You'll be inside to confirm it's him."

The two men nodded, expecting as much.

"The rest of us will provide support and exfil once the kill is confirmed. Wilks and Cole will be stationed in a van with Anwar on one side of the restaurant to provide support if anything goes wrong. If nothing, you'll head to pick up Tex and Tyus after the shot. Ryan, Simms, and I will be stationed here." She indicated an intersection down the road from the restaurant. "Along with Mohammed to pick up Gut and Santiago. After that, we head for the Saudi border. Cross over at night. And that's a wrap." She stood back, looking at everyone. "We all in agreement?"

The team nodded, and she glanced over her shoulder. Mila was nodding, too. "Great. Let's get moving."

****

Mohammed turned onto the street where the restaurant and target location was at. It was a narrow street, maybe three car widths wide. Dotted by miscellaneous storefronts. Parked cars lined the road on either side. People strolled the sidewalks going about their daily lives, completely unaware or not caring that the world's number one terrorist would soon be in their neighborhood.

The Arab slowed the van, looking for an area to park, finding a spot a few dozen yards away from the building. A car whipped by, the driver laying on the horn, giving him a scowl as he sped by. Mohammed parked, cursing under his breath, checking the backseat, and meeting the terrified faces of his three passengers, who were holding onto anything they could. "Sorry," he apologized for the rough ride, turning the van off. "Place is over there, across the street. On the corner." He pointed without making too much of a show of it.

After collecting herself, Sophia peered cautiously from behind the blackout curtains. Setting eyes on a busy corner restaurant. People were going in and out. It looked like any corner dining establishment you'd find in a busy city in America. Everyone acted no different than any other civilians, going about their days milling around, conducting their lives as they saw fit. If one weren't caught up in the geopolitical state of the country, one would never know that it was embroiled in a civil war.

Cars continued to whoosh by on the busy street, horns blaring, and music from other nearby stores played at abnormally high volumes. People passed by on the streets. Mostly men, but Sophia could pick out groups of women walking together in full traditional attire—full-length burkas, wondering how it could be comfortable wearing black clothing head to toe in the oppressive heat of the region.

She focused her attention back on the restaurant, which grew in size as she donned a pair of binoculars. "I hope he shows," she said, handing them to Ryan. "Alpha-five, Bravo-eight, you're up," she radioed Gutierrez and Santiago, respectively.

"Copy," they both reported.

Sophia shifted positions, swapping with Simms, who struggled to get around in the tight confines of the van decked out in full tactical combat gear. They shuffled about until Sophia could peek out the back window. The two SEALs, who had swapped their fatigues for traditional Arab garments, turned a corner and headed for the restaurant. Thankfully, they were both about the same size as Mohammed, and he was courteous enough to let the gentleman raid his closet.

The two men approached the restaurant's front entrance. Then disappeared inside.

"All units, the foxes are in the hen house," Sophia radioed to the group. Bravo-one, are you in position?" Sophia and Simms swapped positions again, much to the annoyance of Simms. She clambered to the front of the van, head poking between the front seats, startling Mohammed, searching the streets for Wilks' van.

After a few seconds, Anwar's van turned the corner,

approaching from the north. They pulled off to the side and parallel parked on the other side of the busy road adjacent to the target building—catty corner from Sophia's location.

"We're in position," Wilks answered. "Cargo has been dropped off." He checked his watch. "About five minutes ago. Should be getting into position."

"Alpha-three, you guys set up, up there?" Sophia radioed Tex.

"Copy. Alpha-four and I are settling in."

Earlier, with the help of Mohammed, they'd picked out a perfect vantage point with a clear line of sight to the restaurant's front door—a six-story building directly across the street two blocks from the target location. Tex, now laid in the prone position on the rooftop under a camouflage mesh netting. The bipod legs of his M91A2 sniper rifle extended. He checked a picture of his target one last time, burning the image into his brain. "Yo, drone." He nudged Tyus, who'd finished setting up their M151 spotting scope.

With a grunt, Tyus slithered back from the ledge, crawling out from underneath the camouflage mesh netting and removing his backpack. From within, he pulled out a small, sleek black device. He pressed the power button at the base of the object. A post shot out from the top; three spring-loaded rotor blades extended from it. Another post with two blades attached protruded from the back end. He set the dragonfly-looking device on the ground. "TOC, Black Hornet activated."

"Copy, taking control," Richard reported from behind his computer back at Camp Darby. He typed a few commands on his keyboard, activating the Bluetooth long-range controls. The device's blades whirled into motion, spinning at five thousand rotations per minute. The device lifted off. With another couple of keystrokes, the device's cameras were activated. A few more taps and the image displayed on the wall monitors. The hornet briefly hovered above the two SEALs, then flew out over the city. "Looks tight."

"Too tight," Mila responded with trepidation. Worry strewn across her face. Their concern that the satellite couldn't provide an accurate overview was confirmed. The streets of the old city were narrow, and with the plethora of multi-story buildings packed so closely, it would be hard for the cameras to drill down. However, they could still use its thermal capabilities to see people's heat signatures. Their direct visual capabilities were reduced to what the drone could see.

"Great, gangs all here. Now, all we need is the guest of honor." Sophia ducked back into the van's interior upon seeing several people approaching it. They gave it a suspicious look. "So, where is he?" she asked Mohammed.

The Arab checked his watch. "Should be here soon."

"How do you know the man's schedule?" Wilks asked over the radio. It had been bothering him since they'd met the Arab. He seemed to know an awful lot about Hasan's activities when no one else seemed to.

Sophia was now wondering the same thing. She'd taken Gabby's word that Mohammed was a solid asset. But it had still eaten at her. Had she let her biased goals push away any concern, letting her desire to capture Hasan cloud her judgment? Or was he just a well-informed asset, and that's why he'd been kept on the agency's list of contributors?

Sensing the tension growing, Mohammed hurriedly reached across the front seat, diving for the glove box.

"Whoa, don't fucking move." Simms pushed Sophia aside, whipping up his FN Scar and jamming it against the back of Mohammed's head. "One more move, and I'll blow your fucking head off."

Ryan had also drawn down on Mohammed with his sidearm. Sophia leaned out of the way, one hand clutched around her right ear, Simms' rifle barrel inches above her head. But, from her vantage point, she could now see what the Arab was reaching for. Inside the glove box, there was only a slip of paper.

"Stand down, stand down," she ordered, pushing Simms' rifle away. Mohammed, what is that?" she asked, seeing his hand shaking. It's okay; no one's going to shoot," she said, giving both Simms and Ryan a glare, which silently conveyed that no one had better shoot.

"Here, here." Mohammed's trembling hand matched his

quivering voice as he slowly handed the paper to Sophia. "It's a recruitment notice," he managed to squeak out.

Sophia took the paper, glancing over it. "You've got to be kidding me?" she said, shaking her head, unable to believe what her eyes were reading. "It's seriously a recruitment flier. Like a job fair. Jesus, terrorism is now a job." Exasperated, she handed the flier to Ryan.

The paper included a location, time, and what they sought. "We are looking for true believers to fight on the side of Allah against the infidels and sinners. Fight, fight, fight," Ryan read amusingly. "Well, now I've seen it all. Wonder what the benefits are?"

"What's going on over there?" Wilks asked. "You're drawing some unwanted attention. Your van's rocking like a sex wagon."

"Nothing, just getting the answer to your question," she stated, unable to contain her dismay. It was so bold and out of the norm that she couldn't help but be horrified and amused. "They put up recruitment posters all over the city, apparently," she explained.

"What's the benefits package, seventy-two virgins? An explosive work environment, and BTO, blown-up time off," Tex joked.

"My brother-in-law, tell me. Tell me he go to recruitment fair. Text me when he leaves," Mohammed reported, still shaking slightly. "See, same side, same side." His phone buzzed on the dashboard. He asked with his eyes to check. Sophia nodded. He unlocked his phone, read the text, then held it up for her to see.

Sophia read the text. It was a simple notification: 'on his way.' She nestled back into the middle-row seat, sighing deeply. "We're on. He's coming."

****

Ten minutes later, a black sedan passed Sophia's van. "I think that's the second pass from that car," she said, eying it intently. It was an older-style Mercedes four-door coup with pitch-black tinted windows. She watched it disappear as it turned down the street in front of Wilks' van.

"I think you're right," Wilks added before a clicking noise drew his attention toward Anwar. The middle-aged Arab had been fidgeting the entire time with some toy in his hand and had stopped all excessive movements. His hand wandered oddly near the steering wheel, or more so, the steering column.

"TOC," Sophia radioed Mila. "Can you rewind the drone footage to double-check?"

"Copy," Mila answered, ensuring Richard heard the command. He had and was already doing so.

"Five, eight, what's going on inside?" Sophia worked her way to the front of the van and peered out the window. Something was bothering her. In the last few minutes, subconsciously, she'd registered a drop in the level of sounds that just now triggered an unwelcomed thought—peeking between the front seats. The atmosphere of the once busy, chaotic street that had dozens of cars whipping by and throngs of pedestrians meandering about the sidewalks had slowly morphed into a quieter scene in the last few minutes.

Gutierrez and Santiago had taken seats near the rear of the dining area, steadfastly watching the front door. Upon entering, the pair had taken note of the high number of male patrons until realizing that this was a Muslim country that believed and enforced Islam's strict rules. Women weren't allowed out without a male escort unless they were with other women doing household chores.

However, they had taken note of the demographics of the men. Most of the patrons were military-aged males, with a few older individuals sprinkled in the group. There weren't a lot of people inside either for a busy mid-afternoon day. Plus, most didn't have meals in front of them, and those who didn't were all facing the windows on the street side.

They gave each other worried, knowing looks, sensing a change in tone. Most of the conversations inside had slowly trickled out since they'd entered. "I think we may have an issue," Gutierrez whispered under his breath into the mic.

"Folks, I think that Mercedes is coming back around," Tex

reported. The glint from its window as it turned the corner two blocks down had caught his eye. "Headed your way."

"TOC, I need that confirmation now!"

"Hey, what are you doing," Wilks shouted, drawing his sidearm and pressing it against Anwar's temple. It was a small, almost imperceptible movement, but the SEAL's keen eye had caught it. "What the fuck did you just do?" The Arab gave the SEAL an expressionless side-eye glare.

"What's going on over there?" Sophia asked, staring through the binoculars and peering through the windshield, seeing the van rock about. It appeared Wilks had his gun to Anwar's temple. No immediate reply came. "Bravo-two, what's happening?"

****

Tyus, lying beside Tex, was surveying the area through his monocular scope and spotted a blinking light coming from Wilks' van. Its blinker had been activated. "Oh shit." He realized that the flashing signal was set to alert Hasan's men of their location. "It's a trap." As he warned, another flash of movement from the other side. The Mercedes had sped up and was now racing down the street, converging on Sophia's van from the rear. "Tex."

"Oh no the fuck, you don't." The sniper shifted positions, locking onto the speeding car. Looking through the scope, the scowling face of the driver appeared. "Say cheese, asshole." He fired.

With a *whump,* the hypersonic projectile exploded from the barrel, traveling at twenty-seven hundred feet per second.

In the blink of an eye, it smashed through the windshield, blowing a ragged hole in the man's chest and spraying blood all over the dashboard. The car swerved without its driver to hold its course. The speeding Mercedes veered left, then right, cutting back across the road and smashing into the back end of a parked gray Hyundai Accent.

At over seventy miles per hour, the front end of the Mercedes crumpled upon impact, and the lifeless body of the driver was immediately ejected through the windshield, impaling into the back window of the Accent. The Mercedes pole valuated into the air, flipping over, crashing down on top of the Accent in a mangled conglomerate of twisted metal.

The crash sent the few pedestrians that were left on the street scattering everywhere. People were running in every which direction, screaming. Several good Samaritans rushed to the vehicle's aid.

"One," Tex called out with a smirk.

"Second car," warned Tyus upon seeing another black sedan tear around the corner, racing towards the accident.

Tex lined up another shot, seeing the new driver's stunned face. He hadn't expected to see his buddy's car flipped over in a smoldering heap of junk.

The Texan fired.

The second round hit just as the first had: center mass. The vehicle swerved right and then left before hopping the curb and plowing into a building, disintegrating the mud-brick facade, burrowing into the car-shaped hole, and lodging itself halfway in.

"Two."

The few people who ran to the first car now realized what was happening. They turned and fled for cover.

****

The commotion of the crash drew Wilks' attention for half a second, giving Anwar a slim opening to make a move. "Allahu Akbar," he roared, reaching for a weapon tucked away in his door pocket. "Allahu-"

Wilks squeezed his trigger. The 9mm round at close range punched a hole through Anwar's skull, shattering the window and sending a red mist into the street. "Go find your virgins, asshole," he quipped, "Simms, shoot that fucking Arab," he bellowed into his radio. Assuming that since Anwar was working for the AIA, so, too, was his cousin. "Cole, let's move." The SEAL reached across the center console, grasping for the door release to dump Anwar's body.

"Bravo-two on your three!" Sophia's warning call came over

the radio. They hadn't worked together before, but the pitch of her voice sent up warning flares. It was a threat, and it was imminent.

Wilks lifted his head over the dashboard.

A few feet from the front of his van, there was an alleyway. Six men with AK47s appeared as if they had been spawned by some video game AI. The men leveled their weapons at the vehicle. "Fuck. Cole get down," he spat, throwing himself to the floor of the van's back, clamping his hands around his head.

The firing line of terrorist let loose their AKs. The 7.62mm rounds punched fist-sized openings through the thin sheet metal of the van, dotting the exterior with holes as they continued to unleash their barrage. The spent brass shells piled up at their feet.

****

"We've got to help them!" Sophia shouted, pushing Simms' rifle away from Mohammed's head, which was ducked between his legs. "I told you no! Help your team." Simms cursed under his breath, throwing open the van's side door and leaping out. "Three, take'em out."

"Yes, ma'am."

The sniper angled his powerful rifle toward the beleaguered van. Putting the head of one of the shooters into his crosshairs. He squeezed. The man's head exploded, showering the terrorist next to him in pink mist and brain matter. "Three." He lined up another. *Whump.* Brains, blood, and skull fragments sprayed the wall behind Tex's second target. "Four."

"Five, eight, get out of there. Rally on my van. We'll cover you." Sophia ordered the men inside to evacuate. Simms opened fire from behind the hood of the van, giving cover fire. "Ryan, we need to get them." He nodded.

The SEAL kicked open the back door to the van, leaping out, clearing the street. All civilians had evacuated the shooting range like it was some rehearsed school drill. Checking the turned-over vehicle, sending a burst of fire through the passenger's side, making sure anyone inside wasn't going to pose a threat before angling up the road heading north to Wilks' location.

Several shooters sprang from the restaurant's front doors, going in opposite directions: a group headed north, another south moving towards Sophia's van, sending a spray of bullets in Simms' direction. He ducked down as storefront windows behind him exploded in a shower of glass.

Ryan opened fire on the newcomers, downing two immediately before receiving a volley of fire of his own for his efforts. The SEAL threw himself behind a parked car on the side of the road, moving behind the tires, unleashing a fusillade over the hood, scattering the shooters.

****

From inside the restaurant, Gutierrez and Santiago could hear the gunfire as it erupted. In a flash of a second, several groups of the men sitting at the tables sprang up, kicking chairs across the room. There was a man behind a counter, and he started tossing weapons at the men as they ran for the front doors. While more barraged out from the kitchen, rushing for the front.

The first set of terrorists made it out into the street, while the second group, having to contend with the strewn furniture, haphazardly and clumsily made their way, following their companions, eager to join the fight and kill Americans.

They wouldn't get the chance.

Waiting for the flapping doors to stop, the two SEALs eyed one another, getting ready—a nod, followed by a fist bump. *Go time.* They stood kicking over their table, whipping out Glocks. A pair of strangers heard the table and chairs flip, turning to see what had happened.

The pair's heads snapped back, taking a round to each. Their trigger fingers seized in the instant of death, clamping down, sending a spray of bullets around the restaurant. The men ducked behind their cover.

Several rounds tore into their fellow countrymen. Some were grazing shots, others direct hits to vital body parts. Not everyone was in on the ambush; those who weren't were caught unawares by the onslaught. Their bodies hit the floor, followed by outcries from the other unsuspecting patrons.

The man behind the counter who was doling out the weapons took an errant round to his forehead for his trouble.

Two other terrorists that hadn't made it out the front doors paused, hearing the clatter of machine gun fire from *inside*. Spun, seeing the two dead men lying on the ground. They whipped up their weapons, about to fire at their killers. But they were too slow. Gutierrez had already recovered and sprung from cover, unleashing several rounds, dropping the men.

"Santiago, let's move." Gutierrez scooped up one of the AKs checking the mag, then pilfered several others from one of the fresh corpses. Santiago followed suit. Gutierrez locked squarely onto the eyes of one of the older gentlemen while digging in the dead man's pockets. "Don't you even think about it, old man," he warned. The man snarled, then gave the SEAL the middle finger.

"Gut, we're moving," Santiago said, throwing himself against the door jamb on the right side of the front door. Gutierrez joined him, stacking up on the left, keeping a watchful eye on the old man. He didn't move, just held a hateful gaze.

****

"Five," Tex crowed, downing a third shooter from the firing line, assaulting the van, and aiming at a fourth shooter. The mud-brick ledge in front of them exploded, kicking ages of dried dirt into their face and throwing off Tex's shot. "Damn," he cursed, pulling back from the edge.

"They've got our location," Tyus warned. "Roll." The two SEALs clambered back, quickly moving and setting up shop a few feet from their previous location.

Tex threw himself back to the ground, bipod digging into the earthen work. Peering down his scope, he saw that two groups of fighters had emerged from the restaurant. A group headed north up the road to Wilks' van and the other south towards Sophia's location. "You guys have to get out of there," he warned, acquiring a new target. "Six." The gunman running toward Ryan's location fell, sliding face-first across the ground.

****

Wilks lifted his head, no longer hearing the gunfire. All that was left were shouts and screams. "Cole, you good?" The man patted himself up and down, flashing a thumbs up. "Great, let's take the fight to them now."

The gunfire had ceased because the firing line had either run out of ammunition or were dead.

Wilks threw open the side door, poking his SCAR out, unleashing a volley. The rounds tore through the last remaining shooters, bodies and limbs flailing. The AKs dropped to the floor seconds before the bodies.

He climbed out of the van, checking north, then south. Nothing and no one coming from up the street. To the south, though, a group of men were rushing their way. Cole had followed behind, popping two more shots into the closest terrorist. "That's for shooting at me," he spat, kicking the body.

"Save that energy, sailor. We've got company." A round snapped by Wilks' head, and a second twanged off a street sign nearby. "Good thing the assholes can't shoot. Fucking Stormtrooper accuracy." Drawing and opening fire on the encroaching group. "We need to get to the other van." Eying the smoking wreckage of theirs. "Alpha-two, we're coming to you."

****

Sophia had stayed low in the back of the van, an occasional bullet pinging off the vehicle. Mohammed urgently clambered into the back with her. "Whoa, get back," she ordered, scrambling to draw her sidearm, bringing it up to the Arab's face. "Did you know? Did you fucking know?" she shouted, gun steadfastly staying pointed at his face. The man aggressively shook his head, looking as shocked as she was. "Don't lie; just because I stopped Simms from shooting you doesn't mean I won't." She clenched her jaw, staring straight ahead.

"No, no, I no know," Mohammed stammered. "Ali, my brother-in-law, and I wanted to go to America. The agency says we help here; we go afterward. Thought Anwar was going to come with us. I know, not of this plan."

Sophia stared at the man, judging his story. Was he truly not in on this? If he was, she reckoned they would've hit them at the safe house while they slept. Right? The man seemed genuinely taken aback by the ongoing firefight outside the van. "Fine, I believe you." She lowered her weapon. "But-"

Before she could finish her sentence, Mohammed threw himself at her, bowling her over and knocking the gun from her hand. The two wrestled as Sophia tried to push him off of her when three shots hit the headrest of the driver's seat, right where her head would've been.

"I save! I save!" Mohammed exclaimed, letting her up.

She rolled, and another round punched through the bed of the van beside her. Another roll and she snatched up her Glock, pointing it out the back of the van. Two men were running up the street at them, AKs at the ready. They'd climbed out of the second sedan. Sophia fired two shots. The one charging on the left went down in a heap, rolling head over heels. The second man tried to veer right, only to take a round to the kneecap. He stumbled, falling forward. To save himself from face-planting, the terrorist instinctively tried to brace his fall with his hands. He was still holding his rifle.

The butt of the gun struck the earth perpendicular, with the terrorist falling chin first on it. The barrel of the rifle sprang from the top of the dead man's head, blood oozing down it.

Sophia cringed at the sight before spotting something else, or rather someone else.

Hasan Althani.

He was limping away from the crashed car, headed south for an alleyway. "Oh, hell no. You are not getting away." Sophia knew they'd never find him again if they lost him now. The fact they were there had meant Stone betrayed him. With that, he would go underground and most likely never be found again. She couldn't let that happen. "Alpha-two, Hasan's here," she radioed. "He's getting away; I am going after him." She jumped out of the van, running south.

"Alpha-zero, don't." Ryan turned to see her running down the street toward Hasan.

"I've got him. He's hurt," she said, running full speed to catch up. He stopped just before reaching the alley and turned. The two locked eyes. She'd let her hesitation get in the way the last time they were this close. And she wasn't going to make the same mistake.

She stopped, drawing her weapon. He smiled. She fired.

The round smacked into a mud-brick wall behind him as he disappeared. "Shit," she spat. "He's running. I'm going after him."

CHAPTER NINE

RYAN watched Sophia disappear into the alley. "Zero, hold. Wait for backup. I am coming. Three cover us."

The SEAL clambered to his feet and charged after the CIA agent, only to be halted in his tracks as a series of rounds smacked into the pavement in front of him.

He scrambled back to his previous position, taking cover behind the car as the glass above his head shattered, raining small chunks over him. Some managed to slip under his vest and were digging into the chest. Bullets binged and ricocheted off metal and asphalt as the barrage continued.

Another group of AIA appeared from around the street corner half a block ahead, spraying wildly at the American.

Tex heard the heavy clatter of machine gun fire from an area of the street that had been quiet. Readjusting, he spotted a new group of assaulters bearing down on Ryan's location. Turning his rifle, he picked out his first target. "Seven," he counted off as one of the shooters fell before he could reload. "All alphas converge on two," he radioed, searching for his next victim.

"We're coming one, hold on," Wilks radioed. "Bravo-six, cover him. Cole, we're moving."

Ryan rolled his eyes. What else could he do other than hold on?

Simms shifted positions, redirecting his fire southbound toward the new group. Wilks and Cole sprinted up the sidewalk, lying down suppressing fire. Gutierrez and Santiago exited the restaurant just in time to see Wilks and Cole sprint by. The pair shrugged at each other and followed suit.

The team quickly felled four more of the approaching terrorists in a flash of a second, racing up the street.

****

Mila and Richard had been watching everything unfold in shock and horror. How had a seemingly perfect operation gone completely awry in minutes? The pair observed the SEALs, the most elite fighting force the US military had to offer, do their thing. As the men converged on Ryan, her next immediate thoughts went to her friend.

Sophia was in pursuit of one of the most dangerous men on the planet and in his own backyard. Luckily, judging by the flow of the fight, she'd be able to get company in a few seconds.

The team was mopping up the last few of Hasan's men that had ambushed them. "Don't worry, Sof. They're coming to help you," Mila whispered.

"Milli, I think we have a problem. A huge fucking problem!" Richard called out from behind his computer—voice reeking of concern.

"What is it?" Mila was almost too nervous to ask, judging by the look on the young man's face. After a few keystrokes, he pointed to the screen. Her mouth fell agape at the scene.

On a hunch, upon seeing the one-time city block, now turned war zone, had emptied of any potential innocents, he'd switched the satellite feed to thermal heat signatures. While some of the reddish-orange blobs seemed to be taking cover, others were rapidly approaching the city street. He pulled the view out further, only to get a bigger shock. Dozens more heat signatures were collapsing on the team, encircling them.

Two of the objects were fast approaching—vehicles—one from each side of the road.

"Oh my god." Mila's hand went to her mouth. "They've walked into a suicide mission. We've kicked over the hornet's nest."

The last of the assaulting AIA group fell, with a round from Tex's rifle, as he happily called out his tenth kill. "All right, team, time to get Alpha-zero," Ryan radioed, seeing the last man hit the ground.

Mila composed herself, took a deep breath, and pressed the mic button. "All units, all units, you have multiple tangos, I repeat, multiple hostiles headed your way. Two technicals as well. They're *all* coming for you," her voice quivered.

"Alpha-two, to TOC, say your last again."

"You have multiple hostiles inbound on your location! Two

technicals. Approaching from North and South." Mila turned at Richard's snapping fingers. He was trying to get her attention. She shot him a glare before realizing what he was pointing at. More heat signatures were making their way towards the street, coming from every direction. "Correction. They're coming from everywhere." She slumped into her seat. "Get out of there now!"

****

The street erupted again, rounds zipped by Ryan's head, so close he could hear the sizzle of the heat from them. Others pounded into the pavement around the assembling group.

The first of the vehicles peeled around the corner. A Toyota Hilux pickup with a mounted heavy machine gun in the bed barreled down at the team.

The new arrival sent the SEALs scattering for cover. Ryan dove out of the street as chunks of asphalt exploded where his feet had been. "Technical, technical," he called out. The roof of the car he dove behind disintegrated under the barrage of the .50cal machine gun fire. Street signs and lamp posts were cut in half. Gaping holes punched through the walls of the stores.

Wilks and Cole threw themselves through a glass window of a store as rounds punched through, exploding bags of chips and eviscerating soda cans, raining debris down on them.

Santiago and Gutierrez dove into a nearby alley. The latter bowled over a trashcan, coming to a rolling stop, only to be met by a volley of small arms fire from deeper in the alley.

The rounds clanged off the trash can as Gutierrez and Santiago recovered. Sending a volley of their own up the alley, taking out two shooters. The others ducked into any recess they could find.

Hundreds of rounds lanced up the street, shredding everything they came into contact with. One of the men from inside the restaurant stumbled out, ready to take up the fight against the Americans. He was instantly cut in half, chunks of flesh ripped off his body. One of his arms flew into the store, hitting Wilks in the face.

"Someone take that fucking thing out," Wilks screamed,

batting the limb away.

Tyus rose, reaching for his rifle. Snatching it up, he pulled out a 40mm high explosive round from his vest. He unlocked the barrel of his M203 grenade launcher attached to the bottom of his SCAR. He dropped the round into the tube, then aimed at the moving vehicle. "I've got this," he whispered. Considering the vehicle's speed, his angle of fire, and the launch point needed to hit the speeding truck. He fired.

Frump!

The grenade spiraled from the barrel, arching toward its target, striking pay dirt.

With an explosion, the truck was ripped into two parts. The bed, where the gun and gunner were, disappeared into a great ball of flames. The cab veered into a parked car on the side of the road, and the driver was unable to compensate for the sudden weight distribution as its back end had been torn away.

The driver hopped out of the cab, his back engulfed, flames licking into the air as he ran down the street screaming. "Eleven." Tex counted, sending a round between the man's eyes, putting him mercifully out of his misery. "Now that's a burning man concert."

The fight wasn't over yet. Smoke from the destroyed vehicle was now wafting into the air and across the street. Blocking the view of the SEALs. Seconds later, several AIA soldiers appeared from the cloud, firing and keeping the SEALs pinned down.

As the fighters emerged from the cloud of smoke, the second vehicle tore around the street, coming from the other direction, unleashing vengeance.

"Four, take'em out," Ryan ordered. Even taking out the technical, though, he knew they were in trouble. More soldiers were advancing from behind the truck, along with the clatter of gunfire erupting from an alley where he assumed members of his team were engaged, and then, peering north where the smoldering remains of the destroyed Hilux were, saw another group of revenge-hate-filled soldiers pouring through the haze. They were pinned in. A glance toward the alley where Sophia had disappeared, knowing that there was no way he'd be able to get to her now. "Three."

"Go for three," Tex responded.

"We're hemmed in. You need to go get our girl. You know chief will be pissed we lose her. The rest of us. We're fighting till the end."

"Copy, three in route." Tex aimed his last shot at the speeding Hilux. "Parting gift." He fired. The round tore through the head of the driver, turning his neck into a bloody stump. The vehicle swerved, rocking back and forth before finally pitching over, throwing the gunner clear of the truck as it rolled down the street.

Two tons of metal flipped side over side. The glass shattered, spewing over the street, and the side mirrors ripped away, along with other body parts, with each revolution. Littering the street with more debris. The gunner, who had been ejected twenty feet, had thought his ordeal was over until he looked back and saw the rolling truck barreling down on him.

He frantically tried to crawl from its path, but he was too slow. The tumbling truck came to a sudden stop as it rolled over him. His pained screams were silenced as the vehicle smashed him under two tons of metal. A puddle of blood oozed from underneath.

****

Sophia had briefly lost sight of Hasan after he rounded the corner at the end of the alley, but she wasn't far behind. At their current pace, she figured she would catch up to him by the time the team caught up to her.

In a dead sprint, she could hear her boots clacking against the flagstones echoing in the tight corridors of the alleys. Building entrances whooshed by her as she ran. The thought in the back of her mind that someone could spring out from any of the recesses and take her out flooded in. But she had one narrow focus: Catching Hasan.

She rounded the corner, figuring her prey would be closer than before. Except he wasn't. Somehow, he'd managed to increase the gap between them. His limp seemed to have vanished in the time it took her to round the bend. He was now running normally. Adrenaline and fear having kicked in at the thought of being captured, maybe?

Something that she could remedy quickly. Drawing her Glock, putting the fleeing terrorist in her sights—back center mass.

A fleeting thought, she could end it all right here. But she wasn't a murderer nor a coward. Only a coward shoots a man in the back while he's running away.

She lowered her sights. Taking out a kneecap, though, was entirely acceptable.

The agent closed her left eye like she'd been taught, taking a breath. She held it for a second and applied pressure to the trigger. She squeezed.

A loud explosion rocked the area, sending dust and dirt wafting down the narrow alley as the buildings seemingly swayed by the concussive blast. The unexpected *boom* caused Sophia to flinch, sending her shot high, pinging off a power junction box attached to the side of a building.

Sophia reflexively looked back. A cloud of smoke was snaking its way skyward. *What was that*, she thought. An inclination to race back and help the team. But, she felt something else, eyes staring at her. She turned to see that Hasan had stopped and was staring back at her with a sardonic smile and a menacing gleam in his eye. He'd planned the perfect ambush.

"All your men will die in this city," he shouted. Sophia whipped up her pistol again. He was no longer running. So, shooting him wasn't cowardly. She fired, but he ducked down another corner.

"Fuck," Sophia spat, indecision gripping at her heart. She paced, starting to go back to the team. Then stopped, looking back to where Hasan had disappeared. "What to do? what to do?" Running scenarios rapidly filled her head. "Fuuuuck!" She kicked a basket down the alley, slamming her palm against a wall. "Zero, to TOC, what was that?" she radioed.

"A technical. The team took out a technical," Mila answered. They're still bogged down. They're not coming for you. You're on your own." Mila hoped that telling Sophia the situation that there was no backup coming would force her to give up the pursuit.

"Copy." She took a long look at where Hasan had been standing, making a decision with tightly pursed lips, hoping it was the correct one. She thought *they'd be fine; they're highly trained special operators.* "Continuing pursuit," she radioed back.

Mila slumped into her chair, burying her head in her hands. Her friend was too determined not to lose Hasan.

****

Tex shoulder barged through the door to the apartment complex's roof into the square spiraling stairwell. Bouncing off the far wall, nearly losing his balance.

Recovering, he bounded down the flights of stairs three to four at a time, using the handrails for support. One gave way under his weight, falling into the center void. He could hear it rattling off the mud brick on its descent, clattering to a halt at the bottom. He peered over the ledge after it. "Only three more flights to go," he huffed, gripping his chest mic. "Alpha-three to TOC, I need to know where I am going. Re-task the drone to guide me."

"Roger alpha-three, re-tasking," Mila responded.

"If we re-task the drone, we'll lose direct visuals of the team." Richard objected, taken aback by Mila's willingness to reroute the drone without a second thought.

She rounded on the young computer operator. "We still have them on satellite, and Tex needs to know where to go to find Sophia. So, re-task the damn thing, and find her!" Mila snapped. She wasn't about to lose her friend.

Leaping down another flight of stairs, a shot cracked over Tex's head, slamming into the wall just above him. The surprise shot caused him to lose his footing upon landing. He tumbled over, slamming shoulder-first into the wall on the second-story landing.

Finding himself in a lying position, half his body leaning against the wall, dazed, his head ringing, he felt the back of his skull. He could already feel a knot forming, and he saw two of everything. The world around him took a moment to focus. His hearing hadn't been affected, though. The sound of shuffling footsteps snapped him back into alertness.

Instincts kicked in, and he drew his sidearm. The top of an alquaweq appeared—a typical headdress worn by Yemeni men. Or, more appropriately, two that merged into one came into view, cresting the steps.

Tex fired. The round punched through the headdress easily, splashing the earth-toned brick behind him in a Jackson Pollock splatter painting of red and gray.

Another alquaweq-wearing man appeared, leapfrogging over his dead friend. He soon joined his compatriot in the afterlife, taking two rounds to the chest. "Hope you don't have to share your virgins," the Texan quipped, getting to his feet. A series of AK rounds pockmarked the wall behind him. Two more terrorists raced up the steps. Each received a round to the head, crumbling to the floor. "Damn, I am *so* going to get fined for littering." He looked around for anyone to appreciate his joke. There wasn't anyone present aside from the fresh corpses. Looking down at one of the dead men, he remarked, "I wouldn't suppose you'd find that funny, though. I am going to have to remember that one for later. Now let's see what you got for Papa."

He collected the dead man's AK and several magazines from the bodies before continuing his trek down the stairwell, eventually hitting the ground floor, exiting the back entrance of the building, and finding himself standing in the middle of a quiet street—the constant clatter of gunfire just on the other side of the building.

"Alpha-three, we've got you on satellite. Zero is about four, no five blocks north of your location." Mila relayed what they were seeing from overhead. Richard had managed to track down Sophia. She was still following Hasan. The pair were weaving their way through alleys. "She still has Hasan in her sights."

"Alpha-three good copy," he responded, flipping over his wrist and checking his watch. It had a built-in compass, getting his bearings which way was north and sprinting off after deciphering the correct direction. "Alpha-four, you need to move. They have your location. I took out a welcoming party on the way down. But they'll send more."

Tyus slapped the last magazine for the sniper rifle into its well, drawing back the charging hammer and taking aim at a terrorist who was charging Ryan's location. With a *whoomph,* the man fell. "Alpha-three, that's a good copy. Good looking out. Was just about out of party favors anyway," he said, firing again, watching another AIA member fall on the other side of his scope.

CHAPTER TEN

THE narrow road quickly filled with smoke as it wafted down the street from the burning Hilux. The screen of gray haze was beginning to obscure both sides' views of each other. The crackling of automatic machine gun fire, though, wasn't letting up. The AIA soldiers let off magazine after magazine of indiscriminate fire. Hoping that, at some point, they'd hit someone.

The SEALs, though, knew they had to make every shot count. Slamming another mag into his rifle, Ryan looked around. His men were scattered. They needed to consolidate and figure out a plan to get off the street and go after the others. "Four, I need you down here," he radioed to Tyus, who was still on the roof.

"Copy. Coming down," Tyus responded, packing up the rifle and scope, hastily jamming everything into his pack, and slinging the rifle across his body. Shouts arose from behind. He looked back. Tex had knocked off the hinges of the door to the roof. He could hear the shouts of a group of AIA coming up the stairwell. "Welp, not going down that way." He rummaged back through his pack and pulled out a coil of rope. Unrolling it, he wrapped one end around what he hoped was a sturdy piece of ventilation pipe protruding from the roof before quickly making a harness around his waist. "Two, I am coming over the side. Have incoming tangos."

"Four good, copy?" Ryan looked up to see Tyus step up onto the ledge of the roof, twisting, then taking a first step over. His feet pressed against the side of the six-story building. A crack of gunfire, immediately followed by a puff of dust, feet from the dangling SEAL. Ryan rounded on the direction of the shots. Two AIAs had spotted Tyus and shifted fire to the defenseless repelling man. Ryan returned their gesture in kind, dropping both soldiers. "All numbers, cover four."

Simms opened a barrage on several AIA who'd materialized through the smoke cloud, seeing a dangling American from the side of a building. Wilks and Cole, who'd clambered out of the market after the technical had been taken out and were using a car for cover, also opened fire on a group that had appeared from an alley.

Tyus spun, facing the stairwell, hearing the footsteps growing louder. He tentatively leaned backward, testing the support harness. The rope pulled tautly around his genitals. The rope was secure.

He leaned back further, bracing both feet against the side of the building, taking a step back. A cloud of dust kicked into his face as a burst of gunfire strafed across the building several feet from him—the volley followed by another one. But the pitch of fire told him it was a SCAR. His team was covering his descent. Reaching into his vest pocket, Tyus drew a small baseball-sized object, pulled the pin, and clamped his hand around the spoon trigger release. Listening, waiting. The shouts were practically on top of him.

He released his grip, and the spoon sprang away, falling sixty feet with a ping. He counted: *one, two, three.*

The first of his visitors appeared in the doorway, bringing his AK to bear. Tyus lobbed the grenade. It hit the ground with a *thud,* rolling to the feet of the would-be shooter, who looked at it, uncertain of what it was for a brief second.

Realization as to what it was dawned on his face a second later. Tyus flipped the man the bird, then leaped away from the building in a bound, unfurling the rope as he descended.

The grenade went off. A loud explosion rattled the area, sending debris raining over the ledge and down onto Tyus, covering him in earth particles as he continued his descent one bound at a time.

He hit ground level, quickly undoing the rope around his waist, drawing his rifle at an AIA who came around a car. But the rifle barrel snagged against the rope—the terrorist's rifle about to bark. Then, the holder's head popped in a shower of mist.

"Move your ass, Ty!" Simms shouted, selecting a new target who was racing across the road, downing him, too.

Seeing Tyus land, Ryan turned and mowed down several more encroaching AIA. "All numbers collapse on the van."

Wilks and Cole responded, sending a fusillade up an alley

several other AIA had appeared from, downing the running terrorists. "Five and Bravo-eight are still pinned, breaking off to get them."

The two men returned to where they'd seen their friends dive when the truck had unloaded on them. There were several cracks of gunfire. They popped around the corner, seeing a rapidly approaching AIA group. Cole lobbed a grenade down the alley. "Down."

It went off, sending deadly projectiles piercing through flesh and bone in a gruesome explosion, severing the leg of the closest terrorist. Another was thrown against a wall, and a jagged piece of metal speared through his heart, choking off any cries of pain. Others littered the ground, wailing.

"Gut, Santiago, let's move. Exfil now." Wilks turned to see two more soldiers appear from behind the flipped-over Hilux. Snapping up his rifle, he sent a burst down range. The rounds hit their targets. "Moving to the van."

Wilks, Cole, Santiago, and Gutierrez broke across the street. Simms, Tyus, and Ryan laid down, suppressing fire, covering their journey as they made their way.

"RPG!" shouted Ryan.

An AIA came out of the thickening, churning now black smoke. Propped onto his shoulder was a military green cylindric object with an explosive warhead on the tip. Ryan and Simms fired simultaneously, striking the grenadier in the head. But it was too late. He'd pressed the button.

A spark of explosion followed by a trail of white smoke lanced from the tube-

The warhead bounced off the ground harmlessly as it hadn't traveled the necessary distance to activate the fuse. It careened through the air, striking a street sign, before lodging into the wall next to Simms and Tyus. The latter threw himself clear before the warhead ignited.

Simms was too slow to react. The warhead exploded in a thunderous *boom*. The shock wave threw the SEAL bodily into the front of the van with such force he left a human-sized dent in the fender. Hot, burning shrapnel tore into his flesh, slicing off chunks as they embedded into his skin searingly.

"Simms!" Wilks shouted, seeing a member of his team blown up. He raced across the road, the others taking down the remaining members of the AIA. "Quick, someone get me a tourniquet." The blast had almost torn Simms' right arm off. It dangled precariously by a band of skin. The SEAL moaned, writhing in pain. "Morphine, get him some fucking morphine." Ryan and Cole raced over, handing him a first aid kit and morphine syrettes.

"Gut, Santiago, Cole, set up security. Tyus, are you okay?" Ryan asked, watching Wilks go to work on his teammate.

Sitting up, shaking his head, Tyus gave Ryan a thumbs up. "Just got a little rung. I am still in the fight, boss."

"Copy, security. Mohammed." Ryan rounded the back of the van to find that the Arab was still hunkered down, having wrapped a blanket over his body to shield himself. "What the fuck are you doing. Get your ass in the driver's seat. You'll drive Wilks, Simms, and Santiago to the exfil point now." He peeked around the van at Wilks. "We've gotta move him. Let's get him in the van." He helped Wilks lift Simms. The man cried out in agony at the shifting of his body as they carried him to the back. Loading him inside. Wilks hopped in after. By now, Mohammed had jumped into the driver's seat. "He's going to drive you to the border and exfil you."

"What about you?"

"Gut, Ty, and I are going after Tex and Sophia. Then we'll exfil."

"That's suicide. The whole fucking city knows we're here, and most hate us," Wilks countered.

"All the more reason to not leave two team members behind. Now go. Cole, Santiago, get your asses in the van." Wilks' team peeled away from their sectors. Cole climbed into the passenger seat. Santiago joined Wilks and Simms in the back. "Get home." Ryan slammed the door shut, pounding on the side. Mohammed started the van up and sped away.

"What are we going to do, boss," Gutierrez asked.

Ryan surveyed what was left of the street, spotting an SUV that seemed undamaged by the gunfight. "Go get our people," he replied.

****

Sophia rounded another corner, racing down the alleyway chasing after Hasan, who was managing to stay just ahead of her. The city's back alleys were a winding maze, blending into one overly used backdrop—tight corridors of dull earth-toned, flagstoned laced causeways. Spikes of sunlight lanced from above through the cloth awnings stretching between the buildings.

As she ran, she passed numerous potential threats. Doorways blitzed by without incident, head on a swivel as a rifle barrel could poke from any number of windows above and end the footrace.

After the fifth new corridor entered, the echoing of the firefight had eased and became a low thrum of intermittent pop shots. Which either meant her team had won or she was now the last American in a hostile city chasing after a terrorist leader.

As she pounded after Hasan, he disappeared again, rounding a corner. Before doing so, he glanced back at her with a malevolent smile.

Seconds later, she rounded the bend after her prey. Her luck or fortune, or both, ran out. As she whipped around the corner, bounding off the far wall and running too fast to turn sharply, two figures appeared from a doorway, AKs in hand. Sophia's eyes widened.

They drew-

She drew-

The CIA-trained agent was faster. Whipping up her Glock, she fired.

Sophia's gun barked first. Two rounds struck center mass of the nearest terrorist. He crumbled to the floor. She quickly shifted targets, firing seconds before the other man could let off. One shot between the eyes. His head snapped back, trigger finger spasming, sending a harmless volley of rounds into the wall just above her head.

The second man fell in a lump of collapsed flesh. Sophia staggered to a halt, panting, eyes still wide, shifting between the pockmarks in the wall and the two lifeless bodies—a moment of both shock at still being alive and self-impressment at how quickly she'd reacted.

Hands on her knees, bent over, breathing heavily, she looked up to see Hasan at the end of the alley, staring back at her, equally stunned.

Sophia snapped back to the moment, raising her gun towards Hasan. She fired.

But he was already gone. The bullet smacked into the wall. "Shit," she spat, continuing after him.

****

Tex bounded down an alley, searching for a way to turn up to head north, hearing the chatter of automatic gunfire dying down. The last few shots he heard came from American firepower. He knew the boys had won. Then came another shot.

This one came from a Glock 22. The sound was unmistakable as it reverberated through the alleys, bounding over the buildings. It wasn't too far. He continued, seeing a "T" junction at the end of the corridor.

"Three to TOC; which way am I going?" he radioed, slowing to wait for an answer.

"Richard," Mila barked at the computer analyst. They'd lost sight of Sophia under the cover of the awnings for several minutes. A flash of blond appeared on the drone's camera.

"He needs to go right."

"Three turn right," Mila relayed. While Richard was following Sophia with the drone, Mila was watching Tex via satellite, trying to help guide him to Sophia.

"Where's my boys," Tex asked, slowing as he reached the junction, sliding to the right of the alley, pressing against the apartment complex wall, AK in hand. He peered down the left corridor—no one in sight. Swinging around the corner, two Arab militants in fatigues were standing in the middle of the alley, back turned to him. "Phwwwwwhht," he whistled. They turned, only to take several rounds a piece to the chest. Dropping both men, he leaped over their bodies, continuing.

"Alpha-two, what's your status?" Mila radioed Ryan.

"Securing wheels. You're going to need to guide us to the others."

"Copy. Three, you hear?"

"Roger, be quick. We're going to need a fast exfil when I catch her. The alleys are crawling with baddies." Tex rounded the next alley, finding two more armed men. He let off another volley, killing them instantly.

****

Sophia heard the clatter of an AK nearby. It wasn't coming from the streets, but from the alleys, she guessed by the echo. Someone from the team was still alive and coming after her. She reached for the mic button on her vest, pressing it. No squelch followed. Mid-stride, she looked down to find her radio missing. Figuring it must've fallen when she rounded the last alley after hitting the wall.

Still running, she looked up to see a small black dot in the sky buzzing overhead between awnings—the drone.

Mila was following her and guiding the team to her. The drone sent a reassuring pulse through Sophia. Rounding the next alley, Hasan was almost at the end already. A shot rang out.

Sophia flinched, expecting to either feel the burning sensation of metal piercing flesh or a crack of air from the missed shot.

Neither came. She stopped, gun raised, searching the alley for the source. The drone crashed beside her, shattering into pieces.

Someone on a rooftop had taken it out. With no way for the team to track her visually now, she heard another short series of shots. This time closer. Whoever was coming for her wasn't that far.

Raising her gun, Sophia let off three shots into the air before continuing. If they couldn't track her by sight, then sound would have to do it.

****

"Vögeln," Mila screamed in German, seeing the drone feed go black. Seconds before, there was a flash of fire from a nearby rooftop. Someone had shot down the drone. "Three, the drone's out. Someone took it out. You need to get to zero, NOW!"

Something had been bothering Mila the whole time. If Hasan had known that they were there, why did he even bother showing up? If it was a trap, he could've sent all of his AIA forces and taken everyone out before the team could even react. What was he playing?

"Copy," Tex responded. Three shots rang out, two alleys over, he figured by how loud they were. *Good girl, echolocation.* "I think I have her location. En route." He fired a responding volley into the air.

Three more militants entered the alley, hearing his shots. Tex lowered his rifle and let loose on them. Emptying his magazine, slapping in his last mag before continuing.

****

Sophia pressed on hearing the AK fire. They were really close. She bounded down the alley after Hasan, who'd already disappeared around another bend.

She rounded the corner. Ahead at the end of the corridor was her target. Hasan stood at the mouth of the alley draped in shadows. Behind him, a street, several cars whooshed by, seemingly unfazed by the fierce gun battle that had just been raging on several blocks over.

He was just standing there. Hands on hips. He was waiting for her.

Sophia drew, moving up the alley. Hasan was unarmed still, so she couldn't shoot. "Don't move," she shouted, inching her way closer. Every alarm bell in her head went off. Something wasn't right. He could have easily vanished in the crowd once he exited the alleys. Knowing that an American team in Sanaa couldn't just go traipsing around town going door to door.

Now, halfway to him, he still hadn't moved. Was he taunting her? The shadow that blocked his face faded as she drew nearer. He was grinning.

Two more men came around the corner, flanking Hasan, sneering at her. They stood by his side for a second, receiving orders. Then they advanced on her.

It was a trap. And she'd fallen right into it.

Sophia backed down the alley, still facing the two men. Gun flicking between them. Behind her, she heard the scuffling of footsteps, followed by the sounds of closing doors. She peered over her shoulder to find five more men standing in the alley, blocking her path of retreat.

She gulped.

They hadn't shot her yet, which was a good thing. But why? It quickly dawned on her. They wanted to kidnap her. Maybe extract information out of her or worse. She'd seen dozens of videos of Americans being beheaded on TV. She wasn't going to let that happen. She wasn't going to be used as a propaganda pawn to be beheaded on camera. She wasn't going to subject those who cared for her to risk their lives to save hers or watch it taken on TV.

With both groups advancing on her, she stared up, basking in the glow of the sunlight piercing between the awnings. She closed her eyes and took a deep breath. She had never imagined for a second before that this was how her life would end.

She snapped up her Glock to her head, pressing it against her temple. Finger tightening around the trigger. At least, this would be quick.

A door burst open, and out came a charging terrorist. Out of instinct, Sophia snapped her eyes open and reflexively fired at the new danger.

The charging man dropped, sliding to a stop at her feet. The two groups charged. Panicked, she brought the barrel back to her head. Feeling the red-hot steel press against the side of her head. She squeezed-

The spring slammed into the firing pin of the chambered

bullet's primer. Igniting the gunpowder inside, causing it to spark, setting off a chemical reaction of gases, which exploded, sending the bullet rifling down the barrel to meet Sophia's brain.

An intense pain swelled in her stomach before any in her head. Jarring her eyes open, she saw the muzzle flash of her Glock and felt the wind from the ejected projectile blowing in her face before she hit the ground with a thud.

The bullet lodged into the wall behind her.

Sophia bounced off the ground, the back of her head smacked with a sickening *thunk* against the flagstones. The world went black for a second. Dazed, she could feel the body of one of the AIA soldiers on top of hers—his hot breath against her cheek.

Gun still in hand, she raised it, squeezing the trigger, but the man managed to smack her arm aside just in time, sending the bullet wide. Sophia brought her left hand up, striking at his face, only managing to deliver a glancing blow. She didn't have the leverage to deliver a more forceful punch.

The man hauled her off the ground, delivering a gut punch, knocking the wind out of Sophia's lungs. Gasping, she desperately clawed at the man's eyes, digging a finger into his left eye socket.

He wailed, recoiling from her. She swung out her leg, kicking at his genitals. Before she could make contact, another man threw his arms around Sophia's entire body, wrapping her in a bear hug, squeezing. Still winded from the punch, she gasped for breath. The two men exchanged heated words in Arabic.

The first man produced a black bag from his pocket opening. He approached, blood oozing from the corner of his eye. Sophia tried to kick him away, but the man holding her swung her around. Then, the world around her went black. The feeling of her own breath pressed against her face as the bag went over her head.

Sophia continued to struggle, but she was being dragged along. Her boots scraped against the cobblestone ground. The screeching sound of car brakes, juddering a vehicle to a stop, cut through the bag.

She was being taken.

****

Tex approached the end of the alley; he could hear the sounds of some kind of struggle, where three shots had just come from. Rounding the corner, he froze. The sight be-folding in front of him gripped at his heart. Sophia was surrounded by eight AIA soldiers being drug to a waiting SUV. Hasan Althani eagerly held open the rear door, awaiting his prize.

"Hey," he shouted, bringing up his AK. The group turned to find Tex standing in the middle of the alley. He brought the AK up, aiming at the group. But they were too tightly packed surrounding Sophia. If he shot, he ran the risk of hitting her.

Three AIA peeled away from the pack, racing towards Tex.

The stout Texan chucked the AK at the one that reached him quicker. The man batted the rifle away, sending it bounding off the wall. Before he could recover, he ate two rounds to the chest from Tex's sidearm.

The other two men continued charging. Tex fired four more shots. Hitting both of them. They fell.

Hasan ordered four of his five remaining men to attack. The fifth continued to drag the kicking and squirming Sophia to the SUV.

The four AIA charged at the American.

Tex shifted targets from the two that he'd just shot to the closest of the encroaching four. He squeezed the trigger. The slide of his pistol was open. No more rounds; he was empty. He tossed the gun at the attacker. The soldier batted the pistol aside.

Tex had already drawn his K-bar knife from his vest, flipping it over in his hand. Snapping his arm forward, the knife embedded into the soldier's chest, the tip piercing his heart. The running soldier spasmed, tripping over his feet and falling forward.

Tex lunged, wrapping his left hand around the knife's hilt, driving it deeper into the man's chest cavity, twisting it before ripping it back out. The man collapsed to the ground.

The second AIA soldier swung, reaching Tex. The American quickly shifted the knife to his right hand, blocking the blow with his left arm, then drove the K-bar into the temple of the second attacker before he could strike again. Ripping it out, blood oozed down the steel blade.

The two remaining AIA soldiers stopped, drawing level, seeing their two compatriots easily felled by the elite special forces operator. They decided to coordinate their attack. The pair stretched out across the alley as far as they could go to divide the American's focus.

Tex, still holding the blood-soaked knife, waited to see who would make the first move. All three stood, the two parties sizing each other up. Beyond them, though, he could see that Sophia was about to be loaded up and whisked away to God knew where. He couldn't wait any longer.

Tex lunged at the man to his left, stabbing at him with the knife, catching and cutting open his shirt, slicing a gouge in his side. The man reeled back, hand clamping around his abdomen. The guy to Tex's right sprung, launching himself fist first.

Tex moved to block, but it was a feigned attack. Instead, the soldier delivered a kick to the American's side. Catching him off guard, staggering him. The Arab moved to follow the strike with a punch, only to be intercepted as Tex delivered a punch of his own.

The blow struck with such force that it spun the Arab around, sending him reeling into the wall before Tex could press his advantage. The other man charged, thrusting his shoulder into the burly Texan, driving him back a few inches across the dust-covered ground.

Tex managed to regain traction, stopping himself. "Big mistake," the Texan growled, delivering a hammer blow to the back of the man's neck.

He dropped face-first to the cobblestones. Tex raised his boot to stomp on the back of his neck. Before he could deliver the death blow, the other man recovered, leaping at the American. Tex caught him mid-air, slinging him into the wall.

The Arab smacked with a bone-splintering *thud*, flush against the mud-brick facade, cracking and crumbling the wall where he'd hit, slithering to the ground, moaning.

The American turned his attention back to the other soldier, who was scrambling, trying to get back up. Tex drove his boot down on the back of the man's neck. It snapped with a wet crunch; his body fell lifeless.

A quick check of the other guy proved he was out of commission. Tex rounded, snapping his attention to the end of the alley. The other Arab was forcing Sophia into the SUV. Hasan climbed into the passenger seat, waving at the American.

Tex raced up the alley, scooping up the AK. The SUV backed up and peeled out of the alley, bursting onto the street, and nearly striking a passing car in a cloud of white smoke. The American reached the mouth of the alley seconds later, unleashing a barrage at the speeding SUV, blowing out the back window as it turned a corner.

Tex clawed at his mic. "Three to TOC, they got her! They fucking got her! Two, where the fuck are you."

****

Mila's heart sank into her stomach upon hearing those first three words. Her friend was gone. Now, in the hands of a terrorist. Tears welled in her eyes, not knowing what to do next. She wasn't trained for this.

"TOC, where is three?" Ryan's voice crackled over the radio. "TOC come in. I need to know where he is." No reply. "Three, where are you?"

Tex looked around, not knowing where he was, but down the road, he could see a group of military-aged males amassing and pointing at him. "Oh, shit. I am five or eight blocks from the target location. It's about to get hairy down here." The group started making their way towards him.

"Mila, the sat. We can track Hasan's vehicle using that,"

Richard said. "Mila!"

Snapping out of her trance, "Copy, follow the SUV. Two, make your next right. Three head south."

Seconds later, Ryan's SUV swung around the corner, skidding to a halt in the middle of the street. Tex jumped into the back seat. "Go, go, go. We need to catch up to Hasan. He's got Sophia."

"Fuck," Gutierrez spat, pressing the accelerator harder. Swerving around the gathered crowd that had now rushed into the street, throwing bricks, rocks, bottles, and whatever else they could at the speeding vehicle.

"Turn left, left here," Tex shouted, pointing to the street Hasan's SUV disappeared down. "TOC, where are we going next?"

Richard and Mila poured over the screens, searching for the SUV. Mila spotted it, picking its way through a street two blocks east of where the team was. A warning flashed across the screens. The satellite was about to move out of range. Their mission wasn't expected to take this long. "They're two blocks east of your location."

"Great, keep guiding us," Ryan responded. "Everyone, keep your eyes peeled."

"Alpha-two, we are about to lose the satellite link. But they are still headed east of your current location. Wait, they're turning. Looks like they are getting on the main road heading out of the city." The screens went black. "We've lost visuals," Mila announced, defeat in her voice. "There's nothing more we can do for you from here."

"Great, just fucking great. In a hostile city, hostile country, with half our team, and we have no idea where they're taking her." Tex slammed his helmet against the back of the passenger seat.

"Guys, hate to bring more bad news," Gutierrez hesitantly added. "But, we're running out of gas. What do we do?"

Ryan analyzed the situation and, with deep regret, had to make a call. One that would be very unpopular. "Gutierrez, get us out of the city into the mountains. We'll regroup and try to find Sophia later. They're not going to kill her," he added. "If they were going to do that, they would've done it already. Hasan wants her for something. Let's get the rest of the team together again, and we'll track her down."

****

Mila quickly strode from the room, slamming the door behind her. Standing in the hallway, the young German fought to keep her tears back. What would Sophia say? What would she do? No amount of crying was going to find her friend, let alone get her back.

Stiffening her jaw, she stood straight up. She calmly walked into their other command ops room. Gabby and Jerry weren't there. They'd gone to bed sometime before her mission had begun. Wallace's team was on their way to the Embassy in Saudi Arabia, where they'd planned to rendezvous before heading back to the States.

He had to know.

Mila went to Jerry's workstation and radioed the plane. A few moments later. The radio came to life.

"Mila, what's up? We're on our way with Stone and West's families to interrogate them. How'd the mission go?" Wallace asked.

Mila gulped before answering. "They… they have her. We lost Sophia."

Wallace plopped down in a nearby seat, a thousand-yard stare on his face, stomach curling in knots. Stunned, not knowing how to respond. "Wha…what…what do you mean, they have her."

"It was a trap. The informant's cousin betrayed the team and told Hasan we were coming after him. They… they…" Tears began to swell in Mila's eyes, doing all she could to hold them back. "They took her," she finally said. "We lost her. Ryan and the team weren't able to follow. What are we going to do?"

Wallace thought for a second, stunned by the revelation. "Let me work on that. In the meantime, pull the team out to Oman."

"But… but, how are we going to find her?"

"I'll find a way. I'll find a way to find our girl." Wallace hung up the phone, then marched to the cockpit, poking his head in.

156

"Gentlemen, change to the flight plan." He handed the flight crew a slip of paper before returning to the cargo bay as the plane altered course.

"We changing plans?" Walsh asked, approaching with a bottle of beer in his hand, handing one to Wallace, who refused the beverage.

"Boys, listen up." Walsh, Johns, and Alwani gathered up. "The Yemen mission went sideways. Sophia's been kidnapped. We have no idea where she's been taken. But we're *going* to get her back. We have to make a detour first.

CHAPTER ELEVEN
MILWAUKEE, WISCONSIN

A gentle breeze wafted through the closed screen, creating a barrier between the buzzing world outside and the tranquility within the garage. The distant chirping of baby birds, eagerly awaiting their mother's return with food, provided a soothing backdrop of nature sounds to the smooth jazz melodies emanating from the radio.

Fred Jones laid on his back on top of a creeper, wrench in his hands, twisting a bolt on his newfound hobby. Legs spread out, half protruding from underneath a 1967 Oldsmobile 442 soft-top convertible. Leg hairs wisping with the breeze, singing along, albeit off tune, to the record.

His off-tune singing along with the music had almost muted the grating sound of the garage door closing. But he'd sensed something was off when the natural outdoor lighting had begun to evaporate, replaced with the yellowish tinge of artificial light. His suspicions were only confirmed when he felt something grab his ankles.

In a flash, he whooshed from underneath the metal body of the pristinely beautiful classic car, only to be confronted with a more beautiful, heavenly site—at least in his opinion, which was all that mattered.

Standing over him, looking down, wearing a face of *you've got to be kidding me*, stood his wife, Sherry Jones, with wet shoulder-length curly red hair dripping, hands thrust on her hips, in a bathrobe. Her angelic blue eyes stared down at him. "Mr. What do you think you are doing right now?"

Fred gave her a shrug before scrambling to his feet, striding over to his workbench, and placing the wrench back into the open drawer he pulled it from in the very specific spot it had called home. He turned to face his wife. "Just making a few more tweaks. The engine didn't sound quite right," he answered.

Sherry approached, "You know we have dinner reservations for date night. And *now* look at you, you're covered in oil and smut," she said, whipping a small grease trail across his face. "This is not what I had in mind when I suggested you get a hobby after retirement." Glancing back at the classic car, almost enviously.

Fred sighed. "I needed something to do while you're out planning parties. Besides, you know that it's one of my fondest memories of my father. How we'd spend hours in his garage working on people's cars." He sat in a nearby chair, sipping a glass of lemonade, shifting his focus between the car, remembering his father fondly and his loving wife—a sinister growing smirk on his face. "Anyways, the reservation isn't for like two hours," he said, standing, meeting his wife. "Plenty of time for us to take a shower," he added with a batting of his eyebrows.

"Oh no, you don't," Sherry protested, trying to back away as fast as she could. "Fred, don't you dare-"

It was too late; he'd already lunged forward, snatching the sides of her face with his oil-laden hands, pulling her in, and planting a huge kiss on her lips. The two embraced lovingly for a few seconds before she pushed him off. He managed to smear the newly deposited oil over her face even more before stumbling back.

"Now we've both got to shower," he said with a laugh, broad smile on his face, sitting back in the chair.

"Frederick Batholomew Jones," Sherry huffed, seductively encroaching. Fred sat up straight, eyes wide. "I can't believe you did that, you *bad* boy," she whispered, slowly reaching for her robe's cincture. Fred gulped. She tugged the binding, and her robe dropped to the floor, exposing her naked body. She leaned over, spreading his legs open, kissing him on the forehead, and standing back up. She turned and walked back toward the door to the kitchen and gave a seductive glance back, "You coming?"

"Hell yeah," Fred shouted, jumping up and racing after her. He chased her all the way to the bathroom.

****

Fred stood in front of the mirror, taking in his reflection, hand-picking through his hair. He thought that, fortunately, his hairline was not yet receding, as his fathers had done around his current age of forty-six. Yet, he'd stopped counting the mounting gray hairs several years back that were more prevalent now than ever before.

"Honey, I am going to lay out your clothes for you. I want you to wear something nice for once," Sherry said from the bedroom.

"Babe, do you think I should dye my hair?" He could hear a small chuckle from the other side of the door. He poked his head out, seeing his wife slip into a nice, sleek black dress. "Really, that's funny to you? You dye-." He stopped mid-sentence as she whipped around, finishing putting on an earring and giving him a death stare.

"Go ahead and finish that sentence. If you do, you'll be waiting a long while before we do that again, with a lot of cold showers between now and then."

"I…I wasn't going to finish." Making an exaggerated show of zipping his lips.

"That's what I thought, Mr.," she said with a wry smile. "But what you can do is get rid of that beard on your face. You know it pricks my chin when we kiss."

Fred's face turned up, hand protectively going to his face, stroking his fully formed beard. Having been retired from the FBI now officially for the last six months had allowed him the freedom to let it grow out. He promptly returned to the bathroom, once again checking out his reflection. "I…I guess I could." Giving it another stroke before opening the medicine cabinet and retrieving his razor. "I suppose if I want to keep kissing you, I should," he added.

"That's right, and when you're done getting dressed, meet me in the den. I need to go over a last-minute venue change for the Singers' birthday party."

"Yes, dear."

Fred emerged from the bathroom completely clean-shaven, seeing the clothes that Sherry had picked out for him—a black suit with a white undershirt. He stared pensively at the ensemble, reminiscing about when that would've been his normal weekday attire for work. Putting on his clothes, he heard a crash from the living room. Something shattering, he raced out the door down the hall to find Sherry standing in the living room, trembling, staring out the window.

"No…no…no, god no." She looked back at Fred, hands covering her mouth. "Oh my god, this can't be."

Fred rushed to her side. "What, what is it?" He looked outside to see two men approaching the house. The way they carried themselves immediately told him they were military. He'd know that Sophia was somewhere abroad tracking down former Senator Roy Stone. A subtle gasp escaped his lips, and his heart suddenly grew heavy. The doorbell rang. Fred moved to answer it. Sherry grabbed his arm.

"Don't. Don't answer it," she pleaded. "If we don't hear it, then it's not true."

Fred gently removed her hand, grabbed her by the arms, and led her to the couch, sitting her down. "You know it doesn't work that way," he said, striding to the door. "Besides, if it were bad, they'd be dressed in military uniforms," he added as reassurance, not just for the benefit of his wife but also his. The bell rang again as he reached the hallway. He sighed deeply, fixing his suit, and opened the front door. "Gentlemen, what can I do for you this evening?" he said, greeting the pair. The sun had just started its descent, casting an orangish tint over the neighborhood.

"Sir, my name is Master Chief Marshall Wallace, and this is Petty Officer Second Class Ahmed Alwani. We-"

"You're part of the task force that's working with Agent Sophia Evans," Fred cut in, having remembered Wallace's name. "Sophia's talked a great deal about you. She admires you and your men."

"And we her, sir. May we come in?" Wallace asked.

"If you've come to tell us she's de-." Unable to get the word out initially, fighting back the hitch in his voice. "Dead. Then just say it, son."

Wallace gave Alwani a side-eyed glance. "It's not that simple, sir. Please, can we come in?"

Fred contemplated for a moment, then opened the screen, inviting his guests inside. He led them to the living room, taking a seat next to his wife and offering the two men a seat. He embraced Sherry, who was visibly shaking. Wallace took a seat in a recliner across from the couple. Alwani pulled up a dining room chair. "So, what's this complicated matter? She's either gone or not."

"She's not dead," Wallace bluntly said, though Fred could see a hint of anguish in his face at the words. "At least not to our knowledge."

"Wha…what does that mean?" Sherry quivered.

"She's missing, isn't she?" Fred inferred.

Wallace took in the grieving pair, then Alwani. "What I am about to say is highly, highly classified, and I could face a court martial for telling you because I haven't got it cleared. But, Sophia's talked a lot about you too, how you've become a father figure to her, and that you're former FBI and worked on the Stone case before retiring. So, I believe you need to know. And we need your help."

"Spit it out, son."

"She's been kidnapped by Hasan Althani."

Sherry gasped, unable to hold back the tears anymore. They began to stream down her cheeks as she sobbed. Fred held her more tightly, waiting for the rest with bated breath.

"She was on a mission with part of my team in Yemen. We had credible evidence that he was going to be there recruiting. Unfortunately,, our informant's cousin turned on us and tipped him off. It was a trap. He led her away from the team and took her despite my men's best efforts. They've since disappeared off the radar. We have no idea where they've gone. Why he took her, or how long he'll hold her for before-"

Fred threw up a finger, pausing the SEAL leader as Sherry buried her face into his side. He knew Wallace was about to say, 'behead her.' "What do you want from me? How can I help?"

"Sophia said multiple times that aside from her, you would be the next best expert on Hasan and the AIA, including how they operate, where they operate, and how they think. So, we need your help to get her back."

Sherry raised, stifling the flood of waterworks streaming from her now-beat-red face. "Fred, you do anything and everything to get our girl back. You hear me?" She stood, using the couch for support, her knees weak. "I don't give a goddamn what you need to do. You bring her back." She fixed a gaze upon the two SEALs. "And the two of you, you'd better make sure that my whole world comes back to me. Do you understand?"

"Yes, ma'am," the two intoned.

Sherry weakly made her way down the hall to the bedroom, slamming the door shut.

The three men stayed seated in the living room quietly, looking at each other, trying to figure out where to go from here. Fred took out his cell phone, his thumb flicking up its face, activating the screen. "Well," he said, sifting through his contacts, stopping on his old friend Tobias Stevens. "I've got a good place to start, but it's going to require clearance and a trip." He pressed the call button.

****

Fred exited his car, followed by Wallace and Alwani. The trio proceeded up the small footpath to the front of the house they'd just parked in front of. The car ride over was taken mostly in silence, with Wallace divulging a few other facts about the mission they were on.

The former agent felt a little more comfortable, having changed out of his going-out attire and back into his everyday regular clothes. As they neared the front door to his friend's house, he stopped to face the two men. "Tobias is a great friend of mine and is the Special Agent in Charge of the Milwaukee Field Office for the FBI. He can help." Fred rang the doorbell.

Tobias Stevens, a tall, bald African American, opened the door, eyeing the three men standing on his doorstep. "Fred?"

He nodded, and the two shook hands.

"By your tone on the phone and the fact that you've brought company, I am assuming this isn't going to be a social call."

"Assumption right," Fred answered. "This is Master Chief Marshall Wallace and Petty Officer Second Class Ahmed Alwani." Introducing the pair, they exchanged handshakes. "May we come in?"

"Of course." Tobias stepped aside, letting the trio enter. Let's go to my office, you know the way."

Fred led the way through the hallway and to a pair of staircases: one leading up to the second floor and the other down to a basement. He'd been to Tobias's house a thousand times before and was as familiar with it as his own home. He proceeded downstairs, the rest following suit. Once they reached the bottom, Fred and the SEALs parted, allowing Tobias to squeeze by. He unlocked a door at the end of the small hall. The three men filed in after him.

Tobias circled behind an old oak desk to a small bar behind it, popping the top off a bottle of whiskey. He poured himself a glass, turning to face his company. "Fred, I know you don't drink, so I am not going to bother offering. But would the two gentlemen like a glass?"

"No sir, but thank you," Wallace answered.

"Me neither," said Alwani.

"Ok, drinking alone." Tobias shrugged, taking a seat at his desk. Fred pulled up the chair in front of him. Wallace and Alwani settled for a couch off to the side of the room. He took a sip from his glass. "So, what brings a retired FBI agent and two Navy SEALs to my doorstep this late at night?

Fred glanced over to Wallace, who gave him a nod. "Tobias, Sophia's been kidnapped." The generally very laid-back, calm man shot straight forward in his chair, setting the glass of whiskey down with a gulp.

"What, where, when? Is there a plan to get her back?" Tobias had spent months working with Fred and his FBI team tracking down the AIA cells responsible for the attack on the Harley Davidson Museum a year ago. Over that time, he'd become very fond of the CIA agent.

"Yemen. She was following up on a lead about Hasan. His team…" Fred pointed to Wallace. "Was betrayed by an informant or someone working with their informant. It was a trap, and Hasan took her."

"When? Shouldn't this be all over the news, or at the very

least, government back channels? An American CIA operative has been captured. That's some headline news."

"Yesterday," Wallace cut in. "Our task force has been deemed highly classified and off the books. In fact, the simple act of us being here could be a court martial as I haven't cleared it with the head of the operation, James Owens. We came straight here after I found out. Sophia always said the only other person with as much knowledge about how the AIA operates was Mr. Jones," the SEAL said, pointing to Fred. "We were hoping that he could give us some insight into how to find her. Half of my team is currently in Oman awaiting orders."

"Ok, this is some heavy shit." Tobias leaned back, taking another sip, processing what had just been dumped on him. "Fred, you know that I'd do anything to get her back. But, I am not sure how I can help."

"I need access to Adeel," Fred answered bluntly. Adeel was one of the terrorists that he, Sophia, and another undercover agent, Naseem, used to infiltrate the AIA cell in Orlando. He also gave up the information that led to Sophia and the SEAL team capturing Tarik Salem, an arms dealer who had been supplying the AIA. "And I need clearance to work on this."

"Fuck, Fred, that's a huge ask." Sitting down his drink and rubbing the top of his head. "One I am not even sure I can grant." He looked at Wallace. "Can't you get access to him?"

"I don't even know who this guy is," Wallace countered. "I think… again, I think that once I get a hold of Owens, I can get Fred on the task force. But this Adeel character, I don't know."

"Isn't he in Federal custody?" Fred asked. "He committed crimes on US soil. That's Federal jurisdiction."

"Department of Homeland Security had him transferred to their custody shortly after your ordeal in Orlando."

"Why didn't you tell me that?" Fred asked, confused.

"Because you were in a coma after the crash, and I didn't really think it was relevant to tell you once you came to, then retired," Came Tobias' sarcastic retort.

"Can you do anything? This is fucking Sophia we're talking

about here. I…I can't not do anything."

"Ok, ok, bring it down," he said, seeing that his friend was starting to get visibly upset. He knew how much Sophia meant to him. "I'll tell you what. I'll call in some favors tomorrow morning and see what I can get you—not making any promises here. But I'll do what I can. And for the two of you." He faced Wallace and Alwani. "I highly recommend you do what you can to get in touch with Owens and get yourselves cleared even to be discussing this with anyone, let alone a civilian. Because once I start making calls. People are going to be asking a whole lot of questions."

"Copy that, sir," Wallace responded.

The quartet rose. "Now let me see you out, as I now have a lot of work to do tomorrow."

Tobias led everyone out, shaking Fred's hand again and giving him another reassurance that he was going to do everything that he could.

Fred drove Wallace and Alwani back to their car outside his house. "Tobias will come through," he said to the men. "I know him, and he's never let me down. I'll need a number to get a hold of you when he calls." He handed his phone to Wallace. The SEAL quickly plugged his number in, handing back the phone. "Thanks; I'll see you guys tomorrow."

****

The elevator doors opened, and Fred stepped out onto the landing, taking in what he'd expected to be the familiar surroundings of the office he'd called his second home for the better part of a decade.

However, upon entering the double doors to the office, he found an alien space. Standing on the top step, he looked out across what used to be the section called the bullpen, where the lower rank and file agents did the bulk of their work at desks in an open floor plan.

The office had been completely renovated. Now, in the bowl of the bullpen, everyone had their own cubicle-styled office sections, each complete with a sliding glass door. However, he did notice there were quite a reduced number of cubicles compared to desks that once dotted the floor.

The wrap-around walkway leading to the back of the room, with the familiar offices tucked away, was still around the floor. An agent exited the room titled 'break room' holding a cup of coffee. She turned and spotted the bewildered former agent.

"Fred!" she shouted, latently realizing she was shouting a bit too loud as several agents poked their heads out from their workstations. "Oops, sorry." She waltzed over, embracing him. "How have you been?"

Agent Michelle Ramirez, a Hispanic woman of medium height, was a former agent under his command. "I've been good. You know, enjoying that retired life and driving the wife crazy," he added with a sly smile.

"I doubt that," she said. "What brings you in?"

"Came to see Tobias."

"He's in his office with two rather sexy-looking men." Her face suddenly blazed red. Her hand shot up to her mouth, lightly covering it. "Oh my god, I can't believe I said that to you," she whispered, shocked at her candidness.

Fred laughed, "It's ok. I am not your boss anymore. Tobias' office is still in the same place?" Still not over the shock by her open, candid remark, the young agent nodded and pointed. "Thanks, Michelle." Fred slid past her and continued to the back of the room, ascending another small flight of steps to find another familiar face: Jill Giolito, a young brunette woman sitting at her desk outside Tobias' office.

"Fred," she said happily with a broad smile, looking up from her computer. "It's so nice to see you again. Go ahead in; Tobias is with your guests already."

"Thanks, Jill," Fred said, breezing past her, opening the door, and walking in to find Tobias at his desk and the SEALs sitting opposite of him.

"Fred, come in and have a seat," Tobias said, looking up from his phone. The FBI Agent pointed to the device, alerting Fred that someone was on the line. Fred nodded, finding his way to a chair quietly. "Ok, so everyone's here. I guess I'll let you take it from here, Director Owens.

Fred's eyes shot open. He knew the name but had never met or spoken to the man. He was the Director of the CIA's Clandestine Services and Sophia's boss.

"Great. Thank you, Agent Stevens." Owens' voice filled the office through the speaker phone. "Mr. Fred Jones." Even though the man wasn't in the room, Fred felt as if his eyes were staring at him. "Agent Evans speaks highly of you, and your work with her on Amell's case was good."

"Thank you," Fred said.

"But," Owens cut back in. "I was not happy when the Master Chief told me last night he'd come to see you and divulged classified information without my approval."

"Sir, I think he was-."

"However," Owens cut Fred off again. His voice came through hard and biting. "I do see the reason, and after discussing it with him, you have my full approval. I want Agent Evans back at any cost." The Director's voice softened. "After speaking with SAC Stevens, I think we've come up with a plan."

"What's the plan?" Fred questioned.

"I've already consulted with my counterparts from the DOD and DOJ, and we've come to the conclusion that we are going to make you a civilian contractor, which will give you complete access to all top-secret information on the mission and authorize you to be in theater with the team if need be."

"Thank you, thank you very much, sir," Fred said, releasing a deep breath he hadn't noticed he had been holding in. He was clearly nervous that he'd be kicked out before he got the chance to start.

"You can thank me by bringing home Agent Evans."

"You can count on that," Fred added.

"Great," Owens responded. "I have one thing for the team as well. During my last conversation with Agent Evans, we discussed the potential of a mole somewhere within the operation who was providing Stone with information to stay a step ahead of the team." The occupants in the office could hear the rustling of papers. "From my personal investigation," he continued. "I am sure that the leaks are not coming from anyone on the team."

"Where is he getting his information from then?" Wallace asked, speaking up for the first time.

"Still looking into that, but I have a suspicion."

Everyone waited for him to elaborate.

"So, when do we leave?" Fred asked, sensing the Director wasn't going to give details. "Time, as we know, is of the essence here. They haven't made any formal demands or broadcasts saying that they have an American spy. So whatever Hasan wants her for. She's still of use to him. Which is good for us."

"I'll let SAC Stevens address that. I have another meeting to attend. Mr. Jones, happy to have you aboard and bring back my agent."

"Will do, Director," Fred added before the line went dead.

All eyes shifted from the phone to Tobias. "Well, with all that said," Tobias started. "I made a few phone calls and inquiries as to the location of Adeel."

"Let me guess, Guantanamo Bay?" Fred interceded.

"Yup," Tobias confirmed. "Along with Tarik Salem as well."

"Great, so no way to question them."

"Generally, no. But, with some added support from Director Owens and an old friend, we were able to get you clearance for both of them."

Fred chuckled. "Our good friend, the Attorney General, I suppose."

Amy Sanchez, the sitting Attorney General and an old classmate and crush of Tobias', had helped Fred and Sophia secure the arrest warrant for Senator Stone the previous year at great risk to her political career, which had only taken off since she was the one to receive a great deal of notoriety for rooting out the corrupt Oklahoman Senator.

"She has a debt of gratitude for what the two of you did last year. So, when I called her, she was more than on board to help."

"Great." Fred stood, "When do we leave?"

"Once the papers from Director Owens come through and you sign them *in front* of me, making it official, you'll be on your way to Cuba," Tobias stated, rising with his friend.

"Awesome. I guess I'll swing by later. Thank you again for your help." The two shook hands, followed by Wallace and Alwani.

"Fred, hold up." Tobias let Wallace and Alwani depart before asking, "Sherry. What does she think of all this? She wanted you to retire to avoid dangerous situations. Now you're going to Cuba to interrogate a terrorist, then who knows where and in harm's way."

"She told me to do whatever it takes to bring her back, and that's exactly what I am going to do. Besides, I'll have a whole SEAL team with me," he said with a grin.

"Good luck, old friend." They shook hands again and embraced each other before Fred departed.

SOPHIA heard footsteps scuffling outside the closet-sized room she'd been thrown into several hours before. Judging by their sounds and the weight they fell with, she assumed it was two men—her 'escorts' from the previous day. One fell heavier than the other. She could tell from the way one had manhandled her that one of them was probably large and bulky.

After being shoved into the SUV in Sanaa and having a black bag thrown over her head and hands cuffed with zip ties so tightly they dug into her wrist with every move, cutting into her flesh. They drove for what felt like hours.

Trying to remain calm despite now being in the hands of Hasan Althani, who'd been known as Amell's torture extraordinaire. She thought back to her Survival, Evasion, Resistance, Escape (SERE) training back at 'The Farm.' The thought of how long she could hold out against any torture that Hasan might cook up rushed to her forethoughts.

She knew that fear in this situation would be counterproductive, so she quickly shoved those thoughts aside. There were more important things to focus on—other parts of her training. For instance, trying to stay focused on where they were headed. In case she was able to escape and find a way to contact the team, she'd be able to give them her location.

She tried to keep track of the time in her head, figuring out that they were headed eastward out of Sanaa. The lack of paved roads had given that away. Most of Yemen's roads weren't paved outside of the larger cities. So, they were no longer in Sanaa. The fact she could feel the heat from the sun on the back of her head. This indicated that they were headed eastward as the sun set in the west. She could tell that they had driven into the night as the warmth from the sun beating into the vehicle dissipated, and the blackness of her world had only gotten darker as time passed. An indication that day had turned to night.

Several hours after the sun had set, the SUV pulled over and came to a stop. The sounds of the car doors opening pierced easily through the fabric hood. A rough feeling hand clamped down on her arm, and the owner of it wrenched her out of the vehicle, dragging her into a building and shoving her into a hard metal seat.

There she sat for an hour, two, maybe even three. It was hard to tell at that point as there was nothing she could use in the fluorescent setting to determine time. She could hear the smattering of conversations taking place. The tones and inflections of the men had suggested they were growing antsy, impatient even. They were getting bored, a sign that at least more than an hour had passed.

Sophia listened intently for any clues as to what her fate would become. Several voices discussed if they would sell her off, ransom her, or just kill her. In her opinion, all three outcomes were of the utmost undesirable nature. The last suggestion, though, rattled Sophia to her core.

Her mind instantly began to play vivid images of American captors of terrorist groups meeting the blade of a sword as some masked terrorists lopped off their heads on the internet for the world to see. *Was that the future that awaited her?*

The one voice, though, that had appeared to be absent was that of Hasan's. She thought he was in the same car as her. However, no one had even said a word in the cabin the whole trip. *Did he leave? Had he even been in the SUV in the first place?* To that point, Sophia's only solace at being kidnapped was that at least Hasan—her target of desire, was close enough that if she were able to escape, she could still kill him.

Now, that possibility was in question.

The same set of rough hands from before gripped her again, dragging her back to the SUV and throwing her into the back seat. She heard the *clacking* of doors slamming shut, and they were off again. Hopefully, no one had noticed that while she had been seated, she managed to remove one of her pouches from her vest, dropping it on the ground of whatever building they had been in.

Leaving a breadcrumb for Ryan to follow—a faint hope that somehow they were tracking her. After all, they had all the sophisticated military surveillance technology in the world. They must be tracking her. Right?

However, that possibility had faded throughout the night as no rescue mission had come to save her. Another terrifying thought entered her mind as she lay on the ground of the room. She didn't even know the fate of the team. *Had they all been killed? Was she truly alone? There was no one to save her?* No, she couldn't think like that. Wallace wouldn't let her down. She was going to fight to stay alive long enough for a rescue.

The sound of dangling keys approaching zapped her back to the present. Her escorts were coming to grab her again and take her off to who knew where. Sophia forced herself up. Kneeling. She felt around her waist blindly. The bag was still on her head. She searched for the clasp on her belt, her hand running across nylon, zipper, button—finally metal.

Her fingers danced spider-like over the clasp, searching for the magnetic lift point. Finding it, she yanked it open, unbuckling her belt.

The scuffling stopped. They were at the door. With her hearing heightened due to the loss of her vision, she heard the sound of a key being inserted. *Shit*, she had to work faster. She tugged on the belt. It slid around her waist, breaking free of the belt-loops restraints, working the accessory free loop by loop.

The handle turned, and the door creaked open. Sophia yanked the belt through the last loop, chucking it into the corner seconds before an ominous presence loomed darkly over her. A shadow enveloped the area, deepening the dark.

Suddenly, she felt weightless as she was hauled off the ground once more. The familiar sandpaper-rough hands embraced her. The man hoisted the lightweight operative over his shoulder. She jarred with every step as he lumbered through what could've been a domicile of sorts. There was a sound of someone else following them—the second 'escort.'

An intense heat wrapped around her, and the feeling of a burning hot spar of light crept up the back of her neck. Night had turned back into day. They'd traveled less than twenty-four hours due to the stops. They were still somewhere in Yemen, Sophia figured. A car door opened, and the heat disappeared as her brutish travel companion chucked her once again into the back seat of the SUV before he and the other person boarded. They set off again, traveling to what she hoped wouldn't be her final destination.

****

An hour or so later, the SUV jutted to a stop on a gravel road. Dust particles wafted through the open window. The vehicle was an older model from what Sophia could remember seeing for a brief moment before becoming a captive in it. The A/C must've died out on it a long time ago.

A thunderous applause followed by shouts from outside the car replaced the thrum of the engine. "Death to America, Kill the American infidel," chants boomed. Sounds of automatic gunfire rang out. Sophia could feel their intense hatred and vitriol in every word.

The SUV rocked, and thuds peppered the side panels of the sheet metal door as Sophia lay stretched across the back seat. The voices grew louder by the second. A part of her felt glad she couldn't see what was actually going on. It sounded like a huge mob had gathered around the vehicle—an angry one and it was all directed toward her.

One of the shouts was so loud it sounded like the perpetrator was inside her head—another series of gunfire. The chanting and screaming lowered only a few decibels. Not that the crowd hushed, but more so that they were forced away from the vehicle.

The door opened, and 'sandpaper' hands hauled her out. Once outside, the deafening screams rolled back in full force. More calls for America's death bellowed. Some of the shouts sounded directly in her ear, then pulled back like an echo to return, but in a different inflection, as if coming from someone different. Yet, they all intoned the same thing—death to the infidel.

Sophia clung to her escort tighter. The irony of her act did not escape her. However, she felt safer with the brute than the screaming mob. She suspected that he had been ordered not to harm her or let anyone else do so, as she could feel him brushing and shoving people away as they walked.

A glob of a liquid substance showered Sophia's face through the bag, dispersing spittle across her cheeks. A hand clamped down on her arm, squeezing it like a vice. The new person pulled her away from the escort; she could feel her body separating from his.

Her protector/captor yanked her back with such force he nearly pulled her arm out of her socket. Then, a muffled sound of someone hitting the ground in a heap followed. She nearly tripped over the crumpled human as her escort continued to pull her through the perp walk.

The sound of a door opening became the sound of relief as the pair crossed the threshold of a building—the door slamming behind them, leaving the muffled shouts of the mob outside.

He continued to lead her through a hallway, with another door opening ahead. The man pulled her through, dragging her to the center of a room. Their footsteps echoed, signaling to Sophia that the room must be devoid of decoration or furniture.

Seconds later, her suspicion proved false. She was forced down onto what felt like a stool. The door shut, further silencing the rabid crowd outside. Inside, it was silent, with only the barely audible noises of a pair of muffled footsteps.

She could feel the man who had dragged her inside looming behind her, though Sophia could also feel the presence of another person in the room. The room was silent compared to the outside, yet it somehow felt more terrifying than the possibility of being ripped apart by the mob.

Someone snapped their fingers. Sophia's dark world exploded with light. It was blinding, having spent the better part of the last day shrouded in darkness.

Her eyes began to adjust. The formless slowly began taking on form. Sophia blinked once, twice, and a third time. When her eyelids opened on the third blink, she was confronted with the face of the man she'd been hunting for the last six months.

Hasan Althani.

The Arab dominated her vision. He was inches from her face and staring unnervingly into her eyes. His black as-night iris' met her pale blue. He didn't blink. It was like he was staring into her soul. His hot breath washed over her face.

He pulled back, standing straight up. He was tall for an Arab, looking around six feet tall. His dark, thick beard covered the lower portion of his face. However, the exposed upper region looked worn from years of worry and fighting. By most accounts, Hasan was around fifty years old, though the face staring at hers looked to be the face of a man in his later sixties.

He strode back a few paces, and the rest of the room took shape. It was barren, sans the stool she was sitting on, a chair, a bucket full of water, and a table.

Sophia's eyes darted to the table. Upon it lay all manner of torture tools—every kind you'd expect to see in a movie. They were strewn across the table. Hasan picked up one. It looked like a toothpick but was made of steel. The tip narrowed into a needlepoint. He tapped it against the table, confirming it was metal. Sophia's body tensed. She instinctively squirmed. The man who had just protected her clamped his oversized palms down on her shoulders—holding her in place.

"You know who I am," Hasan said, circling the table, wistfully staring at his toys. "But I don't know who you are."

Sophia felt her throat run dry. It'd been dry since she'd been plucked off the street, as she'd not been given anything to eat or drink. But this was a different dry—a fearful dry. She smacked her parched lips together, staring at the bucket, a shimmer reflecting off the inside.

Hasan followed her gaze. He put down the needle, scooped up a cup from the table, dipped it into the bucket, and brought it back up. He handed the glass to Sophia. She gripped it with her bound-together hands, raising the glass to her lips and chugging the contents. She drank it so fast that the excess water trickled out the sides of her mouth, running down her chin and cascading down her uniform.

Finishing, Sophia handed the glass back to Hasan, who placed it back on the table. "Thank you," Sophia finally said. "I haven't had anything to eat or drink in a while. It's kind of hard to answer questions."

Hasan affixed her with a gaze. "Ah, yes, who am I? I am a freelance documenter. I do documentaries for Netflix, Amazon, and anyone who wants to contract me. I am working on a documentary for the military right now."

Sophia flashed back to her training. One of the biggest focuses in SERE training was that if you were captured, you should never, ever divulge your mission. However, they'd made it a point to stress that no matter how tough, strong, or resistant the operative is, they will break at some point.

She was determined to hold out as long as she could. The team was coming for her.

Hasan appeared to be completely unamused by her answer. He circled the table, eying a pair of pliers. "Lie," he hissed, picking up the tool and snapping it open and closed. "Who are you? CIA?"

"I am Sophia Grant, filmmaker, and documentarian," she said, sticking to her long-developed cover. "This was the first time I was with…" She tensed as Hasan drew nearer, snapping the pliers at her. "That team," she struggled out. The man behind her clamped his hands around her head, tilting it back.

He forced her jaw open. Sophia's eyes widened as Hasan got closer and closer, the pliers opening and closing. Unable to move or adjust, her mouth was wide open. She tried to turn away, but the man forced her head back straight. She felt the cold metallic tip of the pliers touch her tongue as Hasan tapped several of her teeth, deciding which one he'd pull first.

A tinge of pressure as the tool clamped down on the one he selected. Sophia clinched, holding her breath, preparing for the burst of pain.

"No, no, no." Hasan pulled back, removing the pliers from Sophia's mouth to her surprise, with no tooth cinched between the tips. She let out a sigh of relief. "You can't tell me anything if you can't speak." He retreated to the table, setting the pliers down. "I know you're CIA. I recognize your voice from when I gave you Stone's whereabouts. I don't care. You pigs have been after me for years." He reacquired the needlepoint device. "I want to know how you found me. I suspect it was the senator," he said, waving the needle in Sophia's direction. "But, I want you to confirm it. Then tell me where that piece of shit is hiding."

"I…I don't know what or who you're talking about."

Hasan nodded; the man standing behind Sophia smacked the back of her head. The blow hit with such force that her vision went black for a second—searing hot pain radiated from the impact point. The American struggled to sit back up.

"I don't believe you," Hasan said, voice low and calm. "You are not a filmmaker. You chased me the second you saw me. You are a liar. Tell me, did Stone give you my location?"

Sophia opened her mouth about to answer, then paused, contemplating what type of answer to give. No matter what she said, it would result in pain. She mentally prepared for it. Then spoke. "I don't know-"

The world faded to black again. Another blow to the back of the head. This time, he'd hit her so hard she fell off the stool. The cold concrete against her cheek quickly snapped Sophia back. Tasting a new salty, tangy sensation, she ran her tongue around the inside of her mouth and found a chunk bitten off. Lying on the concrete, she spat a wad of blood out before being hauled back up off the floor and slammed back onto the stool. The whirlwind of movement left her feeling dizzy and faint.

Hasan approached, ready to ask again. Sophia swallowed, collecting all the blood she could. Then, she spat it at Hasan's feet. The Arab moved back just in time. Sophia smiled.

"Farid," Hasan said, snapping his fingers.

The brute reared back and, with a grin across his face, drove his fist into the side of Sophia's face. She could feel her bottom lip split open as she was knocked back off the stool. Farid circled, delivering a brutal kick to Sophia's exposed midsection. Thankfully, she was still wearing her vest, which took a good amount of the blow, but it was still enough to knock the wind out of her.

Expelling the oxygen from her lungs, she curled up into a ball, writhing on the ground, desperately gasping for air. "You…didn't…ask a question," Sophia gasped out.

Hasan gestured again. Farid scooped the American up off the

floor and propped her up on the stool, holding her. Sophia fought to stay up, teetering in and out of consciousness. A bright flash lit the room up, forcing the operative back to alertness.

The Arab grabbed Sophia by the chin, yanking her head up. Their faces met. He again stared directly into her eyes. She, in turn, steeled herself to meet his gaze. Locked in a stare-off, Hasan sneered, then released his hold on her. "Get her out of here," he snapped at Farid. Get her changed. I don't want to see that flag." He pointed at the American flag patch on the sleeve of her fatigue top.

Farid yanked Sophia out of the chair, leading the battered operative to the door. She whisked around. "I hope you don't treat your friends like this. Because I wouldn't be surprised if they did turn on you," she said as the brute forced her out of the room.

Hasan flashed her a dismissive sneer, picking up his phone from the edge of the table. He dialed a number.

****

West opened the office room door of their new hideout, reflexively dodging a flying glass. The whiskey glass narrowly missed hitting the mercenary leader in the face on its path, smashing into the drywall behind him and exploding into a million pieces.

He calmly stepped over the strewn slivers, closing the door behind him, to find Stone irately pacing behind the desk at the far end of the room. Briggs was standing before the older man in the parade rest position, legs slightly open, arms behind him, resting near the small of his back, silent.

"Roy...what's going on in here?" West asked cautiously. Briggs peered over his shoulder, face giving a clear get me out of here expression.

"This man here...this excuse for a merc," he remarked, wagging his finger at Briggs. "Lied to ME!" A quiver of anger exploded as he thumbed to himself, suggesting how one could have the audacity to do so. "Then has the cowardice to stand there and gaslight me, saying that he didn't."

"Sir," Briggs snapped back. "I was merely pointing out that we had a contingency plan, that if we were to be separated, our first priority was your protection and to exfil with you. The family would then rendezvous later."

Stone flung around the desk, pressing up to the mercenary, trying to get in his face, quickly realizing that Briggs had at least six inches on him. Settling for looking upward, he raged, "Well, that…didn't…FUCKING happen!" The last part was shouted with so much fury spittle accompanied the words. "Now, did it? NO. And now, my wife, YOUR wife," he said, directing his ire at West. "Along with my grandkids, are in the custody of that CIA bitch." Stone backed away from Briggs, continuing his pacing.

"Briggs, you're dismissed." West gestured for the mercenary to leave. As he passed, the man mouthed thank you. If Briggs had so chosen to, he could have ended the former senator's life. West took a seat across from the desk, hoping that it would subtly calm the older gentleman down. It had the desired effect. Stone took his seat behind the desk. "We know they're not going to do anything to them. They are not going to torture two innocent women and two kids," he added reassuringly. "Plus, they don't know anything anyway."

"That's beside the point. I want my family." Stone rested his head in his hands.

"And we're going to get them back. It's just going to take a bit of time," West added. "I've learned where they are." Stone perked up. "They were taken to Rabat. I am still working that out. It could be the embassy or a CIA stash house. From what my contact knows, there are few left." Rabat is the capital of Morocco. "I am putting together a plan to figure out where exactly they are."

"Good. Work on that quickly. In the meantime, I'll call my person to help." There was a rapping at the door. "Come in!" Stone shouted.

The door opened, and Briggs reentered the room, holding a phone. "Sirs," he addressed the two men. "Hasan is on the phone. He sounds pretty pissed."

"Well, we did try to kill him and killed what was left of his family," West said sarcastically.

"Bring it here, son." Stone waved for the mercenary to enter. He handed the phone to West.

West set the device on the desk and pressed the speaker button. "Hasan, our business was concluded when you failed to heed my advice," Stone said. "What can I do for you?"

"Die," came the Arab's curt response. "That piece of dog shit, son-in-law, will die first for killing my brother and cousin."

"Now, there is no reason for name-calling here," West interjected.

"Good, you're both there. That'll make it easier for me. I know it was you who sent the CIA after me."

West looked up at Stone, pressing the mute button. "How the fuck would he know that?"

"They must've already tried to get him," Stone countered. "Apparently, they missed."

"Wait. That's how they found the compound. That slimy Arab bastard crossed us. I knew we should've never worked with the Haji dirtbag. Let me send a crew to get him."

"No," Stone fired back. "Getting the family back together is priority one." He turned the mute off. "So, you gave them our location as retribution?"

"At first, yes. Now I am going to kill you myself."

"Well, you'll have to find us before we find you, asshole," West snarked with a grin.

"I won't have to find you. My new friend is going to tell me where you pigs are hiding."

Stone and West gave each other quizzical looks. Hasan's voice conveyed a sense of utter confidence that he'd be able to find them. How could he be so sure?

"Please," West scoffed, "You don't have the resources or knowledge. We, on the other hand, do. So, you might want to stay hiding in whatever shit hole cave you all found," West taunted. Stone listened, wearing a sly grin. He knew that with one communique to his contacts, within a day or so, they'd have his location.

"Oh, but now, I have all the same resources as you. And more,"

Hasan boasted.

"Bullshit," Stone snapped back. "Amell was so much easier to deal with. He knew not to bite the hand that fed him."

"And he's dead," Hasan fired back. "If I were you, I'd check the text I sent. I'll wait."

West's face scrunched, hit with a bout of concern and curiosity. Stone indicated for West to check. He picked up the phone from the table, hit the menu button, and brought up the text app. His eyes shot open, his mouth falling agape, a look of worry creased across his forehead.

Stone immediately signaled for the phone. West handed it over. He then turned to Briggs, whispering silent orders.

Stone stared at the screen, dumbfounded by the image. "How… how?" It was a photo of Sophia sitting on a stool, bound and beaten.

"I am going to make her tell me where you are. Then kill her and come and kill you all. From here on out, you will always be wondering if I am in the shadows of your houses waiting for you." The line went dead.

Stone threw the phone back down onto the desk. Fingers tapping, lost in contemplation.

"Roy," West called, seeing the older man's distant gaze. "How are we going to respond? If Hasan ransoms the CIA woman back to the agency, they will give him our location."

"The West doesn't negotiate with terrorists, mind you," Stone countered.

"We're not exactly US citizens anymore, or at least not on the right side. They will happily give us up to save one of theirs. So again, I ask what we are going to do."

Stone sat silent for a moment, thinking. Finally, an idea began to sprout: "Go work your contacts. Try to find him. And for God's sake, locate our family, too. Let me handle Hasan. When you find him, let me know. I have an idea." He then waved a dismissive hand. West nodded reluctantly and exited the room.

Once he was out, Stone grabbed a key from inside his wallet and unlocked the desk's bottom right drawer. He pulled out a laptop and flipped it open, navigating to the only icon on the screen and clicking it. A dialogue text box opened.

In the box, he typed. 'I have a proposition for The Council. If I can provide information that leads to the safe return of the kidnapped CIA operative, will that provide leverage to secure a pardon?'

He waited anxiously for a reply, staring at the screen. The still flashing cursor slowly became a nightmare as Stone continued to stare. Time seemingly stopped, freezing him in a paralytic state. He could feel his blood rising, a combination of nervousness and anger. It rarely took so long for whoever was on the other end to respond.

Ten minutes went by. Then it began moving. It was a one-word answer. 'Yes.'

Stone smiled.

CHAPTER THIRTEEN
GUANTANAMO BAY, CUBA

FRED shot straight up, dropping the folder that was lying on his chest at the sound of the seat belt light chiming on. The one flight attendant aboard hurried over, scooping the papers up and handing the disheveled stack back to him.

"Thank you," Fred said, sliding them back into the folder before rubbing his eyes. He hadn't slept much in the last day. Too racked with worry. He knew they were on a ticking clock. Sophia had already been in captivity for more than a day. He knew that, at best, they'd have maybe another two or three days before-

He couldn't even finish the thought. He didn't even want to think about it. He couldn't let his mind go there. The plane began its descent, and Fred quickly buckled his seatbelt. Fortunately for him, the despair of what could happen to Sophia was quickly replaced with what could happen to him. He'd never been fond of flying.

Not necessarily the flying part, but more so the landing. He hated the feeling. He tried to fill his mind with other thoughts, like, *how did Owens get him cleared so fast?*

Fred barely had enough time to get home and pack from his early morning meeting with Tobias before he got the call from his friend stating that Owens had come through and the papers were waiting at the office for him to sign. It was a very quick turnaround in his mind, especially for anything political.

Fred hugged and consoled Sherry, vowing to return with Sophia before he departed. On the way, he called Wallace to confirm all of the flight information and told him to meet him at the airport.

The two met a couple of hours later at a private airport on the tarmac. Wallace was waiting in front of a G5 Gulf Stream. He was light some of his travailing companions. When asked, he told him that he had sent his men ahead earlier to Oman to rendezvous with the rest of his team in case they would be needed to do some ground reconnaissance for their inevitable rescue mission.

Fred took most of the three-hour flight to familiarize himself with Sophia's operation briefs and get up to speed on the mission. Bruising through her highly detailed notes, he felt as if he'd been on the mission the whole time—a trait that he'd come to admire about her. The woman was highly detailed in everything she wrote. However, it also put him to sleep, which may have been a good thing, given his lack of rest the previous night.

The plane lurched to a stop. Fred and Wallace collected their things. The attendant opened the door, and a swell of oppressive, wet humidity smacked Fred in the face. He began almost instantly to sweat as they walked down the air steps.

Retrieving a cloth from his pocket and wiping his brow, Wallace gave him a wry smile.

"You ok, their chief?" the SEAL asked.

"I don't like humidity," Fred answered, pocketing the cloth, and dropping his carry-on. "Where's the welcoming party? I assume someone knows where coming."

"There." Wallace pointed. A wide-bodied, camouflaged Humvee came barreling down the tarmac. It stopped a few feet in front of the pair. Two men disgorged from it. "Oh shit." Wallace snapped to attention and saluted the passenger as he approached. "Good evening, sir," he addressed the man.

The man who disembarked from the passenger side was dressed in traditional NAVY fatigues. He was tall, standing stiff-backed with confidence as he approached, his hair white as snow, and he was wearing a pair of thin-framed glasses.

Fred wasn't too familiar with Navy rank insignias. His knowledge catered more toward that of the Army and Marines. However, the silver-encrusted Eagle was prominently displayed on his lapel, and Wallace's shift in demeanor and reverence for the approaching man gave away the idea that he must be of high rank.

The officer quickly returned the salute. "Good evening, sir," addressed Fred, holding his hand out. The officer shook it with a vice-like grip. "I know this is short notice, but-"

"I don't like civilians on my base, let alone ones I don't know," the officer interrupted sternly.

"I understand Captain Gooding," Wallace said, jumping in. "But, Mr. Jones here isn't necessarily a civilian. He's a highly decorated retired FBI agent. And I am-”

“You are Master Chief Marshall Wallace. Of course, I know who you are. Your team is… quite possibly the best I’ve ever seen operate.”

“Thank you, sir. That means a great deal. If you know who I am, then you know we’re here for a specific reason.”

“I do. I’ve been… briefed,” he added with a hint of disdain, indicating he hadn’t been told exactly why they were there. “I am still not completely sure why he’s here, though,” he stated, pointing to Fred. “I am sure it’s highly classified and need to know, which the brass figured I didn’t need to. So, you’ll have to excuse my curtness. I don’t like not knowing why things are happening on my base.”

“I understand, Captain Gooding,” Fred interjected before Wallace could. “I can assure you it is for a good reason, and we’ll be out of your hair the second we get the information we need.”

“Ah, yes, the two detainees. I’ll have them brought to separate interrogation rooms. They’ll be ready by the time we get to the detention center. Mack will drive us there now. As I assume you’d want to get this over with. I understand there is a time crunch,” he said, stepping aside and waving for them to board the Humvee.

“There is,” Fred added, grabbing his bag, and getting in the back seat of the cramped vehicle.

****

The drive to the detention center took a couple of hours due to the area’s hilly, dense vegetation, which prevented the use of any single straight road. Fortunately, the Humvee had A/C for Fred’s sake.

When they arrived at the detention center’s front gates, night had already set in. When they exited the vehicle, Fred looked up to see a clear night sky full of stars. It reminded him of his camping trips away from the city.

“You can leave your bags in the Humvee,” Gooding stated upon exiting. Mack, stay with the Humvee.” Wallace gave the officer a bewildered look. You’ll probably be leaving the second you get what you came for, right?”

“Yeah, sure,” Wallace responded.

Gooding led them inside a building, passing several checkpoints, as the guards waived them through until they entered the detention center proper. The trio walked down the empty corridor, footsteps clacking on the concrete floor. The pair followed a few paces behind the captain. Wallace leaned over and whispered to Fred. “He seems keen on getting us out of here quickly.”

“I noticed,” Fred answered. “I *really* don’t think he likes visitors.”

“We’re not spying on him.” Fred shrugged.

They passed into another area of the old building and through another security point. Halfway down the hall, two pairs of armed guards stood on opposite sides of the hall, outside of rooms. “Tarik?” Gooding asked. One of the guards on the right raised his hand. Gooding whirled to face the pair. “Tarik Salem is in that room, pointing to his left. Adeel Bashar is behind door number 2.” He pointed to the room on his right.

“Should we interrogate them together?” Fred asked.

“I can take Tarik,” Wallace suggested. “I know him; we go way back,” he added with a grin. He’d helped Sophia interrogate him after they’d managed to kill Amell on Perim Island. It was ultimately his information that led Sophia down the rabbit hole that exposed Stone in the first place. “This isn’t going to be our first rodeo.”

“OK, fine. I’ll take Adeel then,” Fred added. “We also have history.”

The two separated, heading toward their respective rooms. “My men will be outside if you need anything. When you’re done, let me know so we can get you back to the airport,” Gooding added.

Fred and Wallace nodded, then entered their respective rooms.

****

Fred closed the door behind him and entered the interrogation room. The familiar atmosphere eased his nerves.

He hadn't expected the surge of nervous emotions. He'd done thousands of interrogations during his career. They'd become a second nature to him. Comically, at least to him, but not so much for Sherry, at times, he would accidentally find himself interrogating his wife about purchases made. That was how at home he felt with the practice.

Though he suspected the cause of the sudden bout of nervousness was due to the stakes. If Adeel and/or Tarik had no relevant information, then they'd be back to square one in finding Sophia, having wasted valuable time.

Wiping his sweaty palms on his jeans, shifting the folder he'd brought in with him, Fred continued toward the table at the center of the twelve-by-twelve concrete room, pulling out a metal chair, sitting down across from Adeel Bashar, and dropping the folder in front of him.

Adeel was the last surviving terrorist of the attempted Orlando strike nine months prior. The one that he and Sophia, along with the aid of another undercover agent, Naseem Girgrah, had stopped.

The brusque six-foot-eight former terrorist sat cuffed; hands propped on the table. A chain wrapped around a looped spike in the center of the table, keeping the prisoner from getting up and attacking. He had affixed a stare of recognition upon Fred with his right eye. His left was covered with a patch.

He and Sophia had gotten into a fight that night as Adeel and his brother Asher had tried to flee the scene. Sophia gave chase, catching up with the two at a textile facility. They scuffled, and Sophia, in a last-ditch effort to save her own life, drove a broken picture frame through the man's eye.

"I remember you," Adeel said, trying to point at Fred, but the cuffs only allowed him to raise his hands barely.

Fred had questioned Adeel once after he'd awoken from his coma due to being involved in a car crash chasing Amell and Hasan that same night. "Good, that'll save me time explaining who I am and who I work for."

"I told you before. I know no more than what I gave that bitch that did this." He thumbed to the eye patch. "I gave her the location of where we were supposed to go after the attack."

Sophia had used attending the cremation of Asher, who was Adeel's brother who was killed in the raid that stopped the attack, as leverage against him to get the information she needed.

"She says hi and thanks for that information. But she's sorry she couldn't come back by to *see* you again. It only takes one of us," Fred remarked, making a dig at his missing left eye.

"What do you want?" Adeel snarled, taking offense to the jab.

"We figured you'd want an update," Fred continued, leaning back in his seat. The initial wave of nervousness was gone. He was back in his element. "The information you gave her led directly to Tarik Salem, who I don't know if you've had the pleasure of running into here." Knowing that wasn't possible as both men had been kept in different cell blocks that never interacted with one another. An advantage of such a large prison was that, at one point, it held two hundred and seventy prisoners. But, now, only around thirty.

"So, I never liked him. Too high brow thought he was better than us freedom fighters because he had money," the terrorist spat disdainfully.

"Ok." Fred shrugged. "How about the fact that he then gave us the location of your little island hideout over there in the Gulf of Aden?" Adeel sat up, punching his chest out.

"Then I should be rejoicing in the death of many Americans. My brothers are formidable fighters and fight for Allah. He will not let us down."

"Ahh, I wouldn't be getting the ticker tape victory parade ready anytime soon," Fred cautioned, wagging his finger in the air. He then opened the folder. It contained Sophia's notes he'd been reviewing on the flight. After the attack on Perim Island and narrowly escaping, having killed Amell, another SEAL unit went back to see if they'd left any useful intel. They didn't, but they still took photos of the aftermath of Wallace's team's assault. Fred slid out two pictures of the compound. "This is what happens when you fuck with America," he added pointedly.

Adeel deflated upon seeing the images. Several buildings were destroyed. AIA soldiers' bodies were still lying all over. The surviving terrorist left in such a hurry they didn't even bring their dead. "It's… it's not possible. There were hundreds of us."

"Light work for our Special Forces." Fred dug through several more papers, finding the one he was looking for. "Oh, I've got one more for you too." Fred produced a third photo, gliding it across to the Arab. His face fell flatter. "I am sure you recognize him." It was Amell himself, dead.

"What more do you need from me," the terrorist said, pushing the photos away. "It appears you've taken everything."

"Not everything. Hasan got away." Adeel stiffened up at the mention of Hasan's name.

"Then Allah is still with us. He'll avenge our fallen brothers. He will make the streets run red with American blood. Hasan is an avenging prophet."

"You see, that's why I am here," Fred disclosed. "I want to learn more about this prophet of yours. What does he want? Should we fear him?"

"All infidels should fear Hasan. He is a warrior for Allah. He is the sword that will spite all infidels. He will rid the world of animals like you." Adeel's tone took on a reverence for the man. His chest swelled again. "As long as Hasan breathes, you should all cower in fear," Adeel boasted.

"How so?"

"He is like a creature of habit, and his habit is ridding the world of infidels as Allah wishes. He is methodical, routine, and ruthless. You will never see him coming. He will strike when most advantageous, then return home to wait for another opportunity. He is like a snake that strikes quickly but paralyzes you when he does."

"Great, thank you. Got everything I needed." Fred stood, collecting the files, and putting them back into the folder. Adeel rocked back, not knowing what to make of what had just happened.

"I… I gave you no information," he stuttered, replaying the conversation.

Though to Fred, he'd just given him a wealth of knowledge.

"But you did." He headed for the door with a smile on his face. He paused before turning the handle on the door. Glancing back, he added. "You just told me how to find him. Thanks, Adeel. Maybe I'll swing back by to *see* you again," he added, holding a hand over one of his eyes.

****

Wallace entered his interrogation room to find its sole occupant, Tarik Salem, sitting at a table in the middle of the drab confines. The dull, faded, water-marked concrete walls made the sleek metal table look more out of place. It was the only thing that looked clean. Two sets of footprints were marked on the floor in dusty outlines. The room looked like it hadn't been used in years.

Wallace approached the table as the prisoner looked up. He'd been wrangling his wrists that donned a pair of silver cuffs. They were connected by a chain that secured them to the looped post securing him in place.

Wallace took his seat. "Too tight?" he asked.

"Yes," Tarik answered. "They treat me like a rabid dog in here. I wonder where this great compassion that you people claim to have is. I've been sitting in here for months. No rights, no trials. Where is this famous Western law that your country champions around the globe? That you use to justify your parasites invading other people's lands to impart on the 'savages.' Huh, where is all that?"

"Those rights that are given to people as part of a contract are for individuals to act rightfully and morally, which can then be taken away when said individual violates that contract. And one could postulate that selling weapons to mass murders and terrorists would preclude anyone from having those rights," Wallace answered. "Do you remember me?"

"I do; you are the commando who helped capture me along with that woman. You are the reason I am sitting here," Tarik snapped. "I don't need a lecture in morality from an American war profiteer. Your country has done far worse than anything I've done.”

Wallace thought for a moment about engaging in that debate but decided not to. That wasn’t the reason he was there. “Sure, we can debate that topic some other time. It’s not what I am here for.”

“What are you here for? I gave Amell’s location. And, from what I know, your team has already killed him. Good riddance.” The prisoner spat on the floor as a sign of disrespect.

“We did, but his number two, the man you met with when we pulled you out from your hidey hole. Hasan. He got away. He’s causing a lot of trouble that I’d like to stop. The problem is, I am going to be honest. We can’t find him. I know that you used to do business with him. I was hoping since there is clearly no love lost between you and the AIA.” He indicated the congealing liquid saliva on the ground. “Maybe you could help me.”

“And why would I help you? What’s in it for me?” Tarik sat back, waiting to hear a proposal.

“Well, I can help you get that trial you were complaining about.” Wallace reached into his back pocket, pulled out a sheet of paper, and set it on the table.

“What’s that?” Tarik questioned. “You don’t negotiate with terrorists. Right?”

“This is true; we don’t. However, technically… you weren’t an actual terrorist—an arms dealer, yes, but not a terrorist.” Wallace made sure to point out the distinction. “As an arms dealer, I am sure you know you racked up quite a *long* list of misdeeds that had put you in the crosshairs of some really big countries. You even managed to get a red notice put out by Interpol. *Tsk, tsk,* you naughty boy,” Wallace added, rubbing his two index fingers against each other. “I am sure your mother would be proud of that,” he jibed. “Anyway, that paper there will guarantee your immediate transfer to the Hague so you can face a trial by the International Criminal Courts so you can face justice for those crimes instead of rotting here.” Wallace threw his arms open, gesturing at the room. “Where no one will ever let you continue to exist.”

Tarik sat in silence for a moment before answering. “Let me see.” He snatched the paper from Wallace’s hand and quickly scanned the document. "Why do you need my help?"

Wallace took a deep breath, slowly exhaling it, steeling his gaze upon the Arab. He stood and walked around the table, lowering his face, and bringing it inches from Tarik's face.

"He has a friend of mine, and I'd like to get her back," he said. "And I believe you have information that'll help me do that. Because if I don't get her back." Wallace lowered his voice to a whisper, but with a coldness and calculating tone, he added. "I will come back here and make sure you find your justice. And believe me, you don't want my brand of justice," he warned.

The two men stared at each other for a moment, locked in an intense contest, sizing each other's wills. Tarik broke, looking down in defeat. "What do I have to do?"

"Great. I had a feeling you'd see reason." He slammed a hand on Tarik's back and returned to his seat. "It's quite simple. Give me information that'll lead to Hasan's capture or termination. Easy peasy."

"I don't know a lot about the specifics of their operations," Tarik began. "I do know that in addition to being funded by Sotor Corps, the AIA would make money on the side kidnapping women, mostly Western women, and selling them off into European sex-trafficking rings."

"I fail to see how that's going to help," Wallace butted in, reaching for the paper and standing up.

"Wait, wait." Tarik tried to reach out and grab Wallace, but the restraints prevented even the slightest movement. Wallace nevertheless stopped, sitting back down. "It's relevant," the Arab continued, rubbing his wrists again. "Because anytime they would do this, they had to stash the woman somewhere. I know where. We made a deal there before. I had watched Hasan make a deal with a Russian as I was getting there. They were loading a group of women into a truck. If he took someone, he would probably stash them in the same place. Hasan keeps to his habits. He doesn't like change. He would use the same place."

"Where is this place?" Wallace questioned.

"It's a town called Al-Hutah in Yemen. That is all I know."

"Ok, good, thank you." Wallace stood, grabbed the paper, and headed for the door.

"Where are you going," Tarik cried out. "Our deal."

Wallace turned, "Our deal is contingent upon his capture or death, which neither has happened. Once it does, if it's because of this information, I'll be back. So don't go anywhere." Tarik frowned as Wallace departed.

****

The two men entered the hallway at the same time, closing their respective doors. Seeing each other, they declared in unison, "I know how to get her back."

"You go first," Wallace deferred to Fred.

"Hasan is a creature of habit. So, he's going to retreat to where he is most familiar. Like… like his stomping grounds. We find that out. We'll find him." Fred concluded. "What's yours?"

"Tarik said that the AIA was involved in basically low-level sex trafficking to make money for supplies. They would normally stash the women in a village called Al-Hutah, which is somewhere in Yemen."

"Okay, great. Let's get the wheels up." Fred turned to one of the guards. "Can you let Captain Gooding know we're ready to go?" The guard nodded and jumped onto his radio.

Wallace was struck by something Sophia had told him before about Fred and that Sherry had forced him to retire, not wanting him to get hurt. "Wait." He grabbed Fred by the arm, pulling his attention away from the man radioing. "I think it'd be best if my team and I handled this. Why don't you go to the embassy in Rabat?"

"Why?" Fred questioned. "We need to get Sophia back. She's still struck in Yemen. A country filled with terrorists and militants. You'll need all the firepower you can get."

"True, but my team can handle this. Besides, once we get her back, you know her. She's not going to stop until Stone is brought to heel. Go to Rabat and question the family. There, you'll rendezvous with Mila Koch and the rest of the operations team. I'll go to Oman, connect with my team, and prepare for the

194

incursion. Once we're ready to launch, you can run the operation from there."

"Fine," Fred acquiesced, seeing through Wallace's ploy. "Not a big fan of the desert anyway."

"What are you a big fan of," Wallace asked as Captain Gooding approached.

"Not a lot."

"Gentlemen, I assume your business here is complete," Captain Gooding addressed the two men.

"Sure is," Fred answered. "We'll just need one thing. I'll need a flight to Rabat, Morocco."

Captain Gooding looked at the former agent bewildered and replied, "If that gets both of you off my base, consider it done."

CHAPTER FOURTEEN

SOPHIA tried to fight against Farid as he led her from the torture room, one hand wrapped tightly around the back of her neck. His fingernails dug into her flesh deeper and deeper with every movement. Each time she squirmed or wiggled to break free, he squeezed tighter. One of his nails eventually broke through her skin.

She could feel the sharp stab of a pinprick puncturing her skin. Even in her dazed state, she could feel the warm blood ooze down the back of her neck. He continued to push her down the hall.

Where was he even taking her?

At one point, she managed to push him away and tried to run. When a rush of searing pain enveloped her skull as her escort grabbed a fist full of hair and yanked her back. He pulled with such force that Sophia thought he was going to rip her scalp clean off in one single tug. She yelped in surprise and pain as her feet came out from underneath her. She landed sidelong on the concrete floor, driving the air from her lungs.

Gasping and fearful he'd pulled every strand of hair from her skull, she shakily reached up and gently patted her head, setting off a firestorm. Thousands of pain receptors lit on fire, triggering a tsunami of pain cascading over her head. The searing sensation was almost blinding, but it wasn't over yet.

The Arab loomed over her, blotting out the overhead light. Sophia eyed him as he stood there like a sadistic animal pondering what to do with his injured prey.

He snarled down at her. "I…I am sorry," was all Sophia could manage to say.

"Get up," he growled. The American reflexively extended her arm for assistance, which was meant by a sneer and then a swift kick to the gut, bowling Sophia over onto her other side. "Where is that American toughness, haha?" he taunted.

Despite her body being on fire, Sophia managed to get up onto all fours. *Don't give up, don't give up, you got this girl.* She thought, and with a push, she stood. Albeit on wobbly legs, her knees trembled. Her right leg buckled, but she caught herself, standing up straight, poking out her chest. She licked the blood from her still-stinging split lip. She took a deep breath and steeled herself, "Here it is fucker," she roared, much to Farid's chagrin.

"Keep moving," he fired back, clamping down on her neck again, pushing her back down the hall.

Farid led Sophia to another room, down the hall, around a corner from the torture room. There, two other terrorists waited just outside the door. One was holding a bucket, the other some type of garment with a pair of sandals on top. Sophia assumed it was an abaya—a traditional piece of clothing for Arabic women.

Farid shoved her inside, and the two men followed.

He continued to bulldoze Sophia across the room, throwing her against the back wall and pressing her against it. He then wrapped his right hand around her throat, pinning her to the wall. His left hand worked across her ballistic vest.

He fumbled for the edge, not breaking eye contact with the American. Both their eyes set on each other. Farid's were full of rage, Sophia's terror as he gripped the edge of the vest, ripping it open and forcing it off of her before throwing it into the corner. Still, with her pinned, his hand continued across her chest to one of the buttons on her fatigue top, unfastening the first, then the second.

Sophia trembled but mustered up a reserve of fight. She flailed, managing to bring her left arm up and dropping it across Farid's extended right arm, chopping it at the elbow. He lost his grip around her neck, creating a tiny opening as her unsuspected resistance caught him by surprise.

He stumbled slightly, losing his balance from the hit, which created an opening. Sophia drew her right leg up, driving it into his gut and pushing him back. "I can change myself," she screamed, hastily unbuttoning the rest of her top, waiting for a reprisal.

Farid seemed incensed about to charge at her when he whirled on the two other men, who'd let out a chuckle. He settled for smacking the two across their faces, then followed the physical insult with a series of berating comments as Sophia finished undressing.

"Give me that." Farid snatched the bucket from the man holding it, turning back to Sophia, who was now standing by herself in her underwear. "You smell American." He tossed the bucket of water onto Sophia, drenching her. He then tossed the abaya at Sophia as she swatted the water from her face. "Since you can undress yourself, dress yourself." Sophia donned the abaya. It was long, covering her from shoulders to ankles. It was a dark gray color. The man holding the sandals handed them to her. She quickly put them over her feet, trembling from the ice-cold water. "Let's go."

"Where are you taking me now?" Sophia demanded.

Farid didn't answer. Instead, he snatched her up again, leading her from the room down several more doors. The two men followed. One darted in front as they approached a door with an outer metal security door. He quickly unlocked it, holding it open, then opened the interior door before they approached.

"Don't get too comfortable," Farid said sarcastically before tossing Sophia inside.

Sophia landed hard against the dusty, dirty concrete floor, rolling side over side, kicking up a caked layer of dirt into the air. The wall at the end of the room was the only thing that stopped her—crashing into it with her back. She felt her vertebrae crackle as her dizzying trip came to an abrupt halt.

Farid slammed the door, cackling in raucous congratulatory celebration. Then, the outer metal door banged, clacking into its metal-framed place, and a twist of keys locked it, hammering in her absolute sequestering.

Their heavy footsteps became increasingly quieter as they walked away, still laughing. Sophia achingly sat up, leaning against the wall, rubbing the small of her back, and finding herself in a dimly lit room. A single overhead circular light in the center blasted a beam down. Everything outside of the beam was cast in a dimming light the further it was from the source. The far corners of the room lay in almost total darkness.

Sophia rested against the wall, breathing heavily in the still silence of the room.

Something moved, and Sophia's head darted in the direction of the noise. Her heart thumped in her chest. *Was there something else in the room with her?* She waited, listening. Nothing.

There it was again, this time on the other side of the room. Sophia tried to scramble back, but the wall prevented her. Something was scurrying about on the outer peripheries of the light against the far edges. She stared into the dark abyss where the last round of noise had come from.

Quietness fell over the room again. Maybe the darkness was playing tricks on her mind, she thought.

Scuff, scuff.

There it was again; Sophia scrunched against the wall tighter, blinking desperately, trying to will her iris' to adjust to regain her sight. She pressed herself against the wall harder as the sound bounced around again. This time more jarringly, and there was a second sound. Similar to the first, but heavier.

"So, help me, God, if you're a rat, I am going to scream," Sophia commented, forcing herself to her feet with no expectation for the rodent to identify itself.

"Hel…lo,"

Sophia's heart leaped into her throat at the response. The hairs on her arms and neck spiked. She wasn't alone. "Who's there?" she called out. Then came a vile smell, an acrid smell of human body odor and excrement blasted her nostrils as she scanned the room, doing a double take, letting her eyes adjust to the lower lighting. She paused her scan, letting her sight linger in the far-right corner of the room, finding a dark mass.

The black blob transformed into the shape of a human as it cautiously crept away from the wall. The person took on more distinct features as they got closer. Sophia's intense standoffish position eased as recognition struck her. It was a woman—a brown-haired, thin woman, encroaching arms outstretched in disbelief.

"Are… are you real?" the woman muttered, her voice cracking, on the verge of tears. "Have you come to save us?"

The woman touched Sophia's face, almost as if to confirm her existence.

"Us?" To this point, Sophia had only seen the woman, but as she continued to caress her face, the woman slightly turned Sophia's face to the other corner of the room. There, another person lay curled up into a ball. The clump of a person appeared to be a man, though he seemed to be shackled to the wall. A heavy-looking chain cascaded down from the wall, wrapping around his wrist. Sophia subconsciously rubbed her own raw flesh.

"Have you come to save us?" the woman repeated. "Come… come sit." The woman led Sophia back to her corner. It was a makeshift bedroom, Sophia guessed. She had a dingy-looking foam mattress and blanket. The woman sat cross-legged on the mattress, signaling for Sophia to sit beside her. "Please sit. How long before you take us out of here?"

Sophia fought the overwhelming need to gag; the smell emanating from the woman and her bedding was unbearable. Her nose wrinkled with every inhalation. Holding the urge to vomit at bay, Sophia sat. She didn't know how to respond to the question. She hadn't come there as a liberator but as a captive like the woman.

Silence once again gripped the room as Sophia pondered what to say. The woman had sounded so encouraged to see another person, and Sophia didn't want to crush her hope, though something about the woman seemed familiar.

She'd seen her face before but couldn't quite… place it, trying to reconcile the photo image of the person she was thinking of with the visage before her.

Sophia knew she'd seen the face before… thinking… there, snatching the memory. Jessica Richards, an aide worker who was kidnapped about a year ago. Though the woman now barely resembled her earlier portrait. The brunette's face had sunken in slightly, and she was about thirty pounds lighter now. Her hair was a bit longer, but the eyes were the same, albeit harboring more horrors behind them than in the photo. She couldn't imagine what she'd been through.

"Are you…Jessica Richards?" Sophia tried to recall as much information from the brief as she could. At the time, it had sent a flurry throughout the agency as everyone wondered if they were another agent's assets. Why else would two random doctors be kidnapped? The headline of the brief was 'American aid workers Jessica Richards and Trevor Spelling abducted from a refugee camp in Kakuma, Kenya. Sophia looked to the other corner. The man hadn't moved, still curled into a ball, but she guessed it was Trevor. *How had they come into the position of Hasan?*

The woman's face fell despondent at the question. "So…so you haven't come to save us?" Jessica's lower lip began to quiver; a solemn tear streamed down her left cheek. "You…you don't even know who we are." She hurried back, snuggling into the corner into the fetal position, sobbing. "We're going to die here!" The dam broke, and a flood of tears washed down the woman's face as she sobbed, smearing the thin layer of dirt that had covered her face.

The overflow of emotion from the woman stirred the lump of a man in the other corner into motion. He sat up on his bedding, waving Sophia over. She looked back to the woman who'd tucked her face into her knees, balling. She wasn't going to get any information from her.

Was she wrong? Was that not Jessica Richards?
Sophia made her way across the dully lit room to the man, kneeling before him. He reeked just as much, if not worse, than the woman. His hair had grown down past his shoulders and was a ratted, tangled mess. He had an equally disheveled-looking beard dropping down to his sternum. He was covered in dirt and grime. Every part of his exposed skin was two shades darker, and his clothes were tattered and worn like he hadn't changed in a very long time. The man she was looking at now resembled nothing of the picture she'd seen. His eyes were dead, defeated. He was vastly more emaciated than Jessica. He was a husk of the man he'd been when the photo she was comparing him to was taken.

"Hi," Sophia addressed him, kneeling in front of him. "I could be wrong, but… are you Trevor Spelling?" The man nodded vigorously, a flash of light behind his otherwise dead eyes. "Ok… ok, Trevor. Is that Jessica?" Pointing to the sobbing woman. Again, he nodded. "OK, good. How long have the two of you been here?”

He started to speak, but the sounds were unintelligible. Throwing Sophia off. She’d expected fully formed words but only got a garbled mix of vowels and breaths. He was trying to say something, but it wasn’t coming out. A rush of despair filled his face, sensing that whatever he was trying to tell her wasn’t getting through. His eyes bugged as he tried to slow down and enunciate the words. However, they still weren’t coming out in sounds that could be understood.

“They… they, cut… out his tongue,” Jessica managed to say between sobs. Trevor opened his mouth wide enough for Sophia to see that half of his tongue was gone. Sophia jerked back, shocked, falling onto her ass. Trevor’s shoulders slumped in defeat at being unable to communicate what he was desperately trying to say. “They didn’t want to hear him praying at night anymore,” Jessica added. “I am sorry. I… I am a little overwhelmed right now.”

Sophia collected herself, dusting off the dirt as she stood. “I am sorry,” she said, apologizing to Trevor. “I want to understand what you are saying.” She took a step back toward Jessica, which sent Trevor into a flurry of agitation. He tried to yell, but it came out as a series of grunts; he frantically waved for her to come back, almost pleading. “I am sorry,” was all Sophia could manage to say. She needed information and knew she wasn’t going to be able to get it from him. She sat down again in front of Jessica, who had by now stopped crying. “So you are Jessica?”

The woman wiped the tears from her cheeks. “Yeah, sorry again. It’s been a while since I’ve been able to speak to anyone. Let alone another American. You’d imagine there are not many of us around here. So, when I heard you, I got excited that you’d come to negotiate for our freedom. So… I take it you’re not.” She eked out a hopeful grin, but the tightness in her pursed lips gave away she already knew the answer.

“No, sorry, sadly, I am not. I would reckon I am now in the same boat as you guys.”

“So, you’re not with the American military or government?”

“No, not entirely. They contracted me,” Sophia said. The

revelation perked Jessica up. "I am a documentarian," she elaborated, not wanting to entice any hope at a rescue further despite herself secretly clinging to that very hope that at any moment Ryan and Tex would break the door down and save her, well, now them. "I was asked to film a documentary on how the Special Forces operated when these people kidnapped me. Who are they?" she asked, not to give away any suspicions. She needed to keep her cover intact.

"Not sure." Jessica shrugged. "We've just got here…" She paused, thinking. "Gee, I don't know how long. Maybe a couple of months. We've been sold. I don't know how many times now. There's always some other group taking us. It started after we were taken from the refugee camp in Kenya. A few days later, we were sold to the highest bidder at a human auction. I can't believe those still exist today," she said, appalled.

"There's still all kinds of evil out there," was all Sophia could think of to say.

"Since then, I don't know, four or five more times. It seems like every time we get moved, it's a different group."

"I am so sorry," Sophia said comfortingly, taking Jessica's hand and squeezing it.

"How'd you know our names?"

"Newspaper," Sophia quickly countered. "I have a pretty good memory. I read about your abduction. You're doctors, right?"

"Were, yeah."

"You were working at the camp treating kids." The woman nodded. "Then one of the local militias raided the camp and wound up taking a couple of you. They found the other two dead not long after."

"Too old to sell off. That is what I overheard one of the men saying, at least."

"That's barbaric." Another shrug. "There was a hope a ransom would be offered, but none came. So, you're a military brat?" Sophia asked, changing the subject, seeing she was about to cry again.

"Yeah, my father and mother were in the Air Force. I'd wanted to go but decided to become a pediatrician. You know, a safer job.

Guess it wasn't much safer," she joked.

"My father was Army. Mother was a civilian but worked at the base," Sophia countered. "I know a little about the life."

"Do you think your parents will try to find you?" Jessica asked, her hope returning.

"They are… not in my life anymore. Mom died in a car accident when I was seventeen, but she'd left my dad before that. Father passed from a stroke five years ago."

"Was your father a hard ass? Mine was," Jessica asked.

"Yeah, he was," Sophia admitted. The two shared an embrace at their shared history.

Sophia shifted to sitting beside Jessica as they continued to hold each other. "We'll get through this," she said, comforting her. "I know we'll get through this." Sophia looked around the room. "Guess I'll take that corner, neighbor."

Jessica managed a faint laugh. "Yeah, that's fine. You'll be better than the previous tenant. Which was a rat, by the way." Sophia shimmied at the word. "I take it you don't like them?"

"Eww, ugh." She shook in disgust. "No, not at all."

Sophia stood about to make her way across the room when Jessica grabbed a hold of her arm. "But we can share my bed until they bring you one." Sadness filled her eyes.

"Ok," Sophia agreed. Despite the smell, she nestled back down next to her new friend, even more determined to find a way to escape—not just for herself anymore, but just as much for her two new roommates.

****

Sophia jolted awake when she heard the ominous creaking of the security door opening and a set of jangling keys unlatching the bolts to the room.

She peered around at her surroundings, lost, not knowing where she was for a flash of a second, having been transported out of a pleasant dream. She snapped back to reality, finding herself seated back against the wall in a cell of sorts, presumably still in

Yemen.

Jessica's head was resting in her lap as the two women had fallen asleep embracing each other. Sophia couldn't tell how long she'd been asleep. However long it was, it felt like an eternity. Having not had much of an opportunity to sleep the previous few days. The snooze felt refreshing of sorts.

She'd wanted to stay awake as much as possible, waiting, searching for her chance to escape. However, locked in a room, she wasn't going to get that chance any time soon. Letting her guard down finally, she'd let herself sleep.

The door burst open, Farid throwing it wide as he and the two other men from her previous encounter rushed in. The flurry stirred Jessica and Trevor to alertness.

"No, no, not again," Jessica screamed, pushing Sophia away, cowering into the corner in the fetal position, shivering, rocking back and forth. "No, no, no."

Sophia jumped to her feet, trying to back up as the three approached, bumping up against the wall. "What's going on?" The two men each grabbed an arm and began dragging her toward the door. "Where are you taking me? I don't know anything." She tried to break away, ripping her arm from one of her escort's grip. The American's face seared as the other man smacked her hard across the face. Allowing his compatriot to regain his hold on her.

"No, don't take her!" Jessica animalistically leaped from her near catatonic, terrified state, clawing for her new friend. "Please, I need her."

Farid effortlessly caught the slender brunette mid-air in a swiping motion with one arm. Cradling her back to the corner, patting her on the head, childishly pacifying the young woman. "Now, now, your buyers will be here in the next few days. I don't wanna harm the goods before they can buy it, so *sit down*," he snapped, turning to the two men holding Sophia. "Take her, Hasan," he ordered.

The pair dragged Sophia from her cell down the hall, turning at the end into another corridor, leading her to the fourth door on the left. The American visually took mental notes of the building's layout. It seemed like some type of larger communal housing or storage building: a tin roof, mud-brick walls, concrete flooring. A security door did not protect most of the doors they'd passed, so the occupants appeared able to roam the building freely.

Her escorts barged her into the same room from the previous day. It had a nearly identical setup as before, except the stool was replaced by a chair with wrist straps. The table of torture devices was back with the same accouterments. However, one new one sinisterly stood out.

A Saif sword. A convex curved blade. It was popularly used by Arab soldiers during their early conquering years. Sophia had seen them used in multiple beheading videos that were sent to the agency for analysis.

She tensed upon seeing the blade. One of her worst fears seemed to be coming to fruition, much to her dismay.

The only other difference in the room was a pair of chains dangling from the ceiling, with Hasan standing in the center of the room.

"Sit," the Arab spoke. Sophia's two escorts pushed her down into the chair, forcing her arms onto the rests and fastening them down with the leather straps before backing away several steps. "Agent Evans." The sound of him uttering her actual last name somehow chilled her to the bone. *How does he know my name?* Must've been Stone, she guessed. "I don't have a lot of time, and I am not one that likes to be trifled with or lied to." He slammed his fist down on the metal table. Several of the instruments jumped. Sophia herself flinched. "I know you work for the CIA. I remember your voice. All I want is to know where West and Stone are." Hasan stood in front of her, setting his eyes upon her. Every fiber of Sophia's being shook. "West killed my cousin and my brother. He will pay, and you will tell me where to find him."

Hasan backed away, and Sophia eased, collecting herself. "I... I told you I don't know who you're talking about. I am- "

"Don't fucking lie to me!" he screamed, slamming his hand again. "I know who you are." He snatched a scalpel-like tool from the table and crossed the room in a flurry; the wind from his wake brushed Sophia's hair back. He jabbed the scalpel towards her. Sophia tried to jerk her head back, but one of the escorts pressed his hand against the back of her skull. She inhaled, holding her breath. The tip of the blade paused millimeters from her right eye, touching her eyelash. Everything around her disappeared. The only thing in her sight was the blade. "Tell me now!"

"I... I... I am Sophia Grant-"

"Lie!" He slammed the blade down.

It pierced through the top of Sophia's left hand, impaling her palm to the chair rest. She screamed as the scalpel tore through flesh and tendon. Sophia gawped at the object protruding from her hand in horror and disbelief; agonizing pain swelled in her hand as her eyes bugged.

"My fucking hand!" she yelled, struggling to break free of her restraints. Every instinct in her body was screaming to pull it out. But she couldn't. Hasan jingled the blade side to side, driving it further down, causing the American to release a blood-curdling howl, throwing her head back, trying to rock the chair.

"Tell me!"

"Fuck you," she growled through clenched teeth. "Fuck you, ahhhh!"

He wiggled the utensil. *Ptch.* Sophia spat in Hasan's face. He recoiled, delivering a slap. The pain from the smack only temporarily elevated the fire going on in her hand.

"I don't know anything!" she raged.

Hasan shot forward after wiping the loogie from his cheek. He grabbed Sophia's right pinky. "You don't." He jerked her finger to the side. A wet crack of bone as he snapped her finger.

Sophia wailed in agony as her hand spasmed. She stared at her hand and her awkwardly angled pinky finger, which now resembled an 'L' shape. She convulsed violently in the chair. "I can't tell you what I don't know," she seethed.

Hasan stepped back, sizing the American up. She was covered in sweat; it beaded down her face, and her abaya was drenched. She scowled at him. "I've heard your training is very intense and prepares you for this. I think you are prepared to endure much. Yes, yes, but." He snapped his fingers. The door opened behind. She couldn't turn to see what was happening, but she could hear something dragging. That something came into view as Farid dragged Trevor past her. "*You* may have been trained to take pain for your country, but what about a fellow countryman? Can you watch him suffer?"

Farid affixed Trevor's hands into cuffs on the chains, pulling a string that tightened them, bringing his arms up over his head and lifting him an inch or two off the ground. Sophia's and Trevor's eyes met; his were filled with fear. Sophia's were laden with guilt and sorrow. She couldn't divulge anything.

"No, no, don't... don't do what you're going to do to him. Please. I don't know anything," Sophia begged.

"And I don't believe you. Why are you protecting these men? They conspired against your country. Helped kill Americans. They are traitors. Why protect them?"

For what it was worth, Sophia knew he was right. There was no need to protect them. They were animals, just like him. However, she wasn't protecting them at this point. It was more so protecting herself. She knew the second she gave up the information Hasan wanted, she would no longer be of use. He'd kill her the second after she talked. Deep down, she was still hoping for a rescue. However, with each passing hour, that likelihood was decreasing.

"Look, sir, I really don't have the answers you are seeking." Switching tactics to a more pleading tone. "I... I," she struggled to get the words out through her own pain. Both hands throbbed; a pool of blood from her hand had accumulated beneath her chair. Her body shivered. She was sweating profusely now. Becoming lightheaded. "I... I would give them to you if I had them. But I don't. Please let him go."

Hasan continued to stare at Sophia. "Once again. Where. Are. They."

Sophia looked at Trevor with a mournful glare, her face flat, her lip quivering, and a single tear streamed down her reddening eyes. *Should she give up the charade?* She shifted her stare back to Hasan. *No, hold out.* "I don't know anything. Please?"

Hasan nodded; Farid cocked back his fist, thrusting it into Trevor's sickly thin body. The blow struck with such force that Sophia heard the cracking of ribs from across the room as he swung violently from the chains. He wailed in pain. Farid delivered another devastating blow. The American grunted in agony as he swung—a third strike delivered to his jaw.

"Where?"

Sophia defeatedly looked to the floor, bitter sorrow encompassing her heart as she heard Farid deliver a fourth strike. "I… I can't," she cried. "I don't know."

Hasan scoped up a baton-looking device from the table. It was a stun gun type of tool. He pressed a button, and a wave of blue light arched between two metal tips with a *crackle*. "Where?"

"Please don't."

Hasan pressed the button and jabbed the device against Trevor's side. The man failed as thousands of volts of electricity coursed through him. Sophia tried to look away, but one of the escorts grabbed her head, angling it toward the gruesome scene. Sophia sobbed as Trevor floundered away, screaming until he began foaming at the mouth.

Hasan stopped, throwing the baton back onto the table. With another finger snap, Farid tugged on the string attached to Trevor's shackles. He dropped to the floor with a thud, unmoving.

Farid continued, proceeding to drag over a bench, placing it in front of the tortured man. He then hoisted him to his knees, dropping him chest first over the bench. Hasan circled the table, picking out his next weapon of choice. "I grow tired of this, as I am sure the two of you are. And by the look of you, we don't have much time left today."

By now, the pool of blood underneath her chair was starting to look more lakish. Sophia was starting to struggle to keep her eyes open. Her head lolled from side to side. Her body temperature plummeted, and she was growing colder despite being in the hot room. Her throat was running dry, feeling the parchedness of barely having anything to drink in the last few days.

"Please stop," she begged, pleading with her captor. "You… you don't have to do this to him."

"I am not, you are. You are hurting him by not telling me what I need to know." Hasan picked up the Saif, sliding it out of its scabbard. Farid grabbed the barely conscious Trevor's arms, pulling them behind him to position the upper half of his torso just off the edge of the bench to where his head barely dangled over.

Sophia began to weep harder, "No, no, no, please… please don't. You don't have to-"

Hasan stood to the side of Trevor's draped body. The prisoner started to stir, coming back to alertness. Hasan raised the blade. "I ask one last time. Where. Are. Stone and West?"

"I… I… don't know. My name is not Sophia Evans, and I don't work for the CIA. I am a filmmaker. My name is Sophia Grant."

"Lie," Hasan snarled.

The Saif sliced down through the air. Sophia screamed as the blade cut through flesh, muscle, and bone. Severing Trevor's head from his body. It plopped to the floor with a wet *smack*. Arterial blood spouted across the room, dousing the American in crimson red.

"You *fucking* asshole, I am going to kill you!" Sophia shouted, wiggling in the chair, trying to break loose despite the blazing pain in both hands.

Hasan casually set the Saif back on the table, gliding to the angry, struggling Sophia, gripping the scalpel. "Take her to her room," he ordered, ripping the surgical utensil out. Sophia's face twisted in agony as black spots dotted her vision. Head lolling side to side, struggling to remain awake. "Maybe you'll be ready to tell me tomorrow."

Those were the last words Sophia heard before her world faded to black.

FRED peered out the tinted window of the SUV as the road passed by. Had he not known better, he'd thought he was driving down any road in any major US city. The buildings were modern, with carpets of lush green grass and vegetation surrounding them. The roads were perfectly paved with asphalt and concrete.

Alas, though, the fact that he was in the back seat of the SUV with two US Marines in the front seat and a third sitting in the back along with him and that they were armed demolished the illusion that he was within the US borders. No, he was in Rabat, Morocco, on his way to the US Embassy to meet up with his new team—Sophia's team.

After the nine-hour flight from Cuba, he landed at the Rabat-Sale International Airport, having obtained the information they needed from Tarik and Adeel. By now, Wallace would be getting close to his destination in Oman, where he would link up with the rest of the SEAL team to begin planning their extraction of Sophia from Hasan's hands.

First, though, he wanted to meet with the families of Stone and West to see if they had any information on where the pair might be hiding.

"Sir, we're getting ready to pull in. You're going to wanna get your identification ready," the Marine in the passenger seat informed.

"Roger. And you can call me Fred." The retired agent dug into the front sleeve of his backpack, producing his credentials, as the SUV stopped and slowed to bob and weave around the alternating off-set concrete barricades, pulling up to the gatehouse.

Despite Morocco being a very West-friendly country, there always stood a chance for danger no matter how pro-West a Middle Eastern North Africa (MENA) country was. The Marines protecting all US Embassy and Consulate installations knew their assignments and were always ready for anything to kick off.

After a quick ID and vehicle check, the gate guards waved the SUV through. It pulled up to the front of a three-story glass building, which was completely sleek and modern. It appeared no expense was spared on the aesthetics.

"Another waste of taxpayer money," Fred grumbled, disembarking the SUV. "You gentleman coming," Fred asked, retrieving his carry-on luggage.

"No, sir Fred." The Marine caught himself seeing the older man's expression change. "This is where we get off. Just head inside."

Fred nodded, shutting the door, and making his way up the pathway to the front doors. There, he was greeted by two more Marines who gave him a quick once-over inspection. Followed by another ID check while the other waved a metal detector across his person. Satisfied, the pair opened the doors.

Fred entered the lobby of the Chancery building, taking in the atrium-style, modern art-deco, marble-floor opulence. He was even more impressed by the eight-acre compound, which seemed complete with all the modern trappings of a high-class office building in the States.

"Agent Fred Jones," a voice called out to him from across the lobby.

Fred looked around for the source, hearing the clacking of high-heeled shoes on the marble floor. A stunningly beautiful woman with long blonde hair and piercing icy blue eyes approached, wearing an outfit that the older, more modest former agent felt was way too revealing. She wore a mid-thigh-high pencil skirt and a white blouse, with the top two buttons intentionally undone, exposing the top of her ample cleavage.

"Mr. Fred Jones," he replied, trying not to look too appalled by her outfit. *How in the world could any government agent be allowed to dress like that*, he thought.

"My apologies, I sometimes forget you retired." Fred picked up a slight German accent. A memory clicked in his head. "I am Mila Koch." She extended a hand.

Fred shook the woman's hand, recognizing the name. "Ah, Sophia's friend, right?"

The young German pursed her lips at the mention of her friend's name, her smile dropping to a more somber expression.

"Yes, and…" She perked up, catching that her sadness wasn't going to help the situation. "With your help, we are going to get her back."

"Absolutely," was Fred's confident reply. In his mind, there was no other outcome.

"I am sure you'd like to get situated and maybe a little sleep before-"

"No, not actually." Fred cut in. "I slept enough on the flight." He checked his watch. "Wallace should be in Oman in… about seven hours. So, I want to be prepared."

"How so?"

"First off, I'd like to meet the rest of the team and talk with Mrs. Stone and Mrs. West."

Mila shrugged, "OK, follow me."

"Lead the way."

She proceeded to lead Fred deeper into the Embassy, taking an elevator *down* a couple of levels and swiping her badge to get through a few sets of locked gates, eventually leading to a room.

Upon entering, there was every manner of surveillance and reconnaissance technology one could ever dream of having—things light years ahead of anything Fred had access to during his FBI tenure.

Several people were already inside; they all turned at the new arrival.

Mila pointed to the far-right corner at an older brunette woman. "That over there is Gabby Wise; she handles data analysis and various other things." She panned to her left. "That is Jerry Dickerson, analyst, drone operator, and linguistics. Then behind the computer is Richard Sparks, tech expert, and overall, Mr. Get it done." She unabashedly blew him a kiss, causing his pale cheeks to flare red as he sat back down. "As for me, I am a hacker extraordinaire, data analyst, and doer of whatever Sophia needs at the time." The German finished introducing everyone.

"Ok," Fred spoke up to address the room. "Well, it's nice to meet everyone, and I look forward to working with all of you. We are going to get Sophia back. We know where she is, and Wallace's team is going to be successful." He turned to Mila.

"Where are the families."

"I'll take you to them," Mila said.

****

Wallace found the bungalow that he'd been directed to by the base Shore Patrol (SP) upon dropping him off outside the base's barracks. He was holding his bag outside the room. A sense of jet lag, having flown from Morocco to Wisconsin, to Cuba, and now to Oman, was finally starting to catch up with him. Yet he was still happy to see his entire team back together again, albeit wishing it was under better circumstances as there was still one member of the team they needed to find.

He entered the building.

"Attention on deck," Ryan shouted upon Wallace's entrance.

"Shut the fuck up, Sands," Wallace fired back, cracking a smirk. The Master Chief was not one for standing on military ceremony amongst his team. Was he technically their superior? Yes, but the team had been together for long enough that it didn't matter. He viewed them all as his equals and family. "Get over here." The two shared a unit handshake and embrace. He followed suit with every other member coming to Tex.

The bulky Texan eyed his commander with a sullen expression. "I tried, Chief. I really did try hard not to lose her."

"Tex." Wallace grabbed the man by the shoulders. "I know. I read the After Actions. There wasn't anything you could do. It was a trap. The fact that any of you all got out is a miracle and a blessing." He hugged the Texan deeply. "Chin up, we're going to get her."

"Where'd you go, Chief?" Tyus asked.

Wallace looked at Alwani and Ryan. "Figured you'd tell us everything once we were all together," Ryan said. "Didn't wanna get anyone's hopes up." He looked at Tex. Who sunk back down on his bunk.

"You all remember that arms dealer we captured last year in Yemen who gave us Amell's location." The team nodded. "Well, it turns out he's a wealth of information. He gave us the location of one of the AIA's way stations where they collect kidnapped Westerners to sell off into the sex trafficking business. That's most likely where they're holding Sophia. So… we're going to hit those bastards with everything we got."

"Hooyah!" the team shouted.

"Also, I picked up a new member of the team," Wallace continued. "You've all heard Sophia mention him on a few occasions. Her former partner. Retired FBI Agent Fred Jones. If you remember, they started the Amell case together. He's the one who suggested talking to Tarik and another AIA member in Guantanamo. In fact, they are putting together the mission right now to get her. So, let's get ready. Get some shuteye for a bit. We need to be ready to roll out once the mission is green-lit."

"Possible daylight mission again, Chief?" Johns asked.

"Time is of the essence on this one, boys. We're not going to leave her in Hasan's sadistic hands any longer than we need to."

****

Sophia shook awake at a stabbing pain in her hand as a rush of life refilled her body. Gulping in a breath of air, heart pounding in her chest, she surveyed the dimly lit room. Only to find herself back in her cell, surrounded by the four mud-brick walls and dingy concrete floor. She was sitting on the dirty, crusted mattress from the day before, with a small bucket and a pile of blood-stained cloths beside the bedding.

A fresh cloth tangled from her left hand, which was wet and not from blood. Someone had tried to dress the wound. There was also a crude makeshift splint wrapped around her broken right pinky.

Sophia's eyes scanned the room, double-taking at a dark mass huddled in the far corner. It was Jessica. She was curled up in the fetal position, quivering, holding the side of her face, trembling. She had a small cloth in her hand.

As her adrenaline subsided, Sophia felt the throbbing pain in her hand flood back, her head ached from Farid's blow, and her knees wobbled as she climbed to her feet. She tried to call out to the woman, but her mouth was dry. The words that had managed to escape were inaudible. Sophia swallowed, wetting the inside of her mouth as best she could.

"Jess, why are you in the corner?" Her foot knocked into the bucket, and a few sloshes of water spilled out. Making it evident that it was Jessica who had been treating her. And when she awoke too violently, she must've startled and hit the poor woman. "Oh, my goodness, did I hit you?" Sophia asked. The woman nodded. "I am sorry, I didn't mean to." She sat back down. "Come on back, it's ok." Sophia patted the mattress beside her. Jessica slowly stood, taking a tentative step forward. "Come." Sophia tried to signal for her to come over, wincing as she instinctively used the hand that Hasan had stabbed.

The wince jump-started Jessica's natural urges as a doctor, spurring her into action. She rushed over and immediately began retreating the wound.

"It's ok; I was just startled, that's all," she said, dipping the cloth into the water and wiping the entry and exit holes. "What did he do to you?"

"He stabbed me with a scalpel, ow." Sophia flinched as Jessica applied a little pressure to the wound.

"I am sorry, I've just got to make sure to get the inside cleaned out as much as possible. Or it's going to get infected. And you don't want to lose your hand. Do you?"

"No, I don't suppose I dooo." Baring her teeth, she tensed at another sweeping wave of pain.

"What else did he do?" Jessica questioned. "I only see this small wound, but-"

"That's all he did to me. Why?"

Jessica's head panned to the pile of cloth that was streaked red. "That's a lot of blood from just this one wound, and it was all over your face and clothes when they dropped you back in here."

"Well," Sophia paused, thinking about the best way to phrase what actually happened.

"Have you seen Trevor?" Jessica cut in before Sophia could answer her first question. "They came in and took him shortly after they took you. Did you see him? I can sometimes hear them torture him. But I haven't heard anything. Did they take him to another room? Did you hear him? Where is my Trevor?"

The woman fired off the questions in a dizzying rapid-fire sequence; Sophia had no idea where to start answering or if she even should. It was clear that Jessica's mental state was on the cusp of fracturing. If she told her that her fiancé was just beheaded, it could send her over the edge.

"Well, um…" Without knowing it, she had already subconsciously given away the answer by glancing at the blood-soaked pile.

"No, no, no." Jessica began shaking her head uncontrollably. "No, no." Tears streamed down her face as she quickly retreated to her corner. "This… this can't be. No, no, he's not dead."

Sophia rushed to the corner to comfort the fragile woman. "Jessica, I am… I am so, so sorry," Sophia said, embracing her. "I can't imagine what you're feeling right now." Jessica buried her face into Sophia's shoulder, sobbing, repeating 'No' over and over. Sophia held her tightly as the woman wept.

"We're going to die in here or be sold off as a sex slave. Oh My God!" she screamed in Sophia's ear, nearly rupturing her eardrum. "We're going to die; I should just die. Without Trevor, there's no use."

"Jessica," Sophia yelled, pulling the other woman away from her shoulder and locking eyes on her. "We. Are. Not going to die here. I promise. Someone's going to rescue us." Despite everything, she still believed that Ryan or Wallace would be busting in at any moment. They had to.

"How… how… how do you know?" Jessica squeaked out between sobs. "We… we thought the same, and now look— Trevor's dead." Jessica's voice cracked, and her lip quivered at his name.

"I can't tell you how I know, but I just do. Someone's coming for us. We need to stay alive and stay together."

"I… I can't." She buried her face back into Sophia's shoulder.

"Your dad was a Marine, right? Mine was Army; I am an Army brat," Sophia stated, not knowing what else to do. She knew that she needed to get Jessica out of her head.

"Yeah," she murmured, still sobbing. Jessica pulled away, propping herself up against the corner.

"Cool. So, you know what it's like having to keep moving and living all over. I think I went to like eight different schools growing up. It always sucked having to leave friends behind and try to make new ones."

"Yeah," she gulped, swallowing her tears. "It was the pits." Jessica wiped her face, stemming the tide of tears. "It was probably easy for you, though. You're so pretty." She caressed the side of Sophia's face.

"Thank you. Speaking from experience, I see. You must've been a stunner, as well, from the photos of you in the papers. You were pretty hot, too."

Jessica finally cracked a half smile. "No, I was an ugly duckling, but I hit a glow-up in college."

"To be a doctor like your mother, right?"

"Yeah, how do you know what my parents did?"

"Your… situation was all over the news when you were taken. Newspaper articles, newscasts." Sophia didn't want to admit how much she knew about her because most of it came from CIA reports that are much more detailed than what journalists push out.

"How did my parents take it?" the woman asked. "We were so close. Gosh, I miss them."

"They're heartbroken. They were on the news, pleading for any information. They filed petitions with the government to launch searches. They did this many times, even raiding some places they thought you were. But I suspect you'd already been sold off to Hasan's people."

"Yeah, it wasn't long before we were moved. They kept moving us from one location to the next—sometimes two or three in a day. The longest stay we had was in Darfur when I got violently ill from a parasite. Trevor…" Her face sank at the mention of his name, recalling the moment. "Risked his life the first time to make sure I got the medicine I needed. I am going to miss him."

"I know." Sophia hugged her counterpart again.

"Wait." Hope struck Jessica. "What about you? I know you said your parents were gone, but what about the film company you're working for? Shouldn't they be sending people out to find you? That's how we're going to get rescued, right?"

Sophia could see the twinkle of hope in her eyes. "You're right; the production company I am working for by now knows I've been taken. They are undoubtedly pleading with the military unit I was embedded with to send out search missions. We're not too far from where I was abducted. We're going to get out of this."

"Sophia," Jessica said, looking up at the Agent.

"Yes."

"Please make sure that nothing happens to me. I don't want to die. I really, really don't want to. But if I do, can you tell my parents that I loved them?"

"I will. But you're not going to die. You're going to see them again. I *won't* let anything happen. I will do anything in my power to make sure you get home safe. *Nothing* will happen to you."

The two women continued to embrace each other, uncertain of what the future would bring. Though, whatever it was, they'd face it together.

CHAPTER SIXTEEN
THUMRAIT AIRBASE, OMAN

A heavy wrapping on the door to the bungalow alerted the occupants that someone was outside. "Tex, check to see who it is," Wallace ordered.

The burly Texan was in the bunk closest to the door and let out a sigh before getting up to open it. A fresh-faced Airman was standing on the other side. "Can we help you?" he asked the awestruck young man. He'd never seen Navy SEALS up close and in person. He'd considered them the rock stars of the military.

"Um… um, is Master Chief Wallace here?"

"Tex, move," Wallace barked, coming to the door. "What is it Airman?"

"You're wanted in the operations room. A Fred Jones is asking-"

"Perfect, give me a minute." Wallace closed the door and retreated to his bunk. "Maybe we've got a mission go." It'd been several hours since his last communication. The whole team had been waiting anxiously for the green light on the mission to rescue Sophia. Tex, for one, was especially eager to get back out there and avenge his perceived failure for allowing her to be taken.

"Should we all go?" Ryan asked, standing and grabbing his fatigue top.

"No, stay put," Wallace said, waving him off. "If it's a go, I'll send for them to get you all."

Wallace opened the door, pounding down the steps. "Let's go, Airman," he told the young man. The Airman led Wallace to a waiting pickup truck. They clambered inside and sped off towards the main building.

Several minutes later, Wallace was escorted to a small room in the operation building. An image of Fred along with Mila was displayed on a large wall monitor. The two were exchanging muted words when Mila noticed Wallace on their monitor. Fred turned around, pressing a button, unmuting the pair. "Wallace, good news," Fred addressed the commando happily. "The brass green-lit the op."

"Bout fucking time. These animals have had her long enough," Wallace replied with measured glee. He'd always been a man of doing over talking. The one thing he hated most about the military was having to wait around for a bunch of pencil pushers to analyze the situation and deliberate on whether or not operation success was most likely, especially in a situation like this one where an American life hung in the balance. A life he cared for.

"Get your team ready, and head to the copter," said Fred, happy to see the man who was entrusted with bringing Sophia home was rearing to go. "You're going to chopper in and be dropped off just outside the village of Al-Hutah. From there, we'll guide you into the location where we believe Sophia's being held."

In the proceeding hours since they last spoke. Fred and Mila had been diligently working on pulling up as much information as possible on their target via satellite imagery and video surveillance.

"Great, hear from you again when we're in the air. Wallace out." He turned to the Airman. "Go pick up my team."

Thirty minutes later, two vehicles pulled up on the tarmac, and two Sikorsky UH-60 Black Hawk helicopters started to spin up their rotors. Wallace's team disgorged from the SUVs in full combat gear, approaching their waiting commander.

Ryan had Wallace's gear in his hand while Tex handed Wallace his rifle. Wallace quickly donned his vest and other various equipment.

"Daylight mission again," Walsh quipped, passing Wallace boarding the chopper. "That's rarely ever a good thing."

"I'll go anytime, anywhere, if it gets Sophia back. So, let's fucking rock," Tex shouted over the increasing windstorm overhead as the blades began to pick up speed. The Texan angled toward the second chopper, still crowing, pounding his chest, shouting into the sky, psyching himself up. Walsh headed toward his Chalk, shaking his head and the Texan's pre-mission ritual. Ryan, Ty, and Gut joined him, boarding Chalk Two. Wallace waited for Alwani and Johns to board the second chopper, Chalk One. With the team loaded, the helicopters lifted off to make the hour-long flight to the target village.

****

Sophia heard the rustling of keys at the door again. She and Jessica had fallen asleep in each other's arms during the night. She nudged Jessica awake. "They're coming back," she whispered.

"Wha… what?" Jessica groggily replied as the door began to creak open. "What do they want from you?"

"They think I have information that I don't," Sophia replied.

Jessica sat up, gripping Sophia tighter and squeezing the agent. Her eyes darted around the room, first to the door, then to Sophia. "They can't take you. I won't allow it. I am not going to be left alone," she whispered, panic filling her eyes and voice.

Sophia pushed the woman off her. "It's ok. I don't have what he wants."

"Then he's going to kill you. Just… just like Trevor." Tears began creeping back into the corners of her eyes. She lunged, grabbing a hold again.

"He's not. At least not yet." Sophia tried to reassure Jessica, pulling her away again. The door opened, and Farid's large silhouette appeared in the frame. Shafts of light shot into the room around him. The other two men who usually accompanied him rushed inside, pulling Sophia to her feet. "It's ok, Jess, it'll be ok," she cried out as the two men pulled her to her feet. Jessica had latched on to her leg with a death grip. "Don't make a fuss," Sophia warned.

"No, you can't take her," Jessica wailed, clutching tightly to Sophia's leg. The two men struggled to drag Sophia away while Jessica clung to her leg. The brunette used her weight to anchor Sophia to the ground.

Farid barged into the room, stomping toward Jessica. "Jess, let go. Don't make it worse. I'll be fine." Catching the brute from the corner of her eye. "No, don't, don't harm her," Sophia pleaded as Farid wrapped his arms around Jessica. "Stop, don't." Farid paused, tentative to rip the two women apart. "Jess, let go, or he's going to hurt you," Sophia pleaded silently with the woman.

With hesitation, Jessica finally reluctantly released her grip on Sophia's leg before Farid forcibly removed her. "Remember what you promised." The two men continued to hustle Sophia from the room. Farid, holding her back. "Remember what you promised," Jessica called out. "Remember." Her screams dissolved into a cry as they dragged the blonde from the room.

Sophia hooked a hand on the doorway, pulling herself back into the room. "I do, and we'll get out of this."

The two men ripped her away from the room and dragged her back to the interrogation room. They marched her to a chair, pushing her down into the seat. This time, instead of the chains dangling from the ceiling, another chair was set up across the room. The concrete was still soaked with Trevor's blood, as was the stool they used to behead the American doctor.

Hasan was waiting inside, seated on a stool by the table adorned with all of the same torture devices from her previous two trips. The two men quickly tied Sophia's forearms and legs to the chair and backed away, taking up positions by the door.

The terrorist leader had taken several long drags from the cigarette he was smoking while they secured her to the chair. Once they'd finished, he dropped the cigarette to the ground, stamping it out with his shoe like he was squashing a bug.

He stood, then lapped around the room a couple of times, not saying a word. Sophia tensed each time he passed behind her. She could feel his eyes staring at her, sizing her up.

He circled a fourth time, reappearing in her right peripheral. He leaned in and took a drawn-out whiff of her. His nostrils flared as he inhaled deeply. His eyes rolled into the back of his head. He was like a dog getting a scent. "You're either a very brave woman or a very well-trained spy. I hardly smell a hint of fear." Which was ironic, but that was almost entirely what she felt with her captor breathing down on her neck. "But, all infidels break. You all have that line because you are not true believers. I will find your line."

He caressed her hair, taking another whiff. Sophia jerked away. "I don't have a line because I can't tell you what I don't know. I don't know this… this Stone guy."

Hasan whirled, delivering a back-handed smack across her face. Sophia's head jerked at the blow. She could feel a metallic liquid taste in her mouth. She spat a wad of blood. He'd smacked her so hard she bit the inside of her raw cheek for the second time. Swallowing some of the blood, she spat out another glob. "It doesn't matter how hard you hit me. I don't know what you want."

"We'll see." Hasan strode back to the bench. This time, not reaching for anything on top but instead for something on the bottom shelf. A battery charger. Sophia only now realized that the chair she was seated in was entirely metal. "I am thinking we'll shock the secrets out of you."

Sophia gulped as he dragged the battery over to her chair, unable to move. He fashioned the positive and negative cables to the legs of the chair while sardonically watching her every expression. Revealing in the thought of how much pain can he cause. How much could the woman endure before divulging what he wanted? Stone's location.

****

"You're getting close to the insertion point." Fred's voice crackled over Wallace's headset. "The pilot is going to drop you just outside of a tree line to the wooded area that borders the village."

Wallace leaned his head outside the chopper's open door; a harsh rush of wind smacked him in the face as he peered out. Through the goggles he was wearing, he could see the outline of a small tree-scape in the distance. The green canopy stuck out in stark contrast to the open desert lands broken up by the occasional rocky features of the desolate region. "Copy that," Wallace answered, pulling his head back in. He turned to the other members of his Chalk. "Get ready, boys, we're about to drop lines."

Moments later, the two helicopters slowed, coming to a hover eighty feet above the ground. The co-pilot gave a thumbs up to the doorman, who quickly fastened a rope to the end of a metal rail that was affixed to a tract inside the chopper. Once the rope was secured, he slid the rail outside. The line followed, uncoiling to the ground. Which was followed by another thumbs up to Wallace, who signaled back. Afterward, the Master Chief leaned out the door, gripping the dangling line in his gloved hands, and pushed out.

Wallace slid down the line, and in seconds, his boots hit the hard rocky ground with a thud, rocks crunching under his feet. Chucking the line aside, he moved ten feet from the rope, unslinging his M4, dropping to a kneeling defensive position, scanning the tree line for any movement. While they were still a bit from the village, the noise from the choppers could draw in anyone who was out for a stroll. Johns quickly joined him. Wallace looked across the open expanse to see that most of Ryan's chalk had already touched the ground while both Alwani and Walsh came into view on his left side.

In a roar and rush of wind that beat down on the team, the two Black hawks quickly ascended, banking hard peeling off to the right, and thundered off to their preordained staging point to await exfil orders.

In moments, the howling thumping of the chopper's rotators disappeared in the distance. An eerie silence fell back over the desert. Nothing but the wind and the dancing heat haze moved. Satisfied that no day strollers had come to see the spectacle caused by the Black Hawks, Wallace signaled for the team to move.

Both teams met up in the tree line. "Bravo, team all here," Ryan sounded off.

Wallace nodded, "TOC, this is Alpha-one; all units on the ground Oscar Mike to target location." He checked his watch. Calculating in his head how long it'd take the team to traverse the small woodland. "Be on target in thirty mikes. Alpha-one over."

"Alpha-one, TOC has a good copy, and we have you on ISR. Establish comms again when you reach the target. TOC out." Fred turned to Mila, who was sitting behind a computer at a desk to his left. Richard to his right. Both Jerry and Gabby were in the back of the room. The embassy had several covert operations rooms tucked away down on the lower levels of the compound. The

Ambassadors team had been letting the group work out of one of them. "It feels weird being on this side," he commented.

"How so?" The German woman asked.

"I am usually the one in the field for these."

Mila smiled, "Sometimes it's just as hard to be on this side too, though." Her grin faded. "Especially when things go wrong."

"Well, let's hope they don't." Fred turned his attention back to the wall monitor—the eight dots on the screen were rapidly moving toward the village.

It took Wallace's team less than twenty-five minutes to get into position, clearing the forested area quickly. They were spurred on, no doubt, by their pending reunion with Sophia. The Master Chief peered through a set of binoculars. The village appeared very nondescript, especially for one that housed terrorists and sex traffickers.

It was laid out almost in a city block configuration. One main paved road stretched through the village, coming off the highway. Several other dirt track offshoots leaked out away from the main street—some snaking for a distance to structures dotted around the village. The main road dead-ended into a cold-a-sack with several multi-story buildings forming a semi-circle at the village's end.

While watching, he could see several terrorists roving the perimeter of the village, though, indicating at least they were in the right spot. He pressed his mike, "Alpha-one to TOC, in position."

"TOC copies, there is a building located near the center of the village, off to the far right, down a dirt road. It has a black flag flying above it. There's been a lot of activity in and out and several deep track marks leading from it. That's where we believe she's being held."

Wallace scanned the horizon, spotting the mast with the flag. It was the AIA flag. Definitely, they were in the right location. "I see the flag," he reported. "Alpha team on the move." He turned to his men. "Let's get our girl back, boys."

A muted Hooyah echoed through the group. They began to descend the small incline from the woodland down toward the village in a wedge formation. Alwani at point.

****

Hasan backed away from the chair after connecting the positive line to the leg. With a sadistic grin on his face, he said, "We'll see if you are telling the truth." He snapped his fingers.

One of the escorts came around to face her. He was holding a bucket, drops of water falling out as he walked. Sophia shook her head. "No, no, you don't have to-." The man chucked the contents of the bucket at her, dosing the American. Streams of water cascaded down her body, the hair on her skin prickled, and tiny goosebumps sprang up all over her body. The water was ice cold. She gulped down what had splashed into her mouth, shaking her head, throwing droplets from the ends of her hair. "Do this," she finished. "I can't tell you what I don't know. I don't know this Stone character. I am a filmmaker!" she shouted the last part angrily, jerking in the chair and slamming her feet like a child.

"And I don't believe you. You work for the CIA, and you've been following me for months now," Hasan said, standing in front of the battery charger. "You will tell me what I want to know." He turned a nob on the charger's face, setting the voltage. "Or-"

Hasan threw the power switch on. A sharp jolt of electricity surged through Sophia's body. Sending her into a spasm, twitching, teeth clenched so tight, she thought they were going to shatter in her mouth. However, the voltage was just high enough only to cause intense pain. Her muscles contracted involuntarily. It felt as if her every nerve ending was on fire, but Hasan had expertly set the current to a level that ensured it wouldn't cause lasting harm, only excruciating agony. He needed her alive to tell what she knew.

He watched with a calculating, cold smile as Sophia writhed and convulsed in pain for a few seconds before powering the charger down. "Where is Stone and West?" he questioned again.

Sophia panted heavily, trying to catch her breath, her head bobbing up and down. Before she could answer, she had to let her nerves and muscles settle. Rotating her jaw to loosen it up. "I…

don't know who that is."

"Lie!" he shouted, flicking the button again, sending another charged current that hit the chair. Again, Sophia's body erupted into a series of involuntary muscle contractions. She shook in the chair, feeling the tingling sensation envelop her body.

****

Wallace signaled for Ryan to take Fire Team 2 and swing around the north side of the cold-a-sac while his team pressed forward. Checking the outskirts of the village for any movement. They didn't have an estimate of how many enemy combatants the village held. They were practically going in blind with very little reconnaissance, none of which mattered. All the team cared about was getting Sophia back.

Fred and Mila watched via the overhead drone as the SEAL team split into two groups. "Are these guys as good as Sophia brags?" the former agent questioned.

"Aside from losing Sophia. Which, by the way, was an impossible situation," she quickly added. "They're the best."

"I know that was impossible. I read the AARs and watched the footage. I think if it were any other team, there'd have been several body bags." Movement on the screen caught Fred's eye. "Alpha-one, two tangos are about to swing into view."

"Copy," Wallace replied. Seconds later, two AIA soldiers rounded a corner coming out of the cold-a-sac on a roving patrol. "Al."

The point man raised his silenced rifle and fired two shots. *Pfft, pfft*. Both bodies dropped. The squad picked up the pace, breaking into a light jog, reaching the same corner the two dead men had just come around. Wallace peeked around the corner, locking eyes with Ryan, who was doing the same on the far side.

Alwani and Johns dragged the two corpses further back, finding scrubs to put over them, but it was a meager cover. Anyone who was actually looking would spot the bodies, but if they were just doing a sweep, they may miss them.

"We see six, no, seven roving guards. There is no telling how many are in the buildings. Move with caution," Fred warned.

"Copy. Alpha-one out." Wallace checked his six. Alwani and Johns had rejoined him and Walsh. "Alpha, move out." He gave the hand signal, and both groups started toward the target building. Ryan's Fire Team 2 was on the north side of the road, with Wallace's Fire Team 1 on the South side.

They continued to move up the street, checking each building as they passed by. Most of the structures on the east side of the village were empty and had been so for a bit, judging by their overall look and emptiness when they peered inside. The whole town gave the feeling of a dying mall—tons of unoccupied shops, all closed up and collecting dust.

Judging by the amount of AIA soldiers, this wasn't actually a village anymore being used as a settlement. But more so, a way station for prisoners as they came through to be sold, the way Tarik had described it.

"Alpha-two, guard coming in view on your eleven between the buildings," Fred blurted into the radio.

Gutierrez, who was running point for Ryan's team, swiveled his rifle to his eleven, catching Alwani, Wallace's point man, on the opposite side in his field of view. Wallace's team had stopped, taking a defensive position. The SEAL waited. Then, a man in a thawb holding an AK appeared in the cut between two buildings. The two men sized each other for a second before Gutierrez squeezed his trigger. The man hit the ground dead before he could react. Both groups resumed movement.

"Oh scheisse," Mila gasped.

"What?" Fred whirled on Mila. "What is that German for shit, right?" Concern filled Fred's voice. Anytime someone started cursing on an op, it was never a good thing in his experience.

Mila clacked a few keys on her keyboard, shooting the image that she was looking at to the larger monitor. She'd been monitoring the broader area for any potential exterior threats. There were two pickup trucks full of what appeared to be enemy combatants headed for the village. "I think our boys are about to have company," she exclaimed.

Fred hit the mike. "Alpha-one, you have two truckloads of

tangos headed your way. They are about ten mikes out. Get a move on it."

"Good copy, you heard him, team. Double time it."

CHAPTER SEVENTEEN

HASAN continued to watch Sophia writhe in pain and agony with a malevolent glare behind his eyes, almost burning the image into his brain to recall later for his pleasure when the door opened, and Farid entered.

The torturer powered down the charger, giving Sophia respite from the pain. Farid strode past her with barely a glance to whisper something in Hasan's ear. Sophia managed to lift her head in time to see a new expression take hold of the Arab's face. Whatever his man had just told him seemed to displease the AIA leader. He responded to the information with a whisper of his own.

"Trouble in paradise," Sophia panted. Her breathing was heavy and labored. She'd endured several rounds of shock, her body fatiguing further with each flip of the switch. "Or do you have dinner plans? Wife's anniversary." In her head, she knew it was probably not a good idea to antagonize her torturer, but she couldn't help herself.

"I've heard America is the land of comedians," Hasan responded, giving Farid his leave. The brute exited shortly after. "You see, I am somewhat of a comedian myself."

"Yeah, tell me a joke," Sophia wheezed.

"What do you call a stupid infidel woman that comes to Yemen in search of a freedom fighter?"

"Looking to date below her class."

"Fried chicken," Hasan snapped back with a laugh before flipping the charger switch, sending another surge of pain through Sophia's body.

****

Both teams bounded up the street, sweeping past the houses lining the dirt road. A man stepped out of one of the houses as Ryan's team passed by. He was startled to see a full group of US military men sprint past him. They were clearly on their way to something important. He snatched his AK and opened fire.

Several rounds rocketed past the four SEALs. The crackle of

air as one of the rounds shot past Tex's head alerted him to the danger. He swung around and opened fire on their attacker. The man fell, crumpling into the road.

The sound of the burst of fire echoed through the village. Anyone who was there would now be alerted to their presence. In seconds, they'd have the village occupants bearing down on them. "Move," Wallace yelled. They broke back in a double time, racing for the target building.

Two more AIA appeared from another house to investigate the gunfire, only to be cut down by a volley from Alwani.

"Gun!" Tex shouted, seeing a barrel protrude from a house that Wallace's team was fast approaching. He let out a fusillade. The rounds impacted through an open window. A burst of red splattered the blowing curtain.

"Cross, cross," Wallace directed Alwani—the Arab angled right to cross the road. A small group of AIA appeared, and several structures were up. Ryan and Johns spread out, opening fire on the group, instantly felling three of the men. The survivors scurried into whatever cover they could find.

The suppressing fire allowed Wallace's team to make it safely across. "Alpha-one, to TOC, how far," Wallace radioed. His team spread out, covering the street in a wide field of fire. Anyone popping out would be spotted and gunned down.

Fred checked their position and traced it to the target. "Four houses up, turn down the path going north, and you should see the structure fifty yards up the road. Follow the tracks."

"Copy, Oscar Mike." The group of SEALs advanced up the road.

One of the gunmen popped out from his cover. Walsh blew the top of his head off, spraying the wall behind him with red splatter.

****

Hasan powered down the device with a look of near admiration toward the American. How had she managed to take five rounds of electrocution and still be conscious?

Although she was still hardly alert at this point, her head lolled side to side between shocks. Her breathing had become more labored with each flick of the switch. A line of drool trickled down from her mouth, pooling on her abaya. Hasan stood before her, cupping her chin in his hand and raising her head to meet his. "You are very strong. I see that." He took out a knife and began cutting loose her restraints. One of the guards moved to the back of the room, dragging another chair across the floor and placing it a few feet across from Sophia's.

Hasan finished cutting the bonds, scooping her out of the chair, dragging her to the new one, and dropping the beleaguered woman down in it. He snapped his fingers. The other man by the door opened it, calling down the hall. "We'll see how strong your new friend is. Maybe you told her something."

Sophia fought to raise her head. "You leave Jess out of this. She knows nothing," the American replied between pants. Faint crackles of automatic gunfire entered the room from the open door. They hit Sophia's ears, causing her to perk up. *Could that be Wallace?* she thought. They were faint but present. Then, something else overpowered the muffled gunfire. Screams. Summing her strength. "Don't you do this, you fucking monster!" Farid appeared, dragging Jessica with him. She was kicking and screaming, but all fighting ceased when she saw Sophia sitting in the chair.

"I am not. You are." Hasan gestured for Farid to place Jessica in the electric chair. "You tell me what I want to know, and she doesn't have to suffer like you just did." Farid forced the other woman down into the chair. The gunfire outside increased in intensity only briefly. Then the smattering disappeared as the door slammed again. Hasan circled back to the charger. "I ask again. Where is Stone hiding?"

Sophia and Jessica's eyes met—the two sharing an almost telepathic communication. Jessica's face pleaded silently to Sophia. All Sophia could return was an empathetic *sorry* before turning to Hasan. Opening her mouth, seemingly on the verge of saying something she didn't want. "I'll tell you…I don't know who that is. I'd tell you if I did."

Hasan shrugged, "Suit yourself," he said, flipping the switch.

Jessica tensed and convulsed, shaking in the chair as the hum of an electrical current pierced the air.

"Stop, stop, I don't know anything." Sophia willed herself to her feet, about to rush at the Arab, when a hand snatched her back, forcing her back into the chair. "Stop!" she screamed, heart thudding in her chest, watching Jessica writhe in the chair she'd just been sitting in.

****

The SEALs fought their way down the street, taking potshots from all directions. AIA members leaped into the road to take a quick shot before darting back into cover.

"These fuckers are like stormtroopers, man," Ty quipped, sights fixated on a spot he'd seen a man pop out of several times, unloading a single burst when he sprang up for what would be his last time.

"Be thankful that they can't hit shit," Tex countered. "Would be a shame to get your nuts blown off."

"Alwani, left turn," Wallace ordered. The Arab point man rounded the corner of a building. A dirt track cut between it and another, forming an alley. It was the path Fred said they needed to take. The sound of an engine entered the area.

"Technical," shouted Gutierrez.

One of the forewarned pickup trucks came rocketing up the street, barreling down on their position. "Johns, blast it," Wallace commanded.

The SEAL plucked a 40mm grenade from his vest, then slid open the breach of the M203 attached to the bottom of his rifle. Sliding the round down inside the tube, he slammed the breach shut with a *chink*. He then proceeded to drop to a knee. He peered down the gun's sights, picking up the moving vehicle. He then adjusted his aim, arching the rifle slightly. He squeezed.

With a *thump,* the grenade launched from its tube in an arch, reaching its apex before tumbling back to earth.

The 40mm round landed in the bed of the truck in a fiery explosion, ejecting its burning occupants into the air in every direction as the truck performed a backward somersault, crumpling to the ground. The burning wreckage was now blocking the main road into the village. "Technical down," Johns pronounced.

"Good job," Wallace congratulated, patting the Johns on the shoulder before cutting up the path toward the structure. It let out into a bowl. Steep rocky hills protected the three remaining sides. Aside from the driveway, there were no other ways in or out once inside. "Johns, Ryan, Alwani, Gut, hold position here and cover of our exfil. Tex, Walsh, and Ty on me."

Everyone responded with an affirmative. Wallace's team pounded up the path toward the building, leaving Ryan's to cover the entrance.

****

Hasan powered down the charger, and a flash of anger swept over his face. "Enough, this isn't working," he roared angrily, fiddling with the dial. "Maybe I need more incentive. Farid?"

The big Arab marched over, hoisting the groggy Jessica out of the chair and slinging her over his back like a sack of potatoes. One of the escorts recoiled into one of the recesses of the room, bringing out the stool they'd beheaded Trevor over the day prior. Sophia watched in horror as Farid slumped the semiconscious woman over it. The other man sat on the ground and took hold of her arms, pulling them out in front, preventing her from being able to move.

"Don't do this. Please don't do this. She knows nothing. She's not even a part of this. Just *fucking* sell her off already. Take my life." Sophia fought feebly against the man who was pinning her down to the chair. A wave of fear washed over her as she watched the two men position Jessica like she was a sacrifice. Hasan retrieved the Saif sword, still covered in Trevor's now-dried blood.

Sophia tried to turn her head away from the scene, only for it to be forcefully jerked back into place by her guard. In the silence of the room, though, the once faint crackles of gunfire were now increasingly louder. Once distant snaps, they'd grown to louder cracks like they were just outside the building.

Hope entered Sophia's mind. But would they get to her in time?

Hasan handed the Saif to Farid, who happily received it like a gift from Allah, and then rounded on Sophia. "I ask again, where is Stone hiding? Before you answer, do you value this woman's life?" Sophia nodded. "Then, for her sake, I hope you'll answer truthfully." An explosion outside caused the four Arab occupants of the room to pause. Hasan rounded on the door, viewing it with a sneer. Dust cascaded down from above.

The blast changed the expression on Hasan's face for a moment. Uncertainty flashed.

There was a loud banging outside, like a door being thrown open, accompanied by several shouts.

Hasan whipped around back to Sophia. "Where is Stone?" he shouted. For a millisecond, Sophia detected fear in his voice. She hesitated to answer. *Could she stall? Was Wallace coming to rescue her?* If so, it wouldn't matter if she gave up anything. "Where is Stone?" the Arab reiterated louder. "I ask one last time," he snapped, and Farid raised the blade. Jessica's eyes snapped open. She tried to move but was trapped.

"Sophia, what's going on? Why is this guy holding my arms and looking at me like that?" The man holding her outstretched arms had a look of bloodthirsty expectation, eyes gleaming with anticipation of the imminent violence. "Help me, please. Please," she begged, squirming uselessly against the man's pull.

****

Wallace readied himself just outside the front door to the structure, Walsh stacked behind him, offset to the right side of the door. Tex and Tyus were across stacked on the left side. The two parties regarded each other. The Master Chief held up three fingers. The group acknowledged they were going on a three-count.

Wallace dropped his ring finger. One. The quartet readied

themselves for what lay behind the door. Middle finger down two. They tensed. Index down… three.

Tex kicked the door open and rushed in. A man in a bright thawb sprinted from a room, yelling. Tex didn't care to understand what; he had an AK. The Texan fired a burst from his M4. A ragged line of bullets strafed across his chest. He hit the floor. Tex leapfrogged the downed man, rushing to the room where he had sprung from checking the interior. No one else inside.

Wallace flooded in behind Tex, followed by Ty and Walsh. "Moving," Wallace said, overtaking Tex as he secured the room. Another AIA flashed into the hallway, sprinting across, firing blindly. The rounds whipped past Wallace's head, impacting the wall, and causing him to jerk his head aside. Still, he managed to cut the shooter down before he could make it to the next room. "Split," the commander called out. He, along with Walsh, pressed against the wall on the right side of the hall. Tex and Tyus were pressed against the left side. They'd come to an intersection, a room on each side. "Go." The two teams sprang into the rooms on their respective sides.

Wallace whipped his rifle around the corner, bursting into the room. The loud chatter of an AK fired. The SEAL had spotted the crouching gunman a fraction of a second before he fired. The rounds blew half-dollar-sized holes in the mud brick behind him as he dove headfirst, letting off a three-round burst of his own— the wall behind the shooter splattered red.

"Chief, you good?" Walsh asked, entering and checking on the slumped corpse. "Here," he said, putting out a hand.

Wallace embraced it. Walsh pulled his Chief up. "All good." The two moved back to the doorway. "Secured," he called out to Tex, who flashed a thumbs up. "Sophia!" he called out.

****

The gunfire outside was so loud that Sophia felt it was now coming from inside the building. However, her hesitation to answer Hasan's question was still growing. *Could Wallace make it to her in time before the sadistic terrorist beheaded someone else in front of her?*

"Where is Stone?" he shouted impatiently, waving his hand. Farid raised his arms, lining the blade up with Jessica's neck.

"Tell him! Tell him, please, Sophia. Tell him what he wants. I don't wanna die. You *promised*." The terrified woman squirmed, trying to break free from her guard's hold. "Oh god, just tell him."

More gunfire outside. "Wallace!" Sophia shouted. "In here."

****

A woman's scream came from deeper inside the building. "Move, move, move," Wallace ordered; Tex took point. The SEALs moved down the hallways, gunning down several more AIA soldiers following the scream.

They rounded a corner, finding two men standing guard outside of a room. Tex gunned both of them down in an instant, rushing to the door—another bloodcurdling scream from inside.

****

"Stone, now!" Hasan demanded. More gunfire crackled outside. "Farid." The man grinned, eying his target—the back of Jessica's neck.

"NO!" Jessica wailed.

"Wallace!" Sophia screamed. "Here!"

Farid swung his arms downward, bearing down on Jessica.

Sophia's eyes bulged as Farid sliced downward. The metal sword glinted as it passed through a spar of light coming through a dingy window.

****

"We're here, Sophia," Tex shouted, rearing back his leg, unleashing a savage kick to the door and blowing it off its hinges. The blow was delivered with such force it unbalanced the Texan. Wallace rushed past him, sweeping his rifle side to side, finding a lone occupant, an Asian woman, bound and lying on the floor covered in wood debris, screaming.

No sign of Sophia.

****

"Wait, I'll tell you," Sophia screamed, closing her eyes, not wishing to see another decapitation.

"Where?" Hasan asked calmly. Sophia cracked her left eye open to see that the would-be executioner had managed to halt the blade inches from the woman's bare neck. "Where is he?"

Her eyes shifted from Jessica to Hasan; they were laced with defeat. "Truthfully, I don't know," Sophia divulged, her shoulders slumping, eyes lowering to the floor in both anger and self-disgust. The mere fact she'd broken, despite it being for a good reason—saving Jessica's life, still tugged at her heavy heart. She'd let the terrorist break her. However, she still clung to the hope that, at any moment, her team would be breaking through the door to save them. "I'd tell you if I knew," she admitted. "My team and I split; half going after Stone, with me and the other half coming here after you," Sophia continued. "I hope he's in custody and they got the job done, but I don't know."

The man, still holding Jessica's arms, let her go. Farid backed away, and the woman stood, dusting herself off. "I told you she'd crack if you applied the right pressure." Sophia snapped up, fixating her bloodshot eyes on the woman's life she'd just saved. Or did she? Jessica glided across the room under Sophia's intense glare, coming to rest by Hasan's side. A smile spread across their collective faces as they embraced each other.

"And by the way, they didn't," Hasan said, pleased with his deception. He'd said it so matter-of-factually that he couldn't be lying. "I've spoken to Stone recently. He escaped their attempt." Sophia cursed under her breath. They'd both failed. "In fact, you were part of that conversation. He seemed... angry and a little bit worried."

Sophia stared at the pair, who were still embracing each other. "I... I don't." She clenched her jaw, realizing she'd been duped. "My team's coming for me right now. I can hear them." It was all she could manage as a retort.

Hasan let out a boisterous laugh, pounding on the door. It swung open instantly. "You can tell them to stop," the Arab commanded. A chain of voice commands echoed down the hall. He returned, coming inches from Sophia's face. "They're not coming for you. You don't get it. You Americans think you're so smart," he chided, tapping the side of his head with his index finger. "This was all show. Your fellow infidels missed. They're currently in the wrong place," he said, gleaming, happy that his trick worked.

"And, as for you," Jessica cut in. "You'll die live for the world to see tomorrow on the internet. Since you don't have any useful information for my Hasan." A malevolent grin stretched across both of their faces as they backed away. "Oh, but don't worry, your friends won't live long enough to see it. Farid, remove this trash." She waved a dismissive hand, turning to Hasan and kissing him."

Farid hauled Sophia off the chair, dragging her back to her cell.

****

"Tex, get her," Wallace barked, his voice laced with suppressed rage. The urgency in his tone was palpable, a reflection of the dire situation they were in. He wanted to teleport back to Cuba and off Tarik for the lie. He'd sent them on a wild goose chase, wasting valuable time. "Let's go, Al point, Ty follow." He grabbed hold of the young woman after Tex cut her ties. "We're going to get you out of here," he said to the woman. Who could only nod. Too stunned to do anything else. "Just follow my men and listen to our orders, and I swear we'll get you home." Her head bobbed up and down like a bobblehead. Alwani and Tyus had already positioned themselves by the door, readying to go. Wallace took the woman's hand and put it on Tyus' left shoulder. "You stay connected to my guy, ok? Tex in line behind; I'll bring up the six. Let's move."

The quintet filed out of the room; Wallace stopped as something caught his eye. A belt. Not just any belt, but a military-issued belt hidden in the corner of the room. Could it be Sophia's? The discovery sent a shiver down his spine, adding to the already tense atmosphere. He rushed back in, grabbing it and slinging it around his body. Perhaps Tarik hadn't lied. There was a woman, and it appeared Sophia may have been there previously. However, Sophia had clearly been moved already. But to where? They'd need answers later, but first, they needed to get out of Al-Hutah while they still could.

"Chief, you coming?" Tex yelled back.

"Roger Oscar Mike."

The team swept back through the house. The AIA that formerly inhabited the building was no longer alive to pose a threat.

"Fred," Mila warned, back in the OPS room in Rabat. Several more vehicles appeared on the satellite feed. Three pickup trucks filled with enemy combatants were descending upon the village. "They need to get out."

"TOC to Alpha-one, you need to exfil immediately. Status?" A long silence. It'd been several minutes since he'd seen the four men enter the building on ISR. "Alpha-one, I need a status. You have multiple technicals baring down on your location." Still radio silence. Then, five dots exited from the building. The group whooped in excitement, their relief palpable, seeing the fifth dot.

However, that excitement would be dashed as Wallace's voice crackled on the radio. "Alpha-one to TOC, we have no joy. We are ex-filing with one hostage, but it's not zero." Sophia's code name when in the field. "I repeat, we do *not* have zero."

A somber hush fell over the room. Gabby let out an exasperated gasp before falling back into her seat, burying her head into her hands. Jerry sat quietly, turning his attention back to his monitor. Richard and Mila embraced each other silently, not wanting to think the unthinkable.

For Fred, the transmission came through like a punch to the gut. His knees wobbled. He stumbled backward like a newborn calf trying to walk for the first time. His heart dropped. He clawed at a nearby desk to steady himself before falling into the chair behind it. They were wrong. *He* was wrong. Where was Sophia?

Was she even still alive?

"TOC to Alpha-one, proceed to exfil," Mila radioed, voice flat, business-like. Taking over for Fred, seeing the thousand-yard stare of defeat on his face. "You have more incoming technicals inbound in five mikes. I'd suggest not being there when they get there."

"Copy TOC. Alpha-one out until we're aboard the exfil choppers," was Wallace's last communique. She watched as the SEALs slink back into the woodlands, moving away from Al-Huatah.

What was their next move? How were they going to find Sophia now? They'd taken their best shot and come up empty. Fred was stuck. He didn't know what to do next.

CHAPTER EIGHTEEN

WEST barged into Stone's new office in the villa they'd taken refuge in, with Briggs in tow. Both men wore triumphant grins as they marched to the head of a desk centered in the middle of the expansive room. Stone peered over the top of his computer screen from behind bespectacled eyes, waiting for one of the two arrivals to speak. "We've found where that piece of shit haji is hiding out," West crowed finally. "He went back home to that shit hole village called Mudhainab. He's got some compound on the outskirts of the podunk place. My men are preparing an assault as we speak." West stood at parade rest, no doubt expectantly awaiting approval from Stone. He'd been itching to get back out in the field since he'd been forced to retreat back in Tangier.

Stone lowered the top of his laptop screen, eying both men with a disapproving glare. Their grins vanished as he sat blankly staring at them. "I didn't tell you to organize an assault now, did I?" Stone huffed, releasing an irritated sigh. "I'd merely asked you to find him."

"Excuse me, sir, but if we're not going to attack, then what?" Briggs asked, confused. They'd been in a holding pattern for several days now.

"There is a larger plan here at work, son," the old Oklahoman practically hissed the words condescendingly.

"And, what prey tell might that be?" West inserted scathingly, stepping closer. Until now, he'd been involved in every plan, step-by-step. Now, it appeared that Stone wasn't telling him everything. Despite all he'd done for the old man.

"That is-" A phone rang. All three men stopped chattering and looked at each other. Briggs grasped for his pocket, checking his cell phone. The noise wasn't coming from his. The screen was still black. West and Stone had also checked theirs. All three were inert. Yet the ringing continued. A flash of acknowledgment flared across Stone's face. "You're dismissed," said Stone abruptly with a dismissive wave of his hand. Briggs snapped to attention, whirled in place, and marched off. West stayed in place. "*Both* of you are dismissed," Stone reiterated pointedly. West glared at the former Senator before following Briggs out of the room. Stone waited for the door to close, then hurriedly retrieved a taped key from underneath the desk, rushing to open a locked drawer. He pulled out a laptop and an old-style flip phone. He drew in a deep breath, slowly releasing it. Then he slid his thumb down the side of the phone, flipping it open, answering the call. He couldn't believe he was actually receiving a call. Since he'd been given the phone by a member of the cabal who had been his benefactor years ago, funding his government races, There'd been no phone communication. A few meets with someone he supposed was his handler. All of the communication between him and the group had been done through a dark web chat to which the laptop had been connected. "This is Stone," he answered.

"The deal is in motion," said the voice on the other line. It was almost mechanical, like a disembodied spirit. "Provide the information to the agent running the operation to bring home the CIA woman. You'll have a signed deal once she has been safely returned to the States. Your immediate family will be absolved of all crimes. You'll spend one year in a minimum-security prison. You WILL not provide any evidence of our dealings. Is this understood?"

"How is that going to be possible? The country knows what happened."

"There will be a cover story."

"Which would be?" Stone questioned. He'd known the group to have concocted cover stories in the past, two personally on his behalf, but those were all local covers. His situation had been of national news.

"The information that came out wasn't complete. You only financed the terror organization but did so unknowingly. Your son-in-law was behind it all. The shootout in DC was them kidnapping you to obtain the rest of your money. The time you'll serve will only be for the financial crimes. Your son-in-law will bear all the blame. Are you ok with that?"

"Completely," Stone said quickly. He'd just gotten everything he'd wanted. "I'll just ha-" The caller hung up on Stone mid-sentence.

****

Fred had excused himself from the command room once Wallace and his team boarded the Black Hawks to return to Oman with their rescued prisoner. Albeit not the one he'd been hoping to return home. Had they just lost their best chance to find Sophia alive?

It'd been almost five days since she'd been taken. How long could she hold out against Hasan? During their investigation into the AIA, he'd come across mountains of information on how sadistic and torturous Hasan was—photos of his former victims. None had ever survived, though. Now, he was subjecting Sophia to those tortures.

Fred leaned against the wall in the hallway, slinking to the floor, trying to shake loose the images of Hasan's former victims that were now flooding his mind. Almost subconsciously photo-shopping Sophia's face onto them. *How could he have failed her?* Another memory jarred loose in his mind: the night he'd led William, his protégé to his death.

Fred suddenly found himself engrossed in one of his worst memories. He was kneeling over the kid's body in the dark alley. He could smell the scent of blood. He could feel the warm night breeze against his back and hear the unmistakable gurgling sound of the young man trying to eke out his final words. He could remember the fear in William's eyes as he was taking his last breath on earth. He'd let the kid down, Sherry down, and himself. He tried to blink the vision away. It wasn't working.

Fred pounded the back of his head on the wall behind him in frustration, anger, sadness, and sorrow. The blow jarred the vision out of his head, his thoughts snapping back to Sophia.

How could he ever face Sherry again if he didn't bring her home? He'd been a failure that night, and he'd vowed never to let anyone down again. But here he was, failing again.

The door to the command room flung open. "Fred, I am sorry, but you need to see this," Mila said, poking her head through the door. Fred quickly wiped away a tear. He hadn't noticed, but several had streamed down his face. He followed the German back into the room. "This just popped up online. Jerry found it scouring the internet for any reference to Sophia." She pointed to the screen. "Play it." Her voice cracked at the order.

The screen flashed as Jerry punched in a couple of keystrokes. An image populated on the wall monitor that sent a terrifying chill down Fred's spine. He'd seen videos start like this in the past. None of them ever ended well. On the screen was a room; in the background, an AIA flag was stretched out. Situated in the middle of the foreground was a stump caked in dried blood. Down tucked into the bottom right corner of the screen was a timer set to ten hours. A man appeared on screen, dressed in military fatigues and wearing a black mask covering his face.

He spoke.

"To the Western world, to the infidels who invade our sacred lands—the lands of Mohammed and think you can take what you want, order our proud people around, infest our countries with your filthy ways of life. Your time is ending. My freedom fighters and I will never stop in our quest to eradicate those who live in error of the true word of Allah. As he commands, we will rid the world of you. In ten hours, the first of your traitorous kind will die. She is unclean, a liar, a manipulator, and an American spy. She was sent here to kill me. A prophet of Allah who is only doing as the one true god commands him. I will make the world bear witness to our strength, to let all know who oppose Allah, what awaits all of you."

The feed cut to black, leaving only the counter at the bottom of the screen. It began ticking.

"When was this broadcast? To where? Who's seen it?" Fred demanded, firing off a series of questions aimed at Jerry. The fervor in Fred's voice startled him, causing a flinch. "Now! Dammit."

The analyst recoiled at the sudden burst of emotion before composing himself. He tapped away, finding the metadata behind the transmission. "This… this was live. All over the internet. Dark websites. It's starting to get picked up by Al-Jeezer networks. It'll be everywhere in a few hours."

"Put a timer on the screen now," he barked to Gabby, checking his watch and setting one of his own. "We have until 6 am to find Sophia before this asshole cuts her head off for the world to see. That is *not* happening!"

A red phone propped up on one of the walls rang. Everyone whirled on the seemingly ancient device. It was rare these days to find a landline. Mila wandered over to it, tentatively like it might spring off the wall and attack her. She picked up the hand receiver. Everyone else in the room froze, a little bit out of the novelty of a landline and a little curious who was calling their clandestine team.

"Patch it through," Mila said after listening to the caller. She pulled the phone away from her mouth. "It's… it's Stone," she said, pure disbelief in her voice. "He wants to talk to the person running the operation."

"Wouldn't he ask for Sophia?" Richard questioned. "I mean, they've spoken before. He knows we're hunting him."

Mila held out the phone to Fred. "I guess that's you right now."

Fred stamped across the room, taking the receiver from the German and pressing his ear to the speaker.

"I would like to speak to the person failing spectacularly at retrieving your missing CIA agent."

The arrogance and condescending voice of the former Senator crackled in Fred's ear. It was definitely him. "This is him," Fred answered through gritted teeth.

"Fred, my old friend," Stone's voice crackled in surprise. The man sounded like he was talking to an old-school buddy. "They dragged you off your couch for this? My dear, this must be serious."

"What do you want?" Fred hissed.

"Ironically, the same thing you want right now."

"Which is?"

"The safe return of our favorite CIA agent." The revelation caused Fred to pause. There was no way, despite how connected he was, that he could have responded to the just-posted video that fast. "No snippy comeback?"

"How do you know she's been taken?"

"I've spoken to Hasan. He was *very* confident that he'd get her to break and tell him where I'm hiding, which would've normally caused a small alarm. However, I also happen to know that since her attack dogs failed their mission, no one knows where that is." He paused, reveling in his small victory. He continued, "Which is probably a good thing. Because even if she does break. She can't tell him anything useful, but on the bad side, if she breaks but lies to buy time, he'll kill her once he finds out. Or she does break and admits she's no good to him; he still kills her."

"Did you call just to gloat?" Fred snapped.

"No, to the contrary, as I said. I want her back safe and sound just as you do."

"I doubt that. She's been hunting you for six months. You know she won't stop. So why help? Isn't Hasan your friend anyway."

"We… had a falling out of sorts. And I am not helping her, per se, as I am mostly helping myself."

Fred figured that this would perfectly fit in line with his actions and motives. Though, he wasn't necessarily sure how he could help and exactly why. "Unless you actually have some information, I have things to do." Finding Sophia's location was paramount. "So goodbye, and I will find you."

"Wait… wait, hold on. I have something to tell you."

"I don't want to hear anything more from you until I put handcuffs on your greedy little hands."

"Even if it's Sophia's current location?"

Fred paused as he was about to hang up. "How would you know that?"

"Jonathan, upon my orders, did some digging once I found out that he had Sophia, trying to find his home base. He found it. Would you like to know where?"

"You know I do," was Fred's only reply. Could Stone be playing a game? Of course, but to what end? It's not like he needed to stall for time. They weren't even looking for him yet. Also, if he knows where they are holding Sophia, he has an entire mercenary company at his disposal. He could solve all of his problems at once by just taking out his enemies. "What's in it for you?" Fred questioned, not trusting the conniving old man.

"Simple, you rescue your girl; I get to come home."

Stone's tone suggested he knew something Fred didn't. The way he said it, Fred had heard the tone before. Back when they first interrogated him in DC. When he thought he had a leg up on them. "What do you mean you get to come home? Maybe to a cell."

"For a bit," was Stone's retort. "A year in minimum security. My immediate family goes free."

"What! No way. You basically committed treason. That's the death penalty. It was all over the news. The American people wouldn't stand for that."

"Don't you worry your pretty little head about that. I'll give you Sophia's location. Your attack dogs rescue her. I tell you where to find me. I'll surrender and get shipped back home, where I'll get a slap on the wrist. My family is all set. Everything goes back to normal. Do you want her location or not, Agent Jones?"

Fred gritted his teeth. He had no leads and was now on a clock to find Sophia. Despite every instinct to not trust the man, he truly had no options. "Fine, where is she?"

"Finally, for some reason. She is being held in Mudhainab, Yemen, which is where Hasan was born. There is a compound on the outskirts of the city. You'll find her somewhere inside. Hopefully, for both of our sakes, she is still alive. Happy hunting, Agent Jones. Can't wait to talk to you soon." The line went dead.

Fred hung up the phone, agitated and not yet believing what just happened. He whisked around to face the room. "Get me,

Wallace, now!"

CHAPTER NINETEEN

WALLACE plucked his way down the cavernous cargo bay of the C-17 Globemaster III, boots falling heavily on the metal-rutted floor. The noise of the engines outside drowned out the stomping. He silently checked on each of his men. Making sure they were all aware of the stakes of the mission. Down to every man, all of their facial expressions betrayed their emotions at this moment, for a group of hardened SEALs who never wore their feelings on their sleeves. They did so now. They had one singular goal: bring Sophia back in one piece, and they'd stop at nothing to achieve that goal. Everyone was ready for the fight at hand.

The plane was en route to the location that Stone had given Fred. Mudhainab. Not that either of the two men fully trusted the disgraced former Senator. However, at this point, they didn't see much of a choice. With the threat made that Sophia was to be beheaded first thing in the morning. They had nothing else to go on. The only hope was that Stone, in an effort to save his backside, was at least for the moment aligned with their objectives. The village itself, from what the hastily gathered intel they could find, wasn't exactly a hotbed of terrorist activity, which was a good thing, but it was Hasan's home village, so how many people there would be loyal to him?

What reconnaissance Fred and Mila's team had been able to cobble together through surveillance drones and satellite imagery was that the compound they were about to assault was pretty big. Easily able to house a couple of dozen fighters. How many more would be just a hop, skip, and jump away in the village that would be able to render support to the AIA forces?

All was up in the air, which for the Master Chief wasn't a very particularly comforting situation. Too many variables were in play. Normally, it wouldn't have been a mission he'd sign off on. However, this one was very different. Personal. They'd taken a member of his team, a friend. He was going to stop at nothing to get her back.

Wallace stopped in front of Tex, taking a seat in the very uncomfortable yet familiar webbed seating next to the brooding

Texan, who, aside from a violent expletive-laden outburst once back at Thumrait that had resulted in a flipped table and some damaged office supplies, he hadn't said a single word, which, somehow, was more disturbing than anything. Normally, it was impossible to get him to shut up. Instead, he sat silently with an eerie calm demeanor, elbows on his thighs, hands laced one atop another, chin resting on top, flattening his beard—a stoic, contemplative look on his face.

Wallace nudged Tex, snapping him out of thought. "Can't believe I am asking," he started. "Penny for your thoughts."

The angry sniper was only now registering that someone had sat beside him and looked at his commanding superior. "I don't think it'd be wise to divulge them, Chief. Most would be considered war crimes." The blank emptiness and low growl in his voice raised Wallace's eyebrow. The man to his left, the jokester of the group, had no joke in his tone. "I don't think they've invented the words for what I'll do to that son of a bitch if he does-"

"Let me cut that shit right there," Wallace intercepted. He wasn't even going to let the words come out. There was no way he'd let them manifest in real life. "That's not happening. We're getting her back. Today. And, Tex, it wasn't your fault. You know how impulsive she is."

"You're saying this is her fault for running off without backup," the Texan blurted, offended at the assertion Wallace was blaming Sophia.

"No, that's not what I am saying. We've been around this game for far too long, you and me. We both know S.H.O.T," the two intoned. "Exactly. Shit happens out there. But, no matter what happens out there." He pointed in a nondescript direction. "What matters is what happens in there," he said, pointing to Tex's chest and head. "The three C's, man, remember them. Keep calm, cool, and collected." The Texan managed a faint smile. "And, besides, I'll be there right by your side committing those non-worded actions." The two men gave each other a fist bump followed by a Hooyah.

A green light overhead switched on, filling the cargo bay a

verdant green. It was time to jump. Two airmen entered the bay from the nose of the plane. "Get ready, men. This time, we're bringing her home."

One of the airmen worked a set of controls near the loading bay ramp, the other helping the SEALs stand and get their lines secured to the rope above. The group lined up in a single file line and shuffle-walked toward the back of the plane. After a final check from the airman at the controls, he turned, flashing a thumbs-up. The green flipped to red; the other man returned the gesture. The bay door opened, and a howling wind flooded into the large, empty hull.

Tyus was the last man in the file. He reached up and tapped the man before him on the shoulder. Who in turn did the same, and so on, the gesture signaling that the man behind was ready. The gesture reached Tex, who was the first in the column. Once, he felt a hand on his shoulder. The Texan launched himself from the bay into the pitch-black abyss.

****

Sophia sat alone in the far-right corner of the semi-lit room that had become her cell, curled up—replaying every interaction she had with Jessica. How could she not have seen that the woman had been turned? She was so good at reading people—the sublet art of being able to tell what a person was thinking, their desires, and motivations.

Those were her favorite courses, especially SADRAT. Which stood for spot, assess, develop, recruit, run, and terminate. How in the world could she not have spotted the tells? Everyone had tells. 'It's just human nature,' she remembered her instructor of the course saying. The only thing is, could someone actually pick up on those tells and translate their meanings?

As she sifted through her memories, she started to see the signs. The first one, oddly enough, came from Trevor—his reactions to her, to Jessica, and their interactions. It was becoming painfully clear to her that he was trying to warn her. How could she have been so blind?

None of that would matter soon. Her failures would never see the light of day—nor her, for that matter. Thoughts of her mother, which was a surprise that was the first person she thought of, flooded her mind despite the woman leaving her and her father. She still felt sadness and sorrow when she died. Memories of her father flashed. All of their father-daughter trips, camping, fishing, shooting. She knew he'd secretly hoped to have a son, but that didn't matter; they had a bond. It was rough sometimes, but she knew he loved her no matter what. His passing had hit her hard, so hard that she wasn't sure if she ever wanted to get close enough to anyone so that when her time came, her loss wouldn't be felt so hard.

At that thought, Fred and Sherry popped into her head. A small gasp escaped her mouth. She had done just that. The couple had practically adopted her, taking her in, Fred becoming a mentor of sorts. She couldn't help but think how hurt they'd be when they found out that she had died. Knowing that the CIA would *never* divulge how. But Fred would know that it was in some far-flung country. Protecting the US. Hoping that that thought would bring some solace to him. She died doing what she loved and protecting others.

Then there was her team. She'd grown so close to all of them over the last six months. Sophia wished with all of her heart that, hopefully, they weren't blaming themselves for what happened. That Wallace would live by his motto, S.H.O.T...

A set of keys hit the door lock. Seconds later, it creaked open. Sophia expected Farid or the other two men were coming to drag her off to her execution. The hope that the team would find her had drained from her body. The way Hasan made it sound, they'd been led into a trap. Hell, for all she knew, they were dead, and she'd be joining them shortly now that she was about to be escorted to her doom.

Instead, the figure that stood in the doorway silhouetted in the soft yellow glow of florescent lighting was feminine. Jessica strode in, freshly bathed, wearing a new abaya. The woman dragged in a folding chair behind her. Sophia wanted to leap up and rip her throat out, but there wasn't any fight left in her. Every part of her body ached; her throat parched, and her stomach grumbled. A part of her wished the deed was done already.

Jessica slammed the chair down, snapping it open harshly. The sound of metal slapping against metal reverberated through the echo chamber of a room. The woman sat down; a smug expression stretched across her face. "Today, you will die," Jessica announced. "Today, an infidel pig will be slaughtered for the world to see. Before you do so, though, you're going to read this." The traitor pulled a slip of paper from a breast pocket, jabbing it out for Sophia to take. The agent tried to raise her hand to receive it, but her body wasn't cooperating. Exhaustion had finally taken over. "Oh, for fuck's sake, I lasted longer." She hauled Sophia's hand up, slapping the slip into her palm.

"H-h-" Sophia tried to speak, but the dearth of wetness in her mouth prevented any semblance of full words from escaping. Jessica snapped her fingers, and another figure bolted into the room with a bottle of water, handing it to her.

"I suppose you can't read that if you can't speak. Here." She tossed the bottle into Sophia's lap. The agent quickly pawed at it, tearing the lid off like a ravenous animal, gulping the liquid contents. Droplets escaped, shimmering down her chin. Half the bottle was gone in a flash of a second.

Sophia spat some of the contents back out, using it to wet her crusting, cracking, dry lips. She let the water seep into every corner of her mouth before opening it again to speak. "How could you turn?" she asked, finally managing words.

Jessica released a laugh that boomed around the room, shooting forward in the chair. "You've only been here for a few days and look at you. You're a shell of the person that was tossed in here with me," the woman started to explain. "I was held prisoner with a group of animals that beat me, threw their shit at me, raped me repeatedly every single fucking night," she hissed with a level of vitriol Sophia had never seen before. "For months as they moved us from location to location. My so-called fiancée did *fuck all* to stop them. He couldn't even ask for them to stop. That's why when I had a chance, I had Farid cut his tongue out. If he wasn't going to use it, why have it." Sophia recoiled at the revelations. "So, when Hasan bought us and saw what our captors had done to me. He killed them all. He gunned every last piece of shit down. Then he showed me what your people have done to this country and to many more like it. He treated me with more respect than any American man had done. Especially that yellow-bellied Trevor." She leaned back. "I would've loved to be in the room when Farid cut his head off." She lingered on the thought, musing for a second. "How was it?" she asked, leaning forward again. "Did he cry, did he beg, did he plead for his life? Like I had to every *fucking* night."

"No, he did nothing." That was all Sophia could manage to say back. Initially, Sophia thought maybe she could reason with Jessica. That thought evaporated the second she started to explain her reason for turning traitor. There was an evil and malice behind her eyes that she'd not even seen in Hasan's. They practically sparkled at the thought of being able to watch her fiancée getting his head cut off.

"Oh well," she stood. "It doesn't matter how the rat died. Only that he did. Speaking of death." She set her eyes on Sophia. "It's about that time for you. Up and at'em, you have a date with the swordsman. Don't want to be late for that. Oh, and better drink the rest of that. Don't want to get tongue-tied on camera."

Sophia guzzled the rest of the bottle as the man from earlier rushed in, hauling her off her feet. The trio marched for the door. "Do I get a last meal?"

Jessica whirled on Sophia. "Oh, Dorthy, you're not in Kansas anymore if you haven't noticed. We don't do that false humane shit here," the woman snarled, then paused, giving it a thought. "But, if it makes you feel any better, when and if we capture any of your team alive, we can extend that courtesy. Now move it *bitch.*" She shoved Sophia into the hallway, pushing the blonde down her own 'Green Mile.'

As she shuffled down the hall, Jessica's words struck Sophia like a lightning bolt. *When and if,* she said. That meant the team wasn't dead; they were still out there. She still had a chance.

****

Wallace's team had touched down on the dark, soft sand two miles from their objective. Despite it being night, they didn't want their parachutes to be spotted bobbing and weaving in the moonlight as it played peek-a-boo through the canopy of clouds.

The conditions were perfect for an early morning assault. The team, well-prepared and alert, was ready to execute their plan. The temperature, as it does just before dawn, had dropped several degrees. The guards around the compound would've been up all night. They'd be weary, and sleep would attack their eyes.

They'd all been on night guard in the desert before. After an entire night of staring out in the blankness of the desert, one's mind starts to wander. The shadows that creep across the ground stir up dreams and thoughts. You begin to believe there are monsters, creatures, and all sorts of demonic things out there that are ready to pounce on you and take your soul. Your guard is up and on high alert until you get the feeling that your senses are just playing the boy who cried wolf on you. Then you let your guard slip a little.

Except this time. This morning, for the men in the compound. Those monsters were about to become very real. Eight of them. They were coming to rescue the captive held within the walls of the fortress and would be taking no prisoners.

The team, fueled by their determination, made quick work of the two-mile jot. They lay in the sand a hundred yards away from the compound, just on the other side of a berm of loose earth. The darkness illuminated a shade of green through their night vision goggles. Wallace checked his watch. Thirty minutes until the timer on Sophia's life was set to expire.

"Alpha-one to TOC, Alpha's are all set. Over." The team united in their mission and was ready to execute their plan. Below, Wallace scanned the compound. It matched verbatim the images sent of him by Mila to their encrypted tablet. The quickness and speed with which the mission was put together left little time to plan—most of it being done on the plane.

The compound was what was left of an old Medieval trade outpost, modified with modern buildings, sitting just outside the village proper. It stretched three city blocks surrounded by an eight-foot wall. A back section of the wall was partially collapsed in one section. That would be their way in. It was covered according to ISR by four men. Light, fast work for the boys. Beyond that was a building about twenty by twenty, a small gathering room, maybe dining. Surveillance had clocked small bands coming and going. A few smaller structures dotted the landscape. Several pickup trucks were scattered around the lot—some with mounted machine guns in the beds.

The main attraction, though, their primary target, was the huge building located near the front gate. A large structure. Indicating the main living quarters or operations area. It didn't matter; everyone inside wasn't going to make it out except Sophia.

"Men, you bring our girl home now," Fred's voice crackled over their headsets. Fred faced the assembled group in the ops room, who had stopped working on whatever they were doing. They stared at the monitor on the wall with bated breath. Mila and Fred exchanged knowing glances. A mutual feeling that this was it. They were going to rescue Sophia, which emanated between the two. The German woman managed a curl of her lips. This was it.

On ISR, the human figures worked their way down the berm, crossing the open terrain to the outpost wall.

The team merged, narrowing into a wedge formation. Walsh was running point, with Alwani, Jones, and Wallace to his left and Ryan, Tex, Tyus, and Gutierrez to his right.

They advanced silently through the desert, using what was left of the night to stalk toward their prey undetected. They were closing in for kill shots. The verdant green of the NVGs made the surrounding area pop. A flare of light sparked as one of the guards drew a drag from a cigarette as he leaned against the wall outside of the compound. His companion followed suit, propping up against the opposite side. Inside the downed perimeter barrier, two other men paced back and forth.

The team closed the gap. Now, within fifty yards. So good, so far, they'd not been spotted. "Walsh, outside right, Tex outside left, Jones inside right, Alwani inside left," Wallace whispered into his mic, calling each man's target. "On my mark." They continued closing in another ten yards. Within 40 yards, there was no way any of his men would miss such an easy shot. "Now."

A series of low, flat *pffts, pffts* pierced the dead night. All four terrorists fell.

The team reached the wall. "Smoking kills," Tex quipped, striding over the man he'd shot. "Guess he didn't get the warning."

"TOC, Alpha units breaching compound, out." The team climbed over the rubble, entering the outpost proper.

"Alpha good copy. Heads on a swivel. Multiple roving guards. There's a fire pit ten yards to your left; three men gathered," Fred warned, taking in the scene.

Wallace gestured; Fire Team 2 broke off. Ryan, Tex, Tyus, and Gutierrez advanced toward the pit. They used a parked pickup to conceal their advance. Reaching the truck, Gutierrez paused, and the other three dropped to their knees to provide cover. He produced a small charge from his satchel, placing it under the rear wheel well and flicking a switch. A red light flickered on. He gave Ryan a thumbs up. The team continued toward the fire pit.

They rounded the front end of the vehicle to find three AIA huddled by a fire, laughing, which would be the last action they would take. The SEALs opened fire. The trio crumpled to the ground.

Fire Team 1, led by Walsh, continued forward. A roving guard came around from one of the buildings. Walsh shifted at the movement without hesitation. He fired. Three rounds burst into the terrorist's body. Two to the chest, one to the throat. Blood choked off a shout, turning it into a gurgle.

The two teams continued to advance, coming up to the presumed dining hall. Wallace's FT1 and Ryan's FT2 split, each going around a different side.

A man rose from the bed of another parked truck. The guard had found himself a place to sleep. He spotted the four dark-clad figures moving across the night, dodging between shadows. For a moment, he blinked, trying to focus his eyes, believing his mind was playing tricks on him.

It wasn't. He scrambled for his weapon, only for his vision to become as black as the night. His corpse thudded back down to the bed of the truck—a perfectly circular hole in his forehead.

Wallace continued forward, following after Walsh. He'd caught the slight hints of movement seeing a man raise his head. Threat neutralized.

The two teams enveloped the building from both sides, meeting at the front door. A shaft of light escaped from under the frame. The team removed their NVGs. Out in the darkness, they were the team's greatest asset. Indoors, however, under lights, they'd be blinding.

Stacking up on both sides, FT1 on the right, FT2 on the left, the group prepared entry. Walsh tried the door handle. Pulling it back, it opened ever so slightly as he pulled. More light flooded the night. Voices beyond inside were in the midst of a conversation. Wallace listened intently, hearing at least six distinct voices.

He held up six fingers, and the team nodded, preparing. On his move, Walsh flung the door open, barging inside, peeling to his right, Alwani bursting in right behind, darting to his left, and the rest of the team filtered in behind. Each man picked a target, catching the six men inside off guard and bewildered momentarily until the realization struck, spurring them into action. Unfortunately for them, that realization struck them a fraction of a second before the bullets did.

The six men had all made their final movements in life. One slumped over a table. One corpse found itself draped over the back of a chair. The others sat slumped in their chairs.

Wallace turned his wrist over, checking his watch—fifteen minutes till the deadline. "Let's move," he ordered the team back out into the night.

****

A surge of energy coursed through Sophia's body. She wasn't going to go quietly, not if Wallace and the boys were still out there looking for her. She tensed herself. The headman's sword wasn't going to get a willing body today.

Jessica strode confidently beside Sophia as they marched down the hall. The guard shoved his captive forward by jabbing the barrel of his AK into the small of Sophia's back, irritating the agent. She was going to have to do something quickly. The end of the hall was coming up. The torture/execution room lay several doors around the T-section to her left. She was going to have to buy time for her rescuers if she wanted to survive.

If she could only find a way to get out of the building, escape her captors, and possibly contact her team.

First, though, she'd have to deal with the annoying guard poking her in the back with his gun and Jessica.

Sophia stopped hard in the middle of the hallway. Using unseen gravitational forces, she planted her feet firmly on the floor. The AIA escorting her walked straight into her, not expecting his prisoner to stop. The barrel of his gun slid down the agent's back, pointing to the floor.

Jessica halted beside her. The man yelled and tried to shove Sophia forward. She held her ground. The man shouted again.

"He said move," Jessica hissed.

Sophia slowly crooked her head toward Jessica. "I know," she said coldly. "I speak Arabic too *bitch.*" Jessica's nostrils flared, and her eyes narrowed. How dare this infidel insult her so acidically. She pulled back her hand to swat at Sophia. "Oh, and you fucked up." Hand held high, about to come down across Sophia's face, but the comment caused pause as a quizzical look crossed her face. "You told me my team is still alive," Sophia snarled.

The agent threw herself forward, catching both Jessica and the gunman by surprise, delivering a vicious head-butt to Jessica's face. A wet crunch of cartilage snapped, blood sprayed from her broken nose, cutting off a scream of pain. Two bits of teeth *tinked* to the floor. The woman staggered backward, smacking head-first against the wall; a river of blood streamed down her face.

Sophia whirled on the gunman, who was bringing his AK up, leaving him open. Sophia drove her foot hard into the man's stomach. With a pained grunt, the blow knocked the oxygen from his lungs, driving him back.

About to press her attack, a primal howl from behind. Sophia turned. Jessica was charging, screeching like a banshee; blood smeared over her face, her front teeth tipped jagged where the head-butt had partially broken them. The woman drove Sophia back, smashing her into the wall, hands clenched around her throat. "I am going to kill you *bitch*," she lisped, squeezing tighter.

Sophia struggled to break free of Jessica's grip. The woman's animalistic rage fueled her with supervillain-like strength. Out of her peripheral, she could see the gunman was recovering from being struck in the mid-section, bringing the rifle to bear on the grappling pair. He wouldn't shoot Hasan's woman. Would he?

Sophia couldn't take the chance that he wouldn't. Returning her attention to the rage-filled woman in front of her choking her. Sophia snapped her right arm up, dropping it across Jessica's outstretched arms at the elbows, causing her to loosen her grip, following up with a punch to the gut, doubling over the howling woman. Freed from the vice-like grip, Sophia inhaled a gulp of air. Checking the gunman, he was pointing the weapon directly at her now, *shit*. He was struggling to pull back the charging hammer. The chambering round jammed.

Temporary reprieve.

Sophia pawed at the recovering Jessica, snatching her arm, yanking her in closer, spinning her, pulling her right arm behind her back, locking it to the small of her spine, wrenching it tighter. The woman squealed in pain, wildly throwing an elbow.

Sophia ducked the incoming blow. "You're going to die!" Jessica bellowed.

The sound of a round being chambered echoed through the hall. "You first, bitch." Sophia propelled the woman forward, charging the AIA soldier, using the woman as a shield.

"No, no, no," Jessica pleaded, waving her free hand in front of her, begging the man not to fire.

It was in vain. The man greedily opened fire.

A maelstrom of bullets violently punched into Jessica's body, jerking the husk of flesh. At such close range, each round tore through flesh and bone. Sophia tucked her body tightly behind Jessica's now bullet-riddled corpse, "Ahhhhh!" she roared, holding the woman-sized shield up, charging. She shoved the body forward as a round bore through, exiting inches from Sophia's face.

The corpse smacked into the AIA soldier, causing him to drop the AK. As the two cascaded to the floor. With Jessica falling on top of him. Sophia, seeing the weapon clatter to the ground, quickly snatched up the rifle. Standing over the Arab, who snarled up at her, frantically trying to throw the dead woman off him. Sophia paused for a moment. Was this murder? *Ah, fuck it,* he'd been part of her torture. She fired. A burst of fire spat from the barrel, pulverizing the man's head. There was nothing left of his face.

Sophia stared at the American woman. A pang of sadness washed over her. Thinking about everything that Jessica had to endure. Would she have turned in those circumstances? Maybe, but one thing was for sure: when she told the woman's parents their daughter was dead, she'd make up a lie about how she died. They didn't deserve to know their daughter turned.

There was no time to dwell now, though; she needed to escape. A bullet sizzled past her head. Sophia spun, dropping to a knee. An AIA soldier had entered the hall, charging at her. She squeezed the AK trigger. A burst spat from the chamber. The rounds found a home burrowing into the running man's chest. He fell forward with a thud, skidding across the concrete floor and leaving a streaking blood trail.

It was time to go. "Giving this hotel a zero-star review." Sophia spat a glob of blood on the dead man, shifting down the hall.

****

The two fire teams continued their quiet march through the moonlit compound, sticking to the shadows as much as possible. Eventually, coming to a pair of Toyota Hilux pickup trucks. "Al, plant." Wallace quietly tapped the side of the truck while silently giving the same command to Ryan through hand signals. Who in turn relayed them to his Explosive Ordnance Disposal expert.

Alwani and Gutierrez both unslung their respective packs, producing gray brick-sized clay blocks and planting them on the undercarriage of each vehicle, fumbling for the activation triggers.

Two men stumbled from one of the smaller structures nearby. One wiping the crust from his eye, the other staggered about. Both were still consumed with the night's rest from which they were waking. Wallace tracked both men as they walked. They could gun both of them down in a heartbeat. But they were in the open. Another roving guard might see two of his comrades lying in the dirt and set off an alarm.

He couldn't risk that. The pair seemed to be headed for the same building they were. They'd take care of them there.

"All set, Chief," Alwani said, zipping up his pack and taking his weapon back up.

"Move out," Wallace ordered.

The fire teams moved on, slinking into the shadow of the building. The door creaked open, and a shaft of light shot into the darkness. Another AIA stumbled from his domicile, half asleep still— must be shift change. The team hugged to the edge of the wall as the man turned, oblivious to the fact Tex lurked in the shadow behind him, stalking him like a predatory jungle cat.

The Texan quietly unsheathed his K-bar, inching closer to the unsuspecting terrorist. The man was about to round the edge, leaving the blocking view of the building to stride into the open— one last chance to take him cleanly.

Tex pounced, hand wrapping around the man's mouth. He quickly and violently rasped the blade across the man's neck. A sprout of blood projected from the gaping wound in his neck. A gurgle of blood choked off any scream he may have wanted to make. The man spasmed in Tex's arms, then went limp. He dragged the man back to the doorway. "Incoming." He hoisted the dead man into the small room, finding both Walsh and Tyus inside, standing over two other men, now in similar states as the one Tex was carrying. Walsh helped Tex lay the third man in a cot. "Night, night fuckers," he said, tapping the boots of the dead man.

"Let's go," Wallace whispered from outside. It was ten minutes until the timer on Sophia's life would run out. By the looks of it, the camp was starting to come to life so that they could witness it firsthand.

A loud burst of automatic gunfire erupted from the target building. The team all looked in the direction of the shots. "What the fuck?" Ryan asked. "They're early."

"That's something else. Move!" Wallace bellowed. "They wouldn't go through all the fanfare of airing a shooting." No, he knew they wanted to cut off her head. So, the gunshots were for another reason.

The team broke from cover to see men pouring out of the houses. All of them scrambled for the main building, weapons in hand, ready for a fight. Johns and Tyus picked out two close targets and opened fire, cutting both running men down. "It's a party now," Johns said.

Another group of AIA that were running toward the building spotted their friends taking a dirt nap and spun, seeing the eight dark-clad figures emerge from the shadows. They had no time to react. A fusillade strafed across their chests. They joined their friends on the ground.

Still, more groups were descending on the house.

"What's going on!" Fred barked over the radio, seeing multiple groups of AIA rush toward the house.

"Shots fired in the house. Something inside is going on." Wallace answered. "Go, go, go," he ordered his men.

The team broke into a double time spreading out across the compound grounds. More men piled out of the smaller houses. Mostly to be met with bullets from the team.

****

Sophia crouched by the man she'd just killed, rolling him over, searching for extra magazines, finding one. She ejected the mag on her AK. Three rounds left. Useless. She chucked the magazine and slid the new one in.

Then continued down the hallway, reaching the T-section. She looked left and then right. To her left, the torture room. To the right, who knew, maybe a way out. She'd been blindfolded when she had arrived. It was a fifty-fifty proposition. Her heart was pounding in her chest; this was her escape: no time to mess up or second guess.

She was trying to think about her route from the days prior when she first arrived. The thought of her being dragged from the car into the building and immediately taken to Hasan was still fresh. She didn't remember ever turning, and it wasn't long after the sun left her skin that she was dragged into the torture room. *Go left*, her mind shouted.

She turned *left*.

Sophia headed up the corridor toward the door at the end of the hallway, gun drawn at the ready. A door to her right flung open. A man stepped into the hallway to investigate the gunfire.

It was Hasan, a snarl stretched across his face upon seeing Sophia gun in hand.

The American paused, seeing her tormentor standing in front of her angrily, snarling, "Fuck you," she spat acidically and opened fire.

Hasan threw himself back into the torture room, dodging the volley, luckily for him.

Unluckily, two men had rushed through the door at the end of the hallway. The one to the right took the rounds intended for Hasan straight to the chest. Ragged holes punched through him, splattering the closing door red. He seized and then hit the floor.

Dammit, Sophia cursed, missing her target.

No time to be angry. The other man opened fire. Bullets cracked by Sophia's head, and several pounded into the concrete at her feet. She exchanged bursts of fire. The other man threw himself into another room on his left as rounds slammed into the mud-brick behind him.

Sophia kept the gun trained, sweeping between both rooms and backing up. Can't go left. Gotta go right. She pounded down the corridor, sending an indiscriminate volley behind her and keeping the men in cover. She rounded the corner at the end of the hall. Another door set into the far end. She barreled for it.

****

Several AIA soldiers entered the house, seeing one of their own lying on the floor. Another emerged from a room wide-eyed. They exchanged concerned looks.

Hasan burst into the hall, seeing a quintet of his men standing around. "The American woman is escaping!" he shouted. "Go after her." His arm shot up, pointing in the direction Sophia had just run. The group ran past him, chasing after Sophia. He turned back to the room. "Farid, stay here, keep getting ready." Hasan then followed after Sophia and his men.

****

The SEALs reached the door to their target. About to breach, a rat-tat-tat of AK fire erupted from behind them, pock-marking the front of the building. The group pivoted to see a half-dozen AIA running at them. "Take'em," Wallace ordered.

The group sent a deadly stream of hot lead across the courtyard. Bullets found their targets with laser-guided precision. Several more men rounded a building. The whole compound was awake now and descending on the team.

"Go, get Sophia," Ryan shouted. "We'll hold them here. Fire Team 2 on me." Tex, Tyus, and Gutierrez stretched out in a fire line. M4s barked at the advancing terrorists.

"Team one, let's go." Wallace kicked in the door to the building to find one dead AIA lying by the entrance. They pressed forward.

Wallace came upon a doorway. Before he could check the room, a large Arab man blasted through it, shoulder-barging the SEAL leader and slamming the two through the adjacent wall. The mud-brick disintegrated upon impact as the two men burst through the other side, turning the space into a chalky swirl. Wallace's M4 skittered across the floor out of arms reach.

The SEAL leader jumped to his feet. Farid charged him again. Wallace unsheathed his K-bar, assuming a fighting stance. The Arab roared, closing the gap swinging with his right arm. Wallace threw up his arm to block the incoming strike. The force pushed him backward, feet sliding across the dust-filled floor. His right heel tapped against the far wall.

Farid followed up with a swing from his left. Wallace countered, blocking that blow, too, seeing an opening. He thrust his blade into Farid's mid-section. Anger flashed across the brute's face. *Oh shit.* The stab only seemingly set the man into more of a rage. Wallace drew back, pulling the knife out. Then repeatedly stabbed the Arab in the stomach, again, and again, and again, and again, driving him back. With each successive stab, he felt the life draining from his attacker until he fell to the floor.

Wallace grabbed his rifle, going back to the hole in the wall the two men had made. Alwani reached a hand through. "All good, Chief?" he asked.

"All good," Wallace replied, dusting the brick fragments from his shoulder. "Where's Sophia?"

The pair came to a T-section; down the hall, three bodies lay strewn across the floor. Wallace's heart sank seeing that one was a woman. Walsh was kneeling beside her, checking for a pulse.

"It's not her," he said, turning back to see Alwani and Wallace standing over him. "But, she is dead."

Johns exited a room, shaking his head. "No one's here."

"Where is she?" Wallace pondered.

****

"Wait, what is that?" Fred questioned, seeing a figure emerge from the opposite side of the house facing out into the village. The figure was running away from the location. "Zoom in," he demanded. Richard quickly obliged the command. Tapping a key on his keyboard. The camera on the overhead drone zoomed in further. The faint image of the person cleared up. A more defined figure took shape. It was a woman. Fred's heart leaped into his throat. "Oh my God, that's Sophia!" he excitedly exclaimed happily. Until he realized she was running *away* from the building and headed toward the front and into the village. "She doesn't know we're there."

"How?" Mila asked.

"Don't know, don't care." He pressed the mic to inform Wallace.

"Wait, what's that." Mila pointed to the screen, and Richard zoomed out a bit. Six men burst from the building, chasing Sophia. "They're chasing her."

CHAPTER TWENTY

SOPHIA burst through the wooden door at the end of the hall; a chill enveloped her body as the cool early morning air took her by surprise. It was the first time in days she'd been outside. The sky above was coming to life with a dazzling array of blues, purples, oranges, and reds. The sun had just crept over the horizon; dull spars of light shot from the orb, reaching out like fingers.

It would've been a beautiful sight to behold if her life wasn't in danger. Sophia scanned her surroundings, letting her eyes adjust to the natural lighting. A gate lay ahead, and beyond that, a city. She could get lost in it, hopefully long enough to find a way to contact her team. She broke for the gate. Behind her, there was a loud commotion. People were running and shouting, and the roar of several truck engines rose over the building she'd just broken out from.

Her escape kicked up a hornet's nest of activity. It sounded like she was running from all of the AIA.

Gunshots rang out through the burgeoning day. Sophia whirled, expecting the shots to have been taken at her. There was no one there. *Who was shooting? And at who?* No time to think about that.

Five men barged through the door, spilling out into the foreground, searching for their target, and finding Sophia staring back at them. She snapped up the AK and fired, scattering the group. One man wasn't so quick to respond and took a round to the thigh. Even from her distance, judging by the way he fell, she could tell the round had shattered his femur. He wailed in agony.

Sophia spun, sprinting for the gate.

Clops of dirt exploded all around as she ran. The balgha shoes she'd been given after her military-issued clothes and boots had been stripped away were a size too big, making her feet slide inside. She stumbled as a round burst into the dirt in front of her. Sophia threw herself into a side dive to avoid the next incoming burst, and they closed in on her.

Rolling head over heels, she popped back up, spun, and sent a volley at her pursuers. Once again, sending them scattering. This time, she didn't score a hit but managed to give herself time to recover. Kicking off the ill-sized shoes, she continued to the fence.

Reaching her escape point, she banged against the barrier. It bowed and wobbled but stayed closed. She glanced down to find a chain wrapped around the bisected gates with a giant padlock that locked the two sides together. *Fuck,* she aimed her gun at the lock backing up a few paces and squeezed the trigger.

Chink, chink, out of ammo.

"Dammit, she shouted, casting the weapon aside. Who'd ever locked it last left a small bit of slack in the chain. She hauled at the gate, prying it apart from its partner. A round zinged by her head, the crackle deafening in her ear. She glanced over her shoulder to see the quartet of men running, bearing down on her. Behind the main group loomed a freighting presence. Hasan. He'd joined the chase.

The site of her torturer spurred a renewed sense of strength. She hauled at the gate one more time, creating a gap wide enough to fit her slender frame. She started to squeeze between the metal bars. Halfway through, her abaya snagged on a protruding spike of the chain link fabric, catching her.

Sophia pulled at the part, trying to tear it loose. Unsuccessful, she peeked back; they were now twenty yards away and closing in fast. A man raised his gun, and a sparkle of fire exploded from the barrel. An explosion of earth came raining down on her. Through the cloud, she looked down where it had come from—a bored hole in the ground inches from her foot.

Wide-eyed at the near miss, she frantically tugged one more time. The fabric ripped apart. She tumbled out onto a small roadway. A round pinged off the post; sparks flew in her face. "Fuck that was close," she whispered, breathing heavily at the nearest death experience she'd ever had. *RUN!* A primal voice screamed in her head. If she didn't want an *actual* death experience, she'd better heed that instinct and run and do so quickly.

****

Fred and Mila watched the two-minute sequence unfold in front of them on the monitor as Sophia made her mad dash for the perimeter fence. Both tried to contain their undulating emotions as they watched her shimmy through the gap in the fence, nearly escaping being shot multiple times.

Fred released a deep sigh of relief, seeing her make it out. He hadn't realized it, but he'd been holding his breath the entire time.

"We need to get her help," Mila declared, watching her friend dart away from the compound and into the city.

Fred slammed his hand on the mic. "Alpha-one, zero is on the move. She's headed for the city."

****

Wallace stood in the hallway of carnage, taking in the scene of three dead bodies, a wry smile on his face. He knew this was Sophia's work. A voice crackled through his headset, distorted. It was Fred's, but the transmission came through slightly gargled. He moved back down the hall toward where he and his men had entered the building. Gunshots still rang from outside. Some were coming from another direction.

"Alpha-one to TOC, say again last?" he asked, pressing his hand to his chest where the talk button was.

"I say again, Zero is on the move; she's headed for the city. Tango's on her six. Hurry."

Wallace whirled; his eyes darted to the right of the T-section. There was another exit. "One to TOC, good copy." He turned to his team. "Move." Fire Team 1 sprinted down the corridor. "Alpha-two, your status?"

"Wrapping up out here," came Ryan's short reply.

"Follow when done. We're going after zero." The team burst out the back door to find an AIA soldier writhing on the ground, wailing. A spar of bone poking through his pants leg. A gunshot wound, for sure. The round had fractured his leg.

"Quiet," Walsh chided, thrusting his leg forward, whipping it across the man's face. The whining man fell silent.

"Thanks," Wallace said, eyes darting around the foreground area. The sun, now having crested the horizon, shot shafts of light across the landscape, partially blotting out his vision. Something shimmered fifty yards ahead, a chain link fence warbled, and one of the gates was thrown open. "That way." He pointed, darting in the direction of the open fence. His men followed behind, and they raced toward the city.

****

Ryan picked out a target charging between the cover of two structures and opened fire—a single round burst. The bullet struck true; the soldier collapsed mid-stride. He gazed out over the grounds; soldiers were darting in and out of cover, but with each successive trigger squeeze from FT2, there were less and less of them.

"Wrapping up out here," he replied to Wallace's question. Peering over his shoulder, Tex had just gunned another fighter down. "Tex, we need to make this quick."

"Gotcha," the Texan replied mid-trigger pull. "Five," he counted off, hunting for his next body count.

The throaty roar of one of the Hilux trucks revved, springing around one of the buildings; the old-fashioned M60 machine gun, mounted in the bed, barked as flames spat from the barrel. "Down," Johns shouted. The team kissed the ground, throwing themselves flat as rounds blasted above their heads, gouging gaping holes into the building behind them. A second truck peeled around, opening fire on FT2.

"Gut, take'em out," Ryan shouted over the cacophonous barrage.

Gutierrez, staying down, rolled onto his back, fishing out the detonator from one of the pockets on his vest. Taking the small black box in hand, he flipped open the case, protecting the buttons from accidental depressing. He slammed both of his thumbs into

274

the buttons.

A second went by, and nothing happened.

Then, a thunderous explosion ripped through the compound, sending a shockwave of dust and dirt roiling over the team. The C4 explosives triggered, sending the two trucks airborne for a second before crashing back to the earth in fireballs. Columns of fire spat fifteen feet into the air. Two flaming men shot out of the columns, running out into the open; their pained screams cut through the early morning air as they flailed about. Their outcries cut off as they quickly suffocated from smoke inhalation before falling to the ground, silent.

The consistent chatter of machine gun fire evaporated as the blast also managed to take out most of the hiding men. The team stood, taking in the fiery scene. "That's a BBQ," Tex quipped.

"You're not right, man," Gutierrez shot back, shaking his head. "Like serious you're loco."

"Don't go getting all Spanglish on me now. You know-" A shot whizzed by Tex's head. FT2 spun, opening fire on the lone AIA member that had trickled out of the grizzly scene, caked in dirt and soot. He was met with a barrage riddling his body. He fell. "Can I count that as mine?" Everyone turned to face Tex as he shrugged. "I shot first."

"Told ya, loco," Gutierrez reiterated, his right index finger circling his ear.

"Stow it, let's move," Ryan ordered. FT2 entered the building, heading for the back door, following FT1's trail. "Two to one, Oscar Mike, to you now. Finished wrapping up welcoming party."

****

Sophia crossed the road separating the compound from the outskirts of the city. More bullets whip-cracked through the air all around her. One narrowly missed her, punching into the wall beside her as she reached the outlying buildings.

The space between them was only two feet wide. She would have to squeeze through the narrow gap. More shots rang out, striking the building and ground. It was like they weren't trying to hit her. Sophia contorted her body to the side, shimming into the crevasse, her back pressed hard against the wall behind her, her hands against the structure in front of her, and her arms crooked by her side at a ninety-degree angle.

She slid deeper inside, becoming shrouded in shadow. The shift in temperatures was a relief. She was sweating profusely already from the adrenaline and running. Her cool, wet skin aided her by allowing her to pass through the narrow gap easily.

Hasan and his men were hot on her trail. *How was she going to be able to get away? Where would she be able to hide? How was she going to communicate her location for a rescue?* All of these were great questions, but she currently had no answer to *any* of them.

Forcing her body deeper down the corridor, reaching the midway point. A shout from behind. She screwed her head around. One of her pursuers had reached the gap. He'd tried to squeeze inside but was unable to get his chunky body through. He yelled something to the effect of stopping. *Yeah, right, like she was going to listen.* To her relief, though, he didn't try to shoot her. *Did Hasan really want to keep her alive so that he could execute her for the world to see?* She might be able to use that to her advantage.

She continued to make her way toward the end, ignoring the Arab's second and third warnings. Almost out. She had no reason to stop if he wasn't going to shoot. More shouts came from behind the blocky man. Orders. A peek over her shoulder. The man jabbed the barrel of his gun into the opening. Whelp, so much for the thought Hasan wanted her alive.

Sophia quickened her pace, and the gun clapped. There was nowhere to go. Incoming.

She thrust forward. Her walled confines disappeared; she fell, face-planting. The rounds zipped over her head. Sophia flipped onto her back, spitting dirt from her mouth; she looked back to where she'd fallen from. The man adjusted his aim to the ground. He fired. Sophia rolled, and the rounds blasted the earth where she'd just been lying.

Phew, close.

She scrambled to her feet, finding herself in a pentagram-shaped cross-section where the tips of five different buildings meant. She looked left, then right. Hunting for a way out, another gap wide enough to squeeze through. There, one to her left, just the right size. A road lay beyond. Her pursuers would have to circle around and find another way to her. This would hopefully buy time to figure out an answer to any of her current problems.

An explosion rocked the area. Sophia spun around, searching for the source of the noise. It sounded like it had come from the compound she just escaped. She peered back through the crevasse to see what it could've been. Her heart thumped at what she saw. One of her pursuers was shimming his way toward her. A lanky, skinny man with dark curly hair had worked himself halfway to her. The two locked eyes. He fished for his sidearm, managing to angle it toward her.

She darted through the other gap before he could shoot.

****

Fred watched the now split screen monitor showing both sets of action unfolding on the ground. He flinched, as did Mila, as two large plumes of fire lit up the screen to his right. If the city didn't know they were there before, they certainly would now.

"Let's hope our intel is correct," Mila quipped. "Because, if not," she said, turning to face Fred. "We've just lost our friends and family," she added quickly.

Every scrap of intel they were able to gather on the city had suggested despite it being Hasan's birthplace. They weren't completely radicalized, which would hopefully help Sophia and the team, as they wouldn't have to contend with an entire village loyal to Hasan and the AIA.

Fred gawped questioningly, watching Sophia move deeper into the city, away from the explosions, putting himself in her shoes. *What would he do?* He'd be trying to find a way to either escape, hide, or communicate because it was clear that she didn't know that the team was already there. "We have to find a way to tell her we're there." Fred thought aloud, turning to the team and looking for suggestions. "Anyone?" A room of blank faces stared back at him.

"What if we drop the drone?" Richard said after a few moments.

"That's insane," Gabby snapped. "We can't do that; it's our only eyes. Not to mention, it's a thirty-million-dollar piece of equipment."

"I am not talking about crashing it," Richard scoffed, almost insulted that she'd think he would so openly call for the destruction of government property. "I am merely saying drop it down to where she can see it."

"If she could see it, then so will the AIA. What if someone takes it out?" Jerry added.

"The human eye can accurately detect objects from three miles away. The standard range of an RPG is sixteen hundred feet." Richard continued to defend his idea. "We drop it so she can tell what it is while keeping it well out of an RPG's range."

"That's too much-"

"Shut it, everyone," Mila growled, taking the room by surprise. It was very uncommon that the normally quiet German raised her voice. She was staring at Fred.

The former FBI agent stood in the middle of the room, arms folded, right hand to his chin, thinking. "You can't be seriously considering this," Gabby protested.

"I am not," said Fred, unfolding his arms, coming to a resolute answer. Gabby appeared relieved. "I am not considering it because we're doing it." Richard pumped his arm like the piston of a car. "Bring it down, son." Mila smacked her hands together in exuberant glee. "And I mean bring it way down. I want it obvious to her and everyone that America is there. Hopefully, it'll scare off anyone that's thinking about getting involved." He turned back to the monitor, steeling his jaw. If America was known for one thing, it was its military might. If he had to flex it to bring home Sophia, so be it.

****

Fire Team 1 pounded across the foreground of the compound, reaching the gate. They glanced around, checking up the road, then down the road, too wide open. Sophia would've made a break for something with more cover. "There," Alwani shouted, seeing the pockmarks on a building thirty yards across the road.

"I see it," they charged forward, reaching the buildings. There was a sliver of an opening between the two of them. Bullet impacts on the walls of both. Someone had shot at Sophia while she squeezed between. Fearing what he'd see inside, he cautiously looked down the passage. To his partial relief, there was no dead body. However, that meant she was still alive but on the run from who knew how many terrorists foaming at the mouth to kill an American. Most of all, Hasan, since he hadn't been one of the bodies lying in the hallway back at the compound. "One to TOC, we need another way into the city.

"TOC copies," Fred answered. "Mila, guide the team in," Fred ordered. He was standing beside Richard, who was typing in commands on his keyboard, taking over the drone controls. "Alright, Richard, start bringing it down. How long will it take to bring down to a mile high."

Richard did a quick stream of calculations in his head. "Safely, two to three minutes."

"Bring it down."

****

Mila ignored the conversation going on behind her, focusing her attention on the four figures standing on the outskirts of Mudhainab. She surveyed the city layout and the locations of Sophia and her pursuers. She wanted to run the team right into them. She traced a line to the nearest main access road into the city. "One go, right? About two blocks up, you'll find a road that leads into the city." She reviewed the monitor; the city itself appeared to be coming to life, and the explosions and gunshots started to draw citizens out of their houses. "Be advised; you may encounter civilians," she warned.

"Fuck them all, none are civilians here," Walsh quipped.

"ROE men, remember your Rules of Engagement. Anyone without a firearm in hand *is* a civilian; remember that," Wallace announced, shooting an icy stare at Walsh. "One copy, en route."

Mila dropped into her seat, a bubbling fear rising inside. The last time she quarterbacked a mission, Sophia was kidnapped, and here, she was given the task of guiding the team to her rescue. Four more figures appeared on screen, exiting the building once holding Sophia. A thought struck her. "Alpha-two."

"Go ahead, TOC," Ryan answered, looking skyward like he was answering God.

"One is headed into the city from the north. I want you to move in from the south. Head to the road directly in front of you and turn left. Make your way…" She reviewed the screen, hunting for an insertion point. Finding one, she said, "Three blocks, there is an inroad into the city."

"Two copies." FT2 set off for the road, then turned left, heading south.

****

Wallace's team rounded the last building lining the outer city perimeter to find the road leading into the city. "Finally," he said, then saw a gathering of people making their way toward them. "Oh shit." Several of the city's residents had crept outside and were looking toward the compound, awestruck by the two billowing clouds of smoke. Some of their facial expressions looked relieved; others were contorted in anger.

A young Arab man who appeared to be in his early twenties burst from one of the houses, AK in hand. He paused, seeing the four men, then whipped up his rifle.

Bang

Johns fired first. The shot sent the crowd running and screaming. Two more men burst from nearby buildings, toting rifles. Alwani and Walsh mowed them down. "Everyone is a civilian," Walsh sarcastically spat, eying Wallace.

"I said without a gun, smart ass," Wallace slapped back. "TOC, where?"

"Continue straight head for the center. Quickly, they're almost on her," Mila relayed.

****

Sophia exploded out of the crevasse, finding herself standing in the middle of a street. She looked left, then right. Which way to go? She glanced back at the lanky Arab who was closing in. She cut right and headed up the road racing. Her legs and arms were pumping as fast as whatever energy she had left could carry her.

Shop entrances rushed by on either side of her as she ran. None were open, or if they had been, the owners were cowering inside. The gunshots were echoing through the city, which had kept most of the residents inside. She looked for a way off the main road. She was too exposed.

A woman in a burka stepped out of one of the shops. Sophia skidded to a halt just before barreling the woman over. "Phone, do you have a phone?" she pleaded. The woman's eyes gave off a mixture of surprise and confusion. Surprise seeing an American woman in the middle of Yemen and confusion as she didn't understand a word coming from her. Sophia switched languages to Arabic, hoping she had the right dialect. This time, the woman understood slightly better. She reached underneath her dress.

A shot rang out. The sizzle of air swam past Sophia's ear. The Arab woman jerked back; a smear of a dark liquid substance blotted over her shoulder. The woman's eyes grew to the size of saucer dishes as they glazed over. She fell, gasping for air, clutching her shoulder, murmuring to herself.

Sophia whipped around; the man chasing her was standing in the road, gun swinging to lock onto her. *Shit!* The American bolted as another shot spat from his barrel. It pounded the earth where her feet had been. She ducked between another set of shops. He continued his pursuit.

The man was quickly gaining on Sophia. Under normal circumstances, she should've been easily able to outpace him. He didn't look particularly athletic, especially as opposed to herself. However, days of torture, abuse, malnourishment, and dehydration, mixed with the growing oppressive heat, had taken their toll on her body.

At this point, she was purely running on adrenaline, which wasn't going to be able to sustain her for much longer. She felt her legs growing weaker with each stride as if she were running in quicksand. Turning another corner, she spotted the other group of AIA chasing her. Hasan in the rear. They hadn't seen her. Good. She turned double backing, rounding back out toward the main street. She looked for another pathway as the other man would soon be rounding on her street. She spotted another passageway. She slid to a stop to make the turn into it.

Pain burst into her side as her pursuer's shoulder met her ribcage. She thudded to the ground sidelong. The side of her head bounced off the hard impacted dirt. The world turned black before fading back in. It was an unfocused, hazy distortion. Everything around her vibrated slowly back into existence. She tried blinking back faster, opening her eyes again to find the man who'd been chasing her straddled on top of her. His rough, calloused hands encircled her neck, fingers snaking across her throat like tendrils closing in, choking off her oxygen. She tried to fight him off when she saw he was about to shout for the rest of his friends.

If he did, it would be over for her.

Summoning what she could, Sophia jabbed her right arm up, catching the man's chin flat across her palm. His mouth snapped shut. A piece of tongue slopped out, smacking across her face with a wet *splat*. Sophia twisted her head in revulsion. The meaty appendage slid off her face. She looked up; the man was scowling down at her, blood gushing from his mouth, sprinkling droplets over her face. His grip had relaxed just enough for Sophia to buck the man off her.

Throwing her hips up and rolling, the two combatants swapped positions, with Sophia on top. She pressed the attack, drawing back her right arm. The man responded with a hip thrust of his own. The two rolled again. It was the Arab's turn to press the attack.

He swung with his left, sitting atop Sophia. His fist pounded into Sophia's face. Her previously split lip that had closed snapped open. New blood trickled out. He pulled back for another strike.

Sophia reached up, digging her thumb into the man's eye socket. He tried to howl, but it was choked off by the blood still pouring from where he'd bit his tongue off. She twisted her body, and the two rolled once more, with Sophia on top. Her thumb was still lodged in his eye socket. A glint caught her eye.

The gun.

When he tackled her, it had skidded away. Sophia leaped off her opponent, pawing for it and scrabbling across the dirt. A hand clamped jaw-like around her ankle. She glanced back, a sinister look on her attacker's face as he hauled at her, pulling her back. She scraped against the hard dirt, and small pebbles dug into her stomach, raking scratch marks everywhere.

Making one last effort, she kicked at him, pushing him back. She rolled, seeing the gun a few feet away, crawling frantically, the toes of her feet finding purchase against the grainy ground. She pushed off, thrusting herself forward, arm outstretched, gliding through the air a foot off the ground.

The man quickly recovered again, clutching her ankle. His palm wrapped around her leg. Sophia felt his sweaty hand against her flesh as she sailed. She stretched even further, closing her eyes, willing her arm to grow another inch or two.

He pulled at her, yanking her back. Sophia's belly flopped, and her chin bounced off the ground, causing another dizzying flare in her vision. One last desperate attempt, feeling her body recoiling back to her attacker like a boomerang. She thrust her hand forward, her fingers wrapped around the gun's grip, ensnaring her coveted prize. She snatched the pistol as he drew her back into his clutches. He was preparing to strike the woman again as he yo-yoed her back to him.

Sophia rolled, whipping the gun up, barrel inches from the man's head. His face washed pale: his eyes bulged, knowing what was about to happen.

"Fuck you!" Sophia growled through blood-stained, clenched teeth, pulling the trigger.

The gun clapped, recoiling in her hand. The Arab's brains evacuated his head post haste, blood splattered across Sophia's face. His body rocked back, lazily falling off hers, thumping to the ground beside her.

Sophia's body fell limp, hands falling to her sides, gun falling from her grip. She wheezed and panted, breathing heavily, exhausted. She lay on the ground, sapped of all energy reserves. She could hear shouts coming from behind her. She tilted her head back, looking up the road. A group of people gathered and pointed behind the crowd. A familiar face matriculated through them: Hasan's. He was coming for her.

For all she had just done, it had only delayed the inevitable. She would still die today.

With no more fight, she lay on the ground, waiting to be taken captive again, staring up at the blue sky soaked in blood. Waiting.

****

"Which way," Wallace demanded. Mila checked Sophia's position. She'd stopped and was double backing.

"TOC, we need to know where to go." Wallace's voice carried the urgency of the situation. More and more people were filing out of their houses and other places to see what was going on, highlighting the need for swift and effective communication.

"Chief?" Alwani fired at two men who'd burst from a small crowd, guns in hand, striking one in the shoulder. He spun to the floor, crying out. The other disappeared into the quickly dispersing crowd, but the danger was far from over. Three more armed men drew. Walsh and Johns put them down. "Chief, we need to get off this street," Alwani expressed again with more urgency. "We can't stay standing here."

"TOC, goddammit," Wallace shouted into the radio.

"Take the street to your left," Mila answered, recoiling from the reverb of the previous transmission.

Wallace took his team left up the new road. Several more gunmen appeared, popping in and out of buildings only to follow their fellow attackers to the afterlife.

****

"We're here," Ryan radioed, reaching the other end of the city. "Where to now?"

"Head into the city; in two blocks, take a right, then a left. You should find yourselves on the main road working toward the center and to FT1," Mila explained. "FT1 has encountered insurgents, and you will probably too. Keep on high guard."

FT2 moved in the direction Mila instructed quickly. The sound in her voice conveyed an urgency like they'd never heard before. Sophia, in danger of being recaptured, or worse, was on all of their minds as they pounded up the road, taking the right turn she'd instructed. Then, peeling to the left the first chance they got. People were streaming from their houses, leaping back in gasps as the men plucked their way through the murmuring crowd fighting toward the center of the city.

So far so good-

A man stabbed out from the crowd with a knife, slashing at Ryan's chest, digging a gash into his protective plate, catching the SEAL off guard. Tex pounded his fist in the man's face, laying him out flat. "You good?" he asked.

"Good," Ryan responded, checking his plate. "Thank goodness for armor," he added. The team continued to move forward. Keeping their eyes peeled.

****

Sophia lay breathing heavily on the ground, reserved to her fate. The sound of Hasan's men drawing closer grew. She closed her eyes, thinking back to the dinner gatherings she had with Fred and Sherry and how she'd never get to see their smiling faces again. The laughter she'd shared with the team. Her great heart-to-heart talks with Wallace. Her dismissals of Tex's flirting. Everything about life that she'd never get to experience again. "I am sorry, I did my best," she mumbled to herself.

A buzzing noise arched down from the sky as she pictured her last moments of life. Something about it was familiar. She couldn't quite put a finger on it. Her eyes snapped open. A spot loomed high over her. It was growing larger. She squinted, trying to block out as much sunlight as she could. She was willing her eyes to focus. The shapeless object started to take on a form rapidly—a distinct form at that.

****

"Get up. Get up, Sophia," Mila urged her friend. The quartet that had been chasing her was now sixty yards from her location.

"Quicker, drop it quicker," Fred barked. Richard jabbed the joystick forward. The monitor displaying the drone's video feed angled sharply downward, perpendicular to the ground, sending the drone into an all-out nosedive. "At a thousand feet, pull it up. Get up, girl!" he shouted at the screen.

Sophia's image enlarged on the monitor as the drone dropped altitude. Her blood-splattered, weary, defeated face enveloped the screen in HD. The room gasped at her appearance as her body lay lifeless on the ground, not knowing if she was even still alive. A dead AIA soldier lay next to her. They could see Hasan and his men closing in on her. Where was Wallace and his men?

****

Realization pounded into Sophia's heart like a jab of an epinephrine needle. The shape hovering above her was a predator drone. A US predator drone. The team knew where she was.

Sophia sat upright with renewed life. *Was the team already here?* They clearly knew exactly where she was. The battered and beleaguered woman slowly climbed to her feet, scooping up the handgun. Every muscle and bone ached, but she wasn't going to give up the fight. She spun, seeing two of Hasan's men break through the crowd, leveling their guns at her. Like a scene from a movie, she was supercharged with a spike of adrenaline. Sophia drew faster, sending two rounds hurtling at the AIA members. Both crumpled to the ground.

The other two, along with Hasan, roared, shoving residents aside and fired. Bullets whipped past Sophia. She squeezed to fire back. The gun's slide locked into the back position, out of ammo.

One of the pursuers locked aim at her. She chucked the pistol at him. It hit him, sending his burst skyward. His comrade lined up his shot.

A bright burst of red exploded out of his chest as he lurched backward, falling to the dirt, a pool of blood seeping out from under him.

"Run," came a booming welcoming Texan drawl. Sophia spun to see Tex standing on top of a building across the street—three other figures by his side. Rounds pounded the area around her. "I said run, dammit," Tex shouted again.

This time, without hesitation, Sophia bolted from the side street, back out onto the main road and down it as Tex and the team exchanged fire with Hasan and his last man.

The two sides exchanged a stream of bullets, holding the two pursuers at bay while Sophia escaped. "One, zeros on the move headed north on the main road. We're holding-"

The top of the facade of the building they were standing on started chipping away to their left. Gutierrez and Tyus spun, shifting fields of fire. A contingent of armed men were advancing on the team's rooftop position. Ryan looked back to the side street where Hasan and his other men were. They were gone. *Shit.* "Hasan is back in pursuit, taking fire," Ryan radioed.

Sophia sprinted up the road, searching for any way to get back to Ryan and Tex's position. She peeked over her shoulder to see Hasan and the other man explode out of an alley back onto the main road. Onlookers disappeared behind their doors as shots rang up the road. Her heart pounded in her chest a thousand beats a minute. It would be a shame to die now.

She zigged off the road down onto another street, hoping to find another way to double back to Tex's location, barreling down the smaller side street, coming to a T-section of alleys. She gave a subtle peek over her shoulder. No one was in sight. *Good,* she thought if she ducked down one of the alleys, maybe she could lose them. Angling to go left, her forward momentum suddenly ceased as she smacked into what felt like a brick wall.

She crumpled to the ground in a heap, jarred by the collision into whatever she'd just run into. Sophia fell flat on her backside. Dazed, she opened her eyes to find herself staring up at Wallace's bearded face. The normally stoic man cracked a smile as he reached down, taking her by the arm and hauling her back to her feet. "Um…um…" Trying to speak, Sophia found her mouth dry.

The smile on the SEAL's face phased out as he cupped her aside with his arm, swinging her behind him and the three other men she knew as Alwani, Walsh, and Johns. All four men had snapped their rifles up. She peeked over Wallace's shoulder to see Hasan and the other man standing at the end of the street—a sardonic glare behind his beady black eyes.

Both sides opened fire, and Sophia's eyes snapped shut at the rata-tat-tat of the dueling bangs. All she heard were bodies and guns clattering to the ground.

"Would you like to go home?" Sophia opened her eyes to see both men at the end of the street, lying motionless on the ground. Hasan's body convulsed, not from one last breath of life but another volley of rounds littered his corpse as Tex, Ryan, Tyus, and Gutierrez appeared, standing over him to make sure he was dead. "So, what do you say? Would you like to go home now?" Wallace asked again.

Sophia could only manage a small head nod before collapsing

in Wallace's arms.

FRED paced frantically between two concrete pillars with a sense of anxiousness he'd never felt before in the underground garage of the Embassy. He hated waiting, as he had always been a man of doing. He wanted to go to the airport to meet the team but was well aware that he was also expecting an important call.

Zooming back and forth with a dizzying pace, the eyes of the embassy workers, military personnel, and medics who were standing idly by to assist the new arrivals tried to keep up with him. They didn't know him, nor any details about what was going on. All they were told was a team of American Special Forces members was bringing someone into the building that would need medical attention and that that person was of high priority.

For that matter, Fred himself didn't know the full extent of the situation. He didn't know the type or severity of injuries that Sophia had suffered. Wallace wasn't very specific with any information as he wasn't able to get anything out of the agent on the account that she hadn't woken up since crumbling into his arms in Mudhainab, leaving him to fear the worst.

Was she alive? Clearly. Was she able to move and be ambulatory? Yes. This was evidenced by her romping through the city to escape the clutches of Hasan, who was finally taken off the board. The world would for sure be a better place without that lunatic running around killing and torturing people.

However, what damage had he been able to inflict on his Sophia? Not just physically but mentally. Would she even be able to continue not only this mission but her career afterward, Fred thought? When they'd met, she was battling with Post Traumatic Stress Disorder from a failed mission years prior. She had only just recently been able to overcome it. *How would this now affect her state?*

"Fred, you need to calm down," Mila snipped at him. She'd been waiting in the garage, too. Somehow, she was managing to hold her stuff together better than Fred. She was leaning against a wall, her arms folded across her chest and her legs crossed one over the other. She caught a glimpse of one of the Marines standing nearby. He was eyeballing her leg; his lingering stare tracked up her long leg to the slit in her skirt. He smiled as she caught him eying her. His expression silently asked for a rendezvous later. She shook her head, mouthing 'as if,' before pushing off the wall to join Fred, who'd stopped pacing on her request. "She'll be ok." She came to rest by his side, eying the ramp descending into the artificially illuminated structure. "She's alive. We got her back."

"I know." The American gave the German a sympathetic glance, sighing. "I am over here pacing around like a nervous wreck, forgetting that she's your friend."

"Best friend."

"How are you holding it together so well?"

"Ha." Mila gave a nervous chuckle. "Practice, unfortunately. I lost my parents when I was sixteen. They were murdered by a Libyan refugee in a mugging went wrong. Plus, I've lost several of my friends through the years. Some were killed in front of me. So, I am no stranger to loss," Mila explained. "Being a hacker for the criminal underworld is decent money. But it has drawbacks, too. One being you can't trust people; two, you lose people."

Fred could tell through her stoic mask she was hurting. That was one of his true talents, being able to read people. He was currently reading her pain.

He continued his pacing after glancing at his watch. The plane had landed ten minutes ago. They'd arranged a police escort to the embassy. They should be arriving soon. "You know…" He whipped around, pacing back toward Mila. "I always wanted kids." The German shot him a look of surprise. "But, Sherry, my wife couldn't have any. So, I filled that void with my trainees. I never lost one until last year. Sure, I've lost partners, but never a trainee. Trainees are different. You teach them, grow them, and get to know them inside and out. Then I lost William. He was my last trainee. He was shot and killed by an AIA cell member. That loss really did a number on me. I never thought I'd ever feel that level of pain again." He stiffened with a sense of pride, reminiscing about the young man and his sacrifice. Then his expression dropped into a somber one. "This...this though; somehow feels worse, and I know she's not dead. I feel... feel like a..." He cupped a hand to his chin, unable to finish his thought.

This was the first time in his life that he truly wished he could've taken someone else's place—Sophia's place and take all the pain and suffering she'd endured on to himself. It was at this moment he surmised the gut-wrenching feeling in the pit of his stomach was what all parents went through when their children suffered something unimaginable. The stark realization hit him. He was a parent.

Maybe not Sophia's biological one, but the two had bonded, and he and Sherry welcomed her into their lives. He viewed her not only as a fantastical agent and person but also saw himself as a proud father of an amazing young woman.

Mila put a comforting hand on Fred's shoulder. "I know she feels the same way. She's told me on multiple occasions that she feels that you and your wife have given her a second chance at having a family and parents again. She's going to be ok."

"How did you two become friends?" Fred asked, trying to pass the time waiting.

****

Sophia forced her eyes open only to be blinded by a bright light that flooded into her iris.' She blinked, turning her head away from the dazzling illumination. "I thought for sure heaven would be slightly warmer," she muttered, a chill slicing through her body.

"You're awake," Wallace beamed. "Welcome back. Here." He slid a blanket over her.

"So, I am not dead?" She tried to sit up only to find herself strapped to a gurney. "Wha... where am I?" Unable to rise, she looked around as best she could, finding herself in the back of some kind of ambulance, picking up the faint warble of sirens. Her eyes came to rest on Wallace's bearded face.

"We're in Rabat, Morocco, on the way to the embassy," he

said, grinning. "You gave us a hell of a scare."

"Why Rabat? We were supposed to meet back in Saudi Arabia." She forced her head up as far as she could, fighting against the bed restraints, her heart's pace quickening. "Can we get these off, please? I've had enough of being restrained for a lifetime." She smacked her lips together, throat dry, her lips cracked and peeled. "Can I get some water too?"

The paramedic in the back with the two looked to Wallace for confirmation if he could. He nodded. The paramedic started to remove Sophia's restraints. Wallace handed Sophia a bottle of water once her hands were freed. "Here."

She took a swig, which became a gulp. The ambulance bounded over a pothole. Sophia's lips popped off the rim, spilling the rest of the contents onto her. "Dammit," she cursed, chucking the bottle in frustration. She sat up, finding herself dressed in a medical gown. "Where's my clothes? How long have I been out? Where's Hasan?"

"Relax." Wallace pushed her back down. "You need to rest; we're almost to the embassy."

"I can't rest. I can't let my guard down. I need to stay strong. I've still got work to do. I need to know what's going on. Did you get Stone? Hasan said you guys missed him." Sophia tried to sit up again, only for Wallace to push her back down.

"You need to rest, woman. For goodness sake, you've been held prisoner and tortured for five days. You don't need to be strong anymore. Not for me, at least. You can relax now. Let it out."

"There's nothing to let out. I am good to go," Sophia insisted, steeling herself, pushing down memories of her torture. She wasn't going to show any sign of weakness. She needed to be ready to continue the fight.

"Bullshit," Wallace countered. "When my SEER training ended, I was a mess for a week. And I knew that was fake—that I wasn't a hair breath away from death every second. You need time. Let it out."

"There's nothing to let out," she insisted. "This isn't over." Somewhere in her mind, the primal instinct to survive was still active. She couldn't break down, not now.

"OK, fine. Damn persistent woman," Wallace grumbled. "You've been out for a day. Just a day." His tone was mocking. "After we pulled you out of Mudhainab, we ex-filled back to the airbase in Oman. When you were evaluated, they said you were suffering from severe dehydration and exhaustion. They re-dressed the wound in your hand, flooded you with antibiotics, and re-splinted your broken finger. Doctors there said you needed rest and would probably be out for a day or two more. I guess they underestimated your stubbornness," he smiled.

"Har har, funny man," Sophia shot back. "Hasan?"

"He's dead. You watched us gun him down," Wallace added with suspicious curiosity. "You sure you're ok? I think you need more rest."

"I'm fine," the agent countered. "I just… I am fine. Like they said, I'm dehydrated. The last thing I can really remember was Hasan pointing a gun at me, then Tex shouting to run."

"Ok, so you missed a few points then. That's fine. The important thing is Hasan is dead, and so is the entire AIA. That was their main compound and last stronghold, according to the intel we pulled out of there. So, the book is closed on the AIA for good."

"Stone?"

Wallace ran a hand through his growing beard. "Yeah, about that." He paused, hesitating if he should give her the full run down or just a cliff notes version and leave Fred to fill in the rest. He decided on the latter. "He got away in Tangier."

Sophia let out an aggrieved sigh. "How the fuck does he keep getting away?"

"It's fine. We'll get him." The ambulance turned, and Wallace's eyes shifted ahead, seeing the gates to the embassy opening. The vehicle passed right through without an inspection. He looked out the back window at the other three SUVs housing the rest of his team; they passed by with no issues as well. "Anyways." He turned back to Sophia.

"How'd you find me?" she interrupted.

"That's for another day. As for now. Someone is eager to see you."

****

A red with white stenciling emergency vehicle bounded over a speed bump at the top of the ramp leading into the bowels of the parking garage. The medical personnel on standby readied themselves, trying to figure out what to expect.

Fred's body tensed. He could feel Mila doing the same. Somehow, unconsciously, they'd found themselves holding hands in support of each other.

The van raced down the ramp, screeching to a halt. The three medical personnel rushed to the back of the vehicle with a stretcher; another pulled a wheelchair around. They were prepared for any occurrence. The two Marines advanced to the doors as the three black SUVs ground to a halt a few yards back.

For a second, everyone waited, startled by a pounding on the back door. The two Marines threw open the doors.

"Bout damn time," Wallace quipped, hopping down. "We're not going to need that," he added, pushing the stretcher away, eyeballing the wheelchair and the woman assigned to push it. "We might need that." He gestured for her to be on standby. He twisted back to the inside of the van, holding his hands out. "Come on, we've got some eager beavers here."

Sophia weakly took Wallace's hands and, with the help of the paramedic, pulled herself off the gurney. It took considerably more strength than she thought it would. Every inch of her body ached. She gingerly stepped a foot out, dropping it to the ground. The hard concrete, a welcomed sign of civilization, penetrated through her hospital socks as she stepped all the way out.

Her knees wobbled, and her legs shook as she fought to stand upright. "So, who's this special someone who's waiting to see me? I doubt I am getting a Presidential medal for being kidnapped."

"No, how about one for bringing down the terrorist group that attacked the U.S.?" Fred stepped out from behind the door, Mila in tow. "How are you doing, kid?" Fred added.

Sophia let out a gasp, seeing Fred's face appear out of the

shadows. Somehow, seeing him standing there in front of her in Morocco, she instantly knew that somehow he was instrumental in her rescue. It was a gut punch. Everything she'd endured over the last several days flooded back. Tears burst from her eyes like the levy of a river breaking as she staggered toward him. Her weakened legs gave out under her weight, and she collapsed.

Fred caught Sophia in his arms. "It's ok, I've got you." He waved off Wallace, who'd bounded to catch her as she buried her face into his shoulder. She tried to speak between sobs, but it was completely unintelligible. "Shhh, it's ok. You're safe now. We got you."

Sophia continued to heave between the cascading waterfall of tears. Then, her entire body fell limp as she passed out.

Fred motioned for the wheelchair. Tex, who, along with the rest of the SEALs, had disgorged from the SUVs, rushed over politely, pushing the nurse aside. "We've got this sir." He pushed the chair behind Sophia. Fred, along with Wallace, gently placed her down in it. "Lead the way." He signaled for the nurse to guide them in. The rest of the team filed into the embassy behind them, Wallace staying behind.

"When did she wake?" Fred asked the SEAL commander.

"Moments before we pulled in."

"What did you tell her?"

"Nothing much. Just that Hasan was dead and that Stone got away, but we'll catch him," he responded, watching his team disappear around the corner.

"So, she doesn't know it was ultimately Stone that helped rescue her?"

"Nope. Figured I'd let you tell her." Wallace slapped a hand on the ex-agent's shoulder, padding across the parking space into the embassy, passing Mila en route and giving her a quick hug.

"Thanks," Fred called after Wallace. "Not sure how I am going to break that one," he muttered, running a hand through his graying hair.

"You'll figure it out," Mila added.

"Sir," Richard appeared in the doorway. "He's on the phone."

"Great." Fred rolled his eyes. "Another conversation I am not looking forward to."

****

Fred strode into the operations room. Gabby and Jerry were huddled in the center, discussing something among themselves. Upon seeing Fred, Jerry turned, and the conversation ceased. He pointed to the red phone on the wall. "He's waiting to be patched back through, sir."

The two agents shared a look of concern. "Are we really going to do this? After all this time and money, loss of life, and poor Sophia's torture. He's just going to get a slap on the hand?" Gabby scowled. The vitriol behind the words was a sentiment shared by all of them. "This is crap," she muttered, shaking her head.

"I know," Fred said, picking up the phone. "Patch him through," he instructed the switchboard operator. "I don't like it either," he added.

"Agent Jones," Stone's voice cracked against the speaker. "I've received word from my contacts that Agent Evans has been successfully recovered. Alive, nonetheless. Congratulations to the team. They finally accomplished something." His tone suggested he meant it more as an insult.

"When are you turning yourself in?" Fred cut straight to the point. He wasn't in the mood for idle chit-chat. He wanted to get this over as quickly as possible.

"Well, you see, I have to put some affairs in order here. Then I have to ensure that you're not going to go against the deal."

"How the fuck can I?" Fred cut in. "It's signed by the Attorney General. And unlike you, I am not into breaking the law, even if it's for my personal gain and satisfaction."

"Everything I did was for my country," the Oklahoman spat back angrily. "I ensured that America would always stay at the ready. Never again would we be lulled into a false sense of security by our comfortable lifestyles, and where the youth of these new generations, with all of their modern luxuries, couldn't get complacent again. It's because of me that our military might have stayed leaps and bounds ahead of the rest of the world.”

“At the cost of lives that had nothing to do with terror. Just innocent bystanders that were enveloped in your evil plot by virtue of wrong place, wrong time,” Fred countered.

“You can’t put a cost on safety and security. I am a patriot.”

“You’re a mass murderer.”

“Time will be on my side. History will judge me as a patriot along with the likes of George Washington, Alexander Hamilton, James Madison, John Adams, and Benjamin Franklin.” Fred could hear the snarl in Stone’s voice. “I will be right. There will be a day of reckoning for our country. One that you will wish we were prepared for. You’ll see.”

“You are delusional if you think your name will ever be mentioned along with their likes.” Fred had tired of listening to Stone’s dribble. The man had somehow convinced himself that he was the ultimate patriot. “Your name will be synonymous with the likes of Timothy McVeigh, Eric Robert Rudolph, and Ted Kaczynski, you lunatic. I can’t wait to get you behind bars. Even if it’s only for a year.” The simple utterance of the short sentence was like acid in his mouth. Hopefully, in that time, they’d find a way to undo the deal and keep him locked away forever.

“We’ll see,” Stone retorted. “Anyways, I’ve got to go and get ready for my return to my country. I’ll be in touch in the next day or two with the details of when and where.”

“What about your son-in-law?”

“I’ll bring him too. You can arrest him along with me,” Stone said coldly. “Although since he’s not part of the deal, he’ll spend a lot longer in prison. So, I guess you’ll have some semblance of justice. Do give my regards to Agent Evans.” The line clicked, going dead.

“Asshole,” Fred spat, slamming the receiver back down, nearly tearing the phone from the wall.

****

Stone hung up the phone on his desk, simultaneously pulling the small flip phone from his back pocket. He speed-dialed the only number on the phone. Someone on the other side picked up. "It's done. I have a few things to set in order. Then I'll turn myself over to the FBI agent. Are you sure that the deal can't be undone in any way possible?"

"No, it can't."

Came the voice on the other line. It wasn't the same one from before. In fact, he'd suspected he'd never communicated with the same person twice in a row. Stone thought the extreme level of detail that had gone into keeping the members of the cabal totally anonymous was admirable. "About my son-in-law. I am going to hand him over at the exchange. Will he be… taken care of." A euphemism for being killed.

"Yes, it'll be arranged. Remember not a word of any of this, and when you get out, you'll be set up for life," the voice added.

"Great. I am sorry that it's come to this. I had every intention of fulfilling my role in the organization. After all, I am a patriot. However, at my age, my family-"

"Family is everything," the voice cut in. "Without it, we are rudderless and a drift. The council understands. And don't worry, Senator. You have absolutely fulfilled your role and obligations. That's why, in a year, you'll be back out and on a road to redemption. The American public loves a redemption story."

"Thank-" The line went dead. "You."

The double doors to the office burst open. West and Briggs barged in dressed in full tactical gear. "The CIA whore has been rescued, and my team has trailed the SEALs to the embassy in Rabat. We are ready to strike," West crowed.

"You know, there is such a thing called knocking," Stone chastised, hastily slipping the cell phone into his back pocket. "As a former military man, you should know better. Have some fucking manners."

"Sorry, sir, it was important," Briggs apologized. West scowled at the old man.

"Did you hear me? I said we have their location. Your wife and daughter, my wife and kids," West ranted. "We're going to get them as you ordered. The strike will be easy. They won't even know it's coming. They'll be completely defenseless. And once we rid ourselves of our ghost trail. They'll be foolish to send another team after us. They'll let us go."

Stone pulled out his oversized puffy desk chair and dropped into its seat. He opened a small cigar box on the desk, plucking one of its contents. He ran a finger down its side, taking a whiff of it. "Cuban. Real Cuban. You know you can get them here," he said, sizing up the two men in front of him. He removed a cigar cutter from the drawer to his right. "You can stand your men down."

"What!" West barked. "What do you mean?"

"I've secured a deal with *our* government." Stone lit the cigar, taking in a drag and casually blowing the smoke out in a ring.

"When were you going to let us in on this deal?" West and Briggs exchanged looks, bewildered. "You promised we'd exact revenge on the woman who ruined my company and way of life," West carried on. "We know where they are. We should take them all out now."

"Son, calm down. As I said, I've secured a deal. Where I'll spend a year max in prison, meanwhile all of you are granted immunity from all perceived crimes committed. We'll have our family back in due time. Plus, get to return to the States."

"I don't give a shit about returning," West fumed. "I want my revenge on that CIA whore who helped ruin my life." He slammed a fist down on the desk. Stone drew another drag.

"What about our family? Getting revenge can put them in danger. No." He shot up. "This deal is happening. I am going to turn myself in. You and what's left of your men will escort me to the deal and collect our family. And that is that. Understood?"

West straightened. "Yes, sir. Yes, Dad. We'll get our family back then. Copy that." He whisked around and marched back out of the office, slamming the doors behind him and Briggs.

"So that's it?" Briggs asked as the pair walked away. "What about all the men we lost? We don't get revenge for them?"

West turned, glowering at the door. "Something's not right. The old man never rolls over."

"Do you not trust him?"

"I don't. He's always playing some angle. But we'll go to the exchange. There, we'll take everyone out. Someone has to pay for me, losing the company that I worked so hard to build and for all of our fellow brothers who have died. No, I am getting my revenge."

"What about your family, sir?" Briggs asked.

"Fuck'em, I can always create another one. Maybe this time, I'll have a wife who doesn't let herself go after kids."

CHAPTER TWENTY-TWO

SOPHIA stirred, feeling her aching body tremor; her restless nerve endings twitched, springing her consciousness back to life. A quiet thought deep in the recesses of her mind ambled to the forefront, telling her, *your job isn't done.* The voice that had started was a mere murmur, a sound just above a whisper. It was growing louder and louder with each passing second until the timid octave became a beastly lion-like throaty roar, unable to ignore it any longer. Her body jolted. Beeps once buried silently in her ears became a shrill cry—another jolt.

Her eyes sprang open. She sucked in a deep breath. The beeps reached their crescendo, then began to fade to background noise as the rest of her senses became overwhelmed by her surroundings.

Sophia's eyes darted around the room, taking in the sterile scene. She lifted herself with considerable effort into a sitting-up position to find herself lying in a bed. No, it was a hospital bed. Directly in front of her, a pristine white wall with several white boards attached poked out from behind a pair of partially opened privacy curtains. She blinked twice, focusing her sight on the writing sprawled across it. It denoted her name along with several times written beside it. The floor was titled, and it was also a bright white. The overhead lights seemed to be cranked on high, forcing her to squint. A low buzzing noise wafted down from the ceiling.

To her right, the source of the now mundane beeping was discovered—a vital sign monitoring machine. The screen displayed her heart rate, blood pressure, oxygen levels, and various other stats. Above it was a clear bag dangling from a hook containing a clear liquid with a tube running down. She traced the tube and found its trail ending at the crook of her arm, which was attached to a catheter tube.

As the rest of her senses began to filter back to life, a stinging sensation throbbed in her hands. Turning her attention from the needle that had pierced her skin, accessing the vein where the liquid was flowing to her hand. She noticed a splint on her right pinky finger. A thought lingered in her head: *how'd that happen?*

Along with that, she wondered how did she end up in a hospital. Another more painful sensation stopped that thought temporarily. The source came from her left hand.

She glanced over to see that her left hand had been wrapped up with a large dressing. Trying to close her hand, a shockwave of pain flared through her arm to her brain, sending up a flash to stop. The pain was too great.

Along with the blast of pain in her body, a gut punch of realization rolled in with it. She remembered how she got there and the events that preceded it. Her body temperature spiked due to a massive flood of cortisol and adrenaline that rushed into her veins. The docile beeping from the machine beside her rose into a blaring alarm. Her heart raced, thudding in her chest. It felt like it was about to burst out and flop down onto the bed.

"It's okay, it's okay." A pair of hands reached out and scooped hers into theirs. Fred plopped down on the bed to her left. "It's okay. You're at the embassy in Rabat, Sophia. You're fine; there's no danger."

Her heart rate and pulse dropped rapidly, seeing Fred's familiar face smiling at her. The beeping to her right subsided as well. Her eyes continued to dart around, though, looking for signs of danger. "Hasan? The AIA?" she questioned.

"Dead and gone," Fred answered, despite knowing that she'd already been told that information from Wallace, he reiterated it. He didn't want to press the issue that she'd been told before and yet still couldn't remember. She'd just been through an ordeal. Her brain subconsciously was fighting to suppress the events of the last week.

"Are you sure?"

"We're very sure. The boys made sure of it before ex-filling from Mudhainab. We won't be hearing from that group anymore."

Sophia relaxed, laying back down, her heart and pulse dropping back to a normal reading, or so the machine suggested. "How, why, when?"

"Wallace came for me," Fred began to answer, already knowing the slew of questions she would have. "When he found out that Hasan had taken you, he came to Milwaukee. He said that you had always told him the only other person who knew the AIA as well as you was me."

"I do say that a lot," Sophia whispered, a smile breaking across her face for the first time in what felt like ages.

"Once he told me what happened, we devised a way to get me on the team. Owens was on board immediately. From there, we flew to Cuba and spoke to Tarik and Adeel to get information."

"Guess they were helpful since you found me."

"Sort of. Tarik gave us the location of a place where Hasan could've been holding you. The team went in to get you, but I suspect we missed you by a few days. You'd already been moved. Though they did wind up rescuing another woman before she could be sold."

"That's great. But how did you find me then if I'd already been moved? Interrogate some of the AIA?"

"There wasn't enough time. It was a trap. Hasan, I guess, knew the team would hit that spot and sent a group to take them out."

"Everyone's fine, though, right?"

"Yeah, the team made it out."

"So, again. How did you all find me."

Fred paused, thinking best how to parse what he was sure would be a series of follow-up questions for his next answer. "We... kind of... had help."

Sophia's brow furrowed, thinking who in the world would've been able to help, coming to no answer. "I don't understand. No one knew where he was keeping me. If they did, the team would've gotten me out sooner. So, who helped?" Fred's eyes wondered about, suppressing a nervous laugh. There really was no way of sugarcoating what was about to follow. "Fred Jones," Sophia's tone dropped to a register he'd only heard from his mother and wife. "Who helped?"

"You're not going to believe or like it, but.... Stone." Fred instantly recoiled, knowing what was about to happen.

"No fucking way," Sophia shouted. Her voice echoed off the walls of the sterile room. "I don't believe you. Why? He wants me dead."

"Actually... he..." Fred absolutely didn't want the next series of words to come out but knew they would have to. "Used your capture to broker a deal to return to the States serving only a year for financial crimes committed in the furtherance of unknowingly aiding a terrorist group," he spat the words out as fast as he could, hoping they'd just all congeal into a mesh Sophia wouldn't want to unpack.

Each successive word punched at Sophia's heart and stomach like she was in a boxing match with Mike Tyson. The world spun around her dizzyingly.

"He what?" The machine roared back to life in a cacophony of whirs and beeps. The vital sign readouts gave away a giant spike in her blood pressure. "No fuck that, put me back. I'll endure years worth of Hasan's torture before I let that piece of shit get away with a slap on the hand. No fuck that. I wanna go back." She couldn't believe what she was hearing. "How could anyone agree to that deal? He is a traitor to his own country."

"Calm down, please, Sophia." Fred clocked the rise in her vitals. "No one wanted to see your death on the internet. That's how."

"Calm down, how can I calm down? Everything we've worked for is about to go up in smoke. A *year*. He gets a *year* in prison. He should be getting the death penalty or, at the very least, life. How?" she fumed. "Call whoever made the deal. Tell them I don't agree. No way."

"Sophia?" Fred took her hands again. "It doesn't work like that. I know you know this. Stone's not an idiot, sadly. He wouldn't have given us your location without a signed deal. It's done. There's no undoing it."

She took a deep breath, calming herself. She knew Fred was right. Her mind was telling her he was right. She had to look at this as at least a partial win. He would do time. Not a lot, and not enough to make up for all the death he'd caused. But she had to believe somehow, somewhere, karma would catch him. "When?" She asked solemnly.

"Soon. He'll call with the place that he's going to surrender."

"What about West?"

"That's the funny part." Fred gave a genuine, happy laugh.

"He's not part of the deal." Sophia's eyebrows raised, intrigued. "The deal was Stone turns himself in. His immediate family is to suffer no consequences as they knew nothing. West, though, Stone's probably planning a way to pin everything on him. So, when we meet to bring Stone in, we're also going to bring West in. Though I surmise it's not going to be without a fight. So, the team's going to go to back me and bring him down."

"Yeah, we are. How are you feeling, Sof?" A new voice entered the room. Wallace peeked around the curtain that had been drawn to give privacy. However, no one else was in the room. "I see you're awake… and shouting."

Sophia blushed. "You heard that?"

"I think the whole embassy heard you," Wallace said, pulling up a chair and pushing the curtain open wider.

Fred's phone, sitting on the nightstand beside the chair he'd been sleeping in, vibrated across the table. He picked it up, reading the message. "I'll leave you two, three," he corrected, seeing Tex come around the curtain. "To talk. I have to see to this. Sophia, I am glad we got you out. My heart would've broken losing you." He visibly fought back tears, leaning over and kissing her on the forehead.

"Fred," Sophia swept up his hand, squeezing it. "Thank you for coming for me."

"They did all the work." He nodded to Tex and Wallace.

"Damn, skippy," Tex affirmed playfully.

Fred took his leave, padding out of the room.

"Boys," Sophia addressed the men. "Thank you. I am definitely submitting the entire team for Distinguished Intelligence Medals."

"You hear that, Tex, you might finally be mentioned in the same sentence as intelligence," Wallace chided.

"Ha, funny. I don't need a medal. Having you back is award enough," Tex said, smiling at Sophia.

She clutched a hand to her chest, "Aw, thanks Tex."

"But, if you wanted to reward me, you could take me up on

my date offer," he added with a grin.

"And… there he is. The Tex I know, adore, and love."

"Mark my words; we will go on a date at some point. I don't care if right now you don't swing my way, but…" He batted his eyebrows. "Never say never. Curiosity will get you."

"I am not a cat, Tex. But, who knows, maybe your charms will persuade me away from the ladies." She gave him a wry smile."

"Anyways," Wallace cut in, disrupting their playful flirting. "What have we learned?"

Sophia turned to face him, giving an exaggerated eye roll. "To stop running off and to always wait for backup. Never go it alone," she intoned with him. It had been a saying he'd repeated to her many times over the last few months. He was trying to break her of her penchant for running off.

"Hopefully, now you'll get it after this." His tone became more serious. "You're stronger with a team. Please, stop doing that. Or next time-"

"I get it," Sophia cut him off. She set her eyes on his. "I really do get it. Never again."

"Good."

"Hey, so about this shitty deal," Tex interrupted, forcing another eye roll from Sophia.

"I don't want to talk about that," she hissed, still boiling mad about it. "How's the rest of the team?" Wallace, Tex, and Sophia continued to chat away. The boys filled her in with as much information as they could.

"By the way, I am sorry," Tex said. "I tried to get to you. I just…"

"It's not your fault, Tex. Remember, S.H.O.T.. At least you brought me back. For that, I will be forever grateful to all of you.

****

Fred padded out of the room and down the hallway away from the embassy's infirmary. He glanced over his shoulder, looking back toward the door, and a small relief rushed over him. His suspicions that Sophia's capture and torture may set back her mental state seemed to be assuaged for the moment, despite the small lapses in memory, which was to be expected. She seemed even more dedicated to the mission.

He guessed that trying to find and put away the man she felt responsible for everything was as good a coping mechanism as one could have.

He reached the end of the hall, pressing the button on the elevator. The infirmary was on the third floor of the building. He needed to get back to the ops center for his call. The text he'd received came from Mila. Stone had finally reached out to set the meet time and location where he would surrender and bring West to be taken into custody. It'd been two days since they'd last spoken.

With one last look back down the hall, his thoughts still lingered on how Sophia would cope after this all came to a resolution. It was one thing when your mind didn't have time to linger because it had to jump to the next problem to solve. However, once there were no more problems to solve and you had time to sit and dwell on things, that's when your mind could be your worst enemy.

The door opened, and Fred stepped into the car, pressing UG3 for underground level 3, where the command room was located. *They'd all find out soon enough what their lives would be like after a year of this foolishness*, he thought as the door closed.

Several minutes later, Fred entered the ops room. Mila sidled up to him. "How's she doing?" she asked.

"As well as can be, I guess," Fred answered. "I suspect we'll know more after this is all over. She's with Wallace and Tex right now. You should head up there, too. I am sure she'd love to see you right now," he added, nudging the woman.

A moment of apprehension stretched across the German's chiseled face; her prominent sharp jawline accentuated. She was stuck between seeing her friend still alive, thankfully, and fear. How would she react to her? She was in charge of the mission, which led to her being kidnapped. "I…"

"She's not going to blame you," Fred cut her off, practically reading her mind. "Just because you were running the mission from here doesn't mean you can control her actions. Deep down, she knows it was no one's fault; things happen." Mila nodded. "Well, I suppose we shouldn't keep this asshole waiting any longer." He stepped toward the phone on the wall. Then stopped whirling back on the German. "Seriously, go up there." He then continued his stride to the phone. He sucked in a deep breath steeling himself for the conversation. Talking to the egotistical, narcissistic, self-absorbed man had quickly become Fred's least favorite thing in the world to do. He picked up the line and instructed the call to be sent through.

"It's about damn time," Stone's southern accent blared through the headset. Fred peeled the receiver away. "I was starting to think you didn't want me anymore. Should I be worried you're not going to honor the arrangement your government made?" the former Senator barked.

"No, unlike you, *I* am a real American who swore to uphold our Constitution. If our government saw fit to make a deal, I am going to honor it. Anyway, when and where?" Fred cut to the chase, again hating having to speak to the man. He wanted to get this over with.

"Tomorrow, noon, there is an old, condemned building out on Rocade South Road far east of Rabat. We'll meet there," Stone said.

The location stuck out as very odd to Fred. *Why not at the embassy*, he thought? "I was hoping we could do this here."

"Not going to happen unless you want to risk a potential shoot out in the middle of Rabat with pictures of American military personnel, with the potential headlines 'American military personnel kills four Moroccans in a shootout with unknown peoples,'" Stone countered.

"Why would there be a shootout?" Fred questioned. "You're willingly handing yourself over."

Stone slapped his palm to his head. Fred could hear the smack over the phone. "It's a wonder the FBI could catch anyone. My son-in-law, duh. If he gets even the smallest hint that he's going to be taken in, too, there will be ramifications."

Fred pursed his lips together angrily at the insult. "You can't control him."

"He'll feel like a cornered animal. This needs to look on the up and up until the end. So, I would suggest bringing those ball-balancing Seals with you." The reference was meant as a dig at Wallace's team, likening them to the circus version of the animal balancing balls on their noses for entertainment.

"Fine. We'll be there."

"One other caveat," Stone interjected before Fred could hang up the phone. "You need to bring my family."

"Out of the question," Fred shot back without hesitation. Was he trying to play a fast one? Get them to bring the family into the open. Using a fake surrender to get them back.

Stone let out an exasperated sigh. "Like I said." His tone was patronizing. "This needs to look on the up and up. I told him that I'd made a deal where I, and *I,* alone, are surrendering basically in exchange for my family. So, if he doesn't see Rebecca, Megan, and the kids, he'll definitely know something is up, and bullets will start to fly. Jeez."

Fred pressed down the swelling anger. He could not recall anyone ever being able to get him so upset and angry as this man could. "Fine," he agreed, against his better judgment. "We'll do it your way."

"Good, and-"

"But, so help me, God," Fred slashed in. "If you are playing a fast one, I will put a bullet between your eyes in a heartbeat. Understood? See you tomorrow." Fred slammed the phone down. He whirled on Richard, Jerry, and Gabby. "I want everything on this building, the location around it, and I want surveillance on it ASAP. If we're walking into a trap, I want to know before we go in," Fred ordered. The three nodded and immediately began working on their assignment.

CHAPTER TWENTY-THREE

FRED stared at the hardened faces of the SEALs, making his closing remarks on the mission they were about to undertake. Each man had been listening intently during the brief after they'd filed into the briefing room, which was conveniently adjacent to the ops room. Mila, Richard, Jerry, and Gabby sat on the opposite side of the room in the back, listening to their part of what was about to unfold.

The culmination of a year's work that had started with him, Tobias, and William after the attack on the Harley Davidson Museum. A conclusion that, up until just over a week ago, he thought that he'd never be a part of since retiring from the FBI. Now, though, due to a series of unfortunate events that had brought him back into the fold, he was briefing an elite team of US SEALs that were going to bring Former Senator Roy Stone, the mastermind behind the events that had caused so much useless death—Williams', along with many others, to heel.

The door to the room creaked open, drawing everyone's attention. Sophia slid inside. Her right pinky was still splinted, and her left hand was wrapped in a ball of bandages. The various cornucopia of bruises and cuts on her face had begun to turn different shades of colors: blacks, blues, purples, greens, and yellows. She tried to make every effort to creep in as quietly as possible, all in vain.

Fred turned, seeing the battered woman slink in. "No, absolutely not," he roared, jabbing a finger at her wagging it. She didn't even need to say a word. He knew her well enough to know her intentions. And, they weren't simply to be a bystander. "Not happening." He shook his head vehemently. "Nope." He quickly slapped the laptop on the desk in front of him closed. It displayed images of the building where they were about to apprehend Stone and, hopefully with luck, West without a fight.

Sophia sheepishly cowered at his fervent denial of a question not even asked. "I just-"

"No," Fred reiterated, declaring definitively his objection.

"What's the harm?" Tex called out. "It's a simple grab."

Fred whirled on the SEAL. "And what if it's not? West is still a wild card; I know you were listening."

"I think she's earned it," Ryan added.

"Yeah, man, she's been through hell for this moment. You can't sideline her now," Tyus crowed.

"That's right, my dude," Walsh kicked in. "She's part of this team more than you."

"Let her go, let her go," Alwani, Gutierrez and Johns chanted.

Fred blustered at the defiance but was also proud that she'd completely won over an entire SEAL team with her efforts.

"Enough!" Wallace shouted. The room quickly fell silent.

"Thank you," Fred said. He turned back to Sophia. "I know you want to see this through, but I don't think it's a good idea, not in the field. See it through from the Ops room." He gestured to the room next door.

"Fred, come on, I want, I *need* to be there. Please, don't make me beg for this?" Sophia pouted, painfully steepling her hands together in the prayer gesture.

Fred folded his arms across his chest like a father would, being stern with a pleading child, shaking his head.

"Sir, if I may," Wallace broke the tense moment. "What if she stays in the car."

"Yeah, I'll stay in the car," Sophia jumped in, smiling at Wallace. "I won't get out. I promise."

Fred looked back at the rest of the team. Every one of them stared blankly back at him, silently telling him the same thing. Even Mila, Richard, Jerry, and Gabby's faces conveyed the same message. Fred inhaled deeply before speaking. "No." Everyone gasped; Fred cracked a smile. "Getting out of the car." He continued, throwing up his arms in defeat. "Who am I to say no to the will of everyone, apparently," he complained in mock defeat, his face screwed into a wry smile as he and Sophia exchanged nods. Within an instant, the grin on the older man's face swept away, replaced by a more earnest expression like a wave erasing markings in the sand. His face scrunched; his eyes narrowed. He leveled them upon Sophia. "Let's finish what we started together. Let's bring this asshole in."

Sophia felt the sincereness in Fred's voice. "Abso-fucking-lutely," she replied, steeling her resolve. Every square inch of her body felt sore and broken, but she wasn't going to let that stop her from seeing this mission through.

The room broke into clapping and cheering.

****

West sidled up beside Stone, who was staring anticipatory at the flapping plastic material covering maw between the steel frame of the half-finished four-story factory building on the outskirts of Rabat in an abandoned warehouse district. Stone picked the meeting spot to ensure they were far away from the city in case anything went wrong with the surrender.

"So, what was the full deal you made?" the CEO asked. "I know there's some angle you're working. As you always do." West's words were more accusative than seeking clarification on a ponderance. Briggs stalked up from behind the pair nestling to West's left. His head bobbed up and down, alerting West that he'd completed his mission.

Stone lazily cocked his head toward West as a beam of sunlight from overhead darted through the fluttering tarpaulins wrapped around the exterior support beams, drowning out the scowl on his son-in-law's face. "Excuse me, son," the older man snapped. "I don't like your tone." The former Senator bristled at the accusation leveled that he hadn't been forthcoming with information. That was true, but Stone couldn't let that on.

"I don't give a shit if you like my tone," West fired back. "I want to know the full deal you made. Since you'd decided to cut me out of the decision."

"I didn't cut you out," Stone retorted acidically, straightening up, puffing up his chest. "It came together rather quickly. I saw an opportunity to reunite *our* family and took it. You weren't around to mull it over with. I am sorry if that offends your sensibilities.

314

But I figured you'd be fine with being reunited with your kids and wife. My daughter."

It was West's turn to flex his alpha, arching his back before turning to face the older man. "I am just confused after everything we've done to keep America prepared for the inevitable attack that will come. Now, you're just going to give up. Roll over. I don't surrender, and neither do my men," West spat, and Briggs grunted in agreement.

Stone reflexed, shying away from West; he needed to de-escalate the situation to buy time for Fred to arrive. He turned back to face the entrance, willing Fred to hurry up. "We're not giving up. There's more than one way to skin a cat. It's easier from inside than out, son." West's face contorted into a sneer about to interject. "Get right, boy, here they come," Stone cut him off, seeing two black SUVs approach from beyond the tarp covering the front entrance between flaps.

****

Fred peered out the windshield of the SUV as it approached the skeletal frames of several unfinished office buildings. The area gave off an ominous impression of a graveyard of dead buildings. Weather-tattered tarps wrapped tightly around their exteriors. Giant rips and gashes exposed the steel support beams behind them like skin-protecting bones. The supports jutted toward the sky: some were only a story high; others were two or even four. "Slow down," he said, his hand patting the air down. Wallace eased off the accelerator, dropping the vehicle to a low crawl. The rocky gravel of the road crunched under the weight of the three-quarter-ton Chevrolet Suburban. A set of brakes squealed behind them. After a quick check in the side mirror, the trail Suburban eased to a stop. Both vehicles halted.

"What is it?" Sophia asked from the back, leaning forward and poking her head between the front seats.

"Not quite sure yet," Fred answered. His eyes darted around the landscape. Nothing suspicious immediately popped out. Everything was to be as expected. Stone had picked a spot almost entirely devoid of signs of the human world other than the remains of a forgotten building project. However, something gnawed at him from inside. "Alpha-actual to TOC, check the out perimeter please again." Fred leaned forward, checking around the area as far as his eyes could see.

Mila's team had done a full aerial recon of the area the previous day and again as the capture team departed the embassy en route to the meet. Nothing unusual came up during either recon scan. Everything in a two-mile radius of the site was just as it seemed during the previous checks. Richard had overlayed photos of the area taken on top of each other, and nothing was different.

Mila scanned the images, running them through a computer algorithm she'd built to pick up any variations, discovering none. "TOC to Alpha-actual, all seems to be good," she relayed her findings.

Fred shrugged. "Copy, TOC." He scanned the area again. His heart thumped in his chest. His instincts were all telling him something was off. Things seemed a little too quiet. Fred leaned back, chopping the feeling up to rust. The last time he'd actually been in the field. He and Sophia were ambushed by West's men, and Sophia had been shot. He wasn't too keen on a repeat.

"Am I going to get to speak to Roy before you take him?" Rebecca Stone asked, cutting through the quiet of the vehicle's interior, sitting in the back of the SUV. She studied her three traveling companions. "He's not the monster you think he is. I know Roy; he's a righteous man. If he's done the things you say, he's done them for a good reason."

Sophia leaned back into her seat, her eyebrow twitching at the notion this woman was still somehow defending her husband. She let out an involuntary snort before answering. "Mrs. Stone, the things your husband has done have directly resulted in the deaths of hundreds of Americans—some personal friends of mine. His reasons don't matter. He needs to pay for those crimes."

"Yes, yes, he does. And he will. All I am saying is he's not a monster. Isn't this proof?"

Sophia eyed the woman with an admiring look for her persistence in defending her husband. A moment of doubt crept into the corner recesses of her mind. *He did surrender*, she had to admit. *No*, shaking her head and the thought loose. Stone was an animal, sadistic, narcissistic, and maniacal. He was only turning himself in because it served his purpose. He was also going to lay all of the blame on Johnathan West's head to save his own skin. That's not a righteous man; that's a monster.

"That one." Fred pointed out the window straight ahead to the four-story structure. "Alpha-actual to TOC, what do you have on the building directly in front of us?"

"We are registering three signatures inside the building," Mila answered, gazing at the wall monitor displaying the ISR image of the building from the drone high above. "Richard, will you be a darling and show me the heat," she whispered into the young man's ear, prickling his skin. He did what she asked, clacking away at the keys of his computer. The screen flashed from a grayscale to one displaying vivid colors of oranges, reds, yellows, blues, and blacks. "Nothing on heat either," she reported. "Thank you, dear." She patted him on the shoulder.

"Good. Time to get this over. Proceed." Fred waved for Wallace to continue forward.

The front end of the SUV slowly drove between the two supports, creating what would've been the building entrance. The front end pushed the tarp up and over the hood, then the windshield as it crept forward. The tarp slid off the windshield; the vehicle's automatic headlights flipped on with the shadowing. The beam caught three figures standing at the back of the room. Partially hidden in shadows.

"Here's good enough," Wallace said, bringing the vehicle toward the middle of the floor. His eyes narrowed on West. It was the first time he'd seen the man who had managed to kill two of his fellow SEALs back in Tangier. He and another man to his left were decked out in combat gear. "You ready?" he asked, directing the question to Fred.

"Yup." Fred twisted in his seat, facing the back rows. "Mrs. Stone, this needs to go down exactly how we talked about it. Don't worry, and don't panic; nothing is going to happen to you. The woman nodded. "And you," he said, jabbing a finger directly at

Sophia. "Do not-"

"Yeah, yeah, I know. *Don't* leave the vehicle," she intoned the last sentence in a lower, deeper register of her voice mockingly. Fred's intense gaze burned a whole right through her. She'd gone a little too far. "I know, I get it," Sophia added, softer this time, her voice striking a more sincere cord.

"Good." Fred opened his door and stepped out. Wallace and Rebecca followed suit.

The doors of the second SUV opened, and Alwani stepped out of the driver's side. Megan West exited the passenger side. Walsh, Johns, and the two kids, Jessica and Jacob, disgorged from the back seat. Fred waved them forward. The six occupants from the second SUV met the three from Fred's vehicle. Together, they rounded the front end of the lead SUV. Fred and Wallace took point, with Alwani dropping to the rear—Walsh behind Wallace and Johns behind Fred, with Rebecca and the West's in the middle. The group advanced forward.

Stone's face lit up seeing his family for the first time in over a week. "Sweetie, are Megan and the kids all okay?" Stone called out.

"Yes," Rebecca answered timidly.

"Right here is far enough," Fred snapped, halting the group. "It's time to make our swap." He called out, his voice booming in the quiet structure. Birds who'd been roosting on the upper girders took flight, fleeing the building. "You in exchange for your family."

"No tricks, right? My family goes with my son-in-law, and they are free to go. No charges." Stone covertly side-stepped away from West.

"The deal's already been agreed upon. I can't change it if I wanted to," Fred answered. "Besides, I do what my country asks of me."

"Enough," West bellowed. "We're making the exchange. You take the old man." Stone shot West a glare. "We take the women and children. Send them over."

"Fraid, that's not how this goes down," Fred barked, "Stone comes first. Then we send the family over. We take him and leave.

You get to go free." The plan was to get Stone clear of West before the team made their move to grab him.

****

Mila watched as the two Suburbans slowly rolled into the building. Once inside, she keyed the mic. "Go. You're clear." The four heat signatures that had been camped out in a nearby building exploded into action. They darted across the open territory to the side of the meeting place. Their dazzling, sparkling orange and red hues melted into the buildings, muted blue color scheme.

On Mila's order, FT2 burst into action. Ryan, Tex, Tyus, and Gutierrez sprinted covertly across the open expanse between the two skeletal buildings, picking their way to the edge of the meeting spot.

Tex slung his rifle across his back, quickly and quietly scaling the scaffolding that was still somehow attached to the side of the building. The steel piping of the framework clanged against the steel girder to which it was attached.

Ryan whipped his head up, seeing Tex mid-way up the platform. "Shhh," he hissed. Tex shot him a middle finger as a flock of birds flew out of the gaps in the framework. FT2's leader shook his head, giving Ty and Gut instructions via hand signals. The SEALs picked their way into the building, spreading out.

They slowly made their way to what would've been the lobby of the building where FT1 was making the arrest, using the shadows to stay hidden. They were to be the capture team for West if things didn't go as planned.

"Um," Richard muttered from behind his desk. His screen was mirroring that of the wall monitors. He zoomed in on an area of blue shading from the heat mapping of the vicinity just outside the building. "That's odd."

"What?" Mila glided over to Richard's station, leaning over his shoulder to see what had drawn his curiosity. Her left boob came to rest on the man's shoulder. His face reddened like a tomato.

"Um… um," he gulped, peering out his peripheral and seeing

down the German's blouse. "I think something is off about these cold zones," he said finally.

"How so? Don't they match our previous scans?"

"They do, but they look… almost artificial. Plus, I think that one." He pointed to a pulsating blue clump on the screen. "Moved." He switched angles, zooming back out and clacking away at the keys. He set up the images to be recorded.

"Keep an eye on it," Mila ordered, returning to her station. "TOC to Alpha actual; FYI, there may be something brewing."

****

Fred clandestinely keyed his mic twice to acknowledge Mila's warning. "That's just how this deal goes down," Fred urged. "If not, it's off the table." He turned away from the trio. "Let's go."

"Stop!" Stone shouted. He twisted to face West. "Don't fuck this up, son," he growled. "Alright, I am coming. We're making the swap. Me for my family. Then West leaves."

Fred and company turned back around. "Great. You come over, and once we have you, the family will be released."

"Deal. I am walking now." He shot one last glare toward West. Then, with his hands up, he started walking.

The mercenary and owner of Sotor Corps, though, paid him no attention. Briggs was whispering something into West's ear. The man's face washed with a wave of cool anger like he'd just been given some shocking news that he was expecting to receive.

"Dammit," Wallace whispered.

"What?" Fred asked as Stone began to cross the artificial setup of 'No Man's Land' between the two sides.

"S.H.O.T." Wallace turned his head to Fred, whose scrunched-up face gave away his confusion.

"Shit Happens Out There," Wallace answered the unasked question. "Get ready." His hand slid toward the M4 Carbine dangling from its harness in front of him. He tried to move as slowly as he could, hoping it would be imperceptible. Fred's right hand simultaneously inched for his holstered Glock.

****

"Alpha two, to all units, capture team in position," Ryan radioed as he and the others reached the meet. He cocked his head up to see Tex low crawl to the edge of the atrium overlooking the lobby. The sniper was already peering down his scope, settling in on his target.

The plan was clear. Once Stone was safely on Fred and Wallace's side, they'd inform West that he was also going to be taken into custody, at which point FT2 would converge to give him no option but to surrender peacefully unless he wanted to be taken out.

So far, the plan was unfolding just the way it was drawn up. Stone was close to the halfway point between the two groups. A whispered conversation was taking place between West and the man to his left. It would all be over in a minute or two.

A movement in the shadows on the other side of the room caught Ryan's eye. *Could it have been an animal?* They'd seen several stray cats and dogs rummaging around the area. He fixed his rifle toward the shadows on the far side. "Did anyone see that?" he whispered to Tyus, who had taken cover behind a support beam.

****

"I knew it; I knew it," Richard spluttered. "We've got a problem." He frantically controlled his mouse, punching a few keystrokes. The image on his screen flashed to one of the wall monitors. "Jerry, zoom out," he snapped.

"What is it?" Mila inquired. "We're kind of in the middle of something important."

"This is a time-lapse video." Richard pointed to the screen, rewinding the feed he'd taken. He then fast-forwarded it. "Those cold signatures *are* moving. They've been creeping closer."

Mila's eyes shot wide open. "It's a trap." The thought almost physically hit her as hard as the realization struck her brain.

"We have incoming, too," Jerry exclaimed. He'd done as Richard asked and panned out the drone camera to view a larger area. An SUV was rocketing toward the meeting place.

"We've got to warn them." Mila pounded on the mic control, slamming the button. "It's a trap," she yelled into the mic.

****

"Oh, hey, Roy." The former Oklahoman Senator quickly snapped an about-face, whirling on the younger man, overly appalled by his lack of respect, shouting his first name. "I was never your *son*," West spat with an angry snarl; the words foamed out his mouth like a rabid dog. "My daddy was twice the man you ever were."

Mila's voice crackled over their in-ear comms, shouting trap as West snapped up his rifle.

"Gun!" Wallace shouted. He and Fred drew as well. "Take him."

West's weapon came to bear on Stone. He depressed the trigger. A projectile launched, hurtling toward the man as a burst of fire erupted from the barrel. The slug slammed into Stone's left shoulder, spinning him to the ground, as West himself hit the floor.

The shot went wide due to Briggs tackling his boss, seeing Tex's gun hanging over the edge of the atrium above them. Tex's shot plunged into the concrete floor where West had been. More shots barked as the two scrambled back into the shadows out of the lobby.

The once serenely quiet, desolate, abandoned building erupted into a hail of gunfire. West's men, who'd been lying in wait, shed their thermal cloaks, and opened fire on the team.

"Get the family out of here, now," Wallace barked. He tried to make his way to the downed Stone, only to be forced back by the clatter of fire.

Wallace and Fred shot back at their attackers, pulling back to the SUV, and giving the others time to withdraw with the women and children.

Walsh, Johns, and Alwani pulled the women and children back toward the second Suburban—a shot whizzed by Alwani's head, slamming into the back window of Fred's SUV. The SEAL twisted, pushing Jacob forward into Johns's waiting arms, sending a burst of hot lead into the shadows where the shot had come from. A grunt and a moan followed the volley. Who'd ever taken the shot wasn't going to be a problem any longer.

"Move, go, go," Alwani shouted ahead. Johns flung open the rear door, shoving both Jessica and Jacob inside. "Down," the SEAL shouted, warning his friend.

Two black-clad mercs ran in through the entrance, bursting through a tarp. Alwani fired again, downing one of the advancing men.

Johns spun at the warning, dropping to a knee, a round narrowly missing his head, his M4 sending his own report back. Two rounds slammed into the man's chest, dropping him.

****

Sophia's heart smashed into her rib cage, fighting to escape her body, when West's shot boomed through the echo chamber of the empty space. Her eyes bulged in shock, seeing Stone jerk back, spinning to the ground. Then her instincts kicked in.

She threw herself into the back of the SUV, thudding to the carpeted floor liner. More shots thumped against the side of the Suburban, unable to penetrate the reinforced outer shell. It'd take something akin to a .50 caliber machine gun to cut through the SUV's armor—a welcomed feeling of invincibility from the US government.

Another welcomed feeling was knowing that the embassy-issued vehicle came with a fully loaded kit-out for combat in case such a need were to arise. This was definitely a need. Sophia tore open a rear compartment to find a bulletproof vest and a selection of firearms. She threw the vest over her upper body, rounds still thudding against the sides of the truck, only reminding her time was of the essence to get into the fight.

She secured the vest over her chest, then snatched up one of the Glocks, slapping in a magazine, yanking the slide back, chambering a round, and stuffing two more magazines into their pouches. She clambered back over the seats, dropping into the back row.

Sitting up, a round thumbed against the glass window to her right. It grazed in a delicate pattern out from the impact site in a spiderweb of cracks. Sophia flinched, gasping. The glass was bulletproof as well, but it wasn't as strong as the chassis. Another two or three direct hits, and it would eventually shatter.

Adjusting her attention to the firefight, Stone lay on the ground several yards away from Wallace, who'd tried to retrieve the downed man only to be forced back. The driver's side door flung open. "I can't get to him!" Wallace screamed. The passenger's door swung open. Fred appeared on the other side. Sophia watched from the back seat as the two sides exchanged fire; it seemed West's men were everywhere.

****

Stone rolled, leveraging himself onto his knees, his right hand clamped around his left shoulder, blood pouring out of the wound. The hot, oozing liquid seeped through his fingers. He peeled his hand away, almost in shock to see it soaked with blood. *His* blood.

"You ungrateful piece of shit!" he roared. The raging fight almost entirely drowned out his cry. He clambered to his feet as rounds pounded the concrete around him.

The Oklahoman stumbled forward, seeing an exit from the lobby. Two rounds smacked the ground in front of him, causing him to stagger back. Successfully dodging the shots, he lunged forward, diving through a wall of sheet plastic that was covering the exit doorway.

Sophia threw open the back door, sliding out from inside, taking in the scene. The cacophonous chaos of two highly trained groups slugging it out was a dizzyingly unbelievable thing to take in. The sight of Roy Stone staggering back and forth, dodging bullets, snapped her back to reality. He then disappeared behind a thin layer of sheet plastic hanging over a doorway.

"Shit, he's escaping," Sophia shouted. The roar of gunfire also choked off her warning. *Shit, what do I do?* Her body tingled, and her brain pulsated, running every scenario through in her head and taking in the sight unfolding before her. There was only one thing to do-go after him. "Stone, get back here!" she shouted, sprinting after the old man.

"Woman, don't," Wallace implored. Before he could yank her back, he saw a merc lever his gun in her direction. The two squeezed off a burst at the same time. The merc's rounds pounded behind Sophia. Wallace's rounds struck his target. The man who was on the third story fell over the side. His body thudded to the ground inches from West's position.

Wallace broke cover going after Sophia, only to be forced back by a stream of lead coming from behind a pile of stacked cinder blocks. "He's mine," a voice wafted over the pile.

Fred looked through the vehicle, seeing Sophia narrowly escape being hit. "Dammit, Sof," he growled, returning fire on another merc who'd adjusted his target to the sprinting woman. He never got off the shot. Fred's round burrowed through his temple and out the other side, splashing the wall behind him a reddish-gray hue.

Sophia pounded after Stone, a hailstorm chasing after her. She reached the doorway, stopped, spun, and dropped behind a pile of concrete bags. "Walsh let's go!" she shouted, waving for him to follow.

She wasn't about to run off again without backup.

Walsh slammed the back door to the second SUV, having secured Rebecca and Megan inside. He spun to join the fight when he heard Sophia call for him. "Cover me!" he shouted.

"Covering," Wallace, Sophia, and Fred intoned.

The SEAL sprinted out into the open as the trio unleashed a fury of projectiles at the mercs, keeping them down.

Walsh threw himself into a slide, coming to rest behind the wall of bags and crashing into Sophia. "Let's go," the woman ordered, pulling the SEAL to his feet.

The pair disappeared through the doorway—the plastic sheet flapping in their wake.

CHAPTER TWENTY-FOUR

WEST watched as one of his men fell from somewhere above, splatting on the concrete floor several feet in front of him. The wet smack of body and bone melding to the floor enraged the former SEAL, seeing the mangled face of the dead man: Bobby Smith. He'd recruited him personally out of the Army's Green Berets.

The mercenary leader wasn't angry or sad that the man he knew had been killed, just that he'd failed to pick a competent merc. *How dare he make him look bad?* "We need to end this," West shouted at Briggs over the increasing crescendo of gunfire. "We need to flank them. Where's the others?

Briggs pressed the button on his chest, opening a line of communication via his radio headset. "Mack ETA?" A round sizzled by inches from his face, and another smacked into the steel support pillar he was using for cover. He listened for a response. "Two mikes," he relayed the response to West.

"Good." He leaned over his cover, which was a pile of bricks sending a spray toward the driver's side of the SUV, at whom he predicted was the man named Wallace, the commander of the SEAL team that had been chasing him for the last six months. "Tell them to circle around and come in from the entrance; we'll block off their escape. Briggs reported his commands.

****

"Looks like they have reinforcements coming," Gabby pointed out. The SUV that had been barreling toward the hollowed-out office building abruptly changed course, swinging around toward the entrance.

"Really, no shiza," Mila cursed, seeing it for herself. "Alpha-one, a vehicle is coming to flank you. Be on your backside in a minute," she informed Wallace.

✳✳✳✳

"Al, Johns, get our six," Wallace ordered between shots, taking aim at another mercenary running across the top floor. From below, all he could see was the man's head bobbing. He snapped off a shot; then the man's head disappeared. There was no time to celebrate; a burst of fire sent him reeling, retreating to the SUV. He ripped open the door, ducking behind it. The slugs plopped to the floor, smashing harmlessly into the armor plating of the SUV.

"Copy, Chief. Let's go," Alwani said, giving Johns a fist bump. The two worked their way down the flank of the second SUV, sliding past the tarp covering the entrance. The bright, burning sun splashed their retinas, causing temporary blindness.

Their eyes adjusted to see a speeding SUV headed toward them. "Take'em out?" The pair nodded at each other; glee sparkled in their eyes.

"You know it." The two troopers leveled their weapons at the speeding vehicle. "You got right, I got left." Each angled toward their targets. The left and right front wheels. They sent a barrage hurtling toward the car, peppering it relentlessly; sparks flew off the front end. Two people emerged from the passenger side, guns in hand, sending a retaliatory stream back.

Alwani and Johns didn't waiver, staying locked onto their targets. Several rounds struck paydirt. First, the passenger tire exploded with a loud *pop*. A second later, the tire shredded apart, disintegrating off the wheel. The truck dropped an inch. The steel rim plowed into the dirt track, causing the vehicle to slew to the right. Then, the driver's side tire blew out, ejecting shards of rubber into the air.

The vehicle dropped another few inches, digging both rims into the ground. The SUV weaved to the left. The driver hauled at the wheel, overcorrecting. The truck slewed too far, swinging it forty-five degrees. The steel rims dug a trench into the dirt, catching a buried stone. At ninety mile-per-hour, the truck spun;

top heavy, it rolled. The side slammed to the ground, sliding before rolling twice more, coming to a stop on its roof.

A trail of blood, flesh, and bone streaked behind. It happened so fast that the two mercenaries hanging out the side hadn't had time to get back into the cabin before it flipped. They were smashed and dragged. One of the mangled corpses slumped from the passenger seat.

"Check to see if they're all dead," Alwani inquired. Johns nodded. The two headed toward the upturned vehicle, weapons at the ready.

****

Ryan's eyes needed to adjust to what he just saw. Several men emerged from the shadows of the partially darkened structure, shedding what looked like invisibility cloaks. "What the fuck? I need one of those," he quipped, snapping up his rifle and drawing it at the men across the lobby.

"Get it off their corpses," Tyus retorted. "Time to say hi, the SEAL way." The three men let a fusillade loose, sending some of the mercs reeling for cover and distracting them, giving FT1 time to secure the family and take cover.

****

"Fuck," Tex spat, slithering back from the edge of the atrium as rounds pinged off the steel supports by him. Angry that he'd missed his shot, the face of the man that caused him to miss emblazed into his memory. Something burst through the concrete floor a foot from his body, and then another miniature burst shot through. Someone was on the floor below him and was probing to find his location. Another few blasts strafed a line horizontally toward him, showering the big Texan in concrete dust.

He rolled away from the threat as more geysers burst through.

Several feet later, his back crashed into one of the support pillars, bowing him. Tex's eyes widened, and he realized he had nowhere else to escape as the punctures drew closer.

Suddenly, they stopped. From below, he could hear the clicking of the person's mag running dry, followed by its clatter hitting the floor.

The SEAL snatched his sidearm from the holster on his leg. He peered through the hole closest to him. He could see someone yanking back the charging hammer of an AK.

"I am going to kill you," the man shouted, his voice pierced through the holes.

"Not today, jackass," Tex muttered, jamming the barrel of his gun against the hole. He fired several shots; the brass shells spun from the ejection port. One smacked against his face. The searing hot brass sizzled against the side of his face. Luckily, his thick beard hair took most of the brunt of the damage. There was a thud below. Tex pulled the barrel back, looking through the smoldering gap in the concrete. "One." Tex grinned. "Still time to add," he quipped to no one, hearing the spattering of more gunfire.

Climbing to his knees, he unslung his M4 and crept back to the atrium's edge. A round punched into the beam beside him from above. His head snapped. There were men on the fourth floor, shooting down at him. He needed to get up there. Retreating to what looked like a stairwell, he burst through the doorway, bullets chasing after him.

He pounded up the flight of steps, reaching the fourth floor as fast as an Olympic sprinter.

Pausing just before going through the doorless frame. Figuring if he burst through, he'd be shot. The mercs most likely suspected he would come up after them.

From below, he'd spotted only two men. They should be easy pickings. He steadied himself, his heart racing. It was a long shot of what he was about to do, but he had to.

He pressed his back to the wall, placing his right foot flat against the concrete. He pushed off, propelling himself forward. The blocky Texan threw himself into a Superman-esque dive, exploding from the threshold.

As expected, the men were waiting for him. Rounds

pockmarked the wall behind him in a concentrated burst of fire.

Tex hit the ground, rolled, and popped up. He fired right, then left. Both men dropped. "Three," he said softly. He peeked over the ledge down into the lobby below. One man skittered across on the second floor. Tex aimed and downed the running man. "That makes…" he trailed off, his eyes narrowing at another figure, the one who caused his earlier shot to miss. He was picking his way between support pillars and heading for what looked like an exit. *Hell no,* the Texan thought. He turned and barged toward the stairwell.

****

West leaned out from his cover, exchanging fire with the two men, who were now hiding behind the doors of the Suburban. "You've got to be fucking kidding me," he muttered, seeing Stone stir on the floor, then stagger to his feet. "This fucking old man doesn't know when to stay down." He levered his gun at his father-in-law and fired. The rounds plunged uselessly into the ground in front and behind the lumbering Stone. He staggered off and disappeared behind a sheet of plastic into a dark hallway. "Oh no, you don't. You're not getting away from me."

The woman he knew as Sophia darted out into the open after Stone. She was then followed by the man he assumed was Wallace. It appeared they were going to chase after him. "He's mine," West shouted, sending a barrage in their direction. The rounds impacted all around Wallace, forcing the SEAL commander back. The woman made it to a stack of concrete mix bags unharmed. "Shit," West ejected his spent mag, slapping a new one.

Before he could get another shot off, the woman, now followed by another SEAL, disappeared through the same opening as Stone. West's eyes stayed locked onto where the trio disappeared; an intense hatred filled him, blurring his senses. The chaotic world happenings around him evaporated, disappearing, blacking out everything outside of his tunnel vision. He wanted nothing more in this instance than to kill the man who tried to set him up.

Without another thought, he broke cover and darted for the lobby's exit.

"Boss, no, don't," Briggs shouted in vain; West ignored every word. "Cover the Boss," Briggs ordered the remaining mercenaries to protect West. A smattering of gunfire erupted from every corner of the lobby—some of the barrels concentrated on the SUV. The rest focused on another area where bursts of fire had been coming from. The contingent covering the SUV pelted it with dozens of rounds. The man sheltering behind the passenger door dove inside the SUV for cover. The other used the wheel and engine block for cover. The mercenary's weapons ran dry.

They'd achieved their objective, though. West was no longer in the lobby.

****

Fred watched West sprint out into the open, making a mad dash for the exit, going after Sophia and Stone. He shifted fire to the running man only for a maelstrom of hot lead to rain down on him. It felt like every gun in the world was trained on him.

Round after round, pelted the heavy-duty SUV. The FBI agent threw himself headlong into the cab, sprawling over the front seats. The glass windshield and windows finally succumbed to the barrage, shattered, raining shards of glass down over him.

The storm let up like the eye of a hurricane had moved above the building; an odd silence fell over the lobby. Fred peeked over the dashboard. West was nowhere in sight. He'd made it into the hallway. "Wallace," he shouted. The SEAL leader looked back after exchanging reports and killing another of West's men who'd overexposed himself in an effort to protect his boss. "You need to go help. We'll get you over there," Fred added.

Wallace nodded. "FT2, prepare to cover me," he said into the radio. He slammed another mag into his M4 and then held it out across the seats in the cab. "Last mag," he added, handing Fred an extra magazine from his pouch. He waved for Fred's Glock. The two swapped weapons. He made ready to go. "Now!"

The SEAL burst into an all-out sprint, racing across the gritty floor and hitting a slippery, gravelly patch—concrete grains. The substance had spilled out of the bags after repetitious hits from the small arms fire.

Wallace hit the patch, realizing he was losing traction with his boots. The SEAL harked back to a previous life in his youth. He dropped into a feet-first baseball slide like he was going into second base on a double. He slid the remaining three feet, gliding past the threshold and out of the lobby.

Fred, Ryan, Tyus, and Gutierrez laid down just enough cover fire to get Wallace safely out of the lobby. The quartet then turned their attention to the remaining mercenaries. The smattering of gunfire coming from their side suggested that their numbers had dwindled throughout the firefight.

Several sparks danced from gun barrels in places around the room. After each flared several times, they weren't heard from again, as the SEALs continued to pick off their opponents.

One such set of sparks coming from a shadowed corner, Fred picked out. A flash came from behind a pillar to his right. A round *clanked* off the SUV's side. The agent spun and fired into the void. Nothing sparked from that corner again.

"Finish'em off," Ryan crowed into their headsets. The order was followed by a loud HOOYAH! Which echoed from the first to the fourth floor throughout the atrium.

****

Sophia swiped the plastic out of her way, entering into what appeared to be an incomplete office corridor. The sides still had some of their steel support beams exposed and missing drywall panels. Electrical wires and conduits snaked down from the partially completed ceiling. Several broken tiles lay smashed on the ground. Paint cans and other debris sprinkled the floor. She picked her way through the minefield of grit and trash. "Come on, Walsh." She looked back; he was gawping at his boot, scraping it against the top of a paint can.

"I hope that was animal shit," he chirped, giving his boot one last deep scrape.

"No time, hurry. He's getting away," Sophia stressed, leaping over another pile of excrement. "That's definitely human," she added.

They reached a T-junction; Sophia looked left and then right. "Which way?" Walsh questioned.

Sophia did a double-take of their options. "There," she shouted excitedly, pointing at a blood-smeared handprint halfway down the hall. "Go, go."

They raced down the corridor. The cacophonous echo of the gun battle raging in the lobby dulled further as the pair descended into the depths of the unfinished building. Swinging around another tight corner, Sophia was attacked by a collection of wires and cables dangling from above like a spiderweb.

She pawed at them, swatting them away from her face. "Stone!" she shouted, seeing the man's darkened silhouette at the end beyond a spar of light bisecting the room from a hole in the building's exterior. The man turned for a moment, then vanished into the next section. "You son of a bitch get back here." She set off after him again.

****

Ryan spotted the man who had pulled West into safety during the initial stages of the fight. He was shouting commands into a headset. He skirted to another pillar directly across from him, and he appeared to be giving silent orders via hand signals. Luckily, he spoke fluent hand signals. The bald man was telling two men to flank around to the side of the SUV coming up on Fred's five o'clock, almost directly behind him. "Shit," Ryan snapped off a burst. The tall, Black, bald man ducked back into cover behind a pillar. "Alpha-actual, you're going to have company on your five in less than a minute. Two shooters," he warned Fred, searching down range for a sign of his target.

He sprang out from the other side, sending a stream at Ryan

and forcing him back down behind his cover—a hulking A/C unit that hadn't and wouldn't ever be installed. Shots came from several other directions, pinning the SEAL down behind the A/C unit and pinging off the reinforced steel.

"Shit bro, we've gotta help," Gut shouted over to Tyus, who was slapping another magazine into its well.

"Copy."

The two moved, sliding back into the darkness, and making their way around the rotunda. Gut saw one of the shooters firing on Ryan. "Gotcha." He shot, and the man went down.

Two other mercs materialized from practically thin air, ripping off their camouflage jackets. "Shit," Tyus exclaimed, snapping up his rifle; it barked, and one of the men dropped. The other, slightly quicker to move, dove to the ground, rolling out of the line of fire.

The shot eliminated an immediate threat for Ryan, but it also sadly announced their location.

Briggs spun, sending a fusillade at the two men who were trying to creep up on his right. The bursts sent them scattering for cover of their own. "Briggs to Mack ETA." The merc tried to radio their backup, but there was no response. "Mack, ETA." He tried again, his voice rising a little. "Mack, goddammit, ETA, now." There was nothing but static. It dawned on him that two of the SEALs were missing. It was safe to assume the reinforcements weren't coming.

"Where's Mack's guys?" one of the mercs asked. "I am almost out."

"They're gone," Briggs stated. He looked around; there were only a few of his men left. They'd started with twenty. By his count, there were four fighters left, six, including the men he'd sent earlier, flanked around the SUVs to try and secure the one with West's family, and they could also use it as an escape vehicle.

****

Fred heard Ryan's warning that he had incoming. He slinked back to the second SUV and rounded to the driver's side, setting up shop behind the wheel well and limiting his visibility and target area. He hunkered down, placing the M4's hand grip on the Suburban's hood. He peered through the driver's window; he could see the two women in the back huddled over the two kids.

He thought about how much therapy and counseling those kids were going to need after this. Hell, he may even need some.

Just then, two figures dropped down several yards away. They apparently had scaled up to the second floor to try and covertly drop in behind him. Too bad for them, as they appeared to be searching for him. Guns drawn at the ready, having expected to have already fired.

"Yoohoo, boys," Fred whistled. The two mercs whirled, not expecting him to have the drop on them.

The former Agent opened fire, killing both men instantly.

****

Briggs heard the gunshots and then witnessed the dazzling display of igniting gunpowder. He saw both of his men fall. He was fairly confident that when he and West planned the ambush—twenty against eight—twenty of Sotor Corps' best, going up against a SEAL team. He would've taken those odds any day of the week and twice on Sundays. Fast forward to now. Those odds provided a false sense of security. He didn't like any of the outcomes that were left now.

"We need to withdraw," Briggs shouted to his men. "Ex-fil, ex-fil."

"What about the boss?"

"What about him? He'll find us. Move out."

Briggs and the last of Sotor Corps sprinted for a rear exit, exposing their locations.

Ryan and Gut gunned down two of the fleeing men while Tyus took down another. Fred managed to gun down the fourth fleeing member of Sotor Corps after rounding the SUVs to check on the other two men he'd just killed.

Briggs looked back, seeing the last of his men fall. He dug deep, running faster. In another two seconds, he'd be out the door.

"Oh no, the fuck don't. No one makes Tex miss!" the Texan

roared, soaring down through the air from the second floor, feet first.

Tex's legs slammed into Briggs' back, sending the man flailing forward in an almost comically cartoonish way. Tex dropped heavily to the floor, forcing a deep-down exhale. Briggs slammed head-first into one of the steel support beams with a wet crunch and snap of bone. The mercenary dropped to the floor, his head and neck bent in a grotesquely distorted angle—spires of bone protruding from his neck.

"Nice of you to drop in," Ryan teased; Gut and Ty helped haul the big man off the ground. "And where the fuck were you two?" He asked as Alwani and Johns, along with Fred, joined the group.

"Taking care of the reinforcements." Alwani thumbed outside.

"Guys, we've gotta get to the others. West went after Stone." Fred padded across the room toward the dark mystery door frame. He looked back. "Now!" he urged. The rest of the team followed him out of the lobby.

****

Sophia rounded the corner, where Stone disappeared following the blood trail on the wall, passing several rooms that appeared to be offices. Passing one, she stopped, and Walsh bumped into her. "What is it?"

"The blood trail stops," Sophia said, searching the area. "Why?"

Walsh did a one-eighty, examining the hall they'd just come from. "There," he pointed to a handprint cupped around a door frame to another room.

The pair reversed course, Sophia shoving Walsh back down the corridor to the room. They barged in to find themselves in a large office. More cables stretched down from above like fingers snaking to clutch at something. A folding table stretched across the middle of the room with a set of aging blueprints sprawled across it. Her eyes settled on a figure against the far side of the room. He appeared to be trying to pry open a window with one arm. It was Stone. He hauled at the window again to no avail.

"Stop," Sophia shouted, panting. Stone whirled around to find the CIA woman he'd been running from for months once again pointing a gun at his head.

"Deja vú, Agent Evans," Stone said, breathing heavily himself, blood oozing from his shoulder. "This takes us back what eight months. I remember you pointed a weapon at my head then, too."

"Yeah." She wiped the sweat pouring down her forehead with her free hand, soaking the bandage on her hand. Her Glock wavered in her left hand. She wasn't used to holding a firearm in her left. She was right-handed. But, with the tightly wound bandage on her right, it made it hard to hold a weapon. "I wish I would've put a bullet in you then. Saved us all from this trouble," she hissed through gritted teeth, trying to ignore the pain in her throbbing right hand.

"Thank goodness for our good old friend Agent Jones, then." The Oklahoman smiled. "Are you finally going to do it? There's only one witness." He nodded at Walsh. "Which I am sure he's not as righteous as Agent Jones—being a hired assassin for the government."

"Shut up, old man," Walsh fired back. His weapon was also trained on Stone.

Sophia eased up, tucking her gun into the back of her waistband. "No, even though I should." She pulled a pair of zip-tie cuffs from her vest. "I am just curious; you had a deal in place. Why run? Keep your gun on him," she said to Walsh. "Hands up!" She gestured for Stone to raise his hands. He raised one arm high into the sky. "I said raise your hands," she barked.

Stone's face became grim as he stared blankly at Sophia, tilting his head to the side with a deadpanned expression. "I've been shot in the other shoulder, you dumb bitch," he growled, pointing at the hole in his body and the oozing blood."

"Fine, just keep your greedy hands where I can see them— both." Stone kept one arm raised, and he held up the other as high as he could, opening his palm. "Watch 'em closely," she muttered to Walsh.

"I've got you," Walsh said, side-stepping away from Sophia as she crossed his path, keeping his gun aimed at Stone.

Sophia slowly approached the fugitive she'd been chasing all these months. A sense of closure began to bubble inside her as she crept around the table, grabbing his left arm, pulling it behind his back, and securing it inside one of the loops of the cuffs. Her bandaged hand made it more difficult than usual. She gritted through the pain of having to use it at all.

"I wasn't running from you," Stone growled. "I was-"

A shot rang out, and blood splattered over Sophia's face. Stone's last words became gurgled, muttering as he fell backward, pushing Sophia against the wall. Her head smashed through the drywall panel before Stone's body weight pulled the two down. On the way to the floor, Sophia shucked Stone off.

"Shut up, old man," West barked, snapping his gun to Walsh.

"No!" Sophia screamed.

The SEAL spun and fired at the threat. A slug burrowed into his abdomen just below the vest and above the waist. He reflexed from the pain, sending his shot barely wide.

The round sliced across West's face as he bobbed his head to the left, splitting a gash across his right cheek. "You fucking prick," West bellowed, with a level of vitriol, spittle slushed from his mouth.

While one hand sprung to his face, inspecting the damage. He angrily fired two more shots into Walsh, driving the man back. The SEAL fell, seizing. West, still with his hand to his face, entered the room and walked by Walsh, pumping two more shots into him for good measure. He rounded the table, seeing Sophia pressed up against the wall, wearing an expression of shock, covered in Stone's blood. Stone was on the floor, blood pooling around him, a ragged hole in the side of his neck, somehow still breathing.

"You just won't fucking die, will you," West spat, pulling his hand from his face, then pulled a cloth from a pocket, dabbing the gash in his face. "That's going to leave a scar," he quipped, turning his gun onto Sophia. "And as for you, I have a conundrum here.

Do I finish off the old man and give you that satisfaction? Or get rid of you and just let him bleed out. Oh, what to do." He tapped a finger to his chin. "Ah, fuck it, I'll shoot you first, then him."

Sophia's eyes snapped shut, not wanting to see the bullet coming as if she could. It was more so out of the fear she'd be dead in a second.

Instead of the boom of the gun, there was a crash of a table. She ripped open her eyes to see a bloodied Walsh on top of West, delivering a right hand to the CEO's face, pulling back for another strike.

Sophia lunged forward to help subdue the mercenary leader. A hand reached out, grabbing her. She looked back, her eyes locking with Stone's.

His other hand was clamped around his throat. His lips moved, but no words escaped, just a gurgling sound. His eyes did all the talking for him. They stared up at her like a battered puppy in a shelter pleading to be adopted.

She lingered in hesitation. The two communicated without words.

She could help Walsh, but Stone would die. Did she really care about that? He was a murderer, traitor, coward, and an overall monster. She ripped her arm away, standing to help Walsh, then paused. *Was he a monster?* Rebecca Stone's conversation seeped into her head. How adamant she was, that deep down, he was a good man. Then Fred's voice pounded in her skull. "Don't be like him, we're better."

Did the man deserve justice? Yes, but what kind? She wasn't a judge, juror, or executioner. He may very well deserve the death penalty, but not here. Not in Rabat, Morocco, bleeding to death on the floor of an abandoned building, where only she would witness the justice.

There were many others back home who were left mourning losses due to his actions, and they needed to see him brought to justice as well to get their closure. And she would find a way to get it rightfully and lawfully. Plus, she didn't want his pleading face and eyes haunting her for the rest of her life. She had enough demons already.

Reluctantly, she knelt back down by his side. "You better not make me regret this," she whispered through pursed lips, tearing off one of her sleeves, wrapping it around his neck, and applying pressure to the wound.

****

Walsh somehow managed to climb to his feet, shocked he was still alive, having just taken five point-blank shots. Dark blood poured from the wound in his abdomen, his left leg seeped with red liquid, and his right shoulder seared with pain. His vest had taken the other two shots—a little bit of solace. The plated armor prevented serious injury, but he could feel one of his ribs was cracked and possibly was suffering from a collapsed lung, based on his heavy wheezing, but he was still alive. He staggered, turning around to see West lever his gun at Sophia.

He burst into action.

The SEAL threw himself bodily into West, the two slamming down onto the wooden folding table. It snapped in half under the combined weight, showering the pair in a cloud of wood shards as they dropped to the ground. The gun skittered away from the pair.

West thudded to the floor, partially driving the oxygen from his lungs; his head banged against the hard concrete, and his vision danced black. When it turned back on, he saw the man he'd just shot multiple times straddling atop him; then his sight went black again, turning back on to see the bloodied man draw back, preparing for another strike.

Walsh swung down, pummeling his fist into West's face with a flurry of left hands, striking a second, third, and fourth time. But, with each successive strike, though, he felt his energy draining. Plus, there wasn't too much power in the strikes, having to use his left arm due to the bullet wound in his right shoulder. He pulled back to deliver a fifth blow. His wheezing had shifted to an all-out pant.

West grinned back up at him through bloodied teeth. *Was this prick enjoying it?* He swung down, but before he could connect,

West parried the blow, then drove his index and middle fingers into the hole in Walsh's right shoulder.

The SEAL reared back, howling in pain, then clamped his left hand around West's wrist, yanking the man's fingers out of his body and pinning his arm to the floor. With nothing else to strike with, Walsh rushed forward, delivering a headbutt.

The two men's skulls collided, temporarily blacking out both parties. West was the first to recover. The blow had unbalanced Walsh, as he was too sluggish to follow up the strike. His energy reserves were running low due to the amount of blood loss. He teetered atop the merc leader.

Sensing his opportunity to strike, West bucked off Walsh, thrusting up his hips in the air, sending the SEAL flipping over him.

Walsh thudded to the floor, exhaling heavily, struggling to suck oxygen back into his one operating lung. His vision faded, and he blinked, trying to get it back. Nothing.

West hurried to his feet, unsheathing a knife from his vest. The merc leader lunged forward, plunging the blade down at Walsh's neck.

Walsh blinked again. His vision returned just in time to see West's blood-smeared face snarling down, the tip of a blade rushing at him.

Walsh threw up both arms, crisscrossing them in front of his face as West dropped down onto him. The two combatants' forearms meet inches above Walsh's face; the blade hung precariously above his throat. West forced himself down, using his body's leverage to inch the blade down further.

Walsh fought back, summoning a hidden reserve tank of energy. If BUD's training had taught him one thing, it was to hold back some energy for when it was really needed. That was now.

Walsh's biceps bulged as he pushed up, forcing West's to lever up, pushing the blade back.

West's eyes bugged, not expecting such resilience. A flash of admiration beamed across his face. He should've recruited this guy instead of that useless Bobby Smith. In another life, maybe.

West repositioned himself, gaining further leverage, and

pushed down harder; the blade dropped several inches—just mere centimeters from this opponent's neck.

Walsh struggled to maintain his resistance, drawing on the last ounces of will he had, doing everything he could to push back up. His right shoulder burned, and an intense inferno raged on inside. Blood sluiced out from the wound, pooling around his neck and dowsing his face. He managed to push back up with a grunt, creating more distance between life and death.

West snarled, "Just fucking die," he said, spitting blood into the SEAL's face. He let up briefly, releasing one hand, then slammed it back down, putting all of his weight behind the push.

Walsh's strength gave out, and the knife plunged into his throat with such force it snapped off upon impact with the concrete. The SEAL's body went limp.

Sophia, who'd been ignoring most of the fight while trying to save Stone's life, let out a blood-curdling scream, seeing Walsh's body with the snapped blade protruding from his throat after West rolled off the man.

"You son of a bitch! You're going to pay for that!" she bellowed, seeing the gun glint in a flitter of sunlight that blazed through the room.

She grabbed Stone's hand, driving it to the side of his neck and pressing it down. Then leaped for the pistol, arm, and hand outstretched.

West scrambled to his feet, covering the distance to the gun in two strides, and threw himself into a dive. He snatched it up milliseconds before Sophia's hand could wrap around it. She hit the floor, pawing at the dirt.

"Your turn *bitch,*" West snarled, laying on the floor in front of her, jamming the barrel against Sophia's forehead.

The merc let out a wail, his hand seizing mid-trigger pull. He dropped the weapon involuntarily. He scrambled to his feet, gawping at the knife protruding from his hand. He turned, ripping the blade out to see a man standing in the doorway.

"Shoot him," Sophia shouted, recoiling back to Stone.

West gripped the blade, whipping his arm back, preparing to

return the knife back to its sender. "Fuck you," he spat.

"No, fuck you," Wallace retorted, then fired. The bullet tore through West's bicep, jerking him back. The knife clattered to the concrete. "That's for Shamir Smith," he said, striding into the room. He fired again, taking another step. The next round punctured through West's upper left thigh, severing the femoral artery. Blood sprayed across the room. "That's for Wyatt Johnson." Another step and a thunderous boom bounced off the walls; the round struck West in the left shoulder, and he staggered back. "That's for America. You traitorous piece of shit." With another clap, the slug tore a gaping, ragged hole through the merc's throat, spraying more blood. West, spitting a glob of it out. Wallace's eyes were set on Walsh's lifeless body. "And that's for Petty Officer Michael Walsh, my friend." West dropped to his knees, blood pouring from each wound. Wallace stepped up to the mercenary leader, pressing the barrel to his head. "And this is for everyone else."

He pressed the trigger. The back of West's head exploded, showering the wall red and gray, spraying some of it back at Wallace. West's bullet-riddled body slumped to the floor. Wallace holstered the weapon, spitting on the corpse.

"Are you done?" Sophia asked, impressed. "Because I could use your help. She had returned to Stone and continued applying pressure to the wound.

"Sure," Wallace said, giving West's body one last dismissive look.

Fred burst into the room, almost retching at the grisly scene. Blood covered the walls. Walsh's body lay off to one side. West's was slumped in the middle of the room. Sophia and Wallace were against the back wall, applying pressure to a wound in Stone's neck. "What the fuck happened here?" he asked, entering; the rest of the team filed in behind. They immediately rushed to the downed Walsh.

"Justice," Sophia turned and said. "Or, at least, some form of it." She turned back to Wallace, mouthing a thank you, as the pair's hands intertwined, pressing against Stone's neck.

Wallace replied with an equally quiet, "You're welcome."

"Alpha-zero to TOC. "We need ex-fil and an ambulance ASAP."

SOPHIA reached her location, checked the hallway, and paused outside the door, looking up the hall and then down the hall. No one in sight, she'd beat the entourage. A greedy, wry smile creased her face. It was the day she'd been waiting for months. However, it felt more like years now after the events that had transpired over the last few weeks. She reached for the door to push it open, then paused.

She pulled her arm back as her body shivered with anticipatory zeal. The nervous feeling coursed through her like an electrical current, zapping her. She tried to shake the sensation loose by waggling it from her body. She'd once been told that for a spy, she was a bad liar. In fact, she was told that by the very man she was about to speak to now.

She had a theory, though, and it was time to test it by putting into motion a plan. It was a long shot, but right now, that was all she had.

Shortly after arriving back at the embassy in the wake of the botched surrender, Director Owens contacted the team. He'd finished his investigation into whether there was a mole inside the team. He was very confident in his findings that there wasn't one. So, then, who had been feeding Stone information? Who had helped him work the back-the-channel deal with the Attorney General that guaranteed him only a year behind bars? How had a man who seemingly had given his life to the protection of the country for decades gone so awry that he'd fund a terror group to attack it? There had to be something more behind it all. Or at least that was her hunch.

Capturing Stone only raised several more questions. They all needed answers. And there was only one man who could give them to her. He was lying in a bed, just on the other side of the door. In fact, the same bed she'd occupied a few weeks prior, which was probably another reason for her hesitation. When she left its confines, she vowed never to return to it, nor ever wanted to be in one like it again. Left with nothing to do but twiddle away the hours of the day uselessly. Often trapped in her mind with her demons. Demons that, hopefully, the former Senator was now being attacked by, which would make her job easier.

Sophia steeled herself, turned the knob, and pushed.

She cracked open the door and silently slipped into the room. Finding the light switch in the dark interior, she flicked it. A snap crackled above, and a buzzing noise arched down. The place lit up, bathing the sterile room in a bright light, which was magnified by the pristinely white painted walls. She padded across the room, feeling like the weight of an entire country—her country still rested on her shoulders. Reaching a set of curtains, she pawed at the white fabric, balling each side into her fist.

Another jolt shot down her spine. *Gotta do this,* she whispered. If not for the country, then selfishly for herself.

In one sudden motion, she threw them apart; the metal hooks squelched as they glided across the metal bar. "Wakey, wakey, eggs, and bakey," she serenaded the new occupant of her former bed.

Stone blearily gazed up at the smiling blonde, for a second thinking he may have just wound up in heaven. A smile began to crease across his face at the beautiful woman happily staring down at him until he realized it was Sophia Evans. The glee lurched to a stop, doing a complete one-eighty, turning into a sneer. "What the fuck do you want?" he asked, voice still gravelly. His neck muscles and voice box pressed against the thick bandage wrapped around his throat. "I was sleeping."

"Well, that's a loaded question there, bucko." She tapped his foot, then sidled along the side of the bed, pushing him over to take a seat. "For one, that's no way to speak to the person that saved your life." She pulled her hand to her chest, taking on an offended tone. "Geez and I thought all you big, strong, strapping Oklahoma boys had manners. Guess my momma was wrong," she crooned, putting on her best southern accent, which sounded or tried to sound like Dolly Parton, fluttering her eyebrows at the man.

"Get to the point," Stone grunted, lolling his head to the right, cringing from the obvious fake performance. "And drop this bullshit. You hate me as much as I hate you."

"Ok, have it your way." The fake smile washed away. She leaned in, dropping her face to within inches of his, all pretense gone; she set her jaw, steeling her expression. "Justice, asshole," she said in a biting cold, callousness. "And I am not talking about the sweetheart deal you somehow managed to get. I still don't know how you did it, but I am going to fucking make it my life's mission to find out. But no, I am talking life in prison, *max* prison for the shit you've done."

Every word was spoken with a deep-seated vitriol laced with an intense hatred. "See, I've had a chance to read the deal you made. It only covers the crimes you committed in relation to the terrorist plot. I know you've committed more; a narcissistic asshole like you doesn't start and stop with one." She jabbed an index finger to his face, gesticulating it. "All your little misgivings and deeds you racked up will come to light. I will ensure you're locked away for a long, long time."

The door burst open, and a male nurse with a wheelchair accompanied by an armed Marine strolled in. Sophia shot up from the bed, clapping her hands together.

"Good news," she said in a feigned happy tone, whiplashing back. "The doctor says you're healed enough for travel. We all get to go back home today." She wheeled around, facing the two arrivals. "Gentleman, will you please make sure that Mr. Stone here is dressed properly and makes it safely to the transports."

The two men nodded with confused looks. They clearly hadn't expected anyone to be there.

Sophia slipped out of the room, giving Stone another icy stare.

****

"Take it your conversation went well?" Fred said, sidling up beside Sophia, arms folding across his chest, watching Stone emerge from the building, looking deep in thought. Worry racked across his face.

The blonde cocked her head toward him with a wry grin on her face. "Oh, what makes you say that?" she asked coyly.

Fred let out a small laugh, gesturing at Stone, who was being loaded into one of the SUVs that had been staged for their trip to the airport. They were headed back home.

"I don't know the look on his face," Fred answered. "He looks like he's just seen a ghost. Did you tell him you already found a loophole in the deal?"

"That I did, that I did. I also alluded that I'd find everything he's done and get him on all of it," she answered almost too happily. She and Stone locked eyes for a second before the Marine slammed the door closed. Fred gave her a quizzical look. "I want him to stew on the fact that he may not get what he wants. Maybe then we'll get what we need."

"You really think your hunch is right?"

"It's the only explanation," she said, turning to face Fred. "He's either working for someone or had someone on the inside working for him, feeding him information. That's the only way he would've been able to stay a step ahead this whole time since Owens cleared everyone. I want to who." She pointed to the SUV. "And he's going to tell me because people like him will always do what's best for them. Now that I've given him reason to think that he's going to go to prison for the rest of his life, he'll do what's best for Roy Stone and turn on whoever has been helping him."

Fred stepped back, eying Sophia up and down, impressed by her determination. "Well, hopefully, your plan works then. And, remind me never to piss you off."

"It'll work." She'd laid the foundation of her plan to see if he'd give up the information as to whether or not her theory was accurate. She would have the next nine hours with him to further dig in. She smiled at Fred. "Oh, I'd never do anything like this to people I actually love." She caressed his arm. "Again, thank you for coming to help find me."

"I would've gone to the end of the world to bring you back," Fred responded, hugging Sophia.

"We're ready," Wallace said, approaching the pair, Mila

alongside him. "The team's loaded, and we're ready to head to the airport, although I am not at all looking forward to what comes next." The SEAL commander looked solemnly back at one of the SUVs.

"Again, I am so sorry. I liked Walsh," Sophia said, putting a hand on Wallace's shoulder. He jerked his head to meet her gaze.

"Yeah, I didn't really get to meet him, but I hear he was a good SEAL," Fred added.

"I liked the jokes he told," Mila threw in.

Wallace chuckled. "His jokes were shit, but you're right. Walshy was a good SEAL and a great man. He'll be missed." Tex leaned out of the third SUV in the convoy, slamming on the side door. "Guess he really wants to go."

"Yup. I'll ride with Sophia and Stone. Mila, you drive. Wallace, follow in the car behind us." Fred organized their seating arrangements.

Wallace gave him a thumbs up, striding to the third SUV. The others headed to the second. They were going to be escorted to the airport by Embassy security so they could use diplomatic immunity to skip all customs checks.

The convoy set off.

****

The twenty-minute escorted ride to the airport was taken in almost complete silence by the four occupants of the second SUV. Sophia and Fred gazed out their respective windows, watching the city of Rabat flash by outside.

They communicated silently, their eyes meeting in the rearview mirror every so often. Their unspoken words filled the air, a silent dialogue of anticipation and wonder, all directed at Stone. They were waiting for it to happen when the seeds that Sophia had planted during her chit-chat with Stone would sprout and take hold of him.

The old man, too, was engrossed in the world outside his window, observing the people going about their day in blissful ignorance. He was part of a world within a world, a world where a select few people belonged to an organization that, behind the scenes, covertly orchestrated the lives of many. Or… he was part of that world.

The leaders of this shadow world designed machinations on how they could stay in invisible power and provide everyone the illusion that they were in control of their own lives when, in actuality, they weren't, not even in the slightest bit. No one outside the people in the know had any true control, influence, or power. The people were pawns. They were moved about on a world-sized chessboard, participating in a game they didn't even know they were playing.

He thought about how, for all of his planning and scheming, he eventually came up short. He'd failed his part of the plan. He glowered to his left, staring intently at the blonde.

She caught him staring at her but said nothing. She smirked at him. How dare she be so cavalier and flipped about ruining his life? Suddenly, a thought hit him. *Did he fail?* Sophia's words burned in his ears. He was told there were no loopholes in the deal that he signed. In his haste, he realized that he hadn't thoroughly read the deal. He assumed all would be taken care of by the Council of the Cross. Had *he* become a pawn? Suddenly, the vehicle shifted underneath him like tectonic plates. His world shook violently. Stone sat in contemplative silence.

Mila guided the SUV and its silent occupants around a bend, following closely behind the lead vehicle. They passed a gated checkpoint. The local airport security and customs officers waved them through without stopping any of the vehicles as they passed by—the benefits of traveling in vehicles with diplomatic plates.

The vehicles continued on, making a series of turns, until they pulled out onto the tarmac of a private airstrip. A Boeing BBJ 737 exploded into view through the windshield at the end of the runway. The massive private airliner loomed over the vehicles as they sped on approaching.

Sophia spotted several ground crewmen scrambling about the jet. One detached a hose from it, running it back to a large tanker nearby. Several others began wheeling out a set of steps. The cabin door opened. Someone stood in the doorway, guiding the men hauling the staircase.

The convoy lurched to a halt several yards away from the airliner. The grounds crew had just finished attaching the set of air steps. While the vehicle had stopped moving, Stone's world continued to rock back and forth. The doors opened. Mila and Fred climbed out. Sophia undid her seatbelt to join them.

Stone snatched Sophia around her forearm before she could fully exit, tugging the Agent back. "Don't," he snapped. Fred, seeing the exchange, ripped open Stone's passenger door, grabbing the man by his collar, about to haul him outside to the ground. Stone painfully turned to face him; a look of deep concern written on his face. "Please?" Sophia shook her head. Fred released him. "I need your help." His voice was raspy and low, but it quaked and trembled.

"Fraid I can't help you now. You signed a deal, remember?" Sophia yanked her arm from Stone's clutches, rubbing her forearm as she climbed out of the SUV. He'd gripped her so tight bruises had already started to form. His eyes darted back and forth; the color paled from his face. For the first time since the two had met, his demeanor and expression were absent of his normal arrogant and cocky self-assurance.

"Please?" he begged.

Sophia looked around. The SEALs had already disembarked their vehicles. Some had already set about the task of loading the cargo hold with their gear. Tex, Ryan, Tyus, and Gut had already removed Walsh's casket and were carrying it to the rear of the Jet.

Mila and Wallace, a few paces back, stopped their conversation after seeing the look on Sophia's face. "Everything good?" Wallace asked.

Sophia nodded, then turned back to Stone. "Help you with what?"

"You… you work for the CIA. You guys run black sites. Don't deny it; I sat on the security council."

Sophia shrugged. "What about it?"

"Take me to one."

"Why?" Fred asked. Stone's head turned to the former FBI Agent. "Why, you're headed to a cozy prison cell. Why demand to be taken to a black site? The guards there will treat you…" he tapered off. "Well… as you say, you've been on the security council; you've probably seen the pictures."

"No, not one run by the CIA. A private one. One where only you guys know."

"We don't unlawfully imprison US citizens," Sophia retorted, turning away.

"I have information." Sophia rounded on her heels; eyebrows peaked. "I know things. I can tell you things. I can be a wealth of information."

"About what?" Sophia asked.

"About how the country is really run."

A thin smile pierced Sophia's lips. She shot a gaze across the backseat to Fred. Who silently nodded.

"Ok." Stone relaxed in his seat. "We'll talk about it on the flight. You have nine hours to convince me. Let's get aboard."

Fred pulled Stone out of the back seat and walked him to the base of the steps. Mila, Richard, Jerry, and Gabby had already boarded the jet, along with Johns, Tyus, Alwani, and Gutierrez.

"Here, watch this piece of shit," Fred said, passing Stone off to Wallace before bounding up the steps, brushing past Sophia. He leaned over. "Think you got him," he whispered, ascending.

"Gladly," Wallace answered, holding his charge aggressively around the upper arm. "It's because of you one of my men is dead. I hope you rot in prison," he hissed.

Sophia smiled at Wallace and followed Fred up. A few seconds later, Wallace pushed Stone up the first step.

Fred ducked into the cabin, spinning around to wait for Sophia.

She reached the top and turned, hearing Stone trip on one of the steps. She bent to haul him up, taking his hand. She pulled him to his feet. "You'd better have-"

Blood splattered across her face, and her eyes shot wider than dinner plates. Her heart skipped a beat or two. Stone spasmed in her hands, and a plum of blood spread across the chest of his white shirt.

"Get down!" Wallace shouted. He, Ryan, and Tex dropped to the ground. The Marines that had escorted them to the airport encircled the group, guns up, pointing at the invisible attacker.

"There." Tex pointed off into the far distance at a roof. "Damn, he's good," he muttered under his breath. The sniper, having instantly calculated and deduced the most logical spot to have taken such a shot from.

About two miles to the south of the airstrip sat a line of what appeared to be a series of four and five-story apartment blocks. The shot could've come from any of the windows or roofs. The Marines radioed for assistance and backup; relaying Tex's advised potential location of the shooter.

"Sophia," Fred shouted, wrapping his arms around her and dragging both her and Stone into the Jet cabin. Another round sparked off the fuselage. "Come on!" he said and continued to drag both deeper inside, dropping them to the floor.

"No, no, no," Sophia wailed. With Fred's help, she pushed the man off her, rolling him onto his back. "First aid kit, now," she snapped. Alwani and Tyus rushed toward a sign indicating the location of the kit. Stone wheezed, coughing up blood, his face for the second time in the last few minutes washed a pale white. "You can't die, not before you tell me what you know."

Stone's lips moved, but no words escaped; blood gurgled out, and his breathing labored more.

Tyus passed the first aid kit to Fred. "Here, roll him over. We've got to get his jacket off and pack the wound."

Stone waved them off as they started to roll him. His body spasmed and shuddered. His life drained from his face rapidly. He reached up. His hand was shaking. Cupping it around Sophia's neck, he tried to pull her closer. Realizing what he was trying to do and that he didn't have the strength, she knelt in. He gulped, pooling his last ounces of strength. "The... Council...of the...Cross."

He seized and spasmed again. Then his body fell limp.

Roy Stone was dead, so where were whatever secrets he may

have had? Sans his final words, which meant nothing to Sophia.

355

CHAPTER TWENTY-SIX
WASHINGTON D.C.
TWO WEEKS LATER

FRED, Sophia, and Wallace plodded down the steps of the U.S. Capitol Building in Washington, D.C. For the trio, the last two weeks had been a whirlwind of meetings, interrogations, and the demand for answers from the leaders of Joint Task Force 200.

Some members of the oversight committee wanted to know why no one behind the July 4th attack on the Harley Davidson Museum—the largest terrorist attack on US soil since the horrific events of 9/11 were brought to justice. How did all parties responsible die? Most importantly, how and why was the mastermind behind it all? How was former Senator Roy Stone killed, despite being in their custody at the time of his assassination?

All were questions Sophia had herself. Her and Stone's last conversation had stayed stuck in her head over the last couple of weeks—information that she'd managed to keep between just herself and Fred.

The former FBI agent hadn't heard Stone's last few words, but Sophia had filled him in on the cryptic namedrop of, she guessed, the secret group that Stone claimed really ran the world and that he worked for; 'The Council of the Cross.' They had agreed to keep it just between themselves, vowing to dig into it after the flurry of investigations and questions, which they knew would come with a wealth of scrutiny. Their entire lives would be picked apart.

They reached the bottom of the steps of the Capitol building, and Wallace spun to face his other two counterparts. He was sharply dressed in his Navy Blue uniform, which made his movements seem more crisp and sharp, like he was marching in a parade. "Well, that was fun," he quipped, looking back up at the government building.

"I think you really need to reorient what you consider fun." Sophia smiled.

"Remember, this man runs into dangerous situations, often

staring down the barrel of guns. I am sure for him, staring down politicians' faces is a cakewalk," Fred suggested, also glancing back at the building. "I hate bureaucracy," he decried.

"Actually, after that. I think I'll take the warlord, dictator, or angry militia group any day of the week over that circus," Wallace countered. "At least when they say or do something I don't like, I can shoot them." He let out a laugh like it was a joke, but it wasn't.

"Jeez, I know that battle axe Congresswoman from California; what was her name?"

"Eve Chaplain, I think," Fred answered.

"Yeah, that's the one," Sophia snapped. "I'd hate to be married to her. The look she gave you." She pointed to Wallace. "That had pure malice behind it."

"I felt it. Anyway, lunch." The three nodded their heads in agreement.

Wallace spun about to hail a cab. There was a line of them waiting on the other side of the road when a long, sleek black limousine rolled up, breaking hard in front of them. A man climbed out of the front passenger seat. He was tall, had thick black hair slicked back, and was clean-shaven, and an earpiece dug into his right ear. He paced up to the group. His demeanor and dress suggested he was some sort of private security.

"Agent Evans, Mr. Jones, and Master Chief Wallace." He paused, waiting for them to confirm.

"Yes," Wallace answered for the group. "Can we help you? I thought we were done with the briefings and hearings?"

"Someone would like a word with you all."

"Someone who?" Fred demanded, stepping up to the gentleman.

"My employer," came the man's sharp reply.

"Growing up," Sophia added, sidling up beside her two companions. "My parents always told me, 'Sophia, never get in a car with strangers.'"

The man glowered down at the blonde. Then, the back window of the limo rolled down. A young, strikingly beautiful red-headed woman with jade green eyes poked her head out. "Mr. Bard, there is no need for the cloak and dagger here," she said, her soft, dulcet voice drifting from the car, almost instantly cutting through the building tension. The rear door opened, and she stepped out, exposing her svelte figure, accentuated by a tight, form-fitting black dress. She stood in a way that exuded money and class.

"My name is Mandy Ashcroft, and that," she said and pointed to the man standing in front of the trio. "Is Mr. Frank Bard, head of my security. There, now, we're not strangers. I would like to have a word with the three of you," she concluded.

"About what?" Sophia asked.

"A… job offer," she answered, measuring her words.

"We have jobs. Well, not Fred," Sophia rebutted.

"I think you'll want to hear my offer. Please, if you'd entertain me for a few moments. I can at least give you all a ride back to the hotel. It is pretty cold out." She pointed to the open door, and a draft of heat wafted out.

Sophia instinctively pulled her coat tighter at the mention of the biting cold weather, then looked at the other two and shrugged. "Ok," Sophia answered.

They filed into the car.

The exterior of the limo did very little to prepare the on-border for the opulent interior. Sophia, first to clamber in, found herself taken aback, instantly feeling way underdressed in her modest black dress, covered with a beige blazer as she sidled down the length of the car, using the cushioned bank of a spongy leather couch, nestling into a seat at the head of the back.

Fred climbed in next, following Sophia, eyes wide, expecting it to be darker inside, but the entire area was lit by strands of LED lights running around the top and bottom edges. He took the seat next to Sophia.

Wallace filtered in, mouth agape at his surroundings, inching down the sofa, examining the mini bar across from him lining the other passenger side wall. A row of bottles stretched half the car's length. Below the row, a mini fridge was flanked by a cabinet on the right side. Several TV monitors to the left and back above Sophia and Fred's heads were set into the inlay of the vehicle's siding. Each played silent images of newscasts from around the world.

Ashcroft climbed in last, taking the rearmost seat by the door. Mr. Bard closed the door behind her. A few seconds later, the limo set off.

"Like I said, we have jobs or are happily retired," Sophia started. "So, not seeing how you are going to offer us anything we don't have."

"I may have fibbed a bit." Her thin lips coyly pursed, angling upward into a sly grin, raising her hard, sharp jawline and elevated cheekbones. "It's more of an opportunity," she confessed.

"An opportunity for what?" Fred asked.

"Great question, Mr. Jones." The woman paused, reaching for a bottle of vodka from the row of bottles atop the shelf, retrieving a glass from the cabinet. She poured the liquid half filling her glass, then silently offered her guests a drink. All three shook their heads. She shrugged and continued after taking a sip. "An opportunity to raise the country out of a dark time. A time when a US politician can plot against his own people. A time of pending civil unrest in the country."

"What civil unrest?" Wallace asked.

The woman let out a small laugh. "I am sorry, I forgot that you've probably been so engrossed in your mission that you've not had a chance to watch much of any news. Though I suspect our retired friend here may know a thing or two." She tipped the glass toward Fred.

Both Sophia and Wallace eyed him. "I don't really watch the biased news, but the country seems pretty divided lately," he admitted, agreeing with the red head.

"Very divided," Ashcroft continued. "And it's only going to get worse."

"How could you possibly know that?" Sophia questioned. "Do you have a crystal ball?"

"In a sort of roundabout way, we do," Ashcroft answered, drawing confused looks. Sophia clearly meant the quip to be funny and was surprised at the woman's answer. "Let's say… I represent an organization that, through technology, has the ability to perform predictive analysis. We can predict inflection points in time and within society. Which, we are currently rocketing toward a major one.”

“How so?” Sophia leaned forward in her seat, intrigued.

“Have any of you heard of the group Patriots for America First? PAF?”

“A little bit,” Sophia answered, searching deep in her memory banks. “They’re some type of conservative right fringe group that camps out somewhere in Virginia and some other places if I remember correctly. They’re harmless. Just a bunch of good Ole boys that love the Second Amendment and camping.” She recalled a brief she’d once seen not too long ago. “Their leader is a heavy conspiracist who espouses them on a radio station that is barely listened to.”

“Well, that was before. Now, with the changing winds of society and the open acceptance of things. They’ve gotten a little more aggressive than you remember—much farther to the right of the political aisle.” She reached to her side, producing several manila envelopes, handing them to Wallace, who took one and dispensed the others to Fred and Sophia. They opened them up, and a picture of a man wearing jeans and flannel, with thick black hair and a beard, was attached to a dossier.

“That is Joseph Jefferson,” Ashcroft announced, letting the name linger as if it had any relevance. “He fancies himself as a new-aged revolutionist. Spouting radical ideas about over taxation and corrupt politicians, which recent events with the newly departed Roy Stone didn’t help quail much.” She paused. “It only seemed to galvanize his base. Whereas you said…” She nodded to Sophia. “…No one listened to them; they are perking their ears toward him now. He’s been somewhat of a rallying person for a growing group of radicals. He’s since recently upgraded from radio to podcasting.”

“I don’t see the part where we come in. You said this was about a job,” Fred interrupted, growing a little tired of the monologue, having given the document a cursory glance.

“To the point.” Ashcroft tipped her glass in his direction before taking another sip. “Right. The algorithm predicted that the PAF would grow in support as time went on, which has proved to be correct. It has now predicted an alarming situation, which we would defiantly like to prevent." She took the last sip.

Now, all three audience members edged to the front of their seats as Ashcroft's last sentence left them enticed whether or not she'd done it purposely to draw their attention or to take another drink. The pause served its goal.

"Prevent what?" Wallace finally broke the suspension build.

"The assassination of the President of the United States," Ashcroft revealed to the stunned faces of the trio. She let the revelation fall to sink into their minds, then continued, "That's where your team comes in. We want you to infiltrate the PAF and find out if that's truly where the group is headed and to prevent it from happening."

"Why us?" Sophia asked, and Fred and Wallace nodded in agreement. "I am CIA. He's a Navy SEAL and Fred's retired FBI. Doesn't the government have agencies that do this, you know, like the Secret Service?"

Ashcroft threw one leg over the other, resting back against her seat. "You're right. The official government has the apparatuses for such things. However, if something were to come of this, then all information relating to an attempt of a sitting President would become a matter of record and, therefore, can be subpoenaed. Our group doesn't want the existence of the algorithm to become public record. Therefore, we would rather keep this an off-the-books operation. We are covertly working with the President's people behind the scenes. It was suggested that, based on your recent success, your team is quite uniquely suited for such an investigation. So, we'd like to form a new branch of special operators—a new covert team to handle these types of situations. One that works for my employer, but also directly with the President as well."

"First off, I wouldn't call it a success. Stone was killed," Sophia reminded. "Furthermore, I think I'm speaking for the boys here too." They both nodded. "Who is this group you work for?"

"Great question again," Ashcroft buoyed. "Transparency is a great equalizer when discussing a potential partnership. So, to answer, we are a party interested in keeping America together as a beacon for the free world."

"That doesn't answer my question," Sophia interrupted, giving the woman a deadpan expression.

The redhead pursed her lips, nodding. "Ok, well, then, I work for The Washington Institute. It's a political-"

"Think Tank," Fred cut in.

"Yes," Ashcroft admitted. "We've worked for years on hundreds of bi-partisan legislative works. We want to bridge the gap and divide between our two-party system. We believe the country is strongest when unified under one governing principle. That is what we work to achieve. A unified America is unstoppable. Sadly, we are not very unified at this time. We'd like to get back to that. Because, if not, nothing good comes from a fractured country."

"There's no doubting that," Wallace added, having seen the repercussions of when countries tear themselves apart.

"The inflection point that our algorithm has detected would surely break us apart. We are already teetering on a precipice of falling down a dark path. The assassination of a sitting President would certainly push us over, which could very well be the end of America. And if I am right, the three of you can pull us back. You all swore an oath to protect this country from all enemies, foreign and domestic. At this point, we need to be protected from ourselves. So, that is the job I am offering. Will you help us protect this country?"

Fred, Sophia, and Wallace sat back in silence, each looking from one to the other and back several times. A million thoughts raced through each of their minds. The limo fell silent for a good while; only the thrum of the road beneath perforated the passenger compartment.

"Say we agree that something needs to be done," said Fred, the first to break the silence. "Again, as Sophia has stated, she's CIA, and Wallace is an active member of the US Navy. So, how would this work? Keeping it off books and all. They have people to report to. An operation like this could take months, maybe even years. Money, resources, again, not to mention too many times, but they wouldn't be free to do any of this."

"We have hundreds of contacts throughout the political world, and this wouldn't necessarily be a one-time thing. If you all wish, you can stay on and help us continue to right the ship and work toward a better, more united country. Your team will have any and every resource available to you. Money would be no object, and you'd get to pick your missions and personnel. In an effort to help facilitate that, we can secure Agent Evans' release from the CIA, the Master Chief, and his team's release from military service or suspension of service if they wished to return to their respective roles after the mission has been completed." Ashcroft's eyes darted between the three people sitting across from her, and she saw that her pitch hadn't crossed the finish line yet. "Just as an added perk," she continued. "There is a significant financial windfall for all involved as well. Your services to your country are greatly under-compensated. We can and will correct that deficiency, say to the tune of $20,000 a month."

The trio's mouths fell agape at the figure so wildly thrown out by Ashcroft. "That's, that's a lot of money," Wallace sputtered. "Life changing."

"Indeed, it is, because Master Chief, your actions should you take the offer will change lives for the better."

"I am not going to speak for anyone else at this point," Fred spoke up. "I am not saying I am doing this for the money, but, as you correctly stated earlier, I did swear an oath to protect this country from all that would do it harm. I may have retired, but I will honor that oath till the day I die. So." He paused, biting his lip one last moment to mull over what he was about to say. "I'm in." Ashcroft's face lit up. "But I will need to talk to my wife," he threw in.

"Absolutely," the redhead said, "Family is important, and I am sure that she will see reason."

Sophia released a deep, drawn sigh. Her eyes lingered on Fred, trying to glean why he'd so quickly agreed to the offer and if he was on board. "Well, if he's in, I can't let him do it on his own. If Sherry says yes, you can count me as part of the package." The two exchanged smiles.

Ashcroft craned her head toward Wallace, who also seemed to be deeply mulling over the proposition. She always knew he'd be the hardest sell. A lifelong Navy man and dedicated SEAL. His face gave away no indication as to which direction he was leaning. Though the longer the silence, the greater the risk he'd say no.

After a few uncomfortable seconds passed, which felt like hours. Wallace's lips cracked open. "I cannot, with good conscience, commit my team to any of this." Ashcroft's face fell flat. So did Fred's and Sophia's. "Without talking to each of my men." They perked up. "Plus, I'd need reassurance that our careers would be suspended, not ended. If any of them wanted to go back, they would be allowed without any negative repercussions."

Ashcroft nodded.

"Other than that. I am in. I can't let this one…" He pointed to Sophia. "Run off and do something stupid again."

"Hey," the blonde protested in mock offense.

"Well, obviously," Ashcroft beamed, "I can get all of that to you, and I didn't expect answers today. So…" She reached over and plucked a business card holder from a hidden pocket in the side of the limo. She flipped it open and produced three business cards from inside, handing one to each. Sophia nearly dropped hers, not expecting the weight. They were made of thin, layered metal. The front was all black with a strip of gold trim running across the top and bottom, a silhouetted side profile of George Washington's face stenciled in gold donned the middle of the card. Turning it over, on the back, it read, 'Mandy Ashcroft, President of Consulting.' There was a phone number below.

"When you've spoken to your wife and your team, Agent Jones and Master Chief Wallace, call that number, and we'll get the process rolling," she said, indicating each of them respectively as they rubbed the cards. She tapped a button on what appeared to be a control console at the end of the long leather sofa Wallace had been sitting on. The car lurched to a stop.

"America is at a turning point. We've started down a dark path. It's time to course correct. Exoriemur ex cineribus." She opened the door and shuffled out. The trio followed suit. They were in front of their hotel.

"What does that mean?" Sophia asked of the saying.

"It's Latin for 'Let us rise from the Ashes," she answered, lowering herself back into the limo. Oh, and…'" She popped back up. "Do remember, time *is* of the essence. While the program can predict behaviors, it doesn't say when they'll happen."

With that, the redhead clambered back inside. Mr. Bard shut the door and gazed at the group before walking back to the passenger side and climbing in. The limo set off down the street, reaching a traffic stop.

"You think he makes two hundred thousand a year?" Wallace said, watching the taillights of the limo vanish around a corner.

"Maybe," Sophia added, facing her two counterparts. "So, we are going to do this? Possibly save the President and our country?"

Fred eyed the other two. "As a wise woman once said, abso-fucking-lutly," he answered with a broad smile.

CHASE Green padded across the apartment, plopping down on the couch, sinking into the worn sofa, slamming his feet onto the coffee table, and thrusting himself against the back of the sofa. He made a show of putting his hands behind his head and using them as a support rest. He leaned his head back, closed his eyes, and took a deep breath as a gust of wind carried in the aromas of the street below.

His ears took in all the usual trappings of the hustle and bustle of a busy suburban street in a third-world country from below. People shouted, and car horns blared. The melodic sound of music playing from one of the nearby apartments wafted in.

Sweat dripped down his forehead. It was unusually hot for this time of day in downtown Morocco. As he took in his surroundings, he swallowed, realizing that he felt slightly parched. Licking his lips, he opened his eyes, deciding that he needed something to drink.

"Woman!" he shouted. A beautiful Moroccan woman with light caramel-colored skin whipped around, startled, practically jumping out of her shoes. If she had any on, her long, flowing black hair swung with her, cascading down the front of her body, sticking to her chest. Beads of sweat made her half-naked body glisten as she stood in the kitchen, hovering over a stove in her underwear. "Get me a drink, will ya?" he demanded.

Still shaking from the start, she nervously paced to the refrigerator opening the door. The cool thirty-four-degree air blasted out from inside, washing over her exposed body. The temperature juxtaposition activated her body's sympathetic nervous system. The coldness triggered her hair to stand, prickling her body with goosebumps.

She grabbed a can of soda from the fridge and hurriedly raced out of the kitchen through the living room, handing it to the man on the couch. "Please, here, take," she said in heavily accented

English, offering him the can and bowing her head.

Chase leaned forward, grabbing the can with one hand, and he put the other under the woman's chin, then slowly raised her head. Meeting his bright blue eyes with her dark brown. Her pupils were dilated, almost blocking out the rest of her iris,' and red streaks raced across her sclera. "Don't be afraid," he said, caressing her cheek. "I told you I am not going to hurt you. I just needed your apartment for a few days. Now, you promised me some lunch. Go on and finish." He let go of her face, and she quickly turned; before she could set off, he smacked her across the ass. She rushed off sobbing. "Now, that's a great ass!" he shouted after her as she retreated into the kitchen. He then popped the top of the can and took a huge gulp. He downed half the can in one shot, then leaned back. "It's amazing how coke can taste the same anywhere in the world, he muttered.

Several minutes later, the woman appeared from the kitchen, carrying a plate, and the tears that had once streamed down her face were gone. She knew he didn't like to see that. She'd also fixed her makeup. Knowing that he always wanted her face to be done up.

She put the plate down on the coffee table, presenting it to him like a waiter at a fine dining restaurant, putting her arms behind her back. He shot forward, inspecting the dish and nodding happily. "It is my mother's recipe," she said, managing a smile.

He grabbed the fork and dug in, shoveling the food into his mouth. Gulping down the first bite, then attacking the plate several more times. "You must thank your mother for me," he said through a mouth full of food. A buzzing noise came from the coffee table. A phone vibrated across it. He slammed down the fork angrily, obviously disturbed by the interruption. "Dammit." He flipped open the phone and quickly read a message." Then shot straight up, shoveling one last fork full before downing the last of the can. "Gotta go to work, baby," he said, slipping past her and taking her by the shoulders. She tensed, releasing a gasp, frightened. Chase paid no attention to the reaction. Instead, he lowered her to the sofa. "Now, sit here, and don't say a word."

He shuffled across the living room to the open window and

climbed atop the table that he had set up two days ago. Then, he dropped onto it in the prone position and nestled his shoulder to the stock of a Volodar Obriyu sniper rifle. He peered down the scope, eying his target location. Chase, satisfied he had the best position available, pulled his head back and punched information into a laptop positioned to his right.

He waited a few seconds, and the computer spat out settings. He twisted the dials of his scope to match what the computer displayed, then fixed his eye to the scope again and set about controlling his breathing.

On the other end of the scope, a row of five SUVs pulled up to a waiting Boeing BBJ 737. A couple of Marines disembarked from the lead vehicle and began securing the area. Not his targets. He adjusted his view; several men disgorged from the third, fourth, and fifth vehicles.

He got visuals on all. None were his target. Chase shifted to the second vehicle. A man who looked to be in his forties slipped out of the passenger seat, and a tall, leggy blonde rose from the driver's side. His heart thumped. *What a ride that'd be to climb that peak.* He thought. The rear driver-side door opened. He could see the top of a head. Another blonde woman climbed out. He couldn't quite see her face, but it was a woman. Not his target.

The sniper waited patiently, a trait long drilled into him from his time as a Force Recon sniper. He'd once spent three days waiting in the desert on a hill for his target. This was easy.

Finally, the rear passenger's side door opened. Behind the graying-haired man, his target flashed into the scope's view. He watched and waited. The occupants of the other vehicles moved about the tarmac, several of them loading a person-sized box. Chase figured it was one of their fallen commrades. He'd seen enough of those boxes loaded into planes during his service time.

The tall, leggy blonde was having a conversation with another man who, upon closer inspection, he recognized. The man was practically a legend amongst operators. For a second, a flash of relief hit him. Glad that the bearded man wasn't his target.

The two broke off their conversation. Legs boarded the plane along with a smaller group that looked like computer nerds to him.

Then, some of the men boarded. Several others stayed on the tarmac with the Marines.

Movement from the second SUV. His target emerged. The gray-haired man led him around the vehicle; they met with the other blonde. Something pulsed down his pants, seeing the second blonde. The beautiful blonde sauntered to the base of the steps leading into the plane.

The graying-haired man climbed the steps first, followed by the smoke-show blondie. His target was the third to begin the ascent.

Go time.

Chase's muscles tensed; this was his favorite part of the job. He flexed his index finger several times before laying it on the trigger. He relaxed his breathing, slowing it to almost non-existent.

His finger began to depress the trigger as he held his breath gently.

The man tripped.

Chase quickly eased off the trigger. *Damn, the fool almost ruined my shot.* He thought.

The woman helped the man to his feet, and he climbed the next step, almost to the top.

Chase's finger squeezed the trigger.

The gun went off. The loud *boom* echoed off the apartment walls. The woman, still sitting on the couch, jumped.

The man on the other end of the scope collapsed forward, falling into the arms of the blonde. The gray-haired man appeared again from the plane. He grabbed the woman and started pulling both her and the target into the cabin.

Chase fired another shot, intentionally missing wide. He didn't kill for free and was assigned only one target. He just felt like firing another round.

He could see the SEALs drop; the Marines rushed to circle them. One of them pointed in his direction. The gesture unsettled Chase as it felt like the man was pointing directly at him, which was impossible. He'd picked this exact spot for a reason. It was outside the range for most snipers. No one should've expected a shot to be taken from this far out.

Still, it was time to go.

Chase scrabbled off the table, quickly breaking down his rifle, and stowed the pieces into a briefcase. He collected both of his expended brass shells, slipping them into his pocket. He slid the kitchen table back into place where it was. He padded across the room to the sofa.

The woman tensed, seeing the man stamp toward her. She recoiled, closing her eyes, as he stomped over, expecting the worst. When she felt the wetness of lips smack against her forehead. She opened her eyes to find the man jamming another fork full of food into his mouth.

"Safa, I want to thank you for your hospitality. And for a great last couple of days, especially last night." He gave her a wink. "But, alas, I must go." He dropped the fork and glided to the kitchen, grabbing another can from the fridge. He moved to the door, pulled it open, and looked back. "For the road," he added, holding the can up and then dropping an envelope onto the counter. A stack of hundred-dollar bills slopped out, falling to the floor. "Thanks again." He shut the door.

Chase pounded down the steps of the building, throwing open the door to the outside world. He strolled out and onto the busy street. Sliding in with the crowd of people walking by. He casually and calmly walked down the sidewalk, silently singing Run DMC's 'Walk This Way.' In the far distance, sirens blared. Some sounded like they were heading toward the airport. Others headed toward the neighborhood.

A black town car pulled up beside him and lurched to a stop. The driver's window cracked open. "Get in," a voice barked from inside.

Chase shrugged, opening the rear door, and climbed in. He slid to the middle of the back seat, bathing in the A/C, letting it wash over him.

The car was split by a dividing wall, and a glass window was set into the middle. It rolled down as the car set off. "Mr. Green, the Council would like to thank you once again for your work." The mellifluous voice of a woman carried into the back. A large envelope accompanied it.

Chase leaned forward, taking the envelope and fanning through the stack of money inside it with his thumb. Chase playfully raised and lowered the envelope. "Yup, feels like fifty grand to me," he said, opening the case with his rifle and tossing the envelope inside.

"How would you like your next mission?" the woman's voice asked.

"So soon?"

"Things are going to have to move at a more quickened pace than we anticipated because our good friend back there, Mr. Stone, couldn't keep his mouth shut," the woman snapped acidly. "So, we are going to have to move up timetables. I trust you're ready?"

Chase knew she wasn't asking if he was, more telling him he better be. "Absolutely," he answered without hesitation. Fortunately, he was actually ready. He hated all the downtime between jobs.

"Great to hear," the woman said. "This is why the Council likes you, Mr. Green. Always ready at a moment's notice." She slipped a large manila pocket envelope through the partition window.

Chase took it, undoing the string around the seal, and slid out the first few pages. He quickly scanned the documents. "When and how?" he asked.

"Give it about a month or two, depending on how the next phase progresses. I'll let you know when the time is right. Do it subtle."

"Copy that." Chase added the envelope to his case.

"This looks like your stop. Mr. Green." The car stopped. "Happy hunting, Mr. Green. We'll be in touch," the voice said.

Chase opened the passenger door, squeezing out and reaching back in for his briefcase. "Looking forward to it," he tried to add, but the woman had already rolled up the window. He closed the door, and the car drove away. He watched it merge into the throng of the downtown traffic. "Exoriemur ex cineribus," he said as the car disappeared.

THE END

AUTHOR'S NOTES

Well, here we are, at the end of what I hope was a thrill ride of a journey for all of you. I mean, WOW, what a series of events that Sophia and the team had to endure during HEARTLAND RETRIBUTION.

Sophia being kidnapped, Wallace and team's frantic search to find her, to Fred being pulled back into the life he thought he'd left. Plus, not to mention the bombshell that Stone had dropped before his death. A secret cabal running America. No way. But, hey, in the end Sophia got her man, right? For now.

In the previous installment of "Author's Notes," I took you all on a journey through my life until the point of publication for HEARTLAND STRIKE with the how and why I decided to become a writer. Albeit a sort of abridged version (didn't want to bore anyone, lol. My life's not that interesting.) of a story twenty years in the making.

A story that took some serious twists and turns, but that's life, right? Everyone has their own unique and lived experience, and one that doesn't always follow the paths that we set out on. That's what makes life worth living, isn't it?

If everything was scripted out for us from the moment we're born, until we take our final breaths, why go through it? There'd be no joy in life. No heartbreak, no trials, no successes, no failures. There'd just be a mundane monotony with it.

Sure, having a goal, vision, or path that you plan out is always a good thing. As it keeps us on track and moving forward. However, having a goal and a script are two entirely different things.

In my life, I've had several goals, or pathways that I've charted. With each experiencing its own sets of…let's say, step backs instead of failures. As each one of them has led me to this point. Doing what I've come to really enjoy.

Crafting stories for any and everyone who finds enjoyment in them.

Speaking of crafting stories, HEARTLAND RETRIBUITION was born out of that enjoyment. As previously mentioned, HEARTLAND STRIKE was never supposed to see the light of day. But, after falling in love with the story and characters, I wanted to change that. (See paths change all the time. Sometimes in mid-stream.)

As I drew closer to the end of STRIKE, I didn't want that to be the end of characters that I'd spent months creating and breathing life into. I'd grown attached to them. To their lives, their goals, desires, and paths.

The only problem was the book was supposed to be a one-off. What type of plot could I create? After all, this wasn't the genre that I wanted to write. I wanted more action/adventure, Indiana Jones, Nathan Drake, Lara Croft stories. I was about four books deep into the Nina Wilde/Eddie Chase series from ANDY McDERMOTT (fantastic writer, by the way. If you have time to check him out. I highly recommend his books.) That's the stuff I wanted to write.

Then, as most things do, out of nowhere, I was struck with a potential plot. What if Sophia was kidnapped, and the team had to rescue her? From there, everything else snowballed.

HEARTLAND RETRIBUTION was born from that one single idea. The entire story had been derived from that one thought. Combined with the fact that I realized I had a loose end running around (Hasan. I hadn't wrapped his story arc.) I crafted the story.

I went back and rewrote the end of STRIKE to Stone getting away instead of being killed by Fred. Not a spoiler since I took it out, but yes, the original ending of STRIKE was Fred killing Stone to save Sophia from having to do so.

With the ending changed and an Epilogue introducing West and having the big three (Stone, West, and Hasan) I had my antagonist, and my idea. From there, I set out building around the concept of Sophia being kidnapped.

Everything else just fell into place (after mapping a bunch out.) I knew early in the process what I wanted to do with all the characters and how I wanted to build their relationships. Then it came down to writing it. Which was a process that I needed to refine. By this time, I am in a different job and don't have a lot of free time to commit to writing a book. Though, when you love doing something. You will find the time.

Seven months later, I had HEARTLAND RETRIBUTION done. Another path charted. I had the basis of the series that I'd never expected to write. Though, two books don't make a series. Once again, nearing the end of the book, I had characters I didn't want to give up on and was fully committed to making this a series. All I needed was a third plot. I also wanted to change direction with my writing. I love the action, the chases, the shootouts and doing all of that stuff. Writing those scenes is fun and engaging, but I also think it's time to grow a bit. Branch out into combining a few different genres. Challenge myself.

With that said, The Lord and Universe Willing, Sophia, Fred, Wallace and team will be back for another gripping story in HEARTLAND: HOMEFRONT. Until then, keeping reading and keep experiencing new worlds.

Also, visit my little corner of the web at michael-lee-williams.com. There you'll find some short stories (earlier works), you can reach out and talk to me directly. A chance to sign up for updates on upcoming projects and more coming soon.

In the future there will be a spin-off novella series featuring Wallace, Tex, Ryan and the team as you get a chance to meet them before the books. It's a prequel series that follows some of their missions before meeting Sophia.

They are fun, quick in and out stories with lots of action like that of the main line series. Just told from the SEAL's perspective.

See you all in the next "Author's Notes," and thank you for your support in purchasing my books. You are all appreciated and loved.